Trapped By Malays: A Tale Of Bayonet And Kris

George Manville Fenn

Peter's other hand clutching Archie's left with a force that seemed
crushing to the owner's fingers.

T.

PAGE 364.

TRAPPED BY MALAYS

A TALE OF BAYONET AND KRIS

By

G. MANVILLE FENN

Author of

'Glyn Severn's School-Days,' 'Shoulder Arms!' 'Tention!'
'Stan Lynn,' &c.

WITH EIGHT ILLUSTRATIONS

by

Steven Spurrier

LONDON: 47 Paternoster Row

W. & R. CHAMBERS, LIMITED

EDINBURGH: 339 High Street

1907

Edinburgh:
Printed by W. & R. Chambers, Limited.

CONTENTS.

CONTENTS.

LIST OF ILLUSTRATIONS.

Trapped by Malays.

CHAPTER I.

'TWO BAD BOYS'—SERGEANT RIPSY.

'OH, bother!'

The utterer of these two impatient words threw down a sheet of notepaper from which he had been reading, carefully smoothed out the folds to make it flat, and then, balancing it upon one finger as he sat back in a cane chair with his heels upon the table, gave the paper a flip with his nail and sent it skimming out of the window of his military quarters at Campong Dang, the station on the Ruah River, far up the west coast of the Malay Peninsula.

'What does the old chap want now? Another wigging, I suppose. What have I been doing to make him write a note like that?—Note?' he continued, after a pause. 'I ought to have said despatch. Hang his formality! Here, what did he say? How did he begin?' And he reached out his hand towards the table as if for the note. 'There's a fool! Now, why did I send it skimming out of the window like that? It's too hot to get up and go out to the front to find it, and it's no use to

A

shout, "*Qui-hi*," for everybody will be asleep. Now, what did he say? My memory feels all soaked. Now, what was it? Major John Knowle requests the presence of Mr Archibald Maine—Mr Archibald Maine—Archibald! What were the old people dreaming about? I don't know. It always sets me thinking of old Morley—bald, with the top of his head as shiny as a billiard-ball. Good old chap, though, even if he does bully one—requests the presence of Mr Archibald Maine at his quarters at —at seven o'clock this evening punctually. No. What's o'clock? I think it was six. Couldn't be seven, because that's dinner-time, and he wouldn't ask me then. It must be six. Here, I must get that note again, but I feel so pumped out and languid that I am blessed if I am going to get up and go hunting for that piece of paper. Phee—ew! It's hotter than ever. I should just like to go down to the river-side, take off all my clothes under the trees, and sit there right up to my chin, with the beautiful, clear, cool water gurgling round my neck. Lovely! Yes—till there came floating along a couple of those knobs that look like big marbles— only all the time they are what old Morley calls ocular prominences over the beastly leering eyes of one of those crocodiles on the lookout for grub. Ugh! The beasts! Now, what could crocodiles be made for?—Oh, here's somebody coming.'

For all at once, faintly heard, the fag-end of the 'British Grenadiers,' whistled very much out of tune, came floating in at the window.

'Peter Pegg, by all that's lucky!'

The footsteps of some one evidently heavily laden

came nearer and nearer, till, just as they were about to pass the young officer's quarters, the occupier screwed up his lips and gave vent to a low, clear note and its apparent echo, which sounded like the cry of some night-bird.

The next moment there was the sound as of a couple of iron buckets being set down upon the ground, followed by the *clang, clang* of the handles; a dark shadow crossed the window, and a voice exclaimed :

'You call, sir ?'

'That you, Pete ?'

'Yes, sir.'

'What are you doing ?'

'Fatigue-work, sir. Got to take these 'ere buckets round to cook's quarters.'

'Can you see a letter lying out there anywhere ?'

'For the mail, sir ?'

'Mail ! No, stupid ! A piece of notepaper.'

'With writing on it, sir ?'

'Of course.'

'No, sir.—Oh yes, here it is, stuck in the flowers.'

'Well, bring it to me.'

'Can't, sir, without treading on the beds.'

'Then bring it round to the door.'

There was a few moments' intense silence, during which, in the tropic heat, it seemed as if Nature was plunged in her deepest sleep. Then came a renewal of the footsteps, a sharp tap upon the door, a loud 'Come in !' and a very closely cropped and shaven, sun-browned face appeared, its owner clad in clean, white military flannel, drawing himself up stiffly as he held out the missive he was bearing.

'Letter, sir.'

'Well, bring it here. My arms are not telescopes.'

'*Pouf!* No, sir. Here you are, sir.' And as the letter was taken the bearer's droll-looking, good-humoured face gradually expanded into a broad grin, and then seemed to shut up sharply as the young officer raised his eyes.

'Here, Pete, what were you grinning at? At me?'

'No, sir. That I warn't, sir. I never grin at you. I only do that at the Sergeant when he aren't looking.'

'You were certainly grinning, Pete.'

'No, sir; only felt comf'y-like.'

'Oh, that's right,' said the young officer; and then to himself, 'It is seven o'clock, and it is to get up his appetite, I suppose. Sharpen it on me.—Well, Pete, what have you been up to now?'

'I d' know, sir.'

'Nonsense! You must know.'

'S'elp me, sir, I don't. The patient one has got his knife into me as usual. I expected it was to be pack-drill, but I come off with a two bucket job—water for the cook.'

'Now, look here, Pete; tell the truth for once in a way. The Sergeant wouldn't have come down upon you for nothing.'

'What, sir! Oh, I say, Mr Archie, you can go it! Old tipsy Job not come down upon a fellow for nothing! Why, I have heerd him go on at you about your drill'——

'That will do, Pegg. Don't you forget yourself sir.'

'Beg pardon, sir. I won't, sir; but there have been times when'——

'That will do.'

'Yes, sir; of course, sir—when I have thought to myself if I had been a officer and a gentleman like you'——

'I said that would do, Pegg.'

'Yes, sir; I heerd you, sir—I 'd have punched his fat head, sir.'

'Look here, Peter Pegg; I see you have been having your hair cut again.'

'Yes, sir. It 's so mortal hot, sir. I told Bob Ennery, sir, to cut it to the bone;' and the young fellow smiled very broadly as he passed both hands over the close crop, with an action that suggested the rubbing on of soap.

'Then look here; next time you have it done I should advise you to have a bit taken off the tip of your tongue. It 's too long, Pete; and if I were as strict an officer as the Major says I ought to be, I should report you for want of respect.'

'Not you, sir!'

'What!'

'Because you knows, sir, as I feels more respect for you than I do for the whole regiment put together. I talks a bit, and I never come anigh you, sir, without feeling slack.'

'Feeling slack?'

'Yes, sir. Unbuttoned-like, and as if I was smiling all over.'

'What! at your officer?'

'No, sir; not at you, sir. I can't tell you why; only I don't feel soldier-like—drilled up and stiff

as if I had been starched by one of my comrades'
wives.'

'Well, you are a rum fellow, Pete.'

'Yes, sir,' said the man sadly. 'That's what our
chaps say; and Patient Job says I am a disgrace
to the regiment, that I know nothing, and that I
shall never make a soldier. But I don't care.
Still, I do know one thing: I like you, sir; and
if it hadn't been for seeing you always getting into
trouble '——

'Peter Pegg!'

'Yes, sir. But I can't stop saying it, sir. If it
hadn't been for you, and seeing you always getting
into trouble too '——

'Pegg!'

'Yes, sir—I should have pegged out.'

'What! deserted?'

'Yes, sir. Sounds bad, don't it?'

'Disgraceful!'

'Yes, Mr Maine, sir; but ain't it disgraceful for a
sergeant to be allowed to hit a poor fellow a whack
with that cane of his just because he's a bit out in
his drill?'

'Drop it, Pete.'

'And 'im obliged to stand up stiff, and dursen't
say a word?'

'Didn't you hear me say, "Drop it"?'

'Yes, sir—and one's blood b'iling all the while!'

'Look here; you have been having it again, then,
Pete?'

'Again, sir! Why, I am always a-having of it.'

'What was it, now?'

'I telled you, sir: nothing.'

'That was a lie, Pete.   Now, wasn't it ?'

'Not a lie, sir.   Only a little cracker.'

'Well, out with it.'

'Not enough pipeclay, sir.'

'Oh, I see.'

'Jigger the pipeclay !   It's a regular cuss.   Ah, it's you laughing now, sir.   Can I do anything else for you, sir ? '

'N——n——no.'

''Cause the cook will be howling after me directly, and I don't want to be out with him.'

'No, I suppose not; but what about that bait for fishing ? '

'Oh, that's all right, sir.   I will be ready.   But don't you think, sir, if we was to go higher up the river we could find a better place ?   It don't seem much good only ketching them there little hikong-sammylangs.'

'Eikon Sambilang, Pete.   Don't you know what that means ? '

'That's what the niggers call them, sir.   I suppose it's because it's their name.'

'Five-barbelled fish, Pete, eh ? '

'Just like them, sir.   Then why don't they call them barbel, sir, like we do ?   I have seen lots of them ketched up Teddington way by the gentlemen in punts—whackers, too—not poor little tiddlers like these 'ere.   We ought to go right up the river in a sampan, with plenty of bait, and try in a bit of sharp stream close to one of them deep holes.'

'No good, Pete.   We shouldn't do any good. Those beauties of crocodiles clear out the holes.'

'What ! whacking the water, sir, with their tails ?

I've heerd them lots of times. Rum place this 'ere, sir, ain't it ?'

'Yes, Pete ; rather a change from England. But it is very beautiful, and I like it.'

'Well, yes, sir ; that's right enough. So do I like it. I often think it would be just lovely if old Ripsy would get down with the fever. My word ! what would he be like when Dr Morley had done with him, and he began to crawl about and use his cane to help him hobble, instead of being so jolly handy with it in his fashion ?'

'Peter Pegg, that's a nasty, revengeful way of talking.'

'Is it, sir ?' said the young private, giving himself a twist, as if in recollection of a tap with the cane.

'Yes. You don't mean to tell me that you wish Sergeant Ripsy would catch this nasty jungle fever ?'

'No, sir, I don't want to tell you ; but I do.'

'I don't believe you, Pete. The Sergeant's a fine soldier and a brave man, and I honestly believe that he thinks he is doing his duty.'

'Oh, he's brave enough, I dare say. So are you, sir.'

'Bosh !'

'So am I, sir.'

'Double bosh ! Turkish for nothing, Pete.'

'Is it, sir ? I don't care. I know when the row comes off with that there Rajah Solomon—and there's a pretty bit of cheek, sir : him, a reg'lar heathen, going and getting himself called by a Christian name ! I should like to give him Solomon

—you'll fight with the best of them, sir. I often think about it. You'll fight with the best of them, sir. And 'tain't brag, Mr Archie Maine, sir—you let me see one of them beggars coming at you with his pisoned kris or his chuck-spear, do you mean to tell me I wouldn't let him have the bayonet? And bad soldier or no, I *can* do the bayonet practice with the best of them. Old Tipsy did own to that.'

'Look here, Pete; you are what the Yankees call blowing now. Let's wait till the time comes, and then we shall see what we shall see. And look here; don't you let me hear you call Sergeant Ripsy Tipsy again. One of these days, mark my words, he will find out that you have nicknamed him with a *T* instead of an *R*, and he will never forgive you.'

'Tckkk!'

'What are you laughing at, sir?'

'Oh, don't say sir, Mr Archie! There's no one near. Of course I don't mind when anybody's by, but I couldn't help laughing. Old Patient Job found it out long ago.'

'He did?'

'Yes, sir.'

'And yet you wonder that he has got what you call his knife into you!'

'Oh, I don't think that's why, sir.'

'Well, I do.'

'No, sir; it's his aggravating way of wanting to see a company of human men going across the parade like a great big caterpillar or a big bit of a machine raking up the sand.'

'Never mind. Old Ripsy is a fine soldier, and I advise you not to let him hear you.'

'Pst!'

'What is it?'

'Mr Maine, sir,' whispered the lad; and the subaltern's heels dropped at once from the table upon which they had been resting, for plainly heard through the window, in a loud, forced cough, full of importance, came the utterance, 'Errrrum! Errum!' and Private Peter Pegg's lower jaw dropped, and his eyes, as he fixed them upon the subaltern's face, opened in so ghastly a stare of dread that, in spite of his annoyance, Ensign Maine's hands were clapped to his mouth to check a guffaw. But as the regular stamp more than stride of a heavy man reached his ears, the young officer's countenance assumed a look of annoyance, and he whispered in a boyish, nervous way:

'Slip off, Pete; and don't let him see you leaving my room.'

'I can't, sir,' whispered the lad, with a look full of agony.

'What!'

'He telled me if ever he catched me loafing about your quarters he'd '——

'Don't talk. Cut!'

'I can't, sir.'

'You can.'

'But '——

'Don't talk. Off at once.'

'But I tell you, sir '——

'I don't want to be told. He mustn't see you going away from here.'

'But he's stopped, sir. Can't you hear?'

'No—yes. Why has he stopped?'

'Because he can see my two blessed buckets standing there.'

'Oh, Peter Pegg! Tut, tut, tut, tut, tut!' And as the young subaltern gave utterance to these homely sounds, he was recalling certain sarcastic remarks of the stern master of drill respecting officers and gentlemen demeaning themselves by associating with the men.

CHAPTER II.

A ROWING.

'A GUILTY conscience needs no accuser,' said Archie Maine to himself. 'There's a splendid proverb. It can't mean a wigging this time. But if that pompous old pump, that buckled-up basha, lets the Major know that he caught poor old Pegg in my room to-day, I'm sure to get a lecture about making too free with the men instead of going about amongst them perched up upon metaphorical stilts. Well, whatever he wants to see me about, it can't be for a wigging, or else he wouldn't have summoned me just close upon soup-and-'tater call.'

The smart-looking young subaltern drew himself up, looking his military best, as he made for the Major's quarters, before which, in light undress uniform, a private was marching up and down, crossing the doorway and the windows of the mess-room, through which the lamps of the dinner-table shone, as they were being lit by the servants. The regimental glass and plate were beginning to glitter on the table, while a soft, warm breeze was rustling the tropical leaves and beginning to cool the atmosphere, as it swept from the surrounding jungle through the widely opened casements.

'Yes! Come in!' came in a loud, bluff, rather rich voice; and the next minute Archie was face to face with the fine-looking, white-haired, florid Major in command of the infantry detachment stationed at Campong Dang in support of Her Majesty's Resident, Sir Charles Dallas, whose duty it was to instruct the Malay Rajah of Pahpah how to rule his turbulent bearers of spear and kris and wearers of sarong and baju, in accordance with modern civilisation, and without putting a period to their lives for every offence by means of the sudden insertion of an ugly-looking, wavy weapon before throwing them to the ugliest reptiles that ever haunted a muddy stream.

'Ah! Hum! Yes.'

There was a pause in the strange salute, and, ''Tis a row, then,' said Archie to himself.

'You received my despatch, Mr Maine?'

'Yes, sir.'

'And of course, sir, you are perfectly aware of my reasons for summoning you?'

'No, sir,' replied Archie.

'What! Now, that's what I intensely dislike, Mr Maine. If there is anything that annoys, irritates, or makes me dissatisfied with the men— the gentlemen under my command, it is evasion, shuffling, shirking, or prevarication.'

At the beginning of this speech the young officer felt nervous and troubled with a feeling of anxiety, but his commanding officer's tone and words sent the blood flushing up into his face, and he replied warmly:

'I beg your pardon, sir, but I am neither shuffling nor prevaricating when I tell you that I do not know why you have sent for me.' Then to himself,

'He could not have known about the Sergeant, for that was after he had sent his note.'

He had time to say this to himself, for the Major was staring at him in amazement.

'What! What! What!' he exclaimed. 'How—how dah you, sir? I'd have you to know that when I address my subordinates—ahem!—arrrum!—I—that is—hum—dear me, how confoundedly you have grown like your father, Archibald! Just his manner. I—that is—well, look here, sir; I have been very much put out about you. I promised my old comrade that I would do the best that I could in the way of helping you on and making you a useful officer and a thorough gentleman, and you know, between men, Archibald Maine, it has not been quite the thing. This is not the first time I have had to speak to you and complain of your conduct.'

'No, sir,' said the lad in rather a sulky tone; 'and when I was in fault I never shuffled or prevaricated.'

'Never, Archie, my lad,' said the Major energetically. 'It was bad form of me, but I was angry with your father's son. My words were ill-chosen, and there—there—I apologise.'

'Oh no, sir!' cried the lad, warming up and speaking excitedly; 'there is no need for that. I suppose I have been in the wrong, but I did not really know what I had been doing when you sent your letter.'

'Of course you did not, my boy; but—er—I was not thinking of that. It was about your conduct generally, and I had made up my mind to have you here and give you what you would call a wigging, Archie—eh ?—wigging, sir ! Dreadfully boyish expression !—and then, on second thoughts, I said to myself, " Much better to have the lad in quietly, break the ice and that sort of thing, tell him what I wanted to talk about, and then make him sit by me at the mess, and put it to him quietly over a glass of wine." Understand, my lad ? '

Archie's lips parted to speak, but the recollection of many old kindnesses began to crowd up so that he could not trust his voice, and he only nodded.

'That 's right. You see, my lad, your father and I were boys together—not perfect either. We used to quarrel frightfully. Well, sir, something inside me began to remind me of old times, and make apologies for you, and I was going to talk to you about being an officer and a gentleman—and dignity of manner, and impressing yourself upon your men— just point out that an officer can be kind to his lads and slacken the discipline a little sensibly without losing tone or touch, but there must be a proper feeling between officer and man. An officer need not be a bully and a tyrant, but he must be firm. His men must respect him, and see that the man who leads them knows his duty and is brave almost to a fault; and knowing this, every man who is worth his salt will follow him even to the death if duty calls. It is a grand position, Archie, my lad— that of being a leader of men—and it is shared with the General by the youngest subaltern who wears the Queen's scarlet. See what I mean ? '

'Yes, sir,' said the lad in a deep, low voice.

'Well, sir,' almost shouted the Major, 'that's what I was going to say to you, sir, over a glass of wine to-night, and put it to you that it was quite time that you, a young man grown, should put away boyish things and come to an end of tricks and pranks and youthful follies, and take upon you and show that you are worthy of the great birth-right—manhood, when—confound it all! I was nearly breaking out swearing!—in comes to me that—hang him!—that overbearing bully—Yah! Tut, tut, tut, tut, tut!—it put me out dreadfully, and I am speaking in haste, for Ripsy is a fine, trustworthy man—my best non-com.—to complain to me about you making a chum, a regular companion, of that confounded, low-bred cockney rascal, Pegg. Hang him! I'll have his peg sharpened and make him spin in a more upright manner before I have done with him! Ripsy told me that the fellow was on fatigue-work—takes advantage of the freedom of his position to sneak off to your quarters to hatch some prank or mischief or another; and I had to listen to his complaint and—confound him!—to answer his question, "Is it right for a subaltern to encourage a low-bred rascal like that to come to his quarters?" What do you say?'

'It was my fault, sir, entirely.'

'Yes; and that's your fault too, Archibald Maine. You take a fancy to and make a companion of a private who bears the worst character in this detachment. You see even now, sir, you have made so much of a companion of him that you are ready to take the blame for his fault.'

'In this case rightly, sir,' said Archie, speaking

with firmness. 'I had jerked your note out of the window, and as the poor fellow passed'——

'Poor fellow!' cried the Major irritably. 'There, again!'

'I told him to pick it up and bring it in,' continued Archie firmly; and the Major grunted, for he was evidently cooling down.

'There! Humph! Dinner,' grunted the Major again. 'Now, quick! What have you got to say?'

Archie was silent for a few moments, for the simple reason that he could not speak, only stand trying to gaze steadily in the eyes of the fine old officer, who was watching him intently with a look that forced him to speak at last; but even then his voice shook a little, in spite of his efforts to make it firm and loud. Then the word that had struggled for utterance came, and it was in Latin:

'Peccavi.'

It was only that word, but it was enough to make the old Major lean forward, clap one hand on the lad's shoulder, and half-whisper:

'Spoken like your father's son!' and then, as the door behind him opened, he half-shouted, 'Coming!' Then to his companion, 'Now, my lad—dinner!'

CHAPTER III.

A MALAY FRIEND.

ARCHIE MAINE'S sensations as he marched beside his chief into the mess-room were such that he would far rather have escaped to his own quarters; but he began to pull himself together as he caught sight of a friend, and the next minute he was being in turn introduced by the quiet, gentlemanly Resident to the Rajah Suleiman, a heavy-looking, typical Malay with peculiar, hard, dark eyes and thick, smiling lips, who greeted him in fair English and murmured something about 'visit' and the 'elephants and tigers.' And then, as the Eastern chief, who did not look at home in the English evening-dress he had adopted, turned away to smile upon another of the officers, Archie joined hands at once with a slight, youthful-looking visitor also in evening-dress, who as the youths chatted together showed his mastery of the English language sufficiently to address the subaltern as 'old chap,' following it up with:

'When are you going to get your boss to give you a day or two's leave?'

'Oh, I don't know,' replied Archie. 'Not for some time; I'm in disgrace.'

'Disgrace! What do you mean?' was the inquiry.

'Oh, not sticking enough to my duties.'

'Duties ?'

'Yes; drill and practice.'

'Oh, nonsense! You don't want to be always drilling and drilling and drilling. Your men could kill us all off without any more of that. I shall ask the Major to let you come and stay with me a month.'

'No, no, no,' said Archie, though his eyes were flashing with eagerness.

'And I say yes, yes, yes. I haven't got such a troop of elephants as Rajah Suleiman, but I have got two beauties who would face any tiger in the jungle, and my people could show you more stripes than his could. But perhaps I am so simple at home that you would rather go and stay with His Highness.'

'Look here, Hamet,' whispered Archie quickly; 'you said that to me last time, just as if I had slighted you.'

'Beg pardon, old chap. I didn't mean it; but your people—I don't know how it is—don't seem to take to me. I always feel as if they didn't trust me, and I don't think that I shall care about coming here any more.'

'What!' cried Archie excitedly, as he found that he had to take his seat at the table beside the young Rajah, whose face was beginning to assume a lowering aspect, as he saw that the Major's original intentions had been hurriedly set aside and the chair on the latter's right was occupied by the Rajah Suleiman, that on his left by a keen, sharp-looking gentleman who might have been met in one of the Parisian *cafés*, so thoroughly out of place did he seem in a military mess-room rather roughly erected in a station on the banks of a Malay jungle river.

'What!' said Archie again, in a low tone; and he noted how his companion was furtively watching the attention paid to his brother Rajah.

'I'll tell you presently,' said the young Malay. 'But who is that gentleman?'

'That? Oh, he's a traveller. He's a French count.'

'French count?' said his companion. 'A great friend of Suleiman's, isn't he?'

'Not that I know of.'

'Yes, he is. So one of my people says.'

'Oh?' said Archie.

'Yes; Suleiman met him when he went to Paris.'

'You seem to know all about it,' said Archie laughingly.

'Oh no; I *want* to know everything, but there is so much—so much to learn. I wish I had gone to Paris too.'

'What! so as to get to know the French count?'

'Pish!—No, thank you; I don't take wine,' he added quickly, as one of the officers' servants was filling glasses.

'Won't you have a glass of hock?'

'No,' was the quiet reply. 'And I don't want to know the French count. I don't like him.'

'Why?'

'Because he is Suleiman's friend.'

'That's saying you don't like Suleiman.'

'No. But I don't like him, and he hates me.'

'Why?'

'Because he likes my country.'

'And I suppose you like his?'

'I? No. I have got plenty of land that my father left me. He sent me—you know; I told you—to England.'

'Yes, I know; to be educated and made an English gentleman.'

'Yes,' said the young man, with a sigh; and his handsome half-Spanish countenance clouded over. 'And I did work so hard to make myself like you young Englishmen; but I had not the chance.'

'But you did splendidly. I heard of how high a position you took.'

The young Rajah smiled sadly and shook his head.

'You say that as a sort of compliment,' he said.

'That I don't. I never pay compliments, for I know you don't like them. If you did, you and I shouldn't be such friends.'

The young Rajah turned and gazed fixedly in the speaker's eyes for a few moments, and then turned hastily to help himself from the dish handed to him.

'No, we shouldn't,' he said in a low voice as soon as the dish was removed; and he began to trifle with the food. 'Yes,' he continued, 'those were jolly days at the big school; and it seemed so strange to come back here from studies and cricket and football.' He laughed softly as he turned merrily to look at his companion again. 'I say, how I used to get knocked about! The chaps used to say that it got my monkey up, but I suppose it did me good.'

'No doubt,' said Archie merrily. 'You got over wanting to kris the fellows, didn't you?'

'Of course; and it made me so English that I
don't want to kris the poor fellows now that I have
come back and am Maharajah here in my father's
stead.   But it was all no good,' he added, with a
sigh.

'What ?' exclaimed Archie wonderingly.

'No good,' repeated the young man.   'He sent
for me to come home, but it was only to say good-
bye and tell me that I was to love the English
and be their friend so as to make them my friends.
"They are a great people, Hamet," he said—"a
great people.   We are only little chiefs, but they
can rule the world."   I want to be their friend,
but somehow they don't like me but make much of
Suleiman.'

'Oh, wait a bit,' said Archie.   'I think you are
wrong.   We English are such blunt people.   Why,
our Major—he was my father's schoolfellow—he's
a splendid old chap.'

'Yes; but he doesn't trust me,' said the young
Malay.

'Oh, you wait.'

'I like your doctor.'

'Well, you must like Sir Charles Dallas.'

'What! Suleiman's Resident ?   I don't know
him.   Your English Queen—I mean Her Majesty '——

'Yes, I know,' said Archie, laughing.

'She has not sent a Resident to live in my
country.'

'No.   Do you know why ?'

'Yes,' said the young man coldly.   'She does not
trust me.'

'Ha, ha, ha!'

'Why do you laugh?'

'At you.'

'But why?'

'Because she does trust you—or, rather, our Government does.'

The young man turned sharply to gaze with a searching glance in the speaker's eyes.

'What do you mean?' he said.

'Go on with your dinner, old chap, and I'll tell you by-and-by. Here's Down wants to have a word with you.—Don't you, Down?'

'Ah yes, Captain Down,' said the young Rajah, bowing towards him. 'I seem to know you. Maine says you are such a splendid shot. Are you?'

'Oh, I can pull a trigger, and I can hit something sometimes,' said the young officer.

'Sometimes!' put in Archie. 'Why, he never misses. You ought to know more of him, Rajah. He's like that old country gentleman's two sons who loved hunting and shooting. He's a regular Nimrod and Ramrod rolled into one. Understand?'

'Yes; I read that in the old joke-book. Then your friend will come and have some shooting. Will you not?'

'Rather!' said the Captain; and the general conversation went on till the old English custom was in the ascendant and the Major gave Her Majesty's health and the band played 'God save the Queen;' and afterwards the Major proposed the health of their guest, His Highness Sultan Suleiman, who afterwards rose and bowed two or three times, said a few words very clumsily, and then turned towards the *distingué*-looking guest on the Major's left, and sat down; whereupon the French guest said a few words to the Major, who rose and announced that the Count de Lasselle would respond for the Sultan Suleiman.

There was the customary applause as the Count arose; and in very good English, which he only had to supplement now and then with a strong dash of French, he returned thanks for their illustrious guest, who, he could assure the English officers, had but one aim in life, and that was to be the friend and ally of the great British Queen. His speech was long and very flowery, and he did not forget to say that there was no other country in the world suited to be the Sultan's ally but beautiful France, his own country, he was proud to say, and he was sure that she too would always be the great friend of the Sultan; at which some one at the table uttered in a low voice that was almost like a cough the ejaculation, 'Hum!'

Archie turned sharply, and exchanged glances with Captain Down.

'What did the Doctor mean by that?' said the latter.

'Don't know,' said Archie. 'Shall I go and ask him?'

'By-and-by. Look at your friend.'

'Why? What do you mean?'

'He looks as if he felt that he was being left out in the cold.'

Archie glanced at the young Rajah, who was sitting back picking his cigarette to pieces; and then his attention was taken up by seeing the

big, bluff Sergeant of the regiment making his
way behind the chairs to where the Doctor was
seated.

'It's all right, Maine,' said the Captain; 'you
needn't go. The Major's sent Patient Job, as the
lads call him, to ask old Bolus what he means by
insulting the French guest.'

'Get out! Somebody taken ill. I hope it's
none of the ladies.'

The Doctor nodded, and left his chair, to follow
the Sergeant, just as the Major rose again to propose the health of the regiment's other guest that
evening, Maharajah Hamet, another of the chiefs,
who had declared himself the friend of their Queen
and country.

The toast was quietly received, and quietly replied
to in a few well-spoken words by the young Prince,
not without eliciting some remarks at his mastery
of English; and soon after the party broke up in
smoke, the officers strolling down to the banks of
the river, where the landing-place was gay with
Chinese lanterns hung here and there and ornamenting the two nagas of the Rajahs lying some
distance apart and filled by the well-armed followers
of the chiefs, one of whom was heartily cheered by
those assembled as he slowly walked in company
with his French companion to take his seat, before,
in response to three or four sonorous notes from a
gong, the yellow-uniformed rowers dipped their
oars lightly, to keep the dragon-boat in mid-stream
so that it might be borne swiftly onward.

The young Rajah Hamet remained some few
minutes longer, after taking his leave of the Major

and officers, and then, accompanied by Captain Down and Archie, he walked slowly along to where a guard of the English infantry was drawn up, the chief's men being waiting in their places, ready to push off.

'Don't take this as a compliment,' said the young Malay. 'It is all sincere, and I can make you very welcome in good old English fashion as long as you like to stay—you, Captain Down, and you, Maine. You make the Captain come too. I promise you plenty of sport. My shikaris know their business. Once more, good-night.'

He stepped back, the long, live-looking boat glided off, and the rowers' oars dipped with the vim and accuracy of an eight-oared racer on the Thames. But she made head slowly against the swift stream, while, as the young men watched her, their eyes rested upon the fire-flies glittering amongst the overhanging trees upon the banks, and all at once there was a loud splash just ahead of where the naga was gliding.

'What's that—some one overboard?' said the Captain.

'No, sir,' said a deep British voice from just behind where the young officers stood; 'only one of them great, scaly varmints getting out of the way.'

'Oh, it's you, Sergeant,' said Archie quickly; and then, on the impulse of the moment, the lad laid his hand on the big non-com.'s arm and said hurriedly, 'I've had it out with the Major, Ripsy, and it's all right now. But it was all my fault. Don't be too hard on poor Pegg.'

The Sergeant's reply was checked by a question from the Captain:

'Whom was the Doctor fetched to see? Any one ill?'

The Sergeant chuckled.

'No, sir. It was them rival niggers beginning to cut one another's throats; but I stopped it with my lads, and then fetched the Doctor. It gave him three or four little jobs. Some on them mean a row.'

CHAPTER IV.

THE DOCTOR'S PATIENTS.

THE looking-glass in Archie Maine's quarters often told him that he was rather a good-looking young fellow; that is to say, he gave promise of growing into a well-featured, manly youth without any foppish, effeminate, so-called handsomeness. But nature had been very kind to him, and, honestly, he scarcely knew anything about his own appearance; for when he looked in his glass for reasons connected with cleanliness—putting his hair straight, smoothing over his curliness, and playing at shaving away, or, rather, scraping off, some very smooth down—he had a habit of contracting his nerves and muscles so that a pretty good display of wrinkles came into view all over his forehead and at the corners of his lips and eyes, presenting to him quite a different-looking sort of fellow from the one known to his friends.

The morning after the mess dinner, he had given a parting glance in his little mirror, looking very much screwed up, for his mind was busy with rather troublous thoughts, among which were the events of the past day, especially those connected with his interview with the Major.

Then he had hurried off to take advantage of what little time he had before going on duty, and made for the Doctor's bungalow. It was not much of a place; but the glorious tropic foliage, the distant view of the river, and, above all, the flowers of the most brilliant colours that were always rushing into bloom or tumbling off to deck the ground made it a brilliant spot in the station, and as he neared it his face smoothed, his sun-browned forehead lost its wrinkles, and, just as he expected, he caught sight of the two reasons for the bungalow looking so bright and gay.

One reason was the Doctor's wife busy in the garden with a basket and a pair of scissors, snipping off bunch and cluster ready for filling vase and basin in the shaded rooms; the other was standing upon a chair helping climber to twine and tendril to catch hold of trellis and wire which made the front of the cottage-like structure one blaze of colour.

'Morning, ladies,' cried the lad.

'Morning, Archie,' cried the Doctor's wife, a pleasant, middle-aged, pink, sunshiny-looking lady, whose smooth skin seemed to possess the power of reflecting all sun-rays that played upon it so that they never fixed there a spot of tan. 'Come to help garden?'

'Yes; all right. What shall I do?' cried the lad.

'Make Minnie jump down off that chair, and tuck up the wild tendrils of that climber.'

'No, no, auntie; I don't want him,' cried the owner of the busy hands, as she reached up higher to hook on one tendril, and failed; for the long strand laden with blossom missed the wire that

ought to have held it, fell backwards, and, as if
directed by invisible fairy hands, formed itself into
a wreath over her hair, startling her so that she
would have lost her footing upon the chair had she
not made a quick leap to the floor of the veranda,
bringing down another trailing strand.

'Ha, ha! Serve you right, Miss Independence!'
cried Archie, running to her help.

'No, no, don't. I can do it myself,' cried the
girl. 'Mind; that flower's so tender, and I know
you will break it.'

'Suppose I do,' said Archie. 'No, you don't;
I'll take it off and twine it up myself, even if my
fingers are so clumsy. I say, Minnie, it's lucky for
you that it isn't that climbing rose, or there would
be some scratches.'

He sprang upon the chair, busied himself for
a few minutes, and then leaped down again, to
stand with brow wrinkled, gazing up at his work.

'There,' he said; 'won't that do?'

'Yes,' said the girl, with a slight pout of two
rather pretty lips. 'It will do; but it isn't high
enough.'

'Oh, come, it's higher than you could have
reached.—Don't say the Doctor's out, Mrs Morley?'

'No; but he's got somebody with him;' and the
speaker glanced at her niece, who turned away and
looked conscious. 'I am not surprised,' continued
the Doctor's wife, and she looked fixedly now at her
visitor.

'What at?' replied the lad wonderingly.

'How innocent!—What do you say, Minnie?
Look at him!'

The girl turned sharply, fixed her eyes upon the young officer's face, and laughed merrily.

'What are you laughing at?' he cried, hurriedly taking out a handkerchief. 'Have I made my face dirty?'

'No, sir.—We were quite right, auntie. I can't think how young men can be so stupid.'

''Tis their nature to,' said Archie, laughing, as he replaced his handkerchief. 'But what have I been doing stupid now, Minnie?'

'Sitting in a hot room and drinking what doesn't agree with you, sir.'

'I couldn't help the room being hot,' replied the lad, rather indignantly.

'No, sir; but you could have helped giving yourself a headache and coming here this morning to ask uncle for a cooling draught.'

'Oh, that's it, is it, Miss Clever? Well, you are all wrong.'

'I am glad to hear it, Archie,' said Mrs Morley. 'I thought you had come to see the Doctor.'

'That's right,' said the lad, screwing up his face again and nodding rather defiantly, boy and girl fashion, at the young lady gardener. 'Somebody ill?'

'No, my dear boy. It's only Sir Charles Dallas;' and as she spoke she glanced at her niece again, who had suddenly become busy over a fresh loose strand. 'He's come to ask about the men who were wounded in that wretched quarrel last night.'

'Why, that's what I came for.—Do you hear, Minnie?'

Just then a door somewhere in the interior was opened, and men's voices reached their ears, one being the Doctor's.

'No, nothing to worry about, sir; do them good.'

'Ah, you keep to your old belief in the lancet, then, Doctor,' came in the Resident's pleasant, firm tones.

'In a case like this, certainly, sir. All the better for losing a little of their hot, fiery blood. Set of quarrelsome, jealous fools. Here we are, thousands of miles from home and Ould Ireland, amongst these tribes, all of them spoiling for a fight.'

'Yes, Doctor,' said the Resident, slowly approaching as he crossed the room; 'but I hope to get them tamed down in time.'

'Ha, ha!' laughed the Doctor, as the two gentlemen came in sight.—'Hear him, Minnie! What's the quotation—"Hope springs eternal in the human breast"?'

'I forget uncle.'

'More shame for you.—Hope away, Dallas; but you will never tame the fighting spirit out of a Malay.—Morning, Archie, my lad. What do you say?'

'I say that Rajah Hamet is tame enough, only one ought not to talk about him as if he were a wild beast.—Good-morning, Sir Charles?'

'Morning, my lad,' replied the Resident, with a peculiar smile. 'Have you got a head on this morning?'

'No, sir, I haven't got a head on this morning,' cried the boy angrily, and with his sun-browned cheeks flushing up.

'I beg your pardon, sir. I thought you had come to see the Doctor.'

'So I have,' said Archie, drawing himself up and glancing across at Minnie, and then giving himself an angry jerk as he saw that she was laughing.

'Do you want to see me, Maine?' said the Doctor.

'Yes, sir, if you are at liberty.'

'Yes; all right, my lad.—Don't trouble yourself, Dallas. That will be all right.—Into my room, Maine;' and he led the way into a pleasant, comfortably furnished room looking out upon the clearing at the back, a room evidently the Doctor's surgery more than consulting-room, but whose formality was softened down by the cut-flowers which indicated the busy interference of the ladies of the house. 'Sit down, my lad,' continued the Doctor, as he took a bamboo chair opposite that to which he had motioned his visitor; and gazing searchingly at him, he reached out his hand: 'Head queer?'

'No, no, sir,' cried the subaltern, with his brow wrinkling up again. 'I only wanted to know about last night and the men wounded.'

'Oh! That's what Sir Charles came about. Well, it's nothing much, my boy. It's rather a large pull on my roll of sticking-plaster and a few bandages—rival clans or houses—do you bite your thumb at me, sir?—eh—Montagus and Capulets. Consequence of men carrying lethal weapons—only krises instead of rapiers. Bad thing to let men carry arms.'

'What about soldiers, then, sir?' said Archie merrily. 'Bayonets, side-arms?'

'Ah, but there we have a discipline, my dear boy. But, all the same, it has fallen to my lot to treat a bayonet-dig or two when our fellows have got at the rack. Well, I am glad you are all right. I thought you looked a little fishy about the gills.'

'Not I, sir. I managed a splendid breakfast this morning.'

'Yes, boy; you are good that way. I often envy you, for what with my health and every one's health to think about, doctoring one man for fever, putting all you fellows straight, and patching up squabbling savages, my appetite often feels as if it wants a fillip. A doctor's is an anxious life, my boy—more especially out here in a country like this, amongst a very uncertain people, when a man feels that he has a stake in the country.'

'But you have no stake in the country, sir?'

'What, sir! I? Haven't I my wife and my sister's child?'

'Oh, I thought you meant something commercial, sir.'

'What! I? Pooh, boy! I was alluding to the uncertainty of our position here.'

'Oh! Oh, I see, sir. That's all right enough. Here's Sir Charles with a strong detachment of British infantry under his command, and the native chiefs are bound to respect him.'

'Tremendous!' said the Doctor, with a snort. 'A couple of hundred men!'

'Three, sir.'

'Three indeed! What about the men on the sick-list, and the non-combatants that have to be counted in every squad? Why, if that fellow

Suleiman turned nasty, where should we be, out here in the depths of this jungle?'

'Oh, there's no occasion to fear anything of that sort, sir.'

'What! Not for a boy like you, Archie Maine, with a suit or two of clothes, a razor, and hair-brush. You put on your cap, and you cover all your responsibilities. What about the women, high and low, that we have to look after?'

'Oh, they'd be all right, sir.'

'Would they?'

'I say, Doctor, don't talk like that. You don't think that we have anything to fear?'

'I don't know.—Well, fear? No, I suppose I mustn't mention such a thing as fear; but we are hundreds of miles away from Singapore and help.'

'Oh no, sir. There's the river. It wouldn't take long for the gunboat to bring up reinforcements and supplies; and then, even if Mr Sultan Suleiman turned against us—which isn't likely '——

'I don't know,' growled the Doctor.

'Well, sir, I think I do,' said Archie, rather importantly. 'Why, if he did, there's our friend the Rajah Hamet. He would be on our side.'

'Ah, that I don't know,' said the Doctor again; and he tapped the table with his nails. 'This is all in confidence, boy. I don't think Sir Charles has much faith in that young gentleman. But still, that's the way that our Government worked things in India.'

'I don't quite understand you.'

'Read up your history, then, my boy. Our position in India has been made by the jealousies of the

different princes and our political folks working
them one against another. But there, you didn't
come here to chatter politics. What is it? You
have got something more to say to me, haven't
you?'

'Well—er—yes, sir,' hesitated the lad.

'Out with it, boy. Never play with your medical
man. No half-confidences. I can pretty well read
you, Archie, so out with it frankly.'

'Well, sir, I did half make up my mind to speak
to you, and came this morning on purpose; and then
as soon as I saw you I felt that it was foolish—a
sort of fancy of mine.'

'Well, go on; let me judge. You have got something the matter with you?'

'That's what I don't quite know, sir,' said the
young man, who was now scarlet.

'Well, don't shilly-shally. Let me judge. Is it
some bodily ailment?'

'No, sir.'

'Glad of it. What is it, then? It can't be
money.'

'Oh no, sir.'

'Of course not. No temptations here to spend.
Then you have got into some big scrape?'

'I am always getting into scrapes, sir.'

'Yes; and the Major had you up to give you a
wigging, as you call it, only yesterday.'

'How did you know that, sir?' cried the lad
excitedly.

'The Doctor knows pretty well everything about
people, and what he doesn't know for himself his
women find out for him. Now then, what is it?'

'I am afraid you will laugh at me, sir.'

'I promise you I shall not.'

'Thank you, sir; that's encouraging.'

'To the point, boy—to the point.'

Archie Maine drew a deep breath as if to pull himself together, and then as he met the Doctor's searching eyes they seemed to draw out of him that which he wished to say.

'I am afraid, Doctor,' he said excitedly, 'that I have got something wrong with my head.'

'Why? Pain you? Feeling of confusion?'

The lad shook the part of his person mentioned.

'Dizziness?'

'Oh no, sir; nothing of that sort.'

'Well, go on. A doctor isn't a magician. Have you got a bad tooth? You must tell him which one to attack with his key preliminary to the scraunch.'

'Oh, you are laughing at me, Doctor.'

'Only smiling, my dear boy.'

'I don't see anything to laugh at, sir, because it is a serious thing to me.'

'Good lad. I smiled because I felt happy over you since it didn't seem to be anything serious.'

'But it *is* serious, sir.'

'Let's hear. You say you have got something wrong with your head?'

'Well, I suppose it is my head, sir. But you know I am always getting into some trouble or another.'

'Exactly. You are notorious for your boyish pranks.'

'Yes, sir; and I want to get the better of it.

It 's as the Major said : the troubles I get into are boys' troubles, and not suitable to a young man.'

'The Major's wise, Archie. Then why don't you put off all your boyish mischief and remember that you are now pretty well a man grown, and, as one of our lads would say in his cockney lingo, "act as sich " ? '

'Because I can't, Doctor,' said the lad earnestly. 'I want to act as a man. I 'm six feet two, and I shave regularly.'

'Humph !' grunted the Doctor, who had to make an effort to keep his countenance.

'And whenever I get into trouble I make a vow that I 'll never do such a childish, schoolboyish thing again ; but it 's no use, for before many days have passed, something tempts me, and I find myself doing more foolish things than ever. Can it be that there is some screw loose in my head ? '

The Doctor sat looking earnestly in the lad's agitated countenance, for his brow was one tangle of deeply marked wrinkles.

'I think sometimes I must be going mad, or at all events growing into an idiot, and you can't think how wretched and despairing it makes me. Do you think medicine—tonic or anything of that sort—would do me good ? '

The Doctor gazed at the lad fixedly till he could bear it no longer, and he was about to speak again, when the adviser uttered a loud expiration of the breath, jumping up at the same time and clapping his hands heavily on his visitor's shoulders.

'No, my lad, I don't,' he cried boisterously. 'You are sound as a bell, strong as a young horse. Why,

you ought to be proud of yourself instead of fidgeting with a lot of morbid fancies. You have been
for years and years a boy, fresh—larky, as you
would say—full of mischief, as I was myself'——

'You, Doctor! Impossible!'

'What! Ha, ha! Why, Archie Maine, I have
watched you pretty thoroughly since we have been
friends, noted your pranks, and seen the trouble you
have got into with the Major. Oh yes; I believe
I was much worse than you. And you are now
changing into the man, when most fellows of your
age begin thinking more of others than of themselves; though they are pretty good at that latter,
and particularly fond of arranging their plumage so
as to excite admiration. But you held on to your
merry, mischievous boyhood, so take my advice and
don't worry yourself any more. I hope you have
got many, many years to come, and you will find
yourself serious enough then. So you thought yours
might be a case for medical advice? Not it!'

'But'—— ejaculated Archie.

'But me no buts, as the man said in the book.
You will be cured fast enough in the first real trouble
that comes upon us and makes its genuine appeal to
your manhood.'

'But I get plenty of trouble now, Doctor,' protested the lad.

'Bah! A bit of a rowing—a snub from the
Major! Trifles, boy. Those are not real troubles.
I mean times when you find out that you really are
a man, that others' lives are perhaps depending upon
you as a soldier for preservation. My dear boy, all
you have got to do is not to try to be a man.

Nature will do that. Your full manhood will come quite soon enough. Only try to drop a little of the boy, for you are a bit too young. Well, what are you staring at?'

Archie's face was more wrinkled than ever.

'Ah, I see,' continued the Doctor. 'You are doubting whether you shall believe me. Here's a pretty fellow! Comes to a medical man for advice, and begins to doubt him as soon as the advice is given.—Here, Maria—Minnie!'

'No, for goodness' sake, Doctor! And Sir Charles is there!'

'No, he isn't. I heard him start ten minutes ago.'

'But you are not going to tell them what I said?'

'Do I ever tell my patients' secrets to anybody? Now, look here, Archie; 'you want to jump right into your manhood at once?'

'Of course I do, sir.'

'Well, my lad, I'm afraid you won't have long to wait, for if I'm not very much mistaken your cure is coming.'

'What! mischief with the Malays, sir?'

'This is in confidence, my lad—yes. But look here,' continued the Doctor, lowering his voice, for at that moment voices were heard apparently approaching the Doctor's room. 'Tut, tut!' he muttered. 'They have no business to be coming here now. I suppose they don't class you as a patient. Humph! All right. They are not coming here. Look here, Archie,' he continued, as he threw himself back in his chair; 'mine may only be suspicions, but situated as we are here amongst these people, who, in spite of their half-civilisation, have a good deal of the savage at heart and the natural strong dislike for those who hold them in subjection, it is good policy to be a little too wise and not careless and indifferent over matters that give one food for thought.'

'But, Doctor'—— said the young man earnestly, and with a touch of excitement in his tones.

'There, there, there, don't fly out. I was only going to say that I can't help feeling doubtful at times about our position here.'

'But you don't think that the Malays'——

'Yes, I do—I think that they are very untrustworthy. They dislike us for religious reasons as well as for taking possession of their country, and, in short, there are times when I can't help feeling that we are living on the slopes of a moral volcano which might burst forth at any moment.'

'But, Doctor, they seem so friendly.'

'Yes, my lad; as you say, they seem so friendly.'

'Why, lots of the people quite worship you. See how they come for advice.'

'Oh yes,' said the Doctor dryly, 'I get plenty of native patients; but that doesn't make their own doctors any fonder of me. Still, I dare say I can get on very well, and, as I have suggested, I may be too suspicious. Nothing may happen for years— perhaps never. But you are a soldier.'

'Well, yes, sir,' said the lad, laughing. 'Old Ripsy's trying to make me one.'

'And you *are* a soldier, my lad; and though you mayn't have to fight, you will quite agree with me that it is wise to keep your powder dry.'

'Of course, sir.'

'There's no harm in that, eh?'

'Of course not, sir.'

'Well, men are men, and women are women.'

'Yes, sir,' said the lad, smiling.

'And we don't want to frighten them by letting them see that we are always going to the magazine. See what I mean?'

'Yes, sir. You mean, not let them know that you have any doubts about our position here.'

'Good. I went a roundabout way to put it before you, but you have hit the right nail clean on the head at once. We want to make their lives as sunshiny as we can, and not try to point out clouds where as likely as not there are none.'

'Of course not, sir.'

'Right, Archie. A quiet, thoughtful man would, of course, be careful not to discuss matters before our womenkind that might have an alarming tendency.'

'And you think I, a boy, might, sir?' said Archie, frowning heavily.

'Yes,' said the Doctor; 'but not after such a broad hint as I am giving you now, my lad;' and he leaned forward and patted his visitor upon the knee.

The change in Archie Maine's countenance was instantaneous. The wrinkles of doubt were smoothed out from his forehead, and he stood up, gazing as it were straight past the Doctor into the future, his lips compressed and a general tensity of expression seeming to pervade every feature. Then he started violently, for the Doctor exclaimed:

'Well done! The cure has begun.'

'What do you mean, Doctor?'

'Only this, my lad: that very likely there may

be several relapses, but you are growing up fast. There, our consultation is over, and I suppose you have no more to say to me?'

'Yes, one thing, Doctor,' said the young man in a low tone, for the ladies' voices were heard once more.

'Well, what is it?'

'Only this, sir—private and confidential.'

'Of course. What do you mean?'

'You will not tell Mrs Morley what I have said?'

'Is it likely, my lad?' cried the Doctor merrily, as he clapped his visitor on the shoulder. 'There, be off. You are keeping a patient waiting.'

The Doctor threw open the door and led the way out into the veranda, where Mrs Morley and Minnie were standing beside a black-haired, black-eyed, young native woman, who was squatted down in the shade, and who now started up hurriedly from where she had evidently been holding up a solemn-looking little child of about two years old for the ladies' inspection.

The woman's dark eyes flashed, and she made a movement as if to cover her face, but snatched away her hand directly and stood up proudly for a moment, before bowing low and not ungracefully to the Doctor as he gave her a quick nod.

'Here is Dula,' said Mrs Morley. 'She has brought up her sick child.'

'Yes, I see,' said the Doctor, rather gruffly, as he frowned at the swarthy little patient. 'But I wish Dula could talk English or I could talk her tongue a little better.'

The woman smiled intelligently as she rearranged

the bright-coloured plaid sarong around the child and said in a pleasant voice :

'Ba-be bet-ter.'

The Doctor took a step forward, and the child shrank from him as he laid his hand upon its head and gazed fixedly in its eyes.

'Now, little one,' he said, 'we did teach you to put out your tongue last time.'

'Tongue—tongue,' said the woman quickly; and she held the child towards the Doctor, while Archie and Minnie exchanged glances, and then burst out laughing; for, in obedience to a shake given by its mother, the tiny girl uttered a low whimper, screwed up her face as if about to cry, and then thrust out a little red tongue, drew it back instanter, and buried her face in her mother's breast.

'All right,' said the Doctor to the woman.   'It is getting well fast.'

'Well—fast!' cried the woman, catching up his words quickly; and then, with the tears welling over from her great dark eyes, she bent down, caught at the Doctor's hand, and held it quickly to her lips.

'Oh, oh, that's all right,' said the Doctor hastily, as he drew back his hand and patted the woman's shoulder.

'Look, uncle, what Dula has brought us!' cried Minnie; and she took from the veranda table a great bunch of the beautiful white creeper which the native women were fond of wearing in their black hair.

'Aha!' said the Doctor.   'Thank you.—My fee, Archie.'

'Not all,' said Mrs Morley.   'She has brought

you one of those horrible durians;' and as the Doctor's wife spoke Minnie caught up a little, bamboo-woven native basket, in which, carefully arranged among freshly gathered fern, was one of the peculiar-looking native fruits, the produce of one of the great trees so carefully planted and cared for in nearly every native village. 'Don't! Don't touch the horrid thing, my dear,' whispered Mrs Morley.

'What!' cried the Doctor; and he took the great, hard-shelled fruit from the basket and turned it over in his hands. 'Capital!' he cried. 'A beauty!'

'Ugh!' ejaculated Mrs Morley; and Minnie screwed up her face into a pretty grimace, as she once more exchanged glances with Archie.

'Doc-tor like?' questioned the woman, with an anxious look.

'Yes,' he replied, smiling. 'I like them very much.'

'Like—very—much,' said the woman. 'Dula glad.' And then, soothing her child tenderly, she whispered a few words to it in her native language.

'Oh, come,' said the Doctor, 'I do understand that. Your mother's quite right: I sha'n't eat you.'

The woman smiled again as she hugged her child closer and kissed it lovingly, while the Doctor nodded to Minnie.

'Quite comic, isn't it, my dear? What foolish things mothers are, aren't they? Just as fond of their bairns as Englishwomen, eh?'

'Why, of course, uncle. Such a pretty little thing, too! Look at its eyes!' and, to the mother's great delight, the girl crossed to her, took the child in her arms, and kissed it, while the little thing smiled, raised one hand, and softly stroked the girl's white face.

'There, Archie,' she cried; 'it is pretty, isn't it?'

'A beauty!' said the young man, laughing.

'Come and kiss it, sir,' said the girl imperiously.

'All right;' and without more ado the lad took hold of the child, held it up, and kissed it twice.

'Oh, take care!' cried Minnie. 'How clumsy you are!'

'Well, it doesn't seem to think so,' cried the lad, as he handed the little one back to its mother, who said a few words in her own tongue to the Doctor, and then turned to the two ladies, and after bowing to them with native grace, bent low to Archie, gave him a grateful look, and walked slowly away.

'Oh, you young humbug!' growled the Doctor.

'Why?' said Archie warmly.

'Just to show off before my wife and Minnie. I believe you were growling all the time and calling it a dirty little nigger.'

'That I wasn't! I don't mind babies when they are as big as that.'

'No—don't *mind*,' said the Doctor sarcastically.

'And I didn't call it a little nigger. I was wishing there was some sugar near.—Oh, I say, doesn't your durian smell?'

'Horrid!' exclaimed Minnie.

'All right, my dear,' said the Doctor. 'I can bear it. But you will come down some day, my lady.'

'Never, uncle!'

'We shall see,' said the Doctor. 'My word, what

a beauty !—Here, Archie, drop in this evening and help me to have it for dessert.'

'I'm sure Archie won't touch the nasty thing, uncle.'

'Oh, won't I?' cried the lad. 'Only too glad of the chance.'

Minnie made a grimace and turned away, but turned back directly on hearing Archie's next words :

'I say, Doctor, that woman shows how the people here like you.'

'Well, yes,' said the gentleman addressed, 'I suppose they do feel a little obliged; but I don't think they care much.'

'Oh, uncle,' cried Minnie, 'I am sure they do. See how pleased that boatman was—that man who came up to you out of the sampan, and who brought us that fish afterwards. Why, I believe that he would have done anything for you.'

'I believed once that he was going to do something for me, my dear.'

'Now, don't talk nonsense, my dear,' said Mrs Morley. 'I told you not to talk about that.'

'You did, Mary. But it was an awkward position; wasn't it, Minnie?'

'I agree with aunt, uncle, that a lot of it was invention.'

'Oh, it wasn't invention, Archie. It was an awful position for a poor surgeon.'

'I haven't heard anything about this,' said Archie.

'Well, it was like this, my boy. He was about one of the biggest and fiercest fellows that I have seen here. There was only one good thing about him : he could speak bad English. He came up here one day and tried to make me understand that he was in terrible pain. But that was plain enough, for as soon as he was in my room he began stamping about, pointing to his mouth.'

'What! had he got the toothache?' said Archie.

'Yes—one of those awfully bad ones; and twice over he clapped his hand to his waist and uncovered the handle of his kris as if he meant to use it. It quite startled me.'

'Now, Henry, pray do not exaggerate so. I do wish you wouldn't be so fond of ornamenting your anecdotes.'

'Well, really, my dear, if I didn't touch up a story a little bit, young Maine here wouldn't be able to grasp it.'

'Was he in such pain, then, sir,' said Archie, 'that he wanted you to think he would kill himself?'

'Yes, my lad; and being such a fierce-looking fellow, he made me feel quite nervous, for twice over he looked as if he was going to use a kris on me, and I began to look round my bottles for something to use in self-defence.'

'Chloroform, I suppose,' said Mrs Morley sarcastically.

'No, my dear; something much stronger than that.'

'That's a new improvement, Henry,' said Mrs Morley.

'There, she won't let me tell you, Archie. You ask me, and I will tell you the story some day when we are alone.'

'Oh no, Doctor; you have raised my curiosity, and I want to hear it now.'

'Oh, pray go on,' said Mrs Morley.

'Well, don't interrupt me, then.'

Minnie and Archie exchanged laughing glances, and the Doctor went on :

'Well, I got him down in a chair, and as he lay back he opened his mouth and displayed a tremendous set of the biggest and whitest teeth I ever saw.'

'Ahem !' coughed Minnie, with a merry look at Archie.

'Fine, healthy-looking man he was, but he had the regular savage Malay look in his eyes ; but I gained courage directly I saw what was the matter. There was one great double tooth which was evidently the cause of all the trouble, and I knew at once that he would have no peace till it was drawn. There was a position for a medical man ! And I could not help feeling that I was quite at his mercy. I went to a drawer and took out an instrument, and as I approached him he glared at me more savagely than ever, and laid his right hand once more upon the ugly, pistol-like hilt of his kris. Now, sir, what would you have done under the circumstances ? '

'Bolted,' said Archie laconically.

'I don't believe you,' said Minnie.

'What ! and left two defenceless women at his mercy, sir ? That won't do; will it, Mary, my dear ? '

'Well, then,' said Archie, 'I should have called in old Sergeant Ripsy and a couple more men to hold him. Or why didn't you give him a dose of something to send him to sleep ? But I know. You got tight hold of the tooth and tugged it out.'

Trapped. D

'How are you going to get tight hold of a savage's tooth when you can see him ready to pull out his kris, and your hands are trembling like banana-leaves in a storm ?'

'Well, I should have asked him to give me the kris to put away in case of accidents,' said Archie merrily.

'Ask a Malay to give you his head to put away in case of accidents !' cried the Doctor sarcastically. 'No, sir; I took my courage in both hands and approached him.'

'Why, you were holding the instrument in one hand, sir,' said Archie merrily; and Minnie laughed.

'Ah, you are getting too sharp, sir,' cried the Doctor. 'But I can tell you it was nervous work, and for a few minutes I felt sure that if I operated on him he would operate on me; and if I had thought of it at the time, I think I should have called in my wife to stand sentry with a revolver.'

'Oh dear me !' sighed Mrs Morley, as she drew some work out of her handbag.

'Well,' continued the Doctor, 'I got a good hold of the tooth at last, gave a wrench '——

'And out came the tooth,' said Archie quickly.

'No, it didn't, sir; and as I stood over the man, looking down into his fierce eyes, he snatched his hand from his waist, and I turned cold, for I felt it was all over, when in an instant up came the other hand, and both of them closed over my wrist, giving me such a wrench that it quite startled me; and it was then that the tooth came out.'

'And the toothache was cured, sir ?' cried Archie.

'Minnie, my dear,' said Mrs Morley quietly, 'do you notice any difference in that story since your uncle told it last?'

'Yes, aunt; it is much more flowery than it used to be.'

'Flowery!' growled the Doctor. 'Why, Archie, my lad, that story is as true as true. Indeed, I should have been able to show you the great tooth as a proof, only the man took it away. He was one of my first patients when I came here; and I never had any fee.'

'For shame, Henry! The man is always bringing you fruit or fish. I am sure that he would do anything for you.'

'Well, yes,' said the Doctor, 'he has been grateful in his way; but I never feel sure that those fellows will not make use of their krises.'

CHAPTER V.

THE OFFICERS' WASHING.

'OH, here you are, Mrs Smithers. Aunt was saying just now that she wondered you had not been up. I told her perhaps it was on account of the hot weather, for it has been terribly trying.'

'Oh, bless your heart, Miss Minnie!' said the tall, sturdy, buxom-looking woman who had just set down a big basket in the veranda, 'the weather doesn't make no difference to me. Whether it's hot or whether it's cold, I have got to get my bit of washing done; though I am a bit tried when it comes to that mounsoon, or mounseer, or whatever they call it, when it's such strange, hard work to get the things dry. But even then it ain't fair to complain, for the soft water's lovely, and plenty of it. But I am late again this week, and it has been very hard work to get the officers washed. 'Tain't half-an-hour since I took young Mr Maine's home to his quarters. I hope your aunt ain't cross with me.'

'Oh no, she's not angry. She knew there must be some good reason. We were half-afraid you were ill.'

'Not me, Miss Minnie! I've never no time to be ill; and if I had been, no matter how bad I was I should have been up here to the Doctor for one of his exhibitions, as he calls them. I've brought

his white suit, miss, and it looks lovely. Shall I
show it you?'

'I know how it will be, Mrs Smithers,' said
Minnie, smiling. 'I am glad there has been nothing
wrong.'

'Oh, don't you be glad, miss. It's sorry I am.'

'Why, what's the trouble?'

'Trouble, miss? Oh, my master again. He will
never be happy till he is having the Rogues' March
played over him, and the buttons that I keep sewed
on tighter than those of any man in his company
cut off his beautiful uniform, and him drummed out
as a disgrace to the regiment.'

'Dear, dear!' said Minnie. 'I am very sorry,
Mrs Smithers.'

'Yes; I knowed you would be, my dear, if you
will forgive me for calling you so. You see, I have
known you so long as such a dear, sweet young
lady, with no more pride in you than there is in
one of our Jenny-wrens at home.'

'But what is the matter, Mrs Smithers?' said
Minnie hastily, in an effort to change the flow of
the bronzed, burly woman's words into another
direction.

'You needn't ask, my dear. The old thing.'

'What! surely not drinking again? I thought
he had taken the pledge, and that Sergeant Ripsy
had promised you that he would keep a sharp eye
over your husband.'

'Oh yes, miss, that's all right; and he daren't
go to the canteen, for they wouldn't admit him.
But what's the use of that when he can manage
to get some of that nasty rack, as they call it, from

the first Malay fellow he meets ? I'd like to rack 'em !'

'It's such a pity,' said Minnie. 'Such a good soldier as he is, too. I've heard Mr Maine say that there isn't a smarter-looking man in his company; and my uncle praises him too.'

'Praises him, my dear!' said the woman, looking at the speaker round-eyed. 'Praises him ! A-mussy me, what for ?'

'He says he's such a fine-looking man.'

'Fine-looking ? Oh yes, he's fine-looking enough,' said the woman scornfully.

'And that he is so strong and manly and hearty, and that he never wants to come on the sick-list.'

'Sick-list ! No, my dear, he dursen't. He knows only too well that your dear uncle would know at once what was the matter with him.'

'But he's such a smart-looking fellow—so clean, Mr Maine says, that he is quite a pattern to the others when he comes on parade.'

'Oh yes, that's all right, my dear; but who makes him smart ? Who cleans his buttons and buckles, and pipeclays him, but his poor wife ? Why, many's the time I have had to flannel his face and hands before he went on parade.'

'Well, well,' said Minnie compassionately, 'let's hope he will improve.'

'Improve, my dear ? I've give up hopes. He says that the climate don't agree with him, but when we was at Colchester he used to say he was obliged to take a little to keep off the colic, for the wind off the east coast was so keen; and the same when we were in Canada. That was when we were first married, and I was allowed to come on the strength of the regiment, many long years ago, my dear; and I have done the officers' washing ever since, or I don't know what we should have done. Then when we came out to Injy and it was so hot, he used to say if he didn't have a little something he should be a dead man, because it was so horrid dry; and now we are stationed here he sticks out that he only takes a little to keep off the jungle fever. Any one would think he was fighting against being invalided home, but he don't deceive the Sergeant, and he tells me that Joe will go too far one of these days; and he will break my heart if he does, and I'm always in a skeer as I think and think and wonder how far he will have to go before being sent home. I don't know what's to become of me if I am sent there. Home, sweet home, they calls it, Miss Minnie. I suppose you would like to go?'

'Well, for some things, yes, Mrs Smithers; but I am very happy here.'

'Of course you are, my dear. You are so young and pretty and good.'

'Oh, nonsense, Mrs Smithers! I am very happy here because I think aunt likes me being companion to her, and dear uncle wouldn't like me to go away.'

'Of course he wouldn't, my dear, bless him! for he's a good, true man, though he does talk a bit hard sometimes, and every one likes him. See how good he is to all these Malay folk, who have no call upon him at all. Oh dear! it will be a hard time for every one when you do go away. I know I shall about cry my eyes out.'

'But I am not going away, Mrs Smithers,' said Minnie laughingly.

'Not going away, my dear ? No, not this week, nor next week, nor next year perhaps. But you needn't tell me; it would be against Nature for you to stop here always. Such a young lady as you can't be allowed to do as she likes. All the same, though, my dear, I should be glad to see you go home.'

'You would, Mrs Smithers ?'

'Yes, my dear, for I don't think it's nice for English womenkind to be out here amongst these betel-chewing, half-black people, going about in their cotton and silk plaid sarongs, as they call them, and every man with one of those nasty ugly krises stuck in his waist. Krises I suppose they call them because they keep them rolled up in the creases of their Scotch kilt things. I often lie in bed of a night feeling thankful that I have got a good, big, strong husband to take care of me, bad as he is. For my Joe can fight. Yes, I often feel that we womenkind aren't safe here.'

'Oh, for shame, Mrs Smithers ! Who could feel afraid with about three hundred brave British soldiers to take care of them ?'

'I could, miss, and do often. It's all very well to talk, and I know that if these heathens rose up against us our British Grenadiers would close up and close up till the last man dropped. But what's the good of that when we should be left with no one to take care of us ? Oh, my dear ! my dear !' said the woman, with a look of horror crossing the big brown face.

'Mrs Smithers, you must have been upset this
week, to talk like that.'

'I—I 'ave, my dear; and it's a shame of me to
stand here putting such miserable ideas into your
head; but I had a very hard day yesterday, for my
Joe had been extra trying, and I couldn't get a
wink of sleep, for after being so angry with him
that I could have hit him, I lay crying and thinking what a wicked woman I was for half-wishing
that he was dead; for he is my husband, my dear,
after all, and—— Morning, ma'am—I mean, good-
afternoon,' cried the woman respectfully. 'I am so
sorry to be late this week, and I hope the Doctor's
quite well.'

CHAPTER VI.

ARCHIE OPENS HIS EARS.

THE mess dinner was over, and the officers were sitting back by one of the open windows, dreamily gazing out at the dark jungle and breathing in with a calm feeling of satisfaction the soft, comparatively cool air that floated up on the surface of the swift river.

It was very still, not a word having been spoken for some time; not a sound came from the native campong, while it was hard to believe that within touch of the mess-room there were the quarters of nearly three hundred men. But once in a while something like a whisper came from the jungle, suggesting the passing through its dense tangle of some prey-seeking, cat-like creature. But no one spoke; though, in a half-drowsy way, those seated by the window and a couple of dark figures outside in the veranda were straining their ears and trying to make out what caused the distant sounds. Then some one spoke:

'Asleep, Archie?'

'No. I was trying to make out what was that faint cry. Do you know, Down?'

'Didn't hear any faint cry.'

'Listen, then.'

'Can't. Deal too drowsy.—Lots of fire-flies out to-night.'

'Yes; aren't they lovely?—all along the river-bank. They put me in mind of the tiny sparks at the back of a wood fire.'

'A wood fire? What do you mean—a forest on fire?'

'No, no; at home, when you are burning logs of wood and the little sparks keep running here and there all over the back of the stove, just like fire-works at a distance.'

'Ah, yes, they do look something like that, just as if the leaves of the overhanging bushes all burst out into light.'

'Yes,' said Archie; 'and when the soft breeze blows over them it seems to sweep them all out.'

'Good job, too,' said Captain Down. 'We get heat enough in the sunshine without having the bushes and the water made hot by fire-flies.'

'It's wonderful,' said Archie.

'Wonderfully hot.'

'No, no; I mean so strange that all those beetles, or whatever they are, should carry a light in their tails that they can show or put out just when they like, and that though it's so brilliant it is quite cool.'

'Rather awkward for them if it was hot, in a climate like this. They look very pretty, though.'

'Lovely!' said the subaltern enthusiastically. 'I don't know when I have seen them so bright. You can trace out the whole course of the river as far as we can see; and there above, the sky looks like purple velvet sewn all over with stars, just as if they were the reflections of the fire-flies.'

'Bosh!' said Captain Down, striking a match to light a cigar.

'Why bosh?'

'Fancy—poetry. I think I shall have a nap. It's too hot to smoke.'

'Don't.'

'What! not smoke?'

'No; don't go to sleep. You will get fever.'

'Who says so?'

'The Doctor.'

'Oh, bother!'

'Now then, what do you say to going as far as his bungalow and telling the ladies that the river has never looked more beautiful?'

Plosh!

'Beautiful river!' said the Captain mockingly. 'Like to take them on it perhaps in a boat?'

'Well, it would be very nice, with a couple of good men to pole it along.'

'Of course; and every moment expecting to see the horrible snout of one of those brutal beasts shoved over the side to hook one out.'

'Nonsense!' said Archie impatiently.

'Nonsense? Why, they often upset a boat when they are hungry, and lay hold of a nice, juicy native, to take him down and stuff him in some hole in the bank to get tender for the next feed.'

'Oh, they would never attack a boat when men are splashing about with poles.'

'Well, you don't catch me taking ladies out on a dark night, unless it's in a big dragon-boat with plenty of men on board; and then I should like to have a gun.'

'They are horrible beasts,' said Archie, 'and I

wonder that the Malay fellows don't try to ex-
terminate them.'

'Ah! Go in pluckily and make a decent use of
those crooked krises of theirs. There would be some
sense in having them poisoned then.'

'Old Morley says he has never seen a kris-wound
turn bad, and he has doctored scores. Says it's all
fudge about their being poisoned.'

'Well, he ought to know,' said the Captain; 'but
there's no go in these Malay fellows. I don't
believe they would stir even if they saw one of
their women snatched off the bank where she had
gone to fetch water.'

The officer had been giving his opinions in a
low, subdued voice, and Archie Maine was about to
break out in defence of the people amongst whom
they were stationed; but he closed his half-parted
lips, for the silence within the mess-room was broken
by the voice of the Resident, who suddenly broke
out with:

'To go on with what I was saying at dinner'——

'Eh?' said the Major drowsily; and the two
young men in the veranda turned slightly, to see,
by the light of a faintly burning lamp, the old
officer alter his position and respread a large bandana
silk handkerchief over his head as if to screen it
from the night air. 'What were you saying at
dinner?'

'About its seeming such an anomalous position.'

'What's an anomalous position?' said the Major
more drowsily.

'Why, for me to be supposed to be here, for
diplomatic reasons, to advise Rajah Suleiman as to

his governing his people, and to have you and your strong detachment stationed at the campong.'

'Anomalous!' said the Major, with a chuckle. 'I call it wise. See what emphasis a body of fighting-men can give to your advice.'

'Oh, but that's dealing with the natives by force.'

'Very good force too, old fellow; for I don't believe that thick-lipped, sensual - looking fellow would take much notice of what you say if we weren't here.'

'Yes; but I want to deal with them by moral suasion.'

'Rifles are much better. There's no occasion to use them; it's their being at hand if they are wanted that will do the trick.'

'I don't think it's necessary,' said Sir Charles firmly. 'I am getting on very well with the Rajah, and he listens to everything I advise with the greatest attention.'

'Glad to hear it,' said the Major, with a grunt; 'but it seems to me that he pays a deal more attention to that French chap than he does to you.'

'Think so?' said Sir Charles sharply.

There was silence for a few minutes.

'Let's get up and stroll round the lines,' whispered Archie.

'Sha'n't. 'Tisn't time for visiting posts.'

'But they'll wake to the fact that we are listeners.'

'Let 'em. They ought to know we are here.'

'But they are talking business,' whispered Archie.

'Well, it's our business as much as theirs. Are you afraid that listeners will hear no good of them-'

selves, and the Major will bring in something about your last prank ?'

'No;' and the lad twitched himself a little round in his cane chair, which uttered a loud squeak; and the Resident went on:

'Yes, that fellow is rather a nuisance. His bright, chatty way and deference please the Rajah; and I suppose you are right, for he's always proposing something that amuses the stolid Malay, while my prosing about business matters must bore him.'

'I believe he's an adventurer,' said the Major. 'Don't like him.'

'Well, he doesn't like you, Major; so that balances the account.'

'I don't know. What's he here for?'

'Oh, he's a bit of a naturalist and a bit of a sportsman. Glad of a ride through the jungle on an elephant. Glad of his board and lodging. Bit of a student he thinks himself in his dilettante, Parisian way. Oh, there's no harm in him.'

'So much the better,' said the Major. 'But what about that other fellow — what's his name?— Hamet?'

'Ah-h!' ejaculated the Resident, expiring his breath rather sharply, almost in a hiss. 'I am rather doubtful about that fellow. I'm afraid he's an intriguer.'

'Why, there's nothing to intrigue about in this jungle.'

'Don't you make any mistake, Major. There's as much intriguing going on in this half-savage country as there is in Europe. That fellow Hamet, on the strength of his Europeon education, is very anxious to be friends with me, and his civility covers a good deal.'

'Good deal of what ?' said the Major.

'Politics.'

'Politics ! Rubbish !'

'Oh no, my dear sir; not rubbish. This long, narrow Malay Peninsula is cut up into countries each ruled over by a petty Rajah, and these half-savage potentates are all as jealous of one another as can be. Each Rajah is spoiling for a fight so as to get possession of his neighbour's territory, and if we were not here one or the other of them would swallow up Suleiman's patch, and he, knowing this, submits as pleasantly as he can to the rule and protection of England, which keeps them safe.'

'Do you think, then, that this young fellow Hamet has any of these grasping ideas ?'

'Think ? I am sure of it. He wants to be very friendly with me; and what for ?'

'Well, I suppose,' said the Major, 'he thinks you would be a very good friend, and lend him a company or two of men to help him against one of his grasping neighbours. What do you say ?'

'Between ourselves,' said Sir Charles, lowering his voice, 'I think he goes further than that. He has his eye on Suleiman's rich territory, and would like me to help him to sit in Master Suleiman's place.'

'Ho, ho !' said the Major. 'And what do you say to that ?'

'Nothing,' said the Resident shortly.

'Here, let's go,' whispered Archie; and he started

up from his chair, whose bamboo legs scraped loudly over the veranda floor.

'Who's that out there?' said the Major sharply.

'Down, sir, and Maine.'

'Oh,' said the Major; and then, 'Is it any cooler out there?'

'No, sir,' said Archie sharply. 'I thought it was getting rather warm.'

'Is any one else out there?' said the Resident, leaving his chair and stepping through the Malay French window out into the sheltered spot.

'No, sir,' said Archie.

'None of the servants within hearing?'

'No, sir.'

'Are you sure?'

'Quite, sir,' said Archie, as he laid his hand upon one of the creeper-covered supporters of the roof.

'That's better,' said Sir Charles; and, followed by the Major, he began to stroll along past the mess-room windows towards where a sentry was on duty, watchful and silent, while Archie and Captain Down turned in another direction.

'You needn't be so precious thin-skinned about hearing what Sir Charles said to the old man. I don't see why it should not be confidence for us, and—— Well, what's the matter? Giddy?'

Archie responded by gripping his companion tightly by the wrist, and the two young men stood listening to a faint rustling away to their left, till every sound they could hear came from behind them, where their commander and the Resident were still talking at the end of the veranda in a low tone.

'Hear that?' said Archie.

'Yes. Cat or some prowling thing smelling after the remains of the dinner.'

'If it had been anything of that kind we shouldn't have heard its velvet paws.'

'Perhaps not. What do you think it was, then? Not a tiger?'

'No; I thought it must be one of the Malay fellows—a listener.'

'Not it. What would be the good of his listening to a language he couldn't understand?'

'I don't know,' said Archie. 'Some of these Malays are very deep. Hadn't we better say something to the Major?'

'Rubbish! No! Why, if it had been some one lurking about, the sentry would have seen him.'

'Yes,' said Archie thoughtfully.

CHAPTER VII.

JOE AND THE CROCS.

ABOUT an hour after the last conversation Sergeant Ripsy was giving a few final words of command to the little squad of men whom, to use his own words, he was about to plant, as if they were so many vegetables, at different points about the cantonments, in accordance with the strict military rule kept up, just as though they were in an enemy's country and it was a time of war.

Arms were shouldered, and there was a halt made here, and a halt made there; and this was repeated until a sentry had been stationed at six different points, where the guard could have full command of so many muddy elephant-paths leading away into the black jungle, as well as of two well-beaten tracks which commanded the river.

It was at the latter of these that the Sergeant, whose task was ended until the hour came for rounds, paused to say a few words to the sentry, a well-built fellow who looked as upright as the rifle he carried; and before speaking Sergeant Ripsy glanced through the clear, transparent darkness of the night to right and left, up and down what seemed to be a brilliant river of black ink, which rippled as it ran swiftly, and sparkled as if sprinkled with diamonds, from the reflections of the stars; for, strangely enough, the fire-flies, which had been so frequent amongst the overhanging vegetation, had now ceased to scintillate.

'Here, you, Corporal Dart, hold up that lantern. A little higher. Now left; now right. That will do.'

The non-com., who knew his Sergeant's motive, had opened the door of the swinging lantern, and flashed it to and fro so that its light fell athwart the stolid countenance of the sentry, who stood up as rigid as if he had been an effigy cast in bronze.

'You have been drinking again, sir.'

'Not a drop, Sergeant,' said the man gruffly.

'What's that?' came fiercely.

'Not a drop, Sergeant; nor yesterday nayther.'

'Smell him, Corporal.'

Sniff, sniff, from the Corporal, accompanied by a mild chuckle from the remains of the strong squad.

'Silence in the ranks!' roared the Sergeant. —'Well, Corporal Dart? Report.'

'Onions, Sergeant; not drink.'

'Faugh! Lucky for you, Private Smithers, for there's going to be no mercy next time you are caught.'

'Well, but, Sergeant, this is now, and it aren't next time.'

'Silence! A man who is going on duty must keep his tongue still. Now then, you know the word and what's your duty. Sentry-go until you are relieved. Strict watch up and down the river, for no boat is to land. If the enemy come, take him prisoner; but you are not to fire without cause.'

'Without what, Sergeant?'

'Cause, idiot. Don't you know your own language?'

Plosh!

'Oh, there's one of them big scrawlers. Keep your eyes open, and don't go to sleep.'

'All right, Sergeant.'

'Don't be so handy with that tongue of yours, sir. Listen, and don't talk. Do you know what will happen if you do go to sleep?'

Private Smithers thought of the many scoldings —tongue-thrashings he would have called them— which he had had from his wife, and in answer to the Sergeant's question he drew himself up more stiffly and sighed.

'I said, sir, do you know what would happen if you went to sleep?'

Private Smithers sighed again, deeply, and thought more.

'Do you hear what I said, sir?' roared the Sergeant.

'Yes, Sergeant; but you said I wasn't to speak.'

'On duty, sir.'

'Am on duty,' growled the private.

'Well, I said speak, but I meant chatter,' cried the Sergeant. 'You may speak now, and answer my question. I said do you know what would happen if you went to sleep?'

'Yes, Sergeant.'

'Well, what?'

'Snore,' growled the man.

'Yah! You are turning into a fool. Don't you think you would fall down if you went to sleep?'

'No, Sergeant. When I go off on duty I always stand stiff as a ramrod.'

'Oh! Then you confess, sir, you do go to sleep on sentry?'

'Think I did once, Sergeant, but I warn't sure.'

'Well, now then, look here. You are the most troublesome man in your company, and you are not worth your salt, but your commanding officer doesn't want to put the War Office to the expense of sending you home; and I don't want to have to put a fatigue party to the trouble of digging a hole for you in this nasty, swampy jungle earth, with more expense caused by the waste of ammunition in firing three volleys over your grave.'

'No, Sergeant; that would be 'ard.'

'Bah! Of course not,' growled the Sergeant. 'I made a mistake. You wouldn't be there to bury, because as sure as you stand there, and go to sleep, one of them twelve-foot long lizardly crocs as you have seen hundreds of times lying on the top will be watching you, with his eyes just out of the water, and as soon as ever you are fast he will crawl out and have you by the leg and into the river before you know where you are. So if that happens, be careful and leave your rifle ashore.'

'Yes, Sergeant, I'll mind,' said the man coolly.

'Silence in the ranks!' cried the Sergeant again, for there was the beginning of a chuckle.—'Now then,' he continued, 'that's all. Don't forget the word—Aldershot; and—oh, keep a very sharp lookout for boats, for that's the only way an enemy can approach the campong—— Eh, what?' said the Sergeant, in response to a growl.

'What shall I do, Sergeant, if one of them big evats comes at me? Am I to fire?'

'Fire? No! What for? Want to alarm the camp?'

'No, Sergeant. I don't mind tackling a real enemy, but if it was one of them scaly varmints he would alarm me.'

'Never mind; you are not to fire.'

'Well, what am I to do, then, sir?'

'Fix bayonets and let him have it. Tenderest place is underneath.'

'Well, but, Sergeant, how am I to get at him underneath?'

'Silence, sir! You, a British soldier who has had the bayonet exercise drilled into him solid for years, ask your officer how you are to use your weapon if it comes to an engagement! You will be wanting to know how to pull your trigger next.— Right about face! March! Left incline. Forward!'

Tramp, tramp, tramp, growing fainter and fainter till it died out; and then Private Smithers said, 'Hah!' making a great deal of it; and then sighed and smacked his lips as if thirsty, for the water was rippling pleasantly in his ears. Then, grounding arms, he began to feel in his pocket, and dragged out a soda-water bottle, which felt soft, for it had been carefully stitched up in very thick flannel to guard it from the consequences of casual blows. On his twisting the cork, the neck emitted a peculiar squeak, followed by a gurgling sound, which lasted till the bottle was half-empty, by which time the thirsty private had become fully conscious of its contents.

'Yah!' he ejaculated as he snatched the bottle from his lips. 'Cold tea! Weak — no milk, of course; but you might have put in a bit of sugar.' Then replacing the cork, he gave the yielding stopper so vicious a twist that the neck emitted a screech which sounded strangely loud in the black silence of the night, and was followed by a heavy splash and the sound of wallowing about a dozen yards away. Then, apparently from just below the bank of the river a little higher up, there was a horrible barking sound such as might have been uttered by a boar-hound with a bad sore throat, and then *whop*, as of a tremendous blow being struck on the surface of the water, followed by the hissing *plash*, as of a small shower of rain.

'Murder!' muttered Private Smithers in a hoarse whisper, as he finished corking the bottle by giving the neck a slap, stuffed it quickly into the pocket of his tunic, and then brought his piece up to the ready and began to back slowly from where he had been stationed.

'This is nice!' he growled, as he released his right hand to draw the back across his reeking brow. 'Glad the missus ain't here. He warn't gammoning me, then. My, how thirsty I do feel! It's the prespiration, I suppose. Here, how plaguy dark it is! Course I've seen these 'ere things before, but it never seemed so bad as this.—Not fire? Won't I? Why, if I made out one of them things coming on up the bank, it 'ud be enough to make a decent piece go off of itself. Anyhow, it's fixed bay'nets, my lad; but I wonder whether the tool would go in. Phew! What does that mean?

This is a blessed unked place, and it's getting darker and darker. It aren't fair to a British soldier to put him on a job like this.'

As the man spoke he looked sharply to right and left and out into the river, fixing his bayonet the while.

'Do you hear that, you beggars ? You come on, and you will get the bullet, and a dig as well. A-mussy me, I do wish it was relieve guard ! And I have got to stop here facing this till daybreak almost. It's enough to make a fellow feel ill. I wonder what the missus would say if she knew. Hates—bless her !—hates me to touch the least taste of rum, but if she 'd have knowed what I 'd got to go through to-night she wouldn't have left out the sugar, and she would have put in a double lashing of something strong to keep the heart in her old man, as she calls me—when she 's in a good temper,' he added after a pause, during which he stood breathing hard and trying to make out whence came each splash or lash of a reptile's tail.

'Talk about facing the enemy,' he muttered; 'I don't wish old Tipsy any harm, but I should like him to have this job. It 'ud take some of the starch out of him, I know. Well, what 's to be done ? There ain't so much as a tree to get behind. The Red Book says you ain't to expose yourself unnecessarily to the enemy; but what 's a fellow to do ? If I go padding up and down there, it 's like saying to them, "Here I am ; come on." And they can see one so — them right down in the water and me high up on the bank. Let 's see ; what did the missus say ? Out of two evils choose the least. Well, I know what it is for deserting your post, and that must be leaster than having one of them beggars getting hold of a fellow by the leg and pulling him under water. So hook it, I say; and I might manage to sneak back before rounds.'

Private Smithers stood thinking and watching, hearing many a startling sound of the reptiles with which the river swarmed, evidently fishing after their fashion; and over and over again he took aim and nearly fired at some imaginary monster that appeared to be crawling out of the water to mount the bank. But after straining his eyes till they seemed to ache, he always ended by lowering his piece again and forcing himself to walk up and down his measured beat.

'I never knowed a hotter night than this,' he muttered, as he took off his cap and wiped his dripping forehead; 'and I do call it hard. I can't sneak off, because as soon as I was out of the way, as sure as I am alive somebody would be making extra rounds, so as to drop upon a fellow and ketch him when he ain't there. I can feel it in me to-night as old Tipsy would know it and drop upon me as soon as I had gone; and 'tain't being a soldier neither,' the poor fellow half-whimpered. 'I suppose it's cowardly; but who can help it, hearing them ugly, slimy things chopping the water and gnashing their teeth at you? I want to know what such things as them was made for. Talk about Malays and pisoned krises! Why, I would rather meet hundreds of them. You could bay'net a few of them, for they are soft, plump sort of chaps; but these 'ere things is as hard as lobsters or crabs, and would turn the point of a regulation bay'net as if it was made of a bit of iron hoop. I sha'n't never forget that, Mr Sergeant Tipsy,' he continued, addressing the jungle behind him as he looked in the direction of the cantonments. 'The underneath's the tenderest part, is it? Just you come and try it, old un. Savage old tyrant—that's what you are. Only just wish I was Sergeant Smithers and you was Private Ripsy. I'd make you Private Tipsy with sheer fright, that I would, and so I tell you. No, I wouldn't,' he grumbled, as he cooled down a little. 'I wouldn't be such a brute, for the sake of your poor missus. Ugh!' he growled, as he seemed to turn savage; and he went through the business of shouldering arms, with a good deal of unnecessary energy, slapping his piece loudly, and then stamping his feet as he marched up and down the marked-out portion of the bank, a little inward from the landing-place.

'I don't care,' he muttered recklessly. 'I can't see you, but I can hear you, you beauties! Come on if you like. My monkey's up now. Fire! I just will! It will only be once, though, and then s'elp me, I'll let whichever of you it is have it with a straight-down dig right between the shoulders—one as will pin you into the soft earth. I'll do for one of you at any rate, and then let them come and relieve guard. Relieve guard, indeed, when there won't be no guard to relieve! And old Tipsy won't have any more trouble with poor old Joe Smithers. Nay, my lad, put it down decent, as perhaps it's for the last time. Private Joseph Smithers, 3874, and good-bye, mates and comrades, and bless the lot of

you! Poor old missus! She'll miss me, though,
when she wants the water fetched, but it will only
be larky Peter Pegg doing it twice as often; and she
will be independent-like, for she always washes his
shirt for him every week—a cheeky beggar! But
somehow I always liked Peter, in spite of his larks
as Mr Maine put him up to—chaffing and teasing a
fellow. But he never meant no harm. You see,
it seemed to make us good mates running in company
like, for when the Sergeant wasn't dropping on to
him he was letting me have it, to keep his tongue
sharp. Yes, Peter Pegg will miss me, for they won't
find Joe Smithers when they come; and if I desart
my post, how can I help it if I am pulled under?
But I won't desart it till I am. There,' he cried,
stopping suddenly in his angry soliloquy; and pulling up short, he stood ready, looking inward, forgetting the splashings of the reptiles, which were
repeated from time to time. 'What did I say?
'Tarn't rounds yet, and I should have been ketched,
for here's some one coming. Out of regular time,
too. One of the officers, for that spot of light's a
cigar. Well, glad to see him. Company's good,
even if you're going to be pulled under by a croc.
Wonder who it is.'

CHAPTER VIII.

A STRANGE PRISONER.

PRIVATE SMITHERS had not long to wait, for as the glow of the burning cigar came nearer he challenged, the customary interchange took place, and then Archie Maine took up the conversation with—

'Who's that? You, Smithers?'

'Yes, sir.'

'I say, you have got a lonely watch here to-night. Heard any crocodiles?'

'Heerd any crocodiles, sir? Just you listen!'

'My!' exclaimed Archie.—'I say, Down, why, it can't be those reptiles, is it? What a row!'

'There's no mistake about it,' said the Captain. 'Why, they must be having a party.' For the wallowing and splashing grew louder than ever.

'Here, I know what it is,' cried Archie merrily. 'They can smell Private Smithers here. He's such a big, well-fed chap that they have gathered together for a feast.'

'Yes, sir; that's it,' said the man.

'But they haven't been going on like this before, have they?'

'Just as bad, sir, all the time; and every now and then one of them barks at me just like a wolf.'

'Just like a wolf?' said the Captain. 'What do you know about wolves? You never kept a wolf.'

'No, sir. They are not the sort of things I

should like to make a pet dog on; but I 've heerd
them lots of times in Canady heigh-ho where they
chase the buffalo.'

'Ah, to be sure. You have been in the regiment
longer than I have. Well, these brutes are going
it! Why, Maine, we ought to have brought our
guns and had some shooting.'

'Too dark to see them.'

'Why, what a noise! And they have been going
on like this all the time you have been on duty?'

'Yes, sir; it 's been precious cheerful.'

'But what have you done?'

'Oh, just kep' on the move, sir, so as to baffle
them a bit when they seemed disposed to come ashore
and join one.'

'But surely you haven't seen any of them come
ashore?'

'Well, sir, to be downright honest, it 's been too
dark to see 'em; but I 've seemed to feel one of 'em
crawling ashore now and then; and then I always
went right to the end of the beat, so as to get as
far off as I could.'

'I say, Down, this is horrible!' said Archie.

'Thank you, sir,' said the man. 'It ain't been
nice.'

'Nice—no!' said the Captain. 'It seems like
planting a sentry to act as a bait to draw the brutes
ashore.'

'I don't think, however, that they would attack
a man who was on the alert,' said Archie.

'I shouldn't like to risk it,' said the Captain,
'however much I were on the alert.'

'But the Doctor says from long experience he

never knew them attack any one moving about. Of course he says he wouldn't answer for the life of a man who was lying asleep close to the river's edge, and we know that they will pull in a woman bathing, or who has waded in to draw water.'

'Yes,' said the Captain, 'I can answer for that. Why, they will seize an ox that has walked in to drink. But this is not right. The Major would be angry if he knew of a single sentry being stationed so close to the water as this on a dark night.—Look here, Smithers; move in yonder a bit—up to that hut we just passed. You can well command the landing-place from there, I think?'

'Yes, sir; thank you, sir. No boat could land there without my hearing and seeing it.'

'Well, then, move up there; and when Sergeant Ripsy comes to relieve guard, tell him I changed your position, and that a sentry must not be posted here again on a dark night.'

'Thank you, sir,' said the private. 'It has been awful, sir.'

'Awful—yes, my lad. Well, we are three of us now, but I don't feel at all eager to stay. However, you will be quite safe there—eh, Maine?'

'Oh yes. The heavy, lumbering brutes are not likely to travel up there.—Seen or heard anything else, Smithers?'

'No, sir. I shouldn't think anybody else would want to come.'

The officers stood talking to the man a few minutes, and then turned off to return to their quarters, while Private Smithers hugged himself with satisfaction as he picked up the still burning half-cigar the officer had thrown away, carefully put it out, and deposited it in his cartridge-box.

'You will do to cut up fine for finishing in a pipe to-morrow, my jockey,' he said.

He stood listening till the faint sounds of his visitors' voices had completely died away, and then he settled himself by the hut.

'This is jolly,' he muttered. 'One's safe enough here. That's a capital lookout, for one quite looks down on the water. Yes; no boat could come up here without my hearing it, and I should see any one paddling along. Well, I will say this: our officers are gentlemen, and never want you to do anything that they wouldn't do theirselves. Glad the Captain was there too, for I don't suppose Mr Archie Maine would have ventured to change my place. But I do know what he would have done. I'd bet anybody sixpence, if there was anybody here to bet with and I'd got one, that he'd have stopped to keep me company and—— I'm blessed ! What's that ?'

The man was standing beneath the spreading eaves of the palm-tree and bamboo hut, quite sheltered by the darkness, and he turned his head on one side to listen, for quite plainly from somewhere up the river, and apparently right under the bank on the other side, he heard the sound of paddles, as if a big boat were approaching.

'Why, I shouldn't wonder,' he thought to himself, 'if that boat has been hanging about there waiting till there was no one on the shore. Blessed if I don't think they heard us talking and fancy our officers have took the sentry away. Well, I shall jolly soon know. How rum! It must be a big boat; and it's scared the crocs away, for I can't hear them a bit now. All right; I'm ready for you, whoever you are. Not fire, eh? But I'll tell 'em I will if they don't give up. I wonder who it is. Only fishermen perhaps; but it will give one something to do.'

He drew himself a little closer beneath the projecting attap roof, which extended three or four feet over the sides of the hut, and then felt startled, for suddenly there fell upon his ears, evidently coming from somewhere inland, a rustling sound of footsteps, accompanied by the hard breathing of some one suffering from over-exertion.

'Boat coming ashore! Some one coming down to the landing-place! What does this 'ere mean?' muttered the sentry. 'Well, it's only one;' and he peered carefully from his shelter, trying to make out the approaching figure.

But it was too dark, and he waited a full minute before stepping out boldly; and his rifle gave a loud *click, click,* as he cried:

'Halt! Who goes there?'

His answer was a sharp half-cry, half-gasp of astonishment, and the loud breathing became quite a pant, like that of an excited dog.

'Here—yes—it—is—all right,' came in rather a high-pitched voice, the accents being those of one not fully accustomed to the English language.

'Well, what's the word?' cried Smithers, who, with his piece presented, found himself close up now to a slight man of middle height, wearing a sun-hat, dressed in knickerbockers, and apparently having a fishing-creel slung from one shoulder, something like a tin case from the other.

'The—the—word?' he answered.

'Yes. What's the word?'

'Oh yes; it is all right,' faltered the new-comer, with a half-laugh. 'I was just going down to my boat. What a dark night!'

'Oh yes, it's dark enough,' growled Smithers; 'but what's the word?'

'The word? Oh yes. Good-night—good-night.'

'Halt, I tell you!' cried the sentry in a deep tone. 'That's not the password.'

'Oh no; but that does not matter, my good friend. I tell you I am going down to the pier to my boat, which is waiting for me.'

'Rum time to be going to meet a boat,' growled Smithers; 'and there's no boat waiting there. Can't you hear? They are paddling away down-stream as hard as ever they can.'

The stranger uttered a sharp ejaculation of impatience.

'Oh, this is foolish—absurd!' he exclaimed; and his hands began to busy themselves about his waist.

Private Smithers might have been the worst man in his company, but somehow drill had made him a keen soldier and a good sentry.

'Hands up,' he cried sharply, 'or I fire!'

'Oh!' cried his visitor sharply, 'don't be so foolish. Did you think I was going to do something?'

'Yes, with a revolver, whoever you are. I nearly drew trigger, and you not two yards away.'

'Oh!' said the stranger, with a gasp. 'It is

foolish nonsense, and you have frightened away my rowing-men. Don't you know me?'

'No.'

'I am a stranger. I come out in the forest to-night to collect the beautiful moths—butterflies, you call them. I have some in this case.'

'It's all dark,' said Smithers sourly. 'Gammon! No one can see to catch butterflies at night.'

'Ha-ha! You are a wise man. You English are so sharp. Look; I will show you.'

'You had better mind what you are doing, sir, or my rifle may go off.'

'What do you think of me, my friend? See here. There are many great, beautiful butterfly moths here in this grand forest.'

'Yes; and if you come when the sun shines, with a net, you can catch lots.'

'Yes; and I come at night. I put sugar on the trees. The foolish moths fly round to eat; and then I open this little lanterne, which is not burning now, and then I see to catch the beautiful moths.' As Smithers's visitor spoke, he tapped the dimly seen tin case slung under his right arm. 'If I had time I should show you, sir. But my boat is waiting. I go down to the pier place and hold up my hand. My men see me, and come and take me off.'

'And all in the dark, mister,' said the sentry in his gruffest tones. 'But you are not going down to the pier place to hold up your hand, and your boat-men are not coming to take you off.'

'I do not see what you mean, sir. I say they do come to take me off.'

'Oh, do you?' growled Smithers. 'And I say they don't come to take you off, because my orders are to let no boat come in; and what's more, you are my prisoner.'

'Your prisonare, sir!' cried the visitor. 'You make joke.'

'Oh no, that's no joke, mister,' said Smithers. 'That's only obeying orders.'

'But, sir, I insist. I desire to go much.'

'Can't help it, sir.'

'Then what go you to do? You dare to say you shoot at me?'

'No, sir; not unless you try to run away. My orders would be to stop you, and I should fire at your legs; and it might hurt you very much. But whether it did or whether it didn't hurt, you wouldn't run any more to-night.'

'Sir,' said the visitor pompously, 'you talk like madness. If you do not let me go down to my boat I shall report you to your officer.'

'Yes, sir; that's what I mean you to do.'

'What do you mean?'

'He will be here by-and-by to relieve guard, and then you can say what you like, and he will take you to our Major.'

'What! Faith of a gentleman, this man is too much mad! But there, I forget myself. You like a glass of rack-ponch?'

'Yes, sir, I like it.'

'Then I have none here; but I have in my pocket a Chinese dollar. It is worth shillings. You get many glasses of rack-ponch. You take it?' and as he spoke he thrust his hand into his pocket and drew out in the darkness a broad piece.

'It won't do,' said Smithers. 'You will be only getting me into more trouble, mister.'

'You will not take it?'

'Not me.'

'Then I shall keep it and spend it myself.' With a good deal of gesticulation the speaker thrust the coin back into his pocket, and gave it a heavy slap. 'Now, you say to me that my boat is gone, and you say that my men could not see me if I hold up my hand?'

'That's right, sir.'

'Very well. You are very clever, but I know also two or three things. I shall go down to the pier, and call out to my men, "Ahoy!" and then go into the water and swim till they pick me up and put me in a dry place in the boat. Now, what do you say to that?'

'Only this, mister. What do you think your men, if they come, will pick up?'

'Me—myself, sir, with my butterfly moths and my little lanterrne.'

'Ho!' said Smithers dryly. 'And what about the crocs?'

'I do not understand.'

'I see you don't,' said the sentry. 'What about the great crocodiles that have been waiting about there all night?'

'The crocodile!' said the visitor; and it was not light enough to see, but the stranger's jaw dropped, and he remained silent till Smithers spoke again.

'Understand that, mister?'

'Yes; you say that to frighten me. You talk one minute about using your *fusil* to shoot me, and I am not afraid. Then you say you throw me to the crocodile, and still I am not afraid.'

'Then look ye here,' said Smithers, 'you just give me that little pistol thing you were going to pull out.'

'What! Sir, I re-fuse.'

Smithers stuck the mouth of his rifle against the stranger's breast-bone, and pressed upon it heavily.

'Sit down,' he said.

'I will not sit down! I re-fuse.'

'Mind,' said Smithers. 'I don't want this rifle to go off.'

'You dare — you dare not shoot,' cried the visitor; but as he spoke he began to subside slowly, as if still mentally resisting, till the sentry raised his foot quickly, gave a sharp thrust, and his prisoner went down suddenly upon his back, with the sentry's right foot upon his chest.

'Now then, no nonsense. Hand up that pistol.'

The prisoner's hand went rapidly to his waist as if with the intent of snatching out and making use of his revolver, but quick as a flash the sentry's rifle was pressed down harder now, close up to the man's throat.

'That's right,' said Smithers. 'Now drop it.'

There was a few moments' hesitation, and then the revolver fell softly upon the earth just beyond the shelter of the attap mat.

The next moment Smithers had raised his foot and kicked the pistol aside, but with an unexpected result, for one chamber exploded with a loud bang.

Quick as a flash the sentry's rifle was pressed down harder now, close
up to the man's throat.

T.

PAGE 86.

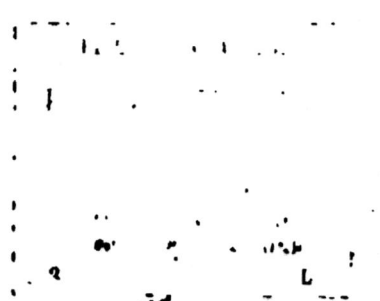

'I've done it now,' said Smithers to himself. 'As for you, you lie still;' and he held his piece pointing still towards his prisoner while he cleverly retrieved the revolver. 'Look here,' he said, 'I had orders not to fire, only if it was wanted particular. Well, I haven't fired, but they will hear that shot and be coming down before you know where you are.'

'What!' cried the prisoner, starting up in a sitting position.

'Look ye here,' cried Smithers; 'do you want me to have an accident?'

'No, no; I want you to let me give you many dollars. You must let me go before your officers come.'

'Nothing of the kind, sir. You must talk to them when they come. You are my prisoner, so just lie still.'

As the sentry was spea[?]the notes of a bugle were ringing out upon the [?]nt night. Hurrying feet could be heard, and it was evident that the night alarm had set the occupants of the cantonments buzzing out like the bees of a hive.

'They don't know which sentry it was,' thought Smithers, and he was raising his piece to fire and bring the relief to his side, when it struck him that he should be leaving himself defenceless if his prisoner should make a dash to escape.

'Second thoughts is best, says the missus,' he muttered, and taking the revolver from his pocket, he fired it in the air, and after a short interval fired again.

'That's done it,' he said to himself.—'Hullo! what's the matter with you?' For his prisoner was rocking himself to and fro as if in pain, and grinding his teeth.

Directly after there was the light of a lantern showing through the trees, shouts were heard and answered by the sentry, and a strong party of the men, led by Captain Down and Archie, surrounded them.

'What's wrong, Smithers?' cried the Captain eagerly.

'Took a prisoner, sir.'

'Corporal, a light here,' cried Archie; and the man doubled up to throw the rays of the lantern upon the prisoner's face as he now rose to his feet.

'The Count!' cried Archie.

'Yes, sir. Your stupid sentry, he make a John Bull blunder—a mistake.'

'A mistake?' said the Captain. 'Why, how come you here?'

'Only I have my lanterrne and collecting-box, and come down the river to catch specimens of the beautiful moth for the naturalists at home in France. I land from my boat, and the boat come to take me away; but your sentry man re-fuse to let me go.'

'Collecting—lantern!' said the Captain.

'Yes, sir. Look. I fear my beautiful specimens are spoiled in the pannier here. He use me very bad.'

'You mean that you were collecting moths?' said Archie dubiously, as he recalled the rustling sounds he had heard below the veranda that night.

'Yes, sir,' said Smithers gruffly. 'I suppose it's right, what he says, about collecting. Here's one of his tools;' and he handed the beautifully finished little revolver to the young officer.

'Humph!' grunted the Captain.—'Well, sir, I 'm sorry if our sentry behaved roughly to you, but he was only obeying orders, and you ought to know that you had no business here.'

'All a mistake, Captain. You will please make signals for my boat to come.'

'All in good time, sir,' said the Captain, in response to a nudge given by his subaltern; 'but you must come up first and make your explanation to the Major.'

'What! It is not necessary, sir.'

'You think so, sir?' said Captain Down. 'I and my brother officer think it is.'

Directly after the relief party and their prisoner were on their way to headquarters.

CHAPTER IX.

THE MAJOR ON HEDGING.

'LOOK here, Dallas,' said' the Major; 'I think your diplomacy and arguing and writing despatches is a great nuisance.'

'You will think better of it some day, sir,' said the Resident.

'Never!' said the Major warmly; and his ruddy, sun-browned face grew redder, while his stiff, silvery-gray moustache and short-cut hair seemed to bristle. 'Of course I know you must have troubles, sir, with other nations, and people like these Malays, who are subservient to us; but when they come, let's fight and bring them to their senses.—What do you say to that, Archie Main

'Spoken like a soldier, sir,' cried Archie quickly.

'Good!' cried the Major. 'Your writing despatches and minutes and red-tape and all the rest of it to a fellow like that Rajah Suleiman is all waste of energy. Here you are supposed to be guiding him.'

'I hope and believe I am guiding him, sir,' said the Resident coldly.

'Bah! He and his people are growing more impudent every day. It's bound to end in a blow-up. These imitation Scotch niggers in their plaid sarongs, as they call them, will be getting up a big quarrel with my men with their bounce and contempt for my well-drilled, smart detachment. Here's every common, twopenny-halfpenny Malay looking down upon my fellows, while there isn't one among my lads who isn't a better man than their Rajah. There will be a row some day; won't there, Archie?'

'I expect so, sir,' replied the lad, who was listening to the conversation, and felt rather amused.

'I sincerely hope, Major, that you give strict injunctions to your officers and men about doing everything to avoid coming into collision with the natives and their traditions.'

'You leave me alone for that, sir. I think I know what to do with my lads. You would like me to confine them to barracks, I suppose?'

'Well, I should be very strict with them, sir.'

The Major grunted.

'I know,' he said. 'Some of you diplomatic people think British soldiers ought to be kept shut up in cages until they are wanted to fight. Don't you criticise me, sir. I have had a good many years with my lads, and they are pretty well in hand. If you come to criticising, you will set me doing the same with your methods. I shouldn't have let that French chap—Count, as he calls himself—go off so easy as you did the other day.'

'What could I do, sir? He is a friend of Rajah Suleiman, and his guest. I communicated with the Rajah, and he answered for him at once, complained of his arrest, and demanded that he should be allowed to return to the Palace at once.'

'Palace!' growled the Major. 'Why, my lads could knock up a better palace in no time with some bamboo poles and attap mats.'

'The natives are accustomed to simplicity in the building of their homes,' said the Resident coldly.

'Oh yes, I know,' growled the Major; 'but I want to know what that fellow was sneaking about our cantonments for in the dead of the night.'

'My dear sir,' said the Resident, 'his explanations were quite satisfactory. He is here studying the natives preparatory to writing a book about the manners and customs of these people, and he is collecting various objects of natural history, as he showed us.'

'Yes; half-a-dozen moths with all the colour rubbed off their wings. Do you mean to tell me that that chap is catching those insects for nothing ?'

'I am not ashamed to say that when I was young I used to collect butterflies, and if I am not very much mistaken, our friend Maine here has done the same thing.'

'Oh yes, lots of times,' said Archie.'

'Of course,' said the Major; 'every boy does, some time or other. I did myself. But I am as sure as sure that Monsieur the Count is playing a double game, and I have been thinking a deal, Archie Maine, about you and Down hearing that rustling as if somebody had been listening outside the veranda to what we were saying.'

' But I couldn't be sure, sir, that it was the Count.'

'Count be hanged! It makes me feel savage. Say Frenchman, boy. No, you couldn't be sure, of course ; but it couldn't have been one of the natives. They daren't have done it, with the sentry close at hand; and it looks very strange that he should be caught later on in the night going down to the landing-place, with a boat waiting for him. Once more, sir, what do you say to that?'

'That I felt bound to be satisfied with the gentleman's explanation, sir.'

'Gentleman!' said the Major sourly. 'I believe he's a mischievous hanger-on, and I should like to see him sent right away. There, I 've done. As you, in your diplomatic fashion, would say, the debate is closed.'

'Yes,' said the Resident, smiling, as he uttered a sigh of relief. 'Why, Major, it has made you quite cross.'

'Not a bit, not a bit; only a little warm. But while we are talking, I do think a little more might be done in support of your position as Her Majesty's representative. And mind, Dallas; I am not saying it unkindly, but on account of the way in which your friend the Rajah swells himself out and behaves to me and my officers.'

'Well, I must confess that his assumption of *hauteur* and the disdain which he has exhibited towards you on more than one occasion has annoyed me very much; but I set it down to his ignorance of England and our power.'

'Yes,' said the Major; 'and I have seen him treat you in a way that has made me ready to kick the scoundrel out of the place, when he has been here.'

'Well,' said the Resident, 'you must make allowances for the natural pride and conceit of these men. We know that they are half-savages, while they, as armed fighting-men accustomed to their petty wars amongst themselves, most likely look down upon us as half-barbarian people, whom they hope some day to subject in turn.'

'Yes, that's it,' said the Major. 'But what I say is, we must teach them better.'

'Well, that's what I am trying to do,' said Sir Charles. 'But I am trying the *suaviter in modo*, while you want to practise——'

'Yes, I know,' said the Major; 'the good old way: the *forti*—what's its name?—What is it, Archie?'

'I forget, sir. *Fortiter* something.'

'Can't you combine the two?' said the Major. 'Let them see something of our strength, Dallas. They certainly are getting more impudent and independent. Now, there's the question of our rations and supplies. The simple country-people are all right, and are glad to bring in all we want, and quite content with what we pay. But this Suleiman's people interfere with them and frighten them; and it's a bad sign, Dallas. What do you say to my arresting one of the most interfering of the Rajah's men and letting my fellows give him a good flogging?'

'For goodness' sake don't dream of such a thing!'

'Then matters will go from bad to worse. You are too easy.'

'And you are too hard, Major.'

'All right; you are one side and I am the other. —Here, Maine, you are a very stupid boy sometimes.'

'Yes, sir,' said Archie dryly.

'What's that? Now, that's a sneer, sir; but let it pass. I was going to say, sir, you have got your head screwed on right, and sharp boys can see what's best sometimes. Now, speak out. I don't know why this discussion has been going on before you, but you have been taking it all in ever since we have been talking. Now then, speak out. Who's right—Sir Charles or I?'

'Oh, nonsense!' said Sir Charles. 'I protest! You are his commanding officer, and he is bound to vote for you.'

'He'd better not,' cried the Major, with his gray moustache seeming to bristle. 'If he doesn't speak out honestly what he feels I will never forgive him. —Now, Archie, who's right—your father's old schoolfellow or the Resident?'

'Both, sir,' said the lad sharply.

'What!' roared the Major. 'You are hedging, sir, and I didn't expect it from you. I wanted you to say exactly what you felt.'

'Well, I am going to, sir; only you cut me off so short. I think you are both right, and both wrong.'

'Well, don't you call that hedging, sir?' cried the Major, looking hotter than ever.

'No, sir. I think Sir Charles gives way too much to these people, these proud followers of the Rajah; but I think it would be disastrous and unfair if you tried force.'

'Humph!' grunted the Major; and the Resident frowned.

'Well, sir,' said the Major, 'have you any more to say?'

'Yes,' replied Archie thoughtfully. 'I have mixed a good deal with the Rajah's people, and they are all very civil to me, but I never feel as if they are safe, and I often think that they are waiting for a chance to use the krises they keep so carefully covered over.'

'There, Sir Charles!' said the Major, smoothing down his bristling moustache. 'It's coming.'

Archie did not seem to heed the remark, and he went on thoughtfully:

'I think as Major Knowle does, sir, that, out of sheer ignorance, they don't believe how powerful we are. You see, they are all armed; every man has a kris; and they are going about with those nasty razor-bladed spears that they can throw so accurately. Most of them carry the point in a sheath, but it is a sheath that they slip off in a moment, and then it is a most horrible deadly weapon.'

'Quite true,' said Sir Charles thoughtfully.

'And then it seems to me, sir, that they feel a sort of contempt for our men, who are armed when they are on duty, but as a rule go about without so much as a bayonet; and even if they did carry that by way of side-arms, it's only a poor, blunt sort of thing that in their eyes does not compare with the kris.'

'Don't you disparage army weapons, sir, that are sanctioned by the War Office and the wisdom of the great Department,' growled the Major.

'No, sir, I don't wish to. But I was thinking that we ought to do something to teach these ignorant people how ready and well provided we are in case of any trouble.'

'Of course,' said the Major; 'we must do something.'

'Better wait patiently,' interposed Sir Charles, 'until we have real cause for using our weapons; and then I am quite for punishing them severely.'

'Stitch in time saves nine,' said the Major emphatically. 'Why not nip the thing in the bud?'

'Why not'—— continued Archie, who, now he was started, gained confidence every minute and did not seem disposed to stop.

'Why not what?' said the Major.

'Have a grand parade, sir. There's the Queen's Birthday next week.'

'Yes,' said Sir Charles.

'Eh?' grunted the Major. 'Grand parade? You mean make a bit of a show? Full review order, and the band?'

'I'd finish off with that, sir,' said Archie; 'but I'd have every man out, and get up a thoroughly good sham fight, burn plenty of powder, make everything as real as could be, and after plenty of firing and evolution, form in line, and deliver a regular good charge.'

'Yes,' said the Major, 'there's something in that. But what's the good of doing it with only the people of the campong to look on?'

'Oh, I wouldn't do it shabbily, sir. I think, in honour of Her Majesty's birthday, Sir Charles ought to give a big banquet here, and invite both Rajah Suleiman and Rajah Hamet to come in force with their followers, and after the sham fight have it all arranged that their people shall be well feasted.'

'But the expense—the expense, sir!' cried Sir Charles.

'You go on, Archie Maine,' said the Major. 'Capital! Hang the expense!'

'But all these things have to be considered, sir,' said the diplomat rather coldly.

'Yes, sir; and I am considering them,' said the Major. 'I think the plan's excellent. It will be killing two birds with one stone. I'll make it so real that we shall overawe the people, and please them and make them more friendly, at one stroke. Why, it will be worth in prestige twenty times as much as the money it will cost.'

'Then you think we ought to do it, Major?'

'Think we ought to do it, Dallas?' said the Major in astonished tones. 'Why, of course. Don't you?'

'I think it's worth consideration, certainly, but I am not for coming to a rash decision.'

'Rash!' said the Major hotly. 'I don't call that rash. What is there rash in it?'

'Several things occur to my mind,' said the Resident.

'Never mind the several; let's have one,' said the Major, with the facial muscles making his moustache twitch sharply.

'Well, sir, we are few in number. Would it be wise to invite these two Eastern princes to come here in force and well armed, so that they could combine and try to sweep us out of existence?'

'What! when our men are hot with excitement and ready to smell mischief in a good sham fight? I should just like to see them try—eh, Maine?'

'Yes, sir,' said Archie, with his eyes twinkling. 'I think they would make a mistake.'

'Yes,' said the Major, leaning forward to give the boy a slap on the knee that made him wince. 'And what about your despised British bayonets then—eh, sir? Eh?'

'Ah!' said the Resident thoughtfully.

'Oh, nonsense, nonsense, Sir Charles!' cried the Major. 'Come, I think this is a grand proposal, and I can only see one failing in it.'

'What's that, sir?'

'That I didn't think of it myself. Why, my dear sir, it's splendid; and I tell you what, we have got a pretty good supply in store. Our fellows shall give them a grand *salvo* of rockets at night from boats in the river, by way of a finish off, the band playing "God save the Queen" the while, with plenty of big drum.'

'And you might make the campong people illuminate all their boats on the river,' said Archie.

'Capital! Of course!' cried the Major.

'Humph! Yes,' said Sir Charles. 'And I might send in my invitation despatch a request to the two Rajahs to arrange that their naga shall be well hung with lanterns.'

'Hear that, Archie?' said the Major, chuckling. 'He's coming round.'

'Well, yes, on further thought,' said the Resident, 'if such a *fête* were made of the matter it would be a great attraction, and must impress not only the followers of the two Rajahs, but the inhabitants of every campong within reach. But I am afraid'——

'I'm not,' said the Major.

'I was going to say, of the expense.'

'Oh, hang the expense! as I said before,' cried the Major. 'Let's do it well, and think about the cost later on. I say that these people, bloodthirsty as they are, quarrelsome, and generally spoiling for a fight, are such children at heart that they would be delighted, and believe more than ever in the followers of her they call the Great White Queen. Now, Sir Charles, are you with me?'

'Yes, Major,' said the Resident, 'I must confess that I am.'

'Settled,' said the Major, drawing himself up. 'The Queen's Birthday, then. We haven't much time to spare.—What's that?' he continued, as Sir Charles left the Major's quarters, where the above discussion had taken place. 'What's that you say —it might be dangerous to bring the followers of those two fellows together, seeing what enemies they are? I never thought of that, Maine.'

'You see, they began using their krises, sir, that night of the mess dinner.'

'Humph! Yes. Then they were hanging about with nothing to do but growl at each other. Oh, I don't think we need study that, my lad. You see, their attention will be taken up—plenty to see; plenty to eat and drink—and we shall have all our lads under arms and prepared for any little *émeute.* Oh no, my lad, we won't seek clouds where there are none. All the same, we'll be prepared.'

CHAPTER X.

PETER TURNS MAHOUT.

IT was the morning appointed for the review, the preparations having been all made on the previous day; and the *réveillé* rang out, making Archie Maine turn over upon his charpoy bed with an angry grunt, for instead of unbuttoning his eyelids he squeezed them up extra tight.

'Mr Archie, sir, don't you hear the call?'

'Hear it? Yes. What does it mean?'

'Look sharp, sir. I'm putting your things straight. Tumble up and tumble in.'

'Be quiet, you noisy rascal! What does it all mean? I say, we are in the middle of the night!'

'Not it, sir. Do look sharp, sir.'

'But what for?'

'It's because of the review, I suppose, sir. The lads are all tumbling up as if there was some alarm. I ain't half dressed.'

'Alarm! Nonsense! Sha'n't get up till the regular time.'

'Hi! Hullo, Maine!' and Captain Down's voice was heard outside. 'Are you nearly ready? Company's all turned out.'

'Ready—no! What's the matter?'

'Don't quite know, but I think we are being attacked. The watch have come in with news that a strong party of the Malays are approaching by the forest path, out beyond the campong.'

'What stuff!' cried Archie, beginning to dress sleepily. 'It's the country-people coming in to see the show.—Here, you, Peter Pegg, why don't you get a light? Who's to see to dress?'

'Slip into your things, man,' cried the Captain irritably. 'No nonsense. Recollect where we are.'

'Oh, all right,' grumbled Archie. 'I know it's only a false alarm.'

'False alarm or no, the Major was half dressed before I came on here.'

'Oh, all right,' grumbled Archie again; 'I'll manage.—Pete,' he whispered, 'try to get me a cup of coffee.'

'Who's that?' cried the Captain.

'Sergeant, sir—Ripsy,' came in that non-com.'s deep, important voice.

'Well, what's up?'

'Well, sir, they may be coming to see the review, but it don't look like it. There's a strong body of well-armed natives just the other side of the campong, and they may be friends or they may be enemies, but we have got to be ready for them, anyhow. You see, sir, it don't look right, because if they had been friends they would have been coming down the river in their boats. These 'ere must have been marching all night; and they have got elephants with them.'

Whatever the body of Malays was, short as was the notice given, they found that the English cantonments were well guarded, and those who approached beyond the native village, where the main body had halted, were stopped before they could get any farther.

It was quite dark, and the whole appearance of the body of men suggested a night attack; but before long native messengers came into camp with a message from the chief officers of Rajah Suleiman to say that they had had a long night march so as to reach Campong Dang before sunrise, on account of the heat, and asking that they might be furnished with refreshments for His Highness, and be given permission for the elephants to be brought into camp by their mahouts, to be placed in the shade of the trees by the parade-ground while the grass-cutters went out for their food.

Messages then began to pass to and fro, and invitations were sent to the Rajah and his officers to join the officers' mess at breakfast and rest, as it would be hours before the military evolutions would begin.

The excitement and bustle quickly calmed down; pickets were stationed, with orders that none of the Malays were to come into camp; and the mess-men were almost ready to announce breakfast, when the Doctor came bustling on to the scene, and one of the first people he stumbled against was Archie.

'Oh, here you are,' he cried, hastily fastening one or two buttons of his white flannels. 'Just the fellow I wanted to see.'

'Morning, Doctor. How are you?' replied the lad.

'Bad. Up nearly all night with a couple of sick people, and I was at last just sinking into a pleasant doze when those wretched bugles began to ring out. All your doing.'

'My doing, sir?'

'Yes—upsetting our regular routine. It will be

just as I expected when the Major arranged for this absurdity. As if Her Majesty couldn't have a birthday without everybody going mad with a desire to get sunstroke.'

'Have some breakfast, sir,' said Archie quietly. 'You will feel better then.'

'Better, sir? Bah! Nothing the matter with me now. Eh, what? Is the coffee ready? Can't be. These princes and potentates haven't all come in yet, and I suppose we shall have to wait for them.'

'No, you won't, sir. Captain Down and some more of us who will have to be on duty have got a snug corner to ourselves, and we are going to have a snatch meal before going out.'

'Oh,' said the Doctor in a more mollified tone. 'Then there is somebody here blessed with brains! Who was it—Down?'

'No, sir; if I must confess,' cried Archie, 'it was I.'

'Oh,' said the Doctor. 'Then you must have been thinking of number one, sir.'

'No, Doctor. My fellow, Peter Pegg, got me a cup of coffee an hour ago.'

Matters soon settled quietly down, and the swarthy-looking Rajah Suleiman, in gorgeous array and attended by quite a staff of his notables—Maharajah Lela, Tumongong, Muntri, Lakasamana, and the rest of them—was haughtily partaking of an excellent breakfast, with a string of followers behind the chairs of him and his suite—pipe-bearers, betel-box carriers, and other attendants; while a picked guard of his finest men in a uniform of yellow satin, all armed with the limbing or throwing-spear and kris, were drawn up in the veranda, carefully watching over their lord in the mess-room, and as carefully watched over themselves by a guard of quiet-looking linesmen with fixed bayonets.

It fell to Archie's lot to be near the clump of trees beneath which the half-dozen splendid elephants that brought in the Rajah were being fed and groomed.

They had come in covered with mud from their journey along the narrow forest path formed of a line of deep mud-holes made by the elephants themselves, every one of the huge animals invariably planting his feet in the track of the one which had preceded him. Their trappings during the journey had been carefully rolled up, and now hung with the howdahs from horizontal branches of the sheltering trees.

As soon as it was light the great beasts had been marched down by their attendants to the landing-place for a swim, and brought out again back to the shelter to be carefully groomed, and now stood partaking contentedly of their morning meal, prior to being decked with their gay howdah-cloths and other trappings.

One of the first men that Archie encountered was Peter Pegg, who was standing watching the mahouts, who in turn were overlooking the attendants whose duty it was to groom the Rajah's stud.

'How is it you are not on duty?' he said.

'Am, sir,' said the lad. 'The Sergeant put me here to keep a heye on these helephant chaps and see as they don't get quarrelling with t'other Rajah's men.'

'Why, they have not come yet, have they—Rajah Hamet, I mean, and his people?'

'Oh yes, sir; and they are out yonder—helephants and all. Joe Smithers is doing the same job with them.'

'Did you see the Rajah?'

'No, sir,' replied the lad; 'only 'eerd he was there. I am to be relieved to go to breakfast in a hour's time.'

Archie nodded and went on. The hour passed, and Peter, who had no further orders, forgot all about breakfast in the deep interest he took in the proceedings of those who had the elephants in charge; while as he waited for the bugle-call which would summon him to the ranks, he stood watching the finishing touches being given to the elephants, now browsing on the plenteous supply of fresh green leafage thrown before them by the grass-cutters, and began to make friends with the mahouts.

He tried one after the other, but on each occasion only to meet with a surly scowl.

He was going to cross to the man in charge of the finest of the elephants—a little, sturdy fellow, who only looked on while the attendants were busy over the showy trappings, the edgings of which glistened with a big bullion fringe, and who himself was showily dressed in the Royal yellow, which suggested that this must be the Rajah's own mount. Pete took a step towards him, but shrank back as if it were not likely that this chief among the others would receive his advances any better, when a voice behind him made him turn his head sharply, to find that Joe Smithers, now for the present off duty, had likewise been attracted by the elephants, and had strolled up for a look.

'Why didn't you come for your breakfast, comrade?' he said.

'Oh—wanted to see these 'ere;' and then, as an idea struck the lad on noticing the canvas haversack slung from Smithers's shoulder, he said quickly, 'What you got in your satchel, comrade?'

'Only bread-cake.'

'Give us a bit.'

'Take the lot,' said Smithers. 'I don't want it. Only in the way. A drink of water will do for me.

Pegg gave him a peculiar look as he hurriedly transferred two great portions of the regimental bread to his own haversack.

'Thank you, comrade. I say—got any 'bacco?'

'Yes; but I want that.'

'Never mind. Give it to me, Joe. I'll pay you with twice as much to-morrow.'

Without hesitation Mrs Private Smithers's husband handed over a roll of about two ounces of tobacco.

'Thank you,' said Pegg. 'Now you shall see what you shall see.'

Peter shouldered his rifle, marched straight up to the gaudily attired mahout, looked him up and down admiringly, pointed at his handsome turban, smiling the while as if with satisfaction, and then tapped the gilded handle of the ankus the man carried, drawing back and looking at him again.

'Well, you do look splendid,' he said.

The swarthy little fellow seemed puzzled for the moment, but Peter Pegg's look of admiration was unmistakable, especially when he walked quickly round the mahout so as to see what he was like on the other side, before saying:

'Have a bit of 'bacco, comrade?'

Not a word was intelligible to the little, bandy-legged fellow, whose supports had become curved from much riding on an elephant's neck; but there was no mistaking the private's action as he took out the roll of tobacco, opened one end so as to expose the finely shredded aromatic herb, held it to his nose, and then passed it on to the mahout, whose big, dull, brown eyes began to glisten, and he hesitated as if in doubt, till the private pressed it into his hands and made a sign as if of filling a pipe and puffing out the smoke. The little fellow nodded his satisfaction, while Peter Pegg smiled in a friendly way and pointed to the huge elephant, which had ceased munching the turned-over bundle of green food at his feet, and now stood swinging his head to and fro and from side to side.

'My word,' said Peter, 'he is a beauty!' And then, looking about him first at one and then at another until he had bestowed a glance upon the other five great beasts, he turned once more to what proved to be the Rajah's special mount, and then spoke again to the little mahout.

'He is a beauty,' he said; and once more his looks conveyed to the driver the admiration he felt. 'May I feed him?' he added, taking out a piece of the white bread he had obtained, and making a sign as if holding it out to the elephant.

The mahout looked doubtful, but the elephant himself answered Peter Pegg's question by slowly raising his trunk, reaching out and closing it round the new white bread, prior to curving it under and transferring it to his mouth.

The mahout nodded and smiled at his new friend,
and the elephant showed his satisfaction by extending
his trunk for more.

'You are a splendid old chap,' said Pegg, breaking
another piece of bread inside his haversack and
offering it to the monstrous beast, now slowly
flapping his great ears.

This was taken, and bit by bit Peter doled out
another portion of the white cake, venturing at the
same time to stroke the animal's trunk.

'I'll risk it,' he said. 'If he tries to knock me
over I can easily jump away.'

But the elephant made no sign of resentment,
only transferring the piece of bread and extending
his trunk for more.

'Here you are,' said Peter; 'only you can't have
any more goes. Wish I'd got a dozen quarterns,
though. I want to mount you, old chap, and hang
me if I know how to set about it. However, here
goes; only I must look sharp.'

The next minute as the elephant's trunk was
extended to him he gave it another scrap of the
bread, and followed this up with a few friendly
touches, which the monster seemed to accept in a
friendly way, before transferring the bread; the
mahout looking on smilingly the while.

The trunk was raised slowly again, and the
mahout uttered a few words, with the result that
the private had to make a strong effort over self
to keep from starting away from an expected
blow; but in obedience to the driver's words
the great beast slowly passed his trunk over
the young soldier's shoulders and breast, and then,

grunting, swung up the end as if asking for more
of the bread.

'Only two bits more,' said Peter; and he turned
to the mahout and made signs to him that he should
mount to the elephant's neck.

The young soldier hardly expected it, but his
meaning was so well conveyed that the mahout
uttered a command, when the elephant passed his
trunk round the driver, swung him up, and
dropped him easily into his seat, raising his ears
the while, and then lowering them over the rider's
knees.

'Bravo! Splendid!' cried Pegg, clapping his
hands; and the next minute, after another word or
two which the elephant evidently understood and
obeyed, the little mahout dropped lightly down and
stood smiling at his admiring audience.

It was not Peter Pegg's words, but the meaning
must have been conveyed by his eyes to the mahout,
for Peter said excitedly:

'There, I'd give a suvren, if I'd got one, to be
able to say to our chaps that I'd had a ride on a
helephant like that;' and then, to his surprise, the
mahout looked at him, smiling, uttered a few words
to him, and held out his hand.

'Eh? What?' cried Peter. 'Let you hold my
rifle? Well, I oughtn't to; but there aren't no
officers near. There, I'll trust you, and I wish I
could tell you what I want.'

To his surprise and delight, as the mahout took
hold of the rifle and examined it curiously, uttering another order to his great charge, Peter Pegg
felt the great coiling trunk wrap round his waist,

swing him up in the air, and drop him astride of the huge beast's neck.

'Oh, but, I say, this 'ere won't do,' cried Peter; 'I am wrong ways on;' and scrambling up from sitting facing the howdah, he gradually reseated himself correctly, nestling his legs beneath the great half-raised ears. 'My word! ain't it nice and warm?' cried the young soldier excitedly. 'Shouldn't I like to ride round the camp now!—I say, Joe, ain't this prime?'

His comrade, who had been looking on admiringly, uttered a grunt, which was followed by an order from the mahout, resulting in the elephant reaching up his trunk, which coiled round the young soldier's waist, twitched him out of his seat, and dropped him at the driver's feet.

'Here, just a minute,' panted the young soldier, thrusting his hand into his haversack and withdrawing the last bit of bread. 'Here you are, old chap;' and he transferred the piece to the raised trunk, which he patted again and again before it was withdrawn.—'Thankye, comrade. You will find that prime 'bacco, and here's wishing I may see you again.'

'Now, Pete,' growled Smithers, for the first notes of the bugle-call rang out.

'All right. Give us my rifle, comrade. I'm off.'

Catching the rifle from the mahout's hand, he followed Smithers at the double; but he contrived to give one glance back at the magnificent beast upon which he had been mounted, with a strange feeling of longing for his lost seat.

CHAPTER XL.

FULL REVIEW ORDER.

'OH, there you are, Knowle!' cried the Resident, bustling up to the Major, who was marching slowly towards the parade-ground in full uniform, carrying his sword under the left arm.

'Yes, here I am. Look all right?'

'Oh yes, yes,' said the Resident impatiently.

'Don't show any spots, do I?'

'Spots?'

'Yes; this confounded, hot, damp climate—specks of mildew on my best uniform. I say: you look capital, Dallas,' continued the Major, running his eye over the Resident's official dress. 'That's the best of you young fellows; you only want a wash and a brush up, and you are all right. Get to my age, sir, and'——

'Oh, don't talk like that, Major. I was not thinking about uniforms.'

'Eh, weren't you? I was. I don't mean about myself, but look at my lads. Aren't they splendid, in spite of all the knocking about and wear? But what's the matter? Not well?'

'No, sir; I am not well.'

'Poor old chap! There's plenty of time; toddle up to the bungalow. Old Morley will give you a pick-me-up, and set you right in no time.'

'I have been there, sir.'

'Oh, that's right,' said the Major, with a chuckle. 'For I am very anxious about the ladies there, and the other women we have in our charge, and I feel more than ever that we have been guilty of a great error of judgment.'

'Eh ? What about ?'

'What about, sir ? Look around you.'

'Eh ? Well, we have plenty of company, but I don't see any error of judgment.'

'Why, my dear Knowle! Company! Look at the crowd.'

'Well, we shall keep them back so as to allow plenty of room for the evolutions.'

'Yes; but, let alone the country-people, every man with his kris, there are the military followers of those two Rajahs in full array.'

'Military! Phit! My dear Dallas!'

'Ah, you laugh, sir. Why, roughly speaking, each of those two chiefs has got a following of about five hundred men—say a thousand.'

'Yes, I dare say,' said the Major; 'but they are not all together.'

'No; they are divided so that we have a strong force on either side. You despise them; but have you thought of the consequences that might follow our being enclosed by two such bodies of men ?'

'Oh yes,' said the Major coolly. 'Might. But, my dear boy, have you thought of the consequences that might follow if I told my lads to close up and face outwards, and began to deal with our visitors ? Look at them,' he continued, as he pointed towards the perfectly drilled detachment drawn up in the centre of the parade-ground waiting for the order to commence the evolutions connected with the military display.

'Oh yes, they are everything that could be expected from a handful of British infantry.'

'Handful, sir! Why, I've got three hundred men on the ground. Every fellow's under arms, and we are going to show these niggers what we could do if ever we were called upon. Error of judgment, sir! The whole thing's a grand idea; and after it's over, these Malays will go away with a ten times higher idea of England's strength than they had before.'

'I don't know,' said the Resident. 'Look at those fierce-looking fellows there gathered round the elephants and their gaudily dressed chiefs. Look at that haughty fellow Suleiman, with his chiefs and spearmen clustering round him looking as if they were awaiting their prince's order to charge down upon us and sweep us all out of the district.'

'Oh yes, I see,' said the Major, chuckling.

'And here on the other side, right away to the river, there is this doubtful fellow Hamet with his lot of elephants and men, a stronger party than Suleiman's.'

'I see. I hope there won't be any row.'

'Oh, don't suggest such a thing!'

'Why not? They are in touch with the others.'

'Yes; and at a word could combine.'

'Ah, I am not afraid of that,' said the Major. 'I was thinking about their jealousy, and the possibility of a row between them.'

'I don't believe in the jealousy. I believe it is all assumed,' said the Resident, 'and that they are ready on the slightest excuse to join forces against us.'

'I don't,' said the Major gruffly. 'I am afraid they may draw knives against each other; but if they do I will give them such a lesson as will prove a startler. But, I say, have you noticed that chap Hamet ?'

'Oh yes, I saw him. He did not march with his men, mounted on one of his elephants, but came up in his dragon-boat.'

'Yes. Quite a fine show, with the amber-satin rowers, and the gongs beating. But you can't grumble about his appearance and theatrical robes. It's quite a compliment to Old England to see a native prince come simply in ordinary morning-dress. Hanged if he hadn't got lavender kid gloves !'

'Oh, don't talk about trifles, Major; but for Heaven's sake be on your guard !'

'Oh yes—guard mounted,' said the Major. 'Why, Dallas, my dear boy, I don't believe you told Morley to give you a pick-me-up. You have been fussing about down there at the bungalow, and fidgeting about what might happen to a certain young lady if the Malays turned nasty and rose against us.'

'Major ! No.'

'Don't be cross, dear boy. I was in love too once upon a time, and fidgeted as much as you do about what might happen if—if—— There, I only say *if.* Now, it's all right, my dear fellow, and it's time for the show to begin. The crowd must be getting tired of waiting; and I only see one error of judgment of which we have been guilty.'

'Ah ! And what's that ?'

'Ought to have begun an hour sooner, for, my word, the sun is hot ! Oh, by the way, I have not seen you since, but we were talking over what to do with our visitors and the crowd generally after the review. There will be the feeding, of course; but we wanted something to fill up time till dark and the fireworks begin.'

'I have heard nothing about further plans.'

'Well, the lads will keep an open course, and there will be some races and wrestling, and Sergeant Ripsy is going to show some encounters with the bayonet and a little sword-play.'

'Well, as you like. I can think of nothing else but getting the affair over and the people dismissed.'

'There, don't you be uneasy. There's a guard mounted to watch over our women folk, so come on.'

The Major went on towards the centre of the parade-ground, while the Resident hurried away, looking hot and anxious, to where seats had been arranged beneath an open tent erected on one side of the parade-ground, partly sheltered by a cluster of palms.

At last, with colours flying and the loud martial strains of the band, doubled by a strange echo thrown back by the dense jungle, the solid little force of infantry, in brilliant scarlet and with the sun flashing from their bayonets, was put in motion; while a strange murmur of satisfaction arose from the crowd of gaily attired campong dwellers, which was caught up by the followers of the two Rajahs with prolonged cries that bore some slight resemblance to the tiger-like *ragh, ragh* of an American crowd.

And then, as the band marched by, Rajah-Suleiman's group collected in front of the great clump of trees left standing when a portion of the jungle had been cleared, and the huge elephants, now gorgeous with trappings, and each bearing its showy howdah, in which were seated the Rajah himself and his principal chiefs, responded to a final blast of the highly polished brass instruments and the thunderous roll of the drums by a simultaneous uneasy trumpeting of their own, with which were mingled the cries of the mahouts, who had to ply their sharp-pointed goads to keep their charges in subjection.

Fortunately for the occupants of the howdahs, this was a final chord from the band, for the huge beasts were thoroughly startled, and the lookers-on noted that similar uneasiness was being displayed by the nine great elephants that appertained to Rajah Hamet's force, these in particular showing a disposition to turn tail and make for one of the jungle paths.

The silence that followed the band's final chord seemed, as Oliver Wendell Holmes says in one of his little poems, to have come like a poultice to heal the wounds of sound, and the great beasts settled down.

Then there was a bugle-call, and the evolutions began in regular review style, with plenty of fancy additions, such as had been planned to impress the great gathering of the Malay people. The troops marched and counter-marched, advanced in échelon, retired from the left, retired from the right, formed column and line, advanced in column of companies, turned half right and half left, formed three-quarter column; there was extended order and distended order, for Major Knowle's force was very small, but he made the most of it. Sergeant Ripsy, with a

face quite as scarlet as his uniform, buzzed about
like a vicious hornet, and, perspiring at every pore,
yelled at the guides and markers, letting fly snapping
shots of words that were certainly not included in
the code of military instructions.   But the men, as
soon as they warmed up—which was in a very short
time—went into the spirit of the thing; and when at
last the officers had got through the regular evolutions, that seemed to consist in weaving and twisting the men under their command into a series of
intricate knots, for the sole purpose of untying them
again, and Archie Maine had been saved from dis-
gracefully clubbing his men by issuing an order
which the said men wilfully disobeyed so as to
cover the lad's mistake, there was a general forming
up again for a rest and cool down, while the band
struck up, and, helped by the echo, filled the parade
with sweet sounds, to the great delight of the
gathered crowd.

There was a burst of cheering here, of a rather
barbaric nature, for from Rajah Suleiman's gathering
there came one solitary boom from a particularly
musical gong.   This rang out like a signal, and was
followed by a score more from as many of the
sonorous instruments, supplemented by an excited
yelling from the spear-armed men.

This ended as quickly as it had begun, and, treated
as a challenge, was repeated from the centre of Rajah
Hamet's party, who followed with a yell that might
have been taken as a defiant answer to hereditary
enemies.

Matters seemed to be growing exciting, and
Major Knowle, who was quiet and watchful as well

as hot, despatched messages to the commanders of
companies to be on their guard.

But now, as the last gong ceased to send its
quivering jar through the heated air, to be reflected
back from the jungle, a burst of Malay cheering
arose from the excited crowd of spectators; the
elephants joined in, trumpeting loudly; and then, as
the strange roar died away into silence, the band-
master took advantage of the opportunity, raised his
instrument, made a sign, the big drum boomed its
best in answer to six of the drummer's heaviest blows,
and to the stirring strains of the favourite old march,
'The British Grenadiers,' the band moved off to take
up a fresh position.

As soon as this was occupied the second part
of the evolutions commenced. The little force was
divided, and took up positions for attack and defence;
men were thrown out, skirmishing began, and the
Malay crowd cheered as the men in scarlet ran and
took cover; and the field was soon after covered
with advancing and retiring men, who ran, lay
down, fired from one knee, fired from their chests,
ran and took cover again; and the musketry began
to roll in sputtering repetitions, till the retiring
force seemed to take courage, gathered together,
repelled their adversaries with half-a-dozen vigorous
volleys, and advanced in turn, gradually driving
their supposed enemies back, till, when the smoke
was rising in a faint, misty cloud to float softly
away over the river, the final stages of the sham
fight were nearly at an end, and for a concluding
curtain to the mimic warfare the two little forces
advanced as if to meet in contention in the middle

of the field. But at a cértain stage a bugle rang
out, and with wonderful precision the men fell into
column and marched away to the far end of the
drill-ground, where they halted, turned, and then,
in obedience to the Major's command, began to
advance in line towards where, on their left, were
the two bodies of armed men comprising the followers
of the two Rajahs, above whom towered the two
knots of elephants, while on their right were the
gathered crowds from the nearest campongs, excitedly
watching for what was to come next.

What was to come next and was now in progress
was Britain's thin red line, and that line was on
that occasion very thin, very, very red, and extremely
long, purposely extended so as to make the most of
the tiny force.

The crowds cheered in their fashion as the train
moved on, and, excited by the yelling, the elephants
began to trumpet as the troops were now nearly half
across the parade-ground. Then the bugle rang out
'Halt!' and the orders followed quickly: 'Fire!'
and with wonderful precision there was the long line
of puffs of smoke as the volley roared and half obscured the advancing force in the thin veil of smoke.

There was a fresh burst of cheers from the
crowds, who now saw that the little line of scarlet-
coated men was marching out of the filmy, gray
cloud and lessening the distance between them.

The next bugle-call was rather unsettling, and
the next still more so, for it meant 'Double;' while
the last of all was more disturbing than anything
that had taken place that day, for it was followed
by a peculiar flickering of light as the brilliant sun

The elephants . . . set the example of making for the nearest
points of the jungle.

played upon the glistening bayonets brought down sparkling in front of the line of men. The bugles now rang out 'Charge!' followed by the good old British cheer given by wildly excited men with all the power left in them, and they bore the bristling bayonets on, racing down upon the spectators in front, as if the mimic advance were real.

The trumpeting that greeted the charge was not defiant, for the elephants turned simultaneously as upon a pivot and set the example of making for the nearest points of the jungle; and to the charging men it seemed as if they formed part of some immensely extended human hay-making machine, whose glittering spikes were about to sweep off a living crowd which, excited and yelling wildly, had turned and fled for safety.

The gaily coloured men of the two Rajahs, perhaps feeling in doubt as to their duty to fetch back the elephants—perhaps not: they may have been in-fluenced otherwise—had dashed off after the huge quadrupeds at once, but the crowd of ordinary spectators were in nowise behind. Shrieking, yelling, and angry with each other as they dashed away, they made for shelter at full speed, and when the charge was at an end and the bugles rang out, the evolution had been so well driven home that a complete transformation had been effected.

Where the great gathering had spread from side to side of the parade, there was the long, halting line of panting and powder-blackened men, who, in spite of their breathlessness, had followed up their British cheer with a tremendous petillating roar of laughter, which ran along the line from end to end and back again—a roar of laughter so loud that hardly a man knew that the band was now playing in full force 'God save the Queen,' with an additional obbligato from the drums—that one known as the 'big' threatening collapse from the vigorous action of the stick-wielder's sturdy arms.

It was only a few of the men who were cognisant of the fact that the Major was lying down exhausted, and wiping his eyes.

'Who's that?' he panted. 'Who's that—you, Maine?'

'Yes, sir.'

'Oh dear! Oh dear! I can't stop it! It's quite hysterical. Give me a water-bottle;' and then, after an application to the unstoppered mouth, 'Oh dear! How they did run! I hope poor Dallas has seen it all. I wish he had been here. Hah! I'm better now. Why, Maine, we've swept them clean away. Are they collecting farther on?'

'No, sir; I can't see a single soul.'

'Who's that?' said the Major again.

'Me, sir.'

'I didn't know you, my man. What is it, Sergeant?'

'Well, sir, I was only going to say, as I was so near, what about them there squibs and crackers as was to be let off to-night?'

'Oh, the rockets and fireworks,' said the Major. 'They haven't gone off in the heat, have they? No accident?'

'No, sir; but there won't be nobody left to see them pop.'

CHAPTER XII.

SEE THE CONQUERING HEROES.

THE line closed up, and marched 'easy' back towards the upper end of the parade-ground, with not a single stranger to represent the spectators, and, half ironically, they were received by the band with 'See, the Conquering Hero Comes.' The review and sham fight were over, and as the officers and weary men were dismissed, and the officers gathered where the ladies and others of the station were assembled, one of the first upon whom they set eyes was the young Rajah Hamet, who had just joined the Resident.

'Well, Dallas,' said the Major, who was mopping his forehead, 'what did you think of our charge?— Ah, Rajah Hamet,' he continued, as he caught sight of the young man, who approached to hold out his hand, 'what did *you* think of our sham fight? Did you see it all?'

'Magnificent, sir; every bit.'

'Where were you?'

'Down yonder, sir, in front of my elephants and men.'

'Then you didn't run?'

'No, sir; I have been to Aldershot and seen a review before.'

'I am afraid we scared your men,' said Archie, to whom the young Rajah turned a few minutes later.

'Well, wasn't it quite enough to scare them?' replied the Prince. 'It seems to me that a body of men, to whatever nation they belonged, would require a good deal of hardening before they would stand firm and receive a bayonet charge.'

'Yes,' replied Archie. 'As far as I know, there are not many who can. It was rather comic, though, to see your men run.'

'Well,' replied the young Prince, 'I don't think my men ran any faster than Suleiman's.'

'Not a bit,' cried Archie hastily. 'I say, I didn't mean to insult you.'

'Oh, I am not insulted,' said the young man quietly. 'I should have run too if I had not known that your men would pull up at the last moment. Well, good-bye.'

'You are not going?' cried Archie. 'You will stop and be our guest to-night? You were invited, of course. There are all the sports to come, and the illuminations and fireworks.'

'Oh no, I must go,' said the young Rajah. 'I have got to rally my men, and see them safely back.'

'Well, but some of your officers will do that, and bring them back.'

'I doubt it,' said Hamet, smiling. 'If I know my people, they will not stop till they get home.'

'Oh, surely not! They will all come here again and see the rest of our *fête*—and Rajah Suleiman's too.'

Hamet shook his head.

'Some of your people from the campongs, who

know you—they may come back, but none of the others.'

'Well, you stop at any rate.'

'No,' said the young Rajah. 'If my people have forsaken me, I must not forsake them. Here, you promised, you know, to come and spend a few days with me, and have some tiger-shooting. When is it to be?'

'When my major gives me leave. Stop! Stop now, and ask him. He or Sir Charles Dallas will put you up for the night.'

'No, Maine; they don't believe in me enough. Somehow they have no faith in me at all, and because I'm Suleiman's enemy—or rather, he is mine, for I have no feeling for or against the fellow —they think that I am opposed to the English, with whom I want to be friends and to get their help to civilise my people. No, I must be off to my boat at once, and try to get in touch with my people as soon as possible. They will keep to the lower elephant-path, as near to the river as they can. There, try and get leave, old chap. I want you to come. I say, you don't mind my calling you "old chap"?'

'Like it,' said Archie, holding out his hand. 'I am disappointed, however, for I should have liked you to stay. But hadn't you better try to bring some of your men back?'

'No. They wouldn't come now, for fear of being laughed at for being such cowards.'

'Well, if you must go, you must; but, as I said, I should have liked you to stay. It would have looked so friendly to my people.'

'I hope they will believe in me some day without that,' said the young Malay. 'But tell me, if you had been in my place, and seen your people scared away by the English soldiers, would you have stayed?'

'No; I'll be hanged if I should,' said Archie with energy. 'I should have felt too mad.'

'Thank you,' said Hamet. 'That sounds frank.'

'It is frank,' said Archie. 'But I say, now, tell me: has it made you feel mad against us?'

'No-o; only sorry for my people. I want to train them up to know you better, and to be ready to fight with you.'

'Fight with us?'

'Yes; not against you—fight side by side with you, so that you may help me to civilise my folks more, and join us to put down the Malay chiefs like Suleiman.'

'You don't like Suleiman, then?'

'Like him!' said the young man scornfully. 'I like no man who cannot stretch out his hand to me and take mine in an honest grasp that I can trust.'

'Of course,' cried Archie. 'But then our Resident believes in Suleiman.'

'Yes, and distrusts me,' said the young man rather bitterly. 'Well, they think they are right; but we shall see. I say, though, I didn't see that French gentleman with Suleiman's people. I expected he would be mounted upon one of the elephants.'

'No,' said Archie; 'he has not been here for the last few days.'

'Forbidden to come?' said the young man.

'No-o,' said Archie; 'he wouldn't be. He is Rajah Suleiman's friend.'

'Yes,' said Hamet quietly. 'That is why I thought he would be here. Do you like him?'

'Not a bit,' said Archie. 'Why?'

'Oh, I suppose it was because I dislike him myself. That is all. Good-bye. As we Malays say, *apa boleh booat.*'

'What is to be will be,' said Archie. 'Good-bye.'

The parade-ground remained deserted for quite an hour, and then some of the campong people had regained sufficient courage to begin dribbling back, to be followed by a few of the inhabitants of the neighbouring villages. But not one of the Malays who followed their Rajahs made their appearance. Consequently there was no attempt made to carry out the sports; but on being consulted, the Major gave orders that the illumination of the boats should be encouraged, and the display of rockets and coloured lights should follow; and as this news gradually spread, some of the nearest village people and fisher-folk joined in, to display their lanterns upon their boats, and a pretty fair gathering of the campong people were present as soon as it was dark, it taking very little in so effective a position to light up the river and jungle banks in a most attractive way.

The Doctor and his wife and niece, in addition to several of the ladies of the station, dined at the mess that night, so that they might afterwards stroll down to the banks of the river and watch the rockets burst and sprinkle the jungle with their stars; and

just as the enjoyment was at its height, and the simple
Malay folk kept on bursting out with their ejaculations indicative of delight, the Major went up behind
the Resident, who had been chatting with the Doctor
and his ladies.

'Well, Dallas,' he said, 'you don't feel nervous
now, do you ?'

'Hush !' was the reply, as the gentleman addressed
looked sharply round.   'More so than ever.   I hope
you have got sentries out to command the river
approaches to the station ?'

'Of course I have.   But why ?'

'Because see what an opportunity is offered for
those two chiefs to take revenge upon us for what
they must consider an insult to their dignity.'

'My dear sir, you are giving reins to your
imagination.   They are well on the way now to
their homes.'   ·

'Perhaps so,' said the Resident in a low, nervous
tone; 'but suppose they have made a halt and are
only waiting till their scouts have announced to
them that we are quite unprepared ?'

'You are assuming, my dear Dallas, that those
two princes are working hand and glove.'

'Well, you are quite of my way of thinking over
that.'

'Humph !   No,' said the Major.   'I am beginning
to think that our lavender-gloved young friend
means well by us.'

'Lavender-gloved young friend !' said the Resident.   'Who knows but those soft kid gloves may
not be worn to cover the tiger's claws ?'

'Ah ! who knows, my dear Dallas ?   But it is

enough for us to know that if we can produce such an effect with blank cartridge and a sham charge, we have it in our power to protect the station and defend the honour of those we love, by using ball cartridge and sending our bayonets home.'

CHAPTER XIII.

THE DOCTOR'S CALL.

IN spite of the Resident's doubts and expressed opinion that the two Rajahs would display resentment, the neighbourhood settled down calmly enough. The village people nearest, notwithstanding their being chased helter-skelter, mixed up with the Rajah's followers, very soon showed that they had thoroughly enjoyed the fun of seeing Suleiman's haughty, tyrannical gang scared away and running as if for their lives.

The people of the more distant campongs came in just as usual, bringing their fruit and poultry to market as before; and though the half-military-looking armed men did not make their appearance, the Resident was bound to confess that this was not a bad sign, as they had rarely approached the cantonments to mingle with the soldiers off duty.

A few days elapsed, and then a present was sent in, consisting of supplies, by Rajah Hamet; and the very next day two of Suleiman's chiefs brought in a letter, written in English, but dotted with French allusions which suggested its source.

It was an invitation for the Major and his officers to a tiger-hunt. This was considered, and then the Major replied in the most friendly way, begging to be excused on the ground that it was impossible to accept the invitation then, but asking for it to be repeated later on.

The weather was lovely, there being a succession of brilliant moonlight nights; while before the moon rose, even the Doctor declared that the display made by the fire-flies in the darkness was simply glorious.

One evening Sir Charles was dining at the bungalow, and, having got over his nervous doubts, upon hearing Minnie express a desire to go up the river and see the fire-flies first, and the rising of the moon after, the Resident at once proposed to have his smaller boat prepared, with a couple of his most trusty native servants to pole it a short distance up the river, and then bring the Doctor and the two ladies back to supper at the Residency.

Minnie was delighted; but, to the Resident's great satisfaction, her aunt declared at once that she would not go up the river by night on account of the crocodiles.

'I don't want to throw a wet blanket over Sir Charles's kindly suggested trip,' she said, 'but I certainly will not go.'

'Oh, there's no danger to be feared, my dear madam,' said Sir Charles. 'The reptiles would never dare to attack a well-manned boat.'

'Never,' said the Doctor emphatically.

'But they might, my dear,' replied Mrs Morley. 'You can go, but I shall certainly stay.'

'You talk very glibly,' grunted the Doctor, 'about my going; but suppose I am wanted?'

'Well, if you are, it will only be for some trivial ailment amongst the native people, and I should know what to give them.'

'What!' cried the Doctor.—'Why, my dear Dallas, the last time she meddled with my bottles she nearly poisoned one of my patients.'

'For shame, Henry!—Don't you believe him, Sir Charles. I am sure I did the poor woman a great deal of good.'

'It's all very fine,' said the Doctor. 'I must confess the woman did get better; and if madam had quite poisoned her, as she was a native it wouldn't have mattered much.'

'Oh uncle, for shame!—He doesn't mean it, Sir Charles,' said Minnie.

'But it would have spoilt my credit,' continued the Doctor; 'and there, I don't want to see a lot of blow-flies with lights in their tails; so, once for all, I sha'n't go.'

'But you ought to go, my dear,' said Mrs Morley, who looked rather annoyed.

'Why?'

'Why? To take care of Minnie.'

'It doesn't take two men as well as a couple of servants to take care of one little girl. Don't talk stuff, my dear. I'm sure Sir Charles will take every care of her.'

Mrs Morley said no more, and Sir Charles left at last with the matter entirely settled to his satisfaction, while Minnie smiled in answer to a few words respecting the old folks leaving them to themselves.

The evening promised to be perfect, and Minnie was waiting for their visitor, when, just as she was beginning to be impatient, a note was brought from the Resident stating that Rajah Hamet had come up the river unexpectedly to discuss a question relating to the possibility of some stronger alliance.

'I am horribly disappointed,' wrote the Resident, 'but it is a Government matter, and your uncle will understand with me that I am only too much delighted to find that this again proves that my doubts were all wrong, and that I am glad to welcome the Rajah here. He evidently means to stop the night, and I have sent in for Major Knowle to join us. Under the circumstances I feel that I dare not come. However, you shall not be disappointed; the boat is waiting with two picked men, and I must beg that your uncle and aunt will be your companions.'

'There, old lady,' said the Doctor as, in a disappointed tone, his niece finished reading the letter. 'It will be rude to Sir Charles, as well as a bitter disappointment to Minnie. Come, there's no cause for alarm. If there were I would not ask you. Say you will come.'

'No, Henry,' replied the lady firmly; 'I will not.'

'Oh, very well,' said the Doctor, as he saw the tears rising in his niece's eyes. 'You sha'n't be disappointed, Minnie. We will risk your aunt giving some poor woman a lotion to take instead of a draught. Get your cloak and veil. We mustn't have any trouble from the night air. I'll take you myself.—Hullo! What in the name of wonder does this mean? An elephant—another Rajah!'

'Two of them,' said Mrs Morley anxiously, 'and they are coming here.'

'Yes,' said the Doctor, stepping out into the veranda of his pretty bungalow to meet his visitors, as the great, soft-footed, howdah-bearing beast was checked by his mahout at the bamboo fence. One of the two Malay officers bent down to inform him that the Rajah Suleiman had been out shooting that morning with his French friend, and that, after firing at a tiger, the wounded beast had leaped upon the Rajah's elephant, and Suleiman and his friend had both been mauled. The bearers of the message stated that the Doctor must come at once.

'Can't help it, my child,' said the Doctor. 'I am sorry for your disappointment, but it is impossible for me to refuse. In an ordinary case I might postpone my visit, but, you see, Suleiman is our friend, and it is most important that I should be off at once.'

'But, my dear,' exclaimed Minnie's aunt, 'it means your being away all night.'

'Of course; and if he's very bad I may have to stay two or three days. There, I can't stop talking. Get me my little bag while I fetch my instruments and some dressing.'

Without a word Mrs Morley hurried to obtain what was required, and the Doctor patted his niece on the shoulder.

'Never mind, my dear. We must give it up. Dallas will be able to go with you another time, and you will enjoy your trip better.'

Minnie nodded.

'I won't mind, uncle—much. But it never rains but it pours: here's somebody else wants you.'

'Young Archie! What does he want?'

He soon knew, for the lad hurried up, glancing at the two Malays upon the elephant, giving Minnie a quick nod, and then catching the Doctor by the arm and hurrying him into the nearest room.

'The Major sent me to know what these two swells want. He thinks they have come to your place instead of to him.'

The Doctor explained at once, and then a sudden thought occurred to him.

'Look here,' he said; 'you know Sir Charles was going to take us up the river in his boat this evening?'

'Yes, I know. He's got Rajah Hamet, and the Major's going into the Residency. That's why the chief thinks those chaps on the elephant have come to the wrong house.'

'Well, look here, my lad; you must take my place.'

'What!' cried the lad, staring. 'I could pour him out a dose of physic, or I could tackle a native, but I wouldn't undertake to dress a Rajah's wounds.'

'What are you talking about, stupid?' cried the Doctor angrily. 'I mean, take my place and escort Minnie up the river in the Resident's boat.'

'De-lighted!' cried the lad excitedly. 'Of course —but I don't know whether the Major will give me leave, as Rajah Hamet's here. Here, I'll run back as fast as I can, and be with you, if it's all right, in no time.'

'Yes, do. I don't want the poor girl to be disappointed; and you will take care of her?'

'Of course!'

Archie was turning to go, when the Doctor caught him by the arm. 'There's no need. I will jump up on the elephant as soon as I have got my bag, and go round by headquarters and make it right with the Major.'

'Yes, sir, do. Capital!—But no, no. He sent me to find out, and he won't like it. I must go, Doctor.'

'What! am I not surgeon to this force, and are not all officers under me? Here, I will make him like it. You mind what I say—I give you leave to go.'

Just then Minnie and her aunt came to the door with the Doctor's bag, and Archie hesitated.

'Look here, Minnie,' he cried, hurrying to her side; 'I am going to—— No, no,' he said, giving his foot a stamp, 'I can't! I will not, Doctor. Here, I will run on and get back. Look here; you see how important it is. Here's Down coming as hard as he can to see why I have been so long.'

'Confound you, sir!' cried the Doctor. 'And when I'd settled the whole thing!—Here, you, Down, what do you want?'

The Captain came up quickly, and the state of affairs was explained, ending with the new-comer being introduced to the two Malay officers.

'Look here,' said the Doctor, turning to the Captain; 'you explain everything to the Major, and tell him I am off at once to Palm-Tree Palace, and am keeping Archie Maine here to take my place for an hour or two. You understand?'

'Quite,' said the Captain.

'Maine thinks, as the Major has sent him with a message to me, that he ought to go back; but your coming and the answer I send by you, I consider, will be sufficient to exonerate your subaltern. What do you say?'

'Oh yes, sir; quite sufficient.'

'Now, Archie, my lad, are you satisfied?'

Archie turned to the Captain.

'Give me your leave too.'

'Certainly. I will make it right with the Major.'

'All right, then, Doctor,' said Archie; and, satisfied now by the Captain going off with the required information, the lad stayed, busied himself with Mrs Morley and Minnie; and after seeing the Doctor mount the kneeling elephant with his bag and instruments, and then wishing him good speed, they stood watching the great, slowly pacing beast till, as it turned off to reach the forest path, there was a final wave of the hand from the Doctor, and the next minute he was out of sight.

'That's being a doctor's wife, Minnie, my child; one never knows what to expect. Well, there, your uncle has gone off to do good. I never liked that Rajah's looks, but I hope he isn't badly hurt. Now then, what about this trip on the water? I really don't like your going, my dear.'

'Oh auntie, how can you be so nervous?'

'I didn't like your going even when your uncle was here.'

'But, Mrs Morley, there's nothing to be nervous about,' cried Archie.

'My dear boy'——

'I say, hang it all, Mrs Morley! you might call me a man now,' said Archie, interrupting her speech.

'Yes, my dear, I have plenty of confidence in you; but it's only you.'

'Why, there will be the Resident's two chief boatmen, won't there?—You said there would be two men, didn't you, Minnie?'

'Yes, of course; and we shouldn't be above an hour or two, aunt.'

'No, I know, my dear; but—but'——

'There, aunt dear, uncle's going away so suddenly has upset you, and it does seem selfish of me.—Look here, Archie, it's very kind of you to offer to take me, but it would be inconsiderate of me to go. I'll give it up.'

'Oh!' cried the lad, 'I am disappointed.'

'Yes, of course you would be,' said Mrs Morley; 'and it's foolish of me to make such a fuss about nothing. There, I am better now. I was a bit flurried by the Doctor going, to be away all night, and leaving us unprotected.'

'And not a British soldier near,' said Archie laughingly.

'Of course; of course,' said Mrs Morley. 'You will take great care of her, my dear boy?'

'Take care of her!' cried Archie. 'Why, Sir Charles would have me out and shoot me, or wring my neck, if I didn't. Look here, madam, I'm too fond of Lieutenant Archibald Maine to run any risks. Now are you satisfied?'

'Quite,' said the Doctor's wife, forcing a laugh.— 'There, my dears, be off as soon as you can—but wait till I get a scarf.'

Archie and Minnie embarking in the Resident's sampan.

'What are you going to do, auntie?'

'See you down to the boat, of course, my dear.'

A very few minutes later the Doctor's wife was standing on the banks of the river watching the Resident's handsomely fitted sampan—not his official dragon-boat—being punted by two sturdy men up the glistening waters, Minnie turning from time to time to wave her hand, and lastly her scarf, just as they disappeared.

'It is foolish of me to be so nervous and frightened about crocodiles,' said Mrs Morley, as she turned her straining eyes from where she had been watching the boat. 'There isn't a sign of any of the horrible reptiles; and if it were dangerous those people would not be going up the river in the same direction;' and she remained watching a small naga with about half-a-dozen men plying their oars, sending the slightly built craft steadily upstream. 'Ah, well, I want to see them back. What a lovely evening it is going to be; but how rapidly the night closes in! I almost wish I had gone with them, for it will be very lovely when the moon begins to rise among the trees.'

The Doctor's wife gave a slight shiver as a faint waft of wind came sweeping over the tops of the forest trees, and she drew her scarf lightly over her head and shoulders as she quickened her steps to return to the bungalow. 'It's not cold,' she said half uneasily, 'and yet I shivered. It's as if the nervous feeling were coming back. Two hours! Well, they will soon slip by.'

CHAPTER XIV.

A GREAT HORROR.

THOSE two hours did soon slip away, and after assuring herself by the clock that the time had really fled, Mrs Morley went and stood in the veranda, gazing out in the full expectation of seeing those for whom she waited coming up from the direction of the river.

The night was glorious. The nearly full moon was silvering the tops of the trees and casting deep, black shadows on the ground. Here and there in the patches of thick shrubbery that had been planted to take off the harsh formality surrounding the parade, there were faint, twinkling sparks that gave a suggestion of how beautiful the river-sides must be where the lights of the curious insects flashed and died out and lit up again in full force; and for some minutes Mrs Morley stood breathing in the sweet, moist perfume of the many night blooms which floated on the air.

'It is very, very beautiful,' she sighed, 'but not like home. One tries to get used to it, and does for a time; but there is always that strange feeling of insecurity which will suggest what might happen— we so few, the people here so many, and always looking upon us as infidel intruders who have forced themselves up here to make a home in their very midst. I am too impatient,' she added, with a sigh, as she turned to walk to and fro in the veranda.

'I am too impatient,' she repeated. 'On such a beautiful night they would easily be tempted to go a little farther up the river than they intended, and they would tell the men to let the boat float gently back with the stream. They have tired the men, perhaps, and have told them to leave the boat to itself. Yes, a lovely night.'

She went in, with a sigh, to speak to her two native servants and tell them that they need not stay up; but she found her care unnecessary, for they were already asleep. Then, obeying her next impulse, she woke them, telling one to wait and the other to walk with her as far as the river-side.

Here she stood with the woman, watching and trying to pierce the soft, gray mist that hung above the water, before looking round for some one—boatman, or any other native whom she could question. But there was not a soul within sight, and as proof of the lateness of the hour, not a light was to be seen.

'Ah!' she cried, with a start, for the woman behind her had suddenly caught her by the wrist with one hand, while she stood with the other outstretched, pointing up the stream. 'What is it?' she said. 'Can you see the boat?'

'No. Listen.'

'Ah! You hear them coming?'

The woman shook her head violently.

'Croc,' she whispered; and her word was followed by a light, wallowing splash.

'Ugh!' ejaculated the Doctor's wife, with a shudder. 'Come back. They may have returned by the other path and called at the officers' quarters.

They are waiting for us by now perhaps,' she added to herself.

Leading the way back to the bungalow, she hurried in, with straining ears, with the hope that the pair would come out to meet her slowly dying away.

'They must have come back directly we went out, learned that we had gone down to the river, and followed us.'

Stepping in quickly to the servants' part of the bungalow, she found the other servant fast asleep, ready to stare at her vacantly and wonderingly as she was shaken into wakefulness. The woman had to be spoken to by her fellow-servant before anything could be got from her; and then it was only to learn that the expected ones had not returned.

'Something must have happened,' said the Doctor's wife, fighting hard now to keep back the horrible forebodings that were troubling her. 'Oh! this is not being a woman,' she said. 'Come back with me to the river.'

The woman hesitated, but Mrs Morley caught her hand, and they hurried back to the river-side, where, before many minutes of excited watching had passed, at least a dozen horribly suggestive splashes had been heard far out upon the flowing stream.

'Come back,' she whispered to her companion. 'I cannot bear it. What!' she ejaculated, as the woman crept more closely to her and whispered something in her ear. 'Those horrid creatures drag people into the river sometimes? Yes, yes; I know —I know. Come back. Perhaps they have come,' she continued, trying to speak firmly; and once more she hurried to the bungalow, to find the other servant again fast asleep.

The clock showed that it only wanted a few minutes to midnight, and setting her teeth hard in her determination, the trembling woman gave herself till twelve before starting for the officers' quarters and the Residency to give the alarm.

As she reached the gate she became aware of lights in the distance, evidently going in the direction of the river lower down. Voices, too, floated on the night air, and her spirits rose, for she was conscious of a merry laugh. It could not mean trouble, and she stopped short, watching the lights that seemed now to have stopped by the river's bank, trying to fit them in somehow with a solution of her trouble. Still all was mental darkness, when she was conscious of a shout or two which made her start, but only to realise directly afterwards as she heard replies, followed by the splash of oars, that some one must be departing in a boat.

Then came the murmur of talking as the little party appeared to be not coming towards her but striking off diagonally in the direction of the officers' quarters and the Residency.

A loud cry escaped her. It was answered, and the next minute hurrying feet were approaching her, and a voice exclaimed:

'Anything the matter?'

'Yes, yes!' panted the agitated woman.

'Who is it? Mrs Morley?'

'Yes. Help, Captain Down—I—I'—— and, trembling and half-breathless, she clung to the speaker as he caught her hands in his.

'The Resident's boat ?' she panted.

'No, no—Rajah Hamet's. We have been to see him off.'

'Oh, you don't understand ! The Resident's boat —Mr Maine'——

'Ah ! What of him ?'

'Went up the river with my niece'——

'Yes, yes—what of them ?'

'Not come back !'

'Oh ! Well, well, don't be alarmed.—Why, you are trembling like a leaf.'

'Yes. I can't help it. It is foolish perhaps. I am terribly alarmed.'

'Oh, come, come ! I will walk back with you to the bungalow.—You go on, Durham ; and you might tell the Resident that I am seeing Mrs Morley home.'

'Yes ; all right !' came out of the darkness. 'Shall I say that the boat's not come back ?'

'Oh yes. You might mention it.'

'Yes—yes, pray tell him,' added Mrs Morley, as the young officer addressed was continuing his route.

'Let's see,' said the Captain ; 'the Doctor's gone off to see to the Rajah, hasn't he ?'

'Yes.'

'Ah, I see ; and you are nervous from being left alone.'

'No, no, Captain Down. I am afraid that something has happened to the boat.'

'Yes, of course ; ladies always are,' said the Captain cheerily, 'when they are sitting up waiting. Now, now, be cool. There are scores of things that might have happened in a little expedition like this. First of all, they may have stopped to watch the fire-flies.'

'Oh yes, but not so late.'

'Well, no ; but they may have gone much farther than they intended. It is very tempting on a night like this.'

'But I begged Archie Maine to be back in good time.'

'Archie Maine is only a boy, and thoughtless ; and I dare say Miss Heath would be delighted with the trip ; and then there would be night-blooming flowers to look at, the noises of the jungle to listen to, and the splashing of the croc '——

'Oh, for pity's sake, don't, Captain Down !'

'Oh, well, I won't. Now then, my dear lady, let's get back to the bungalow, and you give me one of Morley's best cigars—not those out of the old cedar box, please ; one of those will do very well for Archie Maine when he comes—and I will sit down in the veranda and chat with you till the truants return ; and then you can scold your niece, after giving Archie the bad cigar. That will be punishment enough for him, for he will be vain enough to try to smoke it, though a thin cigarette makes him poorly, poor fellow ! Now then, how do you feel now ?'

'Oh, better,' said Mrs Morley. 'And you don't think anything could have happened, Captain Down ?'

'Nothing worse than that they have gone too far and are keeping you up.'

'But you don't think that the boat has been upset ?'

'Certainly not. Why should I ?'

'Boats are such dangerous things.'

'Yes,' said the Captain quietly—'in the hands of

those who don't know how to use them. But Maine
and your niece are not punting, and they have two
of Dallas's best men.'

'Yes,' said Mrs Morley, with a sigh of relief, as
they reached the gate and made their way into the
veranda.

'Thank you,' said the Captain, as Mrs Morley
took a cigar-box from a shelf and then lit a cedar-
wood match at the table lamp. 'I wonder how the
Doctor's going on,' he continued, as he lit his cigar.

'Ah, I wonder too,' said Mrs Morley.

'Hope the poor beggar isn't much hurt. But Mr
Stripes' claws are rather ugly things. Ah, well,
lucky for him that he's got a Doctor Morley to call
into the wilderness. Hullo! Footsteps! What did
I tell you? Here they come! In a hurry, too.'

But the distant sound of steps was not duplicated.
They were those of one only, coming at a rapid
rate; and directly after the Resident dashed open
the garden gate.

'What's this I hear?' he cried excitedly. 'The
boat not back?'

He listened for a few moments to Mrs Morley's
once more excited words; but he half-interrupted
her before she had done, by exclaiming:

'Here they come! I have told the Major, and he
is turning out the men. For Heaven's sake, Mrs
Morley, try and be calm.'

'I am trying, Sir Charles. But my husband
absent! How can I look him in the face when he
comes back?'

'Oh, hush, hush!' whispered the Resident, pressing her hand so hard that she could hardly bear it.

'You are taking the very blackest view of the matter. It may be a trifle—one of the poles broken, or they may have ventured too far.'

'Don't talk, pray,' said Mrs Morley. 'Never mind me. Do something! Act!'

'I am acting, and for the best,' whispered Sir Charles. 'I would give my life to save Minnie if she is in danger, but I feel it my duty to try to comfort you.'

The next minute he was busy with the officers and the men, hurrying along the river-bank and sending off boats up the stream, in one of which— his own, manned by a dozen men—he was standing with Captain Down and the Major, watching the sides of the river; sometimes plunged in black darkness, at others glistening in the light of the moon, which had now risen far above the trees. But they had not been gone above half-an-hour before news came, to run through the ranks of the searchers left behind, some of whom, on the possibility that those sought might have had an accident with the boat and been compelled to land and fight their way through the jungle, had penetrated some distance along the path nearest to the river-side, and been recalled by one of the officers' whistles.

On hurrying back they had encountered the Sergeant going the rounds, who had to announce that the sentry stationed at the hut above the chief landing-place was missing, and no answer could be obtained to the calls that should have reached his ears had he been anywhere near.

It was a night of excitement, misery, and despair, and the short dawn, when it broke, brought not hope but horror and dismay, for all at once, when the morning mist was lying heavily upon the lower reach of the river, the sound of oars was heard approaching the campong, and as it neared the lower landing-place, to which several of the party hurried, it seemed quite a long space of time before the heads of the rowers began to come gradually out of the gray fog; and soon after it was made out to be Rajah Hamet's naga, or dragon-boat, towing behind it a second boat that had been overturned.

The news was passed inward, and this brought the Major to the landing-place, where the Rajah was waiting.

'Ah!' cried the old officer, 'you have brought news?'

The young Rajah bent his head.

'Yes,' he said hoarsely. 'Is this your boat?'

'Yes, yes—the Resident's—Sir Charles's. Been overturned?'

'We found it amongst the trees far down the river. One of my men caught sight of this hanging in a bush;' and he held up a large, thin, gauzy-looking white scarf, torn almost in two.

'Ah!' gasped the Major, as he caught at the flimsy wrapper, now partially dry. 'And—and— you were going to say something else, sir?'

'Yes,' said the young Rajah, with something like a groan. 'But tell me, do you know whose was this?'

He brought forward from behind him an officer's forage-cap, about which a torn puggaree clung like a wisp.

'Great heavens!' panted the Major. 'Oh, my poor, dear boy!—Where did you find this, sir?'

'Part of the boat's bows were crushed in as if by a blow. This cap was held down by one of the splinters.'

Just then voices came floating down the river, indicating that some of the party were returning from their search to the upper landing-place; and soon after the Resident's naga had reached the stage, and the principal occupants sprang out to hear about the missing sentry, and to give no news. The last discovery was whispered to them in broken tones, and as what seemed to be the terrible fate of the small boat's occupants was told by the Major to Sir Charles, he literally reeled away from where he had been standing, and staggered onwards with extended hands, as if making for the bungalow. But before he had gone many steps he stopped short, to whisper hoarsely, 'Who is that?'

'I, Sir Charles,' said Captain Down.

'Thank you. Take my hand, please. I am giddy, and half-blind. Something seems to have gone wrong. I cannot think. Please help me, and lead me home.—No; stop,' he added. 'That poor woman! Some one must tell her. She must know; and I can't—I can't be the bearer. Oh, it is too horrible! My fault, too.—Ah! Who is that? You, Down? I thought you had gone. Don't let me fall. This giddiness again. Yes, I remember now. The Doctor! He was called away to go to the Rajah's help. Has he returned? Has he'——His lips parted to say more, but his words were inaudible, and at a signal from the Captain four of

the men hurried up, to lace their hands into a bearing, and, keeping step, they bore the insensible man
to the Residency.

It was late in the burning afternoon, after the
overturned and much-damaged boat had been lying
to dry in the hot sun for hours, and the terrible
mishap had been canvassed in every detail, when a
sentry passed the word that an elephant was approaching with strangers.

The strangers proved to be the Doctor, one of
Suleiman's officials, and the mahout; while as soon
as the news reached headquarters, Major Knowle
hurried out, bareheaded, to meet his friend, and
stood in the shade of one of the great palm-trees,
signalling to the mahout to stop.

'Morning!' shouted the Doctor cheerily as he
drew near. 'Patient's all right, Knowle, and the
Frenchman only frightened into a fit. Phew! It
is hot, eh? What are you holding up your hand
for? Nothing wrong?'

The Major was holding on by the ordinary trappings
of the howdah, and reaching up as he raised himself
on tiptoe, he almost whispered his terrible news,
while the florid, erst happy-looking Doctor looked
blankly down.

CHAPTER XV.

PETER'S SENTRY-GO.

TRAMP, tramp, tramp, tramp, up and down on the regular beat, sometimes in the full silvery moonlight, sometimes in the shade cast by the hut; one minute only the footsteps to break the silence, or the wallowing plash of one of the great reptiles that haunted the river-deeps.

'That's cheerful!' muttered the sentry. 'Ain't so bad, though, as old Joe made it out when he was doing his sentry-go below there, close to the water. My word, how clear it is to-night! I should just like to have a regular old-fashioned sentry-box down there, close to the landing-place, with a good, strong door to it as one could fasten tight, and loopholes in the sides, and plenty of cartridges ready for a night's shooting. I'd let some of 'em have it! Wouldn't it make 'em savage, though! They'd come out and turn the box over if it was not well pegged down. Wouldn't do much good, though, if I hit every time, for lots more of the ugly beggars would come. Mister Archie says they lay eggs. Pretty chickens they must be when they are hatched. Hullo! what boat's that?'

For the plashing of poles reached his ears, and the dark form of a good-sized sampan came round a curve, with its attap awning glistening softly like dead silver in the moonlight.

The sentry waited in the shade of the hut till the

boat came nearer, and then challenged, when a familiar voice responded :

'That you, Peter Pegg ? '

'Mister Archie, sir ! Yes, sir.'

'It's all right. We are going up the river a little way in the moonlight. Beautiful night ! '

'Yes, sir; lovely, sir. I'd be on the lookout, sir, though.'

'What for ? '

'Them alligator things, sir. I have heard a good many of them knocking about there.'

'Oh, they won't come near us with the men splashing as they pole us along.'

The boat passed on, and as the sentry had a glimpse of a white face and the folds of a veil he stood musing and watching till the boat had passed and disappeared.

'No,' he thought, 'I don't suppose the brutes will go near them. They soon scuttle off when they hear a splash. Nice to be him, enj'ying hisself with his lady. Wonder who it is. Miss Doctor, perhaps. Nice girl. But he's only a boy. Wish I was a officer. I used to think it would be all the same for us when I 'listed. My word, how the Sergeant did lay on the butter and jam ! And talked about the scarlet, and being like a gentleman out here abroad with the niggers to wait on us—and then it comes to this ! Sentry-go for hours in a lonely place like this here, with crocklygaters hanging about to see if you go to sleep to give them a chance to make a grab. Yes, they make a fellow feel sleepy ! Just likely, ain't it ? '

Peter Pegg's thoughts seemed to animate him,

and for a turn or two he changed his pace from a slow march to double.

'Steady, my lad!' he muttered. 'There ain't no hurry;' and he dropped back into the regular pace, and began thinking about the boat and its occupants.

'Nice young lady she is; and I suppose that there Sir Charles is going to make a match with her, for she and Mister Archie always seem just like brother and sister. I suppose he ain't been well. Been precious quiet lately. Can't have offended him, for he was as jolly as could be last time I saw him. He's getting more solid-like and growed up. But my word, what fun we have had together sometimes! And what a row there would have been if we had been found out! It wouldn't have done. But it has cheered me up many a time when I have had the miserables and felt as if I'd like to cut sojering and make for home. It was nice to have a young officer somewheres about your own age ready for a lark. Poor old Mother Smithers, and that brown juice—what do they call it—cutch and gambia?— as dyes things brown. The officers' clean shirts as was washed in that water—haw, haw, haw!—— What's that?'

The listener brought his piece to the ready, and the *click, click* of the lock followed instantly upon a shrill cry which seemed to thrill the sentry along every nerve.

'Is it the crocs?' he thought; and then close upon the distant sound of blows and a splash or two came in Archie's well-known but now excited tones:

'Sentry Pegg! Help!'

The young private obeyed his first instinct, and that was, instead of firing, to give the alarm, to run down as fast as he could to the water's edge and plunge in amongst the scattered, overhanging trees, making as well as he could judge for the direction from which the cries had arisen.

'Here! Coming! Coming!' he panted, as he rushed in where the trees were thickest, to become, directly after, conscious of a figure starting up from behind a bush that he had just passed, and from which, glittering and flashing, came the sparkle of quite a little cloud of fire-flies.

The lad swung himself round as he scented danger, and struck back with the butt of his rifle; but it was only to miss his assailant and expose his head to a blow from the other side—so heavy a stroke from a formidable, club-like weapon that he dropped, with a faint groan, while from the direction of the boat right out towards the middle of the river there was a resumption of the plashing of poles.

CHAPTER XVI.

A STRANGE FEVER.

IT was to Archie Maine like a bad attack of the
fever from which he had suffered when he first
went up-country in the gunboat from Singapore.
There was that horrible beating and throbbing in
his head, only intensely more confusing than it had
been then; and sometimes, when he could think
and everything did not seem mentally upside-down,
he was being puzzled by two questions. One was,
'Is it jungle fever?' the other, 'Is it the throbbing
and beating of the gunboat engines?' And this
latter he favoured the more because he felt convinced that the heat, the burning, scorching heat, in
his head must be because they had put him in a
berth close by the furnace fires.

Throb, throb—burn, burn—and then all nothingness for long enough. He could not move; he
could not speak; he could not think; only hour
after hour in the midst of the throbbing pain he
felt dried up, choking with thirst, and always fighting hard to get back the power to think.

What did it all mean? Where was he? There
was the throbbing as of the engines, and the heat,
but somehow he felt that he could not be on the
gunboat. For once in a way there was a roar as of
wild beasts; then it was not the roar of wild beasts,
for it seemed to be the blast of a bugle, out of tune,
harsh, and blown by some horrible giant, so big, so

vast, so confusing that, as he was trying to think what
it could be and why, everything was all confusion
again. If he could only think ! If he could only
make it out, why it was, and what it was ! And
he was in a hurry to do this. It seemed as if he
was struggling with all his might to be able to
think, before everything was shut down again.

He did not know what was going to be shut
down, or what there was to be shut down. He did
not understand ; but he could feel the awful heat,
the heavy, burning, throbbing pain, and with it—
there was nothing. And what was nothing ? Nothing
but darkness and the great question : why ?—which
grew and grew and grew till it became bigger and
bigger and resolved itself into something going round
and round ; and that something seemed to be why
he could not think.

How long this went on Archie did not know ; but
after a time in the darkness there seemed to come
a faint dawning like a feeble ray of light, which
suggested that he must be at home in England on
a frightfully hot day, lying down on one of the
benches in the Lion House at the Zoo. For there
was that tremendous giant's roar or trumpeting
sound, and this must, he knew, be one of the savage
beasts, and had something to do with his having
suddenly dropped to sleep and being wakened by
the bellowing sound.

Then more darkness—silence—the ever-increasing
confusion and whir, and nothingness, till some time
or other there was a fresh coming of the dawn, in
the midst of which he felt something that seemed
wonderfully cool and moist laid upon his head, and

a voice that seemed to come from miles away whispered :

'Poor old chap !'

Then all was dark again, and he seemed to be dreaming of the fever and the doctor that was talking to him and telling him that there were six of the men just as bad as he was, and that he was to take *that*. He could think now, for he distinctly heard him say :

'Tip it up. It will do you good.'

And somehow the engines seemed to have been stopped, and he felt as if he was being lifted on to some one's arm away from the tremendous heat of the engine fires, and he knew it was the Doctor— good old Morley !—who was holding a very hard wooden cup to his lips for him to drink the medicine. No, it was not nasty ; it was beautifully cool and good. He felt that the Doctor had put in so much water that he could not taste the physic ; and he drank on and on, every drop seeming to make it easier at last to think. And then the cup was being taken from his lips, and he tried to raise his hand to catch it and hold it so that he might drink more ; but his arm fell as if nerveless, and he uttered a deep groan.

'Oh, come !' rose to his ears now, as if from a long way off. 'That's something ! Ain't going to die this time.'

'Not going to die this time,' some one whispered, as if it were breathed with a hot breath upon his lips ; and then he lay thinking in a very feeble way, and feeling the while so tired, as a great longing came over him to go to sleep. It seemed like hours

before that longing was fulfilled; and then he woke
up not knowing why or wherefore, or grasping
anything but that it was dark, black dark; and
then he felt, with a strange sense of agony, that all
his trouble was returning, for the trumpeting roar
thundered through his brain, and he lay perfectly
still as the deep sound ceased, ending with a peculiar
kind of snort and a squeal, feeling that there was no
pain, and beginning to wonder why.

Time passed again—how long a time it was
beyond him to grasp—but there was that peculiar
trumpeting roar once more, and somehow it did not
trouble him so much. The fancy that he was in
the Lion House had faded away, and he became
conscious of the Doctor passing his arm under his
neck and raising him, while the wooden cup was
being held to his lips—cool, sweet, delicious—it
was one great joy to feel the soft draught running
over his parched tongue and down his throat.

Then he started, and he felt some of the contents
of the cup trickle down his chin, for there was a
shrill trumpeting noise again as the desire to exert
himself came, and he exclaimed:

'What's that?'

It was only in a whisper, but the Doctor—no, it
was not the Doctor; it was some one whose voice he
knew—said excitedly:

'Helephants.' And then, 'I say, Mister Archie,
sir, you're a-coming round!'

That was too much for him. He wanted to ask
what it meant—why it was Peter Pegg who had
been holding up his head, and not the Doctor—but
he could not form the words for the deep, heavy

sleepiness which came over him; and then all was
darkness once more, mental and real.

Long enough after, Archie Maine found himself
thinking again, and wondering where he was and
why it was so dark; but he could make out
nothing, till he gradually began to feel about him,
slowly, cautiously, as if in dread of something about
to happen, for the sensation was horrible of being
nowhere and in danger of falling should he move.
Then there was a sudden feeling of consciousness,
for he touched a hot hand, and a familiar voice said:

''Wake, sir? Like a drink?'

'Yes. That you, Pete?'

'Me it is, sir. Lie still, and I will give you
a cocoa-nut-shellful of water, and—and—— Oh
my! Oh my! Oh lor'! I can't help it!'

And Archie lay thinking clearly enough now, and
wondering why it was that the big fellow who had
spoken crouched close by him quivering, and the
hand that had grasped his roughly was shaking
violently, as he lay there blubbering and sobbing
with all his might.

'What's the matter?' whispered Archie, in the
midst of his wonder.

'Oh, it's only me, sir,' cried the lad in a choking
voice. 'I couldn't help it. It would ha' been just
the same if I'd been on parade. It would come.
It's been ready to bust out all this time. I thought
you was going to die, sir—I thought you was going
to die!'

'Die, Pete! No! What for?'

'Don't you know, sir?'

'No-o,' said Archie wonderingly.

'Here, stop a minute; let me give you some water.'

And in the darkness Archie lay listening to the pleasant, musical, trickling sound of falling water; while directly after, as he felt the private's hand passed under his neck, he made an effort to rise, and fell a-wondering again, for he could not stir.

But the next minute there was a fancied feeling of returning strength as he swallowed the cool draught with avidity, drinking till the desire came upon him to sink back with a deep sigh of content, and he felt his companion's arm withdrawn.

'Go to sleep after that, can't you?' whispered the private.

'No; I want to know what it all means.'

'Hadn't you better go to sleep, sir?'

'No!' cried Archie, in a voice so full of the agony of desire that Peter spoke out excitedly:

'Well, we are prisoners, sir.'

'Prisoners! How? Why?'

'I d' know, sir.'

'You don't know!' panted Archie feebly. 'Oh, you are trying to keep it back!'

'That I ain't, sir. I 'll tell you what I do know. Somebody 's took us prisoners—some of them Malay chaps. I think it must be that Rajah Hamet's men, as they says are our enemies.'

'No, no; he 's our friend.'

'Then it must be t'other one, sir. You remember when you come by in the boat that moonlight night?'

'Boat! What moonlight night?'

'Oh, lor' ha' mussy!' muttered Peter. 'He can't be fit to talk.'

'What's that you are saying to yourself? Why don't you speak?'

'Don't you remember hailing me, sir, when I was on sentry-go?'

'No.'

'Nor me telling you to mind the crocs didn't try to come aboard your boat?'

'No. What are you talking about?'

'Oh, my word!' sighed Peter. 'Here's a pretty go! Talk about a poor fellow being off his chump!' Then aloud, as he felt the lad's hand feebly feeling for his, 'It was like this 'ere, sir. You must have got into some row with a boatful of the niggers, and they knocked you over the head.'

'Knocked me over the head?' said Archie dreamily. 'No, I don't remember. Here, give me some more water.'

Peter Pegg hurriedly filled the cup—half a cocoa-nut shell—and Archie drank a mouthful and pushed it away.

'Let me lie down again,' he said.—'Now go on. Knocked me over the head?' he said very slowly and thoughtfully, as if weighing his words. 'Did you know that?'

'Yes, sir.'

'You said you were on sentry?'

'That's right, sir.'

'Then why didn't you come and help me?'

'I was coming, sir, bull roosh, when just as I was running along the river-bank, wondering how I was

Trapped.   K

to swim out to you among them crocodiles, some one
popped out from the bushes and fetched me down
with an awful crack on the pan.'

'Struck you down ?'

'Yes, sir. Hit me crool. There's a lump on the
top now as big as your fist. Regularly knocked me
silly. Just as they must have served you—knocked
every bit of sense out of me. There warn't much
in, as old Tipsy says, but I didn't know no more
till I found myself here, feeling sick as a dog, and
not able to move, for I was lying awkward-like on
my back, with some of them thin rotan canes tied
round my arms and legs so tight that it was only at
times I knowed I had any arms and legs at all.'

'Poor fellow !' said Archie pityingly.

'Yes, I just have been a poor fellow, sir—poor
creature, as they called them up in my part of
the country. Why, I have been quite mazed-like.
That topper I got seemed to do for me altogether;
and when I come-to, here I was lying in this place,
not knowing where I was, and, like you, sir, I
couldn't make out what it meant.'

'And in the darkness, too,' said Archie, 'just like
this ?'

'Like which, sir ? Why, it ain't dark now !'

'Black darkness,' said Archie.

The young private whistled softly and said
nothing, but shook his head and thought.

'But you know what place it is, don't you,
Pete ?'

'Well, I suppose it's part of one of the Rajah's
roosts ; but, as I tell you, my head's felt so muddled,
and just as if some of the works had been knocked

loose, that even now I don't seem to be able to tell
t'other from which. Well, I am getting it clearer
now, and of course it must be at Mr Prince Suleiman's.
Why, to be sure it must; and if my wheels inside
had been going as they should, I should have thought
it out at once. It must be at the Rajah's place, because of the helephants as you 'eerd now and then.
They must have a sort of stable close by here.
And then—why, of course—I'm just as 'fused-like
as you are, sir—that French count chap came in to
see us the other day, and talked to me.'

'He came here?' said Archie in his slow, dreamy
way.

'Yes, sir; that he did.'

'But I want to know,' said Archie, 'why we were
attacked like this and I was so hurt. There seems
to have been no cause or reason for it.'

'Well, I d' know, sir. I can't think much more
than you can. Maybe we shall see it clearly as we
gets better; but it looks to me as if it's his doing,
out of spite, like, for our interfering with him when
he came that night and Joe Smithers arrested him
and gave the alarm.'

'Perhaps so,' said Archie. 'My head's going
wrong again. I can't think.'

'Then you take my advice, sir: don't you try.
Try and eat a bit, for it's five days since you have
had a bite, counting the night we was took.'

'Five days!' said Archie.

'That's right, sir. Think you could eat one of
these fruits—I don't know what you call them—
melons like?'

'No,' said Archie, with a shudder.

'Well, I don't wonder, sir. I couldn't at first. They brought in a lot of bananas with the water, but I couldn't touch 'em at first. When that Frenchman came, though, and saw that I hadn't eaten anything, he turned rusty, and said I was trying to starve myself to death, and that it wouldn't do, because I must remember that I was a horstrich now, and I wasn't to play no tricks like that.'

'Said you were an ostrich?'

'Yes, sir; that's right. I don't know why, and I thought perhaps I hadn't heard him rightly, being so muddled-like. But I'm sure now that's what he said. Perhaps he said it because he thought I was a long-legged one and meant to run away; and I should have been about doing so before now if there hadn't been reasons.'

'What reasons, Pete?'

'Why, you, sir. You don't suppose I was going to cut and leave my mate in such a hole as this?'

'Ostrich?' said Archie dreamily. 'What could he mean by that? Oh—prisoners! He called you a hostage, and we are to be kept as hostages for some reason connected with something that's going on.'

'Ah! that's right, sir.'

As the young private sat on the palm-leaf-covered floor of the wooden building, gazing at his companion in misfortune, and thinking of how changed he looked, Archie slowly closed his eyes and appeared to be asleep, though he was now trying to make up for lost time, and thinking deeply.

'Wonder what's the matter with his eyes,' mused

the young private. 'He can't see, or else he wouldn't keep on talking about its being dark.'

Suddenly Archie unclosed his eyes and said:

'Are your legs and wrists better now?'

'It's my head that was the worst, sir,' was the reply.

'But you said that your legs and wrists were so cruelly tied up that the canes cut into your flesh.'

'Oh yes, sir; that was at first. But when that Frenchie came in he told the Malay chaps to untie 'em, so that I could wait upon you—and precious glad I was.'

'But how did you manage to see to give me the water?'

'I couldn't in the night, sir; but I can now.—It's no use to tell the poor chap that it's quite light, for he's all puzzled-like yet,' thought the private. Then aloud, 'I'd just go to sleep a bit now, sir, if I was you.'

'What for?'

'Rest your head, sir. You will feel a deal better when you wake again, and perhaps see a bit clearer.'

'Perhaps you are right, Pete,' said Archie, with a sigh; 'but I am better now. Most of the pain seems to be gone.'

'Good luck to you, sir! I wish mine had, for there are times when I seem as if I could not think straight.'

Archie made no reply, and as the young private watched him he saw that the poor fellow's eyes were once more closed; and the lad half lay .on the crisp leaves, which rustled loudly at every movement, and mused on their position.

'One would expect,' he said to himself, 'that at any minute a company of our swaddies would be here to fetch us out of this. At the same time, one ought to be ready to help one's self. Can't do anything, of course, with Mister Archie like this; but I have got my ideas about doing something some night if I can get a chance.—Oh, there you are, my beauties! I keep on hearing you, and you set me thinking. Wonder whether I could do it if I tried. I must wait till he comes round a bit more, and then I mean to try. Wonder whether they set sentries over us. Most likely; but if they do they will have to be dodged.'

There was a rumbling noise, which came from one of the elephants stabled near, and Peter Pegg shook his head slowly as if he were imitating the customary habit of a tethered elephant, and in imagination the private seemed to see one of the leg-chained beasts softly bowing its head up and down, and slowly from side to side, swinging it as if it were on springs.

'If I asked that chap who brings the water to let me see the helephants he would see through me, so I won't do it—make him 'spicious; and he wouldn't understand me if I did. His is an awful foolish lingo. Might perhaps get outside the door or window some night and have a look for them in the dark. Ah, there's no knowing what I might do when he gets better.'

Private Pegg started violently, for all at once Archie started up excitedly, and sat with widely opened eyes, gazing wildly straight before him, his hands extended, and trembling violently; while, as his fellow-prisoner leaned forward and caught him

by the arm to try and soothe him, believing him to
be in pain, he snatched his hand away, and in a
piteous cry uttered the one word:

'Minnie!'

Peter Pegg waited for a few moments, half-stunned
by this new form of trouble, and offered the first
palliative that occurred to him.

'Have some more water, Mister Archie,' he said
huskily.

'No, no! Don't you see? Why didn't you tell
me before?'

'Tell you what before, sir?'

'About Miss Heath.'

'About Miss Doctor, sir? It was her, then, as
was with you in the boat?'

'Yes, yes! Why didn't you remind me?'

'Never thought about it, sir. I never — my
word!—I'——

'Yes, yes; I see it all now! It has all come
back. That blindness and misery has cleared off
like a veil. Man, man! when those wretches attacked
me she was with me in the boat; and we stop here,
helpless and prisoners, while she—— Oh for health
and strength! Pegg, there's not a moment to be
lost! We must escape somehow, and get back to
camp. Her poor aunt! What must she think!'

CHAPTER XVII.

DR PEGG MUSES.

'POOR chap!' said Pegg, with a long-drawn sigh, as, utterly exhausted, Archie sank back upon his rough resting-place amongst the palm-leaves, and fell off at once into a deep, swoon-like sleep. 'Oh! if he only won't wake again for hours and hours, for all this worrying and talking must be dreadful for him. Poor girl! She must be here somewhere, a prisoner too. If I could only find out!'

He had been bending over Archie, and was drawing away as softly as could be for fear the rustling of the leaf-bed might wake his companion again, to recommence talking in an excited way about Minnie Heath and her fate, when he heard the sound of voices, the door of the palm and bamboo building was unbarred and thrown open, and a fierce, swarthy-looking, scowling Malay, with the hilt of his kris uncovered, strode swaggeringly in, accompanied by six spear-armed natives of about his own stamp, their leader looking sharply at the two prisoners, and then about the place.

'Here, I say, don't kick up such a jolly row,' said the private in a hoarse whisper. 'Can't you see that the poor fellow has just dropped off to sleep?'

The big Malay turned upon him fiercely, and as he took a couple of steps nearer, the crisp, dry leaves rustled more than ever.

'Will you be quiet?' whispered the private, springing up, and with one stride planting himself threateningly before the offender, who took a step back and flashed his naked kris from its sheath, while his followers lowered their spears for his protection.

'There, put that cook's skewer away,' growled the lad, as he pointed at the kris. 'Can't you be quiet? Can't you see that I have got nothing to fight with? Seven on you to one wounded man! Nice, plucky lot, aren't you? Why, I'm about the youngest chap in my company, but give me my empty rifle and bay'net and fair-play, and I would take the lot on you.'

Then, placing his open hands on either side of his lips as if he were about to hail somebody at a distance, he whispered hoarsely:

'Look at him. Very bad. Thought he was going to die. Can't you understand?'

Lowering his hands, he first pointed to the insensible officer, and then, treating the bared weapons which menaced him with as much contempt as if they were not there, he stepped on tiptoe close to his young companion, and stood pointing down at his terribly swollen forehead, which was not only cut but discoloured.

He stood waiting, but neither of the Malays moved, only looked at their leader as if for orders, and then gazed at one another, till he uttered a low grunt, in response to which the men raised the points of their spears and planted the butts on the ground.

Peter Pegg gave vent to a low, sneering laugh as he gazed half-jauntily at the big Malay.

'It didn't skeer me a bit,' he said, 'queer as I feel; but, between men—you see how bad my poor officer is—I only want you to keep those jockeys of yours quiet. Well, aren't you going to say anything when a English gentleman addresses you?'

The Malay gazed at him as if wondering at the lad's impudence, and then, scowling fiercely, he said, in a hoarse, guttural way, and trying to display his scorn for the sun-burnt, thin-featured lad, 'Ingles— Ingles!'

'That's right, comrade—I mean, enemy. Well, ain't you going to say any more?'

The man made no sign, and Peter Pegg continued:

'Can't you understand plain English? Well, then, take this—*apa boleh booat.*'

'*Apa boleh booat,*' said the Malay, with his face relaxing a little; and he nodded his head slowly, before turning to one of his followers and pointing to the big water-jar standing near the door, which the man immediately took up and bore out as if to fill, while his leader pointed again to a neatly woven bamboo basket in which lay three or four bananas and a half-eaten cake of bread.

This too was borne out, the contents sent flying amongst the trees close by, and the basket brought back, like the big jar, replenished.

'*Apa boleh booat,*' growled the big Malay, and he bowed his head slowly at the young soldier.

'All right; I quite agree with you,' said Peter; 'and now good-morning, or good-day, and don't come and bother me any more, my Royal Highness, or whatever you are, for I want to think.'

The Malay leader scowled at him again, and then followed his men out of the door, which was closed loudly, and as heavy bars seemed to be fitted into sockets, Peter Pegg limped up, as if partly lamed, put his lips close to a crack, and whispered:

'Thank you. Much obliged. A little louder next time, please, for my officer's asleep.'

Then he stood peering through the crack till the footsteps died away.

'Can't see much,' he said; 'but I wonder what *apa boleh booat* means. I meant it for something nasty, but the ugly beggar took it quite pleasant. It's what those sampan chaps say when they come back without catching any fish. To be sure, and I heard another chap say it when the Doctor had done strapping up his cut that time when there was a fight between the two Rajahs' men. I've picked up a lot more, too, of their lingo, but it's all mixed up together somewheres, and my head's about as muddled as poor Mister Archie's. Poor old chap! I got it too, but I'd a deal rather I'd had his topper and he'd had mine, and that's honest; for though he's a gentleman and I have only been a rough recruity, he's always been a good chap to me, and I never liked him so much as I do now when he's in such trouble. I wonder where poor Miss Minnie is.'

Phoonk! came from somewhere outside, and there was a rattling as of an iron chain.

'Oh, there you are, are you?' said Peter. 'The Doctor said in that lecture he gave us chaps that helephants is the most intelligent beasts there is— more so than dogs—that they get to understand

all sorts of words that are spoken to them. That
there *phoonk*, or whatever it was, sounded just like
an answer to something I had said ; but, of course,
it couldn't be. These 'ere are Malay helephants, and
'tisn't likely they could understand English. I wish,
though, this was the one that I got to be so chummy
with on the sham fight day. I 'd give him half
these 'ere bananas and some of the cake, for I don't
feel ready to eat much, and I don't believe that when
the governor wakes up he will take anything but
some more water. Well, anyhow, he 's better than
he has been since we 've been here. How long is it ? '

The lad raised his hand wearily to his aching
brow, and held it there for some minutes, before
shaking his head sadly.

'I d' know,' he said. ' It 's all getting mixed up
again. Oh, my poor nut ! How it do ache ! I
know what would do it good—lie down and try
to go to sleep. But I can't ; for so sure as I did,
Mister Archie would wake up and want some water,
and begin to talk about Miss Minnie. Oh dear !
It 's far worse than mutiny—to go to sleep when
you are on sentry ; and it would be ten times worse
to begin to snooze now, with that poor, half-cranky
chap in such a state. So I 'll have one or two of
them finger-stall fruit things and a good drink of
water, and then lean back against the side and
see how many Malay words I can remember ; and
if that don't keep a poor fellow awake, nothing will.'

He stepped softly amongst the rustling leaves and
bent down over Archie, to find that he was breathing
freely, and evidently plunged in the deep sleep of
exhaustion.

'That's better,' he muttered; 'but I should like
to dip his handkerchy in that fresh, cold water and
lay it on his head.'

His hand was reached out to where he could just
catch a glimpse of the scrap of linen in the lad's
breast pocket; but he snatched his extended fingers
back, and stepped away to where the basket and jar
had been placed.

'Do more harm than good,' he muttered. 'When
I was in orspittle, I remember old Morley said that
sleep was the something that did something to set
wounded fellows up again, and if I got sopping his
head, poor chap! it would wake him up as sure as
eggs is eggs.' Then he went down on his knees,
picked up the cocoa-nut cup, filled it to the brim, and
very slowly trickled the contents down his throat.
'Hah!' he sighed. 'Lovely!' as he held up the
empty cup. 'That's just the sort of stuff as would
do old Joe Smithers a world of good.—Thankye; yes,
I will take another, as you are so pressing;' and with
a contented grin upon his dirty face, grimed with
perspiration and the dried stains from a cut, he
refilled the shell cup, drank the contents, replaced
the little vessel balanced upside-down upon the edge
of the rough earthen jar, and then swung himself
round into a sitting position, wincing and half-
groaning with pain as he did so, leant his aching
head against the thickly plaited palm wall, and
reached out for the basket, from which he picked
one of the largest golden plantains.

'There's plenty,' he said softly, 'and three of
them just about ought to set me up.'

Then methodically breaking off the end of the

one he had chosen, he began to strip off the thick skin, letting each portion hang over his hand, as the creamy, white, vegetable-like fruit became bared half-way down; and then, with a sigh, he took a bite.

'That second cup of Adam's ale was better than the first,' he said appreciatively, 'and this 'ere's the best banana I ever nibbled. We used to say at home that they was like tallow candle and sleepy pear, but this one—my word, it's heavenly!'

He took another bite, munching it slowly, with his head sinking down gently as if to meet his hand, which came up with some effort, ready for the next bite; and then, with his lower jaw impeded by resting upon his chest, it ceased to move, the hand that held the banana sank into his lap, the half-peeled fruit escaped from his fingers, and not one of the many Malay words that he was about to remember obtained utterance, for after the watching and disturbed sleep of nights, Nature would do no more, and Peter Pegg was sleeping more deeply than he had ever slept in his life before.

CHAPTER XVIII.

PETER'S FRIEND.

PHOONK! Then a peculiar squeal and grunting sound, and then once again, *Phoonk!*

Peter Pegg started up into a sitting position, vacant of face and staring at the straightly streaked rays of sunshine that made their way through the plaited and latticed sides of the stable-like building in which he had dropped to sleep.

'What's all that row?' he muttered. 'Where am I?'

He rubbed his eyes; and then, as the grunting, snorting noise continued, 'What does it all mean?' he went on. 'Why, I've been asleep, and was dreaming something about old Bobby Hood's pigs at home, grunting. Am I dreaming now? Them ain't pigs. Here, I know—helephants!'

He turned his face to the side of the place against which he had been leaning, drew himself up, and applied his eyes to one of the cracks, just as a voice seemed to be calling out in the Malay tongue at three of the great, cumbrous-looking beasts which were about a couple of yards away from the building.

'Driving of them, and they won't go,' thought the watcher; and the speaker, a stunted-looking Malay with a short, iron-spiked implement, somewhat like the iron of a boat-hook, in his hand, came into sight between the huge pachyderms and the door, shouting and growling at his charge as he waved the hook and

progged the nearest beast as if trying to drive them
away.

'What a fool I was not to have learned this
precious lingo! They want to come in, and he's
telling them to get on.   Well, there ain't no room for
them here.—Ah, he don't like that!'   For the dumpy
Malay made use more freely of the goad he carried,
and the nearest beast gave vent to an angry half-
squeal, half-grunt, as, shrinking from the prod
delivered at its flank, it made a rush at two
companions, driving its great head first at one and
then at the other, and with a good deal of grumbling,
squealing, and waving of trunks, they shuffled out of
sight.

'Why, I must have been asleep,' cried Pegg, as he
made for another opening where the sun streamed
in; 'but my head—oh, my head, how it aches!   I
can't seem to understand what it means.   It's all of
a '——   'He turned slowly round, staring vacantly,
till his eyes fell upon the basket and jar almost at
his feet.   ''Nanas—water!   Why '——   He turned
his eyes in another direction, and then, with a faint
cry of dismay, he shuffled across the place, making
the dry leaves with which the floor was covered
rustle loudly, as he sank upon his knees beside
Archie.   'I've got it now,' he said to himself.   'I
remember; but my head's as thick as wool.   He
went to sleep, and I sat down to watch till he woke.
Nice watch I've kept!   Well, it's a good job those
great brutes come along and woke me up.   This
must have been their old stable, and if I don't look
out, one of these times they will be shoving that
door down and walking in a-top of us.   Poor old

chap! He's sound enough now. Mustn't touch him. It would be a pity to wake him. I couldn't have been asleep many minutes.'

Peter drew away silently and stood for a few moments watching the bright rays of sunshine that streamed in through the side of the building; and unconsciously he raised one hand and made a peculiar motion with it as if he were following the streaks of light from right to left with his index-finger.

'Seems rum,' he muttered; 'but it's my head being so thick, I suppose. Oh, there's that banana I began to eat;' and he stooped down, picked it up from where it lay amongst the leaves, and then dipped the cocoa-nut cup into the water, and took a deep draught of the refreshing beverage.

'Ah!' he sighed, as he set down the shell. 'Seems to wash the cobwebs out of one's head. Wonder where those helephants were being driven.'

As he muttered he stepped to the door and applied his eye to one of the cracks through which the sun was streaming, and then drew back, for the glare affected his eye.

'Shines hot,' he muttered; 'and it wasn't coming in like that when I looked through just now, before beginning to eat that banana. Well,' he ejaculated, 'it's a rum un! I've got it now! Why, I must have been asleep hours and hours and hours. It ain't this evening. When I looked it was all turning red because the sun was going down. It's to-morrow morning, and I've been asleep all night. I'm a nice sort of a chap, I am, to go on duty and leave my officer in the lurch like that! Well,

Trapped. L

he must have been asleep too. There's no gammon about it, for it is to-morrow morning, and he could not have woke up, because I should have heared him; so that's all right. Poor chap! And it must have done him good. But now I can think again, and my head don't ache so much. I feel better, and there's been no old Job Tipsy to drop upon me.—I wish there was, and a lot of our fellows with him,' said the poor fellow dismally.

He crossed softly to where Archie lay breathing calmly, and then, as if feeling satisfied, he went back to the great earthen jar, refreshed himself with another draught of water, and seated himself by the basket, from which he took one of the bananas and began to eat.

'I'm quite peckish,' he said to himself, 'and, my word, they are good! I don't know how long it is since I felt like this. It must be a good sign. Well, there's plenty of them,' he continued, and he took another, and another. 'Not half bad,' he went on, 'as there's no commissariat coffee. Must leave plenty for Mr Archie, though. But 'nanas don't seem the sort of tack for a poor chap with his complaint. Wishing ain't no good, or I'd do it with both hands, and wish old Jollop was here to look at his tongue and to strap up that head of his. It ought to have all the hair cut off, but one can't do that with a blunt knife. Hullo! what's that?' he muttered, after satisfying himself with the fruit from the basket. 'I believe it's one of those two-tailed pigs grunting and chuntering.'

He went to the opening through which he had peered before, and looked out.

'Can't see anything,' he muttered, 'but it sounds like one of them coming back. Yes, I can! It is—just coming through the trees. Why, he's all wet, and dripping with mud and water. That's it. They have been driven down by their keeper to the river. Yes, there must be a river; and I say, lad, there's something to recollect. This 'ere place is somewhere up the river, or down it. Yes, down it, because up the river the water's clear, and down it, it gets muddy. Oh, I don't know. I dare say there's muddy places up the banks. There, stop that chuntering row. Just like a drove of pigs. He's coming back to his stable somewhere. Why, he's coming straight here, just as if he meant to knock the door down and get in. Well, if he did he wouldn't hurt us. He's only a tame one. That little chap made three of them shuffle off. But what a chance to cut if he opens the door! Oh dear!' he added, with a sigh. 'Talk about cutting, with the young governor like he is! And even if he could walk, we don't know the way. Wonder where we are. It must be the Rajah's place somewhere right up in the jungle where he keeps his helephants, and that there Frenchman put him up to keeping his hostriches, as he called them, up here too.'

Peter Pegg's mutterings and musing were brought to a sudden end by the elephant, which seemed to be quite alone, coming close up to the doorway, grunting and chuntering, as the young private called it, just as if the animal were talking to itself, mingling its remarks with a low squeal which might have meant either anger or satisfaction.

'I believe,' thought Peter, 'it's one of them that came to the sham fight, and I could almost fancy it's the chap I had a ride on. But they are all alike, only one's bigger than another, and t'other's more small. If he had got his toggery on with gold fringes and the big bamboo clothes-basket full of cushions on his back, I should know him directly. But he's what they call disguised in mud.—Here, I say, don't! What you doing on?'

It was plain enough, for the great elephant had seized hold of a portion of the woven, basket-like wall, which began to crack and give way as a piece was torn out.

'I say, don't—don't be a fool! You'll wake the poor governor,' whispered Peter, who began to tremble now with alarm.—'Oh, don't I wish I could remember what the mahout said to him!—Here, I say, don't!—I believe he's gone mad, and if he gets at us—— Here, I say, what shall I do?' And he backed away from where the light was beginning to show more brightly through the woven wall, and took up his position as if to protect his wounded officer. 'If I had only got my rifle and bayonet, I could keep him off, perhaps, with a good dig. Here, they have left me my knife, though,' he said joyously, as he drew it out and opened the blade.

The possession of even this contemptible weapon seemed to give the poor fellow some confidence, and he took three or four steps towards the hole the huge beast was making, just as there was torn away another piece of the elastic palm or bamboo of which the wall between the uprights was formed.

And then the light opening was suddenly darkened.

'Blest if it ain't just like a great horse-leech such as we used to find in the watercrease beds, only about ten million times as big;' and the lad stood helplessly staring as he saw the monster's trunk thrust right in through the wall and beginning to wave up and down and from side to side, wondrously elastic, the nostrils at the end in this semi-darkness looking like a pair of little wet eyes, between which the prehensile part moved up and down like a tiny pug-nose.

Sniff, snuff, snort, and then a little squeal as, after waving here and there for a few moments, the curious member was stretched out straight in the direction of the lad, emitted a deep, damp sigh, and then began to wave up and down and to and fro again, before curling up, to some extent uncoiling, and shooting out straight and stiff again in the same direction.

'Oh lor'!' groaned Peter, 'it's just like one of them there big boa-constructors, and he's coming for me. He means me. There's a sniff! And this knife not a bit of good. If I cut it off it would only make him more wild. Look at it, with its two little eyes seeming to stare at me. Boa-constructor! It's more like an injy-rubber pipe gone mad.'

There was another faint squeal, and the great trunk slowly changed its position, and stretched itself out in the direction of the bamboo basket.

'Here, I say,' thought Peter, 'does he mean them?'

The lad hesitated for a minute or two while the elephant continued its low, almost purring, muttering sound, as the trunk turned once more in his direction, and then became stiffly pointed out again towards the basket, while the wall about the height of the elephant's head gave forth a loud crack.

'He's a-leaning ag'in it, and it's coming through!' gasped Peter. 'Here, there's nothing for it.—All right, mate; wait a minute: you shall have the whole blessed lot. Murder! Don't!' roared the poor fellow; for as he made a dash to reach the basket, as quick as lightning the trunk was curled round his neck, and held him fast as he dropped upon his knees.

'It's all over, Mister Archie, sir,' he groaned. 'And you lying there asleep and taking not no notice! Wouldn't have catched me 'listing if I'd ha' known it meant coming to this!—Oh, I say, do leave go!'

As if his captor thoroughly grasped the meaning of his piteous appeal, the trunk began slowly to loosen its hold; and then, as the poor fellow prepared himself for a dash to get beyond its reach, he found it begin to smooth him over and stroke him gently down from shoulder to arm, playing about as if caressing him, after the fashion in which he had seen the animals treat their mahout when about to be fed.

'Oh dear!' groaned Peter; 'I thought it was all over with me. Does he mean he wants one of them bananas?'

The lad's hand trembled as he reached out, picked up one of the bananas—the largest he could see

—and held it in the direction of the end of the trunk.

There was a loud sniff; the trunk curled round the fruit, curved under, and was drawn back through the hole. The sun shone brightly in, and Peter felt conscious that the banana was disappearing into the great brute's wet mouth. Then in the most deliberate manner the end of the trunk reappeared, gliding towards him like some serpent. The light was pretty well shut out, and as the wall creaked again, Peter somehow omitted to dash right off as far away as he could go, and found himself picking up another banana, which was deliberately taken, disappeared slowly to make way for the light to pass in, and then the process was repeated once more.

'Here, who's afraid?' said the lad, mastering the oppression and panting from which he suffered, as he picked up a fourth banana. 'He means friends, and I'm blessed if I don't believe it's the same one as I tackled at the sham fight. I wish I knew.— Want another, mate?' he continued, as the trunk-end curled towards him again; and as it slowly took the banana from his hand, he passed his fingers beyond the grasped fruit, and gave the quivering member a quick stroke or two.

To his surprise, the trunk remained motionless, and a faint snorting sound or grunt came from beyond the wall.

'All right. Paid for!' said Peter as he withdrew his hand, and the trunk disappeared. 'I do believe it's the same one,' repeated the lad, 'and I shall be all right as long as these 'ere 'nanas last; but when they are done, suppose he comes through to see why the rations have stopped. Well, I must make them last as long as I can; and he's very cool over it, and not in a hurry. Wonder whether it is that one I knew, and he smelt me and come to see. Yah! Stuff! He smelt the fruit. Oh! here he is again.'

The next time the trunk reappeared Peter Pegg was ready with one of the oat-cakes broken in half. This was taken just as readily, and was being drawn through the hole when its awkward semicircular shape caused it to be caught against the sides, and it dropped inside instead of disappearing like the fruit. The trunk was withdrawn unsupplied, and Peter was in the act of stooping to pick up the piece of cake, when the light was obscured again, making the lad glance upwards and catch sight of the serpent-like, coiling member descending slowly upon him.

. 'Here, no larks!' cried the lad, dropping upon his knees and preparing to crawl out of reach; but the thought of what he had suffered before unnerved him for the moment, and he could not stir.

He uttered a faint cry as he felt the touch of the elastic organ; but it only began to stroke him caressingly, and recovering himself, he drew a deep breath, held out the piece of cake, which was smelt directly, taken, and this time disappeared in safety.

It was all done very slowly, and poor Peter thought to himself, 'I suppose he's enjoying of it all—but think of me!' He grew more confident, however, and went on and on, presenting the generous supply of bananas till only four were left, and these and the other cake he thrust farther away, and stripping off his flannel jacket, he covered the remainder in the bottom of the basket.

This he had just done when the trunk reappeared as usual, and summoning up his courage to meet the disappointment and perhaps anger of his visitor, Peter cried aloud:

'There! All over, comrade! No more to-day. Off you go!'

Just as if the huge beast understood him from the tone of his voice, it raised its trunk and passed it about his shoulders and breast; and then the poor fellow uttered a faint groan of despair.

'What a fool I was!' he thought, for he felt the trunk curl round his neck and tighten gently; and his heart began to fail, when it was uncurled, and stretched out again; the wall overhead creaked loudly, and the end of the trunk was dipped in the big earthen jar.

There was a sucking noise, the trunk disappeared slowly, and Peter drew the jar so that it stood just below the opening the elephant had made. As this was done there came the loud squirting sound of the water being sent down the huge beast's throat.

Then the trunk descended, to be recharged and disappear again, and Peter, as the trunk was withdrawn, seized the supply-vessel and drew it right away.

'Don't believe there's half a pint left,' he grumbled. 'What about Mister Archie?—There, no more!' he cried aloud, as the trunk was thrust back, passed over his shoulders again, and finally withdrawn, Peter half climbing up to peer through the hole and see his visitor go slowly muttering away.

'And him grumbling, too,' said the lad—'ungrateful beast! He did give me a fright. But, my eye, what a game! Look at him!' he continued, as the hind-quarters of the monster concealed the rest of its form. 'Just like an awful great pair of trousers walking by theirselves!'

CHAPTER XIX.

PRISONERS.

'HERE'S a pretty go!' he cried, as he lifted the now light basket and put it down again, and peered once more into the earthen jar. 'Suppose they meant the rations and water to last for two or three days! There was a good supply, and that great beast has wolfed and drunk all. Well, it has made him friends, anyhow. He will be coming again. Yes; but who wants a friend like that to keep coming again?'

The lad glanced in the direction of his fellow-prisoner, to find that he was still sleeping; and his next proceeding was to go gingerly about, disturbing the dry leaves as little as possible, and making a more thorough examination of the place.

'Must have been a helephant stable once upon a time,' he concluded at last, 'for here's the great post that one of the big pigs was chained to by the leg so that he could not get at the walls. Walls! They are nothing better than so many fences. Talk about shutting up a helephant! Why, I could pull them down myself if I wanted to get away—least-ways I could climb up the side and make a hole through the roof. Can't call one's self a prisoner. Yes, I can, because I am regularly chained by the leg; for who's going to leave his comrade? Poor old chap!'

At that moment there was a deep sigh, followed by a loud rustling amongst the leaves, as Archie made an effort to change his position, slightly raising his head, but letting it fall back with a low groan, while the young private stepped softly to his side, knelt down, and bent over him.

'Hurt you much, Mister Archie, sir?' the lad whispered quietly, and one hand played over the injured head, hesitated, and was then withdrawn. 'Hurt you, Mister Archie, sir?' he said again, a little louder, for there was only a weary sigh. 'Wish he'd speak,' said the lad to himself, 'for he ought to have something, if it's only a drop more water. What a fool I was to let that great india-rubber thing suck it all up! Why, I couldn't even use some of it now to bathe his poor head.'

The poor fellow seemed to Pegg to be sleeping as heavily as ever, and after he had looked at him carefully for a few minutes, there was a deep, buzzing hum as of some insect, and a great fly flashed across the golden rays which streamed in through the thatch, and hovered around for a few moments as if about to settle upon the sleeping lad's head.

'Would you?' ejaculated Peter Pegg, striking out so fiercely and exactly that he struck the insect with a sharp pat and drove it against the woven wall, with which it was heard to come in contact, to fall directly, buzzing and rustling among the dried leaves. 'That's settled you,' said Peter. 'I know your little game—lay eggs and make a poor fellow's wound go bad. Not this time!'

'Cowards!' came excitedly from Archie, and he once more tried to raise his head, but only for it to sink back wearily. 'Burning—always burning! Oh, how hot—how hot!'

'Like some water, Mister Archie, sir?'

'Water! Who said water?'

'Me, sir. There is a little. Let me give you a taste.'

There was no reply, so Peter quickly filled the cocoa-nut shell, bore it to his companion's side, and knelt down.

'Now then, sir, you let me hyste you up a little. Don't you try—I can do it, and hold the nut to your lips. You will have nothing to do but drink.'

At the first touch Archie started violently.

'Who's that?' he cried.

'Only me, sir. Steady, or you will upset the whole blessed apple-cart, and make yourself wet.'

'Only me—only me,' said Archie, and directly after the poor fellow sank back again with a weary sigh.

'Look at that, now!' said Peter. 'Oh! his head must be awfully bad inside as well as out. Why, if he isn't asleep again!'

It was growing dusk, when, feeling faint, hot, and exhausted, Peter Pegg stood over the basket, looked into it longingly, and then glanced at his wounded companion.

'He's sure not to want anything to eat,' he said to himself. 'A drop of water's about all he will touch when he comes to; and it's lucky I held that cocoa-nut shell tight, or it would all have gone.' He turned to the jar, into which he had poured back the contents of the nearly full shell. 'Oh dear! To think I let that great, gorging fire-hose of a hanimal suck up nearly all that beautiful water, when this place has been like an oven and made me as thirsty as if I had been living on commissariat bacon. Can't help it. He's sure to want a drink when he wakes up. I must leave that.'

As he spoke he turned the jar sideways, and the ruddy light which filtered in through the cracks showed him the cool, clear fluid in the dark bottom of the vessel. He dipped in the shell, and found he could fill it easily.

'More than I thought,' he said joyfully. 'Why, I might have half-a-shellful, and then there would be quite a shell and a half left for the young governor. Can't help it; I must,' he cried impatiently. 'My throat's as dry as a sawpit.'

Dipping the shell as he still held the jar sideways he brought it up again more than half-full.

'Too much,' he said softly. 'Fair-play's a jewel;' and carefully and slowly he let a portion of the precious water trickle back into the bottom of the jar.

'That's about half,' he said, with a judicial look. 'Now then, sip it, mate, and make it go as far as you can.'

Raising the cup to his lips, he slowly imbibed the tepid liquid till the very last drop had been drained out of the shell. Then replacing it where it had been before, he uttered a deep sigh.

'I never used to think water was so beautiful,' he said softly. 'I forget what them people asked for when they had three wishes, but I know what I should wish for now. It would be for that there jar brim-full of cold water, and me to have a throat as long as a boa-constructor, so that I could feel it all go gently down.'

His eyes fell upon the basket again, and the slight draught of water having turned his faintness into a strong desire for food, he could hardly restrain himself from taking one of the remaining bananas. In fact, after resisting the temptation for some minutes, he darted his hand down, caught up one of the soft, gold-tinted fruits, raised it towards his mouth, and dashed it down again.

'Hanged if I do!' he cried angrily; and thrusting his hands deep into his pockets, he had another look at Archie, and then raised himself up so as to peer through the opening the elephant had made, and try to get some better idea of his position.

'Trees, trees, trees,' he said; 'trees everywhere; but there's a path off to the left, and one goes off to the right, and there's another goes straight away. Let's see: off to the right must be down to the river, because that's where the helephants went; and those other paths must go to where somebody lives; but there's no sign of a house—nothing but trees. Not a sound! Oh, what a lonely place it is! And here's all the long, dark night coming. The sun's going down fast. I sha'n't sleep a wink to-night after snoozing as I did. And here I'm going to lie thinking about that upset with poor Mister Archie's boat, and—yes, I shall be thinking more about what's become of Miss Minnie. Here, I say, what a row there's going to be when the Major and Sir Charles know of it all! And me shut up here instead of being with the lads when the governor lets them slip at these Malay jockeys, for I am a bigger fool than I thought for if one of these Rajahs isn't at the bottom of this job. I don't know but what it might be that there smooth young un who dosses hisself up to look like an English gent. If it ain't him, it 's that queer-eyed, big, fat fellow; only I suppose it can't be him, because old Tipsy Job says he 's friends. How comes it, then,' he continued, speaking with energy, ' that the Frenchman has had to do with our being prisoners ? Here, I can't think. It 's making my head ache and things get mixed again. What 's that ? ' he half-whispered excitedly. ' It 's somebody coming ; ' and pressing his face closer to the opening, he strained his eyes round so as to gaze to the left, and then dropped lightly down before throwing himself upon the dried palm-leaves close to where Archie lay, and listening to the coming steps. 'That chap can speak English 'most as well as I can,' he thought to himself, 'and I am going to ask him plump and plain what 's become of Miss Minnie.'

A gruff voice uttered what was evidently a command to halt, the wooden bars were lowered and the door thrown open to admit the deep sunset glow, and the stern-looking Malay with his following marched in, their steps rustling amidst the leaves that covered the floor; and the leader bent down curiously over Archie, scowling at him fiercely, before turning his lurid eyes searchingly upon the young private, who now lay back with his lids half-lowered, apparently gazing down into his chest.

The Malay rose again, then turned and gave an order to his followers, two of whom stepped outside, one of them first standing up the spear he carried in the dark corner behind the door, while their chief growled out something as he pointed at the freshly torn opening in the side. One of the men grunted —it sounded like a grunt to Peter Pegg—and raising his spear, he passed it through the opening, rattled it to and fro, and then stepped outside to pick up two or three torn-out pieces of palm-fibre, brought them in, showed them to his chief, and uttered a half-laugh.

Just then the two men who had passed outside returned, one bearing a fresh jar brim-full of water, the other a basket of fruit and another of the big, roughly made cakes, which were set down.

Then the leader stepped forward, stooped down suddenly over Pegg, his right hand resting upon the fold of the sarong which covered the hilt of his kris, and with his left thumb he roughly raised the young private's eyelids one after the other.

Peter Pegg did not so much as wince.

'Let him think I'm asleep if he likes—an ugly Eastern beast!'

The Malay turned now to Archie to look fixedly at the poor fellow's head, before touching the injured scalp with one brown finger, with the effect of eliciting a deep-drawn sigh of pain.

Then the man rose, and apparently satisfied with the helplessness of the prisoners, he uttered a low, abrupt order, and his little train shouldered their spears and marched out, one of them carrying the empty basket, his companion shouldering the heavy earthen jar.

Peter Pegg lay back motionless, to listen to the barring of the door, half-wondering the while at

Trapped. M

the great change that the closing door made upon
the interior : one moment the last rays of the setting
sun were flooding the great stable with a deep, blood-
red glow ; the next the place seemed by comparison
quite dark.

The lad listened till the last retiring steps had
died away, and then he sat up suddenly, with the
recollection of a little knife and fork given to him
years before by his grandmother, and chuckling
softly to himself, he half-whispered :

'A present for a good boy !—Of course,' he said,
after a pause to make sure that no one was going
to return ; 'I am not going to bounce, but I was
a very good boy for not pitching into that 'nana.
Oh my ! Ain't it splendid !' he continued, turning
over on hands and knees and scrambling like a
quadruped to where the jar and basket had been
placed. There 's going to be such a supper ! But
don't I wish I was going to have company ! Oh,
you beauty !' he cried hoarsely, as he hugged the
great jar to his chest, bent down till he could press
his lips to the thick edge, and then tilting it slightly,
drank and drank and drank.

At last he lowered the jar till it stood firmly in
its place, raised himself upon his knees, and uttered
a long, deep sigh.

'Oh, ain't it splendid !' he said. 'They have
got water here ! Talk about a horse drinking—
well, I suppose any one would say I drank like a
hass or a pig. No, I didn't, because I 've only been
drinking the helephant's share if he comes again—not
yours, Mister Archie. I do wish you were awake.—
Here, I say, let 's have some of that bread,' he said,

half-aloud now; and breaking the cake in four, he placed himself in a comfortable position and took a bite.

'That ain't quite comfortable, though,' he muttered, and raking a lot of the leaves into the corner of the place, he seated himself so that he could rest his back in the angle.

'Not quite right,' he muttered. 'These 'ere big feathers have got a lot of quill in them. Let's have some more.'

He stretched out his left hand in the darkness to draw an armful more of the dried palm-leaves beneath him, when his hand came in contact with something which rasped against the matted wall and fell heavily in the direction of where his fellow-prisoner lay.

'What's that?' said the lad sharply, as, sweeping his hand round over the leaves, his fingers closed almost spasmodically upon what felt like a bamboo cane.

The next moment Pete was upon his feet, staring in the direction of the dimly seen door.

'My!' he whispered hoarsely; and using the cane like a walking-stick, he stepped on tiptoe right to the door, and then whispered softly beneath his breath:

'Hi! Hi! Hi! I say, old un, you've forgot your spear.—Think of that, now,' he continued, half-aloud. 'Why, of course; he stood it up there before he went out to fetch that precious jar. Forgot it! I say—talk about discipline in the Rajah's army, and a chap forgetting his piece! Fancy old Tipsy, and it was me and my rifle!

Plenty of water, plenty of bread and fruit, and a present of one of them spears, as will be handier than a fixed bay'net. Why isn't Mister Archie awake to enjoy all this? Now then, if that chap will only come to-morrow night, and forget another of these sharp-pointed toothpicks for Mister Archie, I shall be very much obliged. But here am I playing the fool like this, and at any moment he may be coming back to fetch this one away. Well, if he expects he's going to get it, poor chap, I'm sorry for him;' and obeying his first impulse, he carried the keen-pointed weapon across the floor, lowered the head, and felt gently to find where it was bare; and the next moment his fingers were playing about over what was evidently a short piece of bamboo of about the same circumference as the shaft, and which fitted tightly over the keen blade like a sheath.

Then going down upon one knee, he thrust the spear carefully in beneath the bed of leaves at the foot of the wall, behind where Archie lay. Not satisfied at once, he withdrew and thrust in the weapon again, feeling if it was well covered; and then going to the far end, and scraping up and bringing a double armful of the dried leaves, he carefully covered his treasure more deeply.

'Ah!' he ejaculated, panting a little with his exertion, 'I don't think it's likely.—What say, sir?' he added, addressing an imaginary Malay fighting-man. 'Have I seen your spear? No, sir. Haven't set eyes upon it, honour bright.—"Always tell the truth, Pete," granny used to say. Well, ain't that the truth? Why, I don't believe a cat

could have seen it; and if I hadn't knocked it
down I shouldn't have known it was there. Now,
between ourselves, I do think I deserve something
to eat after that,' muttered the poor fellow. 'Here,
where did I put that there piece of cake? It must
be lost amongst those leaves. Dropped it when I
was feeling for the spear. What! plenty more
in the basket? No, I won't. Wilful waste makes
woeful want. Why, here it is in my trousers
pocket all the time! So, now then, let's have
another try; and I will treat myself to a banana
afterwards. No, I won't; I'll have two.' And
hurrying to the basket, he helped himself to the
fruit, and then made himself comfortable in the
corner where he had knocked over the spear, and
began to eat with a splendid appetite.

'Oh, don't I wish you was here to help me, Mister
Archie, sir!' he said, half-aloud and rather piteously.
'Poor, dear chap! I'd feed you if I dared wake
you up; but I'm sure it's right to let you sleep.
But won't you be glad when you know about that
spear? If we could only get another, and a couple
of them krises, we should be regular set up if it
come to a scrimmage, as it shall, as sure as my
name's Peter. We are going to escape—somehow;
and if anybody stops us it's a fight. We sha'n't be
able to throw the spears like these Malay beggars
do, but me and Mister Archie can do bay'net practice
with them in a way that will open some of their
eyes. Oh, how good!' half-whispered the lad, as
he finished his frugal supper of bread and banana.
'Don't it seem to put life in a fellow! Now, what
am I going to do? Sit and think of how to escape?

No hurry, lad. I want Mister Archie's orders, and I 'll do the work. Seems to me that the first thing will be for me to get out of here somehow in the dark to go and reconnoitre, and then steal—no, it 's capture, being enemies—another spear and two krises. How ? Knock down an enemy somewhere and take what he 's got. I 'm game. And then '——

That was as far as Peter Pegg got, for he could not partake of so hearty a meal, after refreshing himself in a way that thoroughly quenched his thirst, without obeying Nature afterwards ; and this he did, lying prone, fully stretched out, and not in the painful, cramping position of the previous night.

CHAPTER XX.

ARCHIE THINKS.

HOOMPH! Phoonk!

'What say?' cried Peter, springing up in a sitting position, to find it was daylight once more. 'Oh, it's you, is it?' he cried, for there was a crackling by the door, and the great, tapering, serpent-like trunk of an elephant was waving to and fro and reaching towards the water-jar.

'Yahhh! Burrrr!' came from outside, and there were steps as if somebody were rushing towards the door to chase the intruder away.

The utterer of the yell seemed to have been successful, for the trunk was drawn back quickly, the elephant trumpeted, there were the footsteps of a man, and the shuffling sound of the gait of the great beast, as, springing up, Peter Pegg ran to the door and climbed up to place his eye where the trunk had been, so that he could see what was taking place.

'My! Look at that!' cried Peter cheerily. 'That ain't the way to drive a helephant away. You are going all wrong, comrade.' For, instead of suffering himself to be driven, the elephant opened his mouth, curved up his trunk into something the shape of the letter S, and displaying two finely produced, sharply pointed tusks, he was starting in full chase of the stumpy underling who had been driving him down to the river, but only to turn back and make a call on his new friend for refreshment.

'What a lark!' said Peter, as the elephant disappeared after his quarry. 'It makes me feel as if I should like to keep helephants, if I get to be Field-Marshal and they make me Governor-General of Injy and Malay; for they are such rum beggars. They look just as if when they died they would do to cut up for injy-rubber. And they seem so friendly, too, with any one they like. Sort of things as you can't drive, but have to lead. I should like a good helephant for a pet, but I suppose he would be expensive to keep; and I don't suppose that there grubby-looking little chap feels very comfortable with that one chivying him. Here, I never thought of that,' continued Peter, as he dropped down amongst the palm-leaves. 'My lord was reaching out that big leech of his after our rations. Lucky he couldn't get at them. I ought to have remembered to put them away;' and, to guard against any mishap, Peter Pegg hastened to place jar and basket in the right-hand corner of the building, where they would be handy for replenishing, and out of reach and out of sight of his huge visitor. This done, the young private crossed over to where he had thrust and covered over the spear, and, to his intense satisfaction, he found that unless a searcher well turned over the dried leaves, it would be impossible to find the concealed weapon.

'Is that you, Pete?' said a faint voice; and Archie's fellow-prisoner literally rushed to the speaker's side.

'Me it is, sir. England for ever, and hooray!

Oh, do say you are better, sir !' cried the lad, ending
in a half-squeak as if there were tears in his throat
or he was trying to imitate an elephant.

'Better ? Yes, I think I'm better, Pete,' said
the poor fellow feebly. 'But my head aches dreadfully, and—and—I'm so weak.'

'Ah, I've got to bathe that head, sir.'

'Yes, I think that would do it good. Yes, I am
better, Pete, for I can think. We are prisoners,
aren't we ?'

'Yes, sir, at present,' said Pete confidently. 'Just
till we are exchanged, or escape.'

'Ah !' ejaculated Archie. 'I said I could think
now, and I was forgetting. Look here, have you
found Miss Minnie ?'

'Now, now, now, sir,' cried the young private
in a tone full of remonstrance; 'you have been very
ill, and off your head. It's very horrid, I know,
but you have got to get better, and not make
yourself worse with thinking about that.'

'Yes, yes, I know,' said Archie excitedly. 'But
you don't tell me. Have you found out where she
is ?'

'No, sir; not yet. I couldn't leave you.'

''Not leave me, man ? You must get out of this
place as soon as you can, and either find her or
make your way to headquarters, and let the Doctor
and Major Knowle—oh, and Sir Charles too—know
what has happened.'

'Mister Archie, sir,' said the lad, laying a cool
hand on his young officer's burning brow, 'don't, sir
—please, don't ! They must know all you want to
say long enough ago, and before now they have

got all our brave lads out searching the country; and you may lie still, sir, and think to yourself that nobody will rest until Miss Minnie is found.'

There was silence for a few minutes, during which Peter Pegg half lay beside his wounded officer, listening to words uttered in command that sounded familiar. They were evidently orders addressed to the elephant, which was shuffling by the great stable, making a whining sound as if protesting against being driven.

Then all was still again, till Archie said quietly:

'Yes, Pete, you are quite right, and I pray Heaven that she may be quite safe by now. But tell me, do you think I—I mean we—did all we could ?'

'Mister Archie, sir, once more, don't, please ! I am only a poor, ignorant chap, but I do know this, through having been in horspittle, that you have got to keep quiet and not worry yourself if you are going to get well. First thing, sir, is that you have got to get strong enough so that we can escape.'

'Yes, yes, Pete; that's right ! Escape !' cried Archie excitedly.

'Take it coolly, sir,' remonstrated the lad.

'Well, I will be cool, Pete.'

'That's right, sir. We've got to escape, and I have begun preparations already.'

'Yes, that's right. What have you done ?'

'Got a spear to begin with, sir.'

'Ah, well, that's something.'

'Yes, sir—something for you to handle like a bay'net if they won't let us go quietly.'

'Right—right!'

'And the next thing, sir, is for you to get strong to handle it.'

'Ah, and I am so weak!'

'Of course you are, sir, when you have had nothing but a drop of water for days.'

'For days!'

'Yes, sir; and now your breakfast's waiting. It's only bread and fruit and water, but it's wonderful stuff to put strength in a man, and you have got to begin getting it into you at once.'

'No, no; not yet,' pleaded Archie. 'Let me lie and think a bit first.'

'Not a minute, sir,' cried the poor fellow's nurse. 'You feel as if you couldn't touch anything, of course, but your horspittle orderly says it is only making a beginning; and here you are—cocoa-nutful clear, fresh water, so tip it down at once.'

Archie protested feebly, and then obeyed; and after taking a sip or two from the thick-lipped vessel, he ended by finishing the cooling draught with something like avidity.

Shortly after Peter Pegg was watching his patient crumbling some of the bread-cake and dipping pieces in a fresh supply of water and beginning to eat.

CHAPTER XXI.

PLANS.

'NOW, Mister Archie, sir, you was precious cross with me for bothering you into eating that little bit; but ain'tcher ever so much better now?'

'Oh yes, Pete. That horrible feeling of faintness is going off; but my head'——

'Oh, you let your head alone, sir. That'll come right if only you keep on eating directly you begin to feel faint, if it is ever so little a bit.'

'You must make me, then, Pete. Never mind my turning disagreeable. It's because I am not myself.'

'All right, sir. Now you just tell me what we are to do.'

'Find means for us to escape.'

'That's what I want, sir, so as just to have the way ready. But it's no use to get out and me to have to carry you on my back.'

Archie sighed, for he was forced to accept the truth of his companion's words. He lay thinking then of his interview with the Doctor, and he said to himself:

'I wanted something to take the boyishness out of me, and this has come and swept it away at one stroke and for ever.—Look here,' he said aloud; 'look round and see whether it is possible for you to get out—I mean, just think the matter over so that you may be able to contrive to get outside after dark and examine our surroundings a bit.'

'That's all settled, sir. There's no breaking through the door, but I have been thinking that I might climb up inside here, sir, get as far as them bamboo rafters, and squeeze a way out on to the roof through them palm-leaf mats. Pst!'

'What is it?'

Peter Pegg held up one finger, and then pointed sharply towards the door.

'Some one there? I don't hear anything.'

'No, sir. That topper you got seems to have made you a bit deaf,' said the lad, as he crouched close up to his companion's head. 'I don't suppose if we spoke loud that any one would understand us; but there's some one outside there, and after a bit I am going to look if he ain't gone.'

The lad waited for a while, and then rose and began to pace slowly up and down the front of his prison, and ended by climbing quickly up by the door and peering out through the hole the elephant had made.

He only gave a glance, before descending quickly, to continue his marching up and down for a time, when he ended by throwing himself beside his companion and settling down as if for a nap. The lad preserved silence, lying with his eyes closed, while Archie watched him anxiously.

'Did you see anything?' whispered the young subaltern at last.

'Yes; a chap there in a yellow-and-red sarong, and as I was looking out, the ugly, black-looking beggar was squinting in. I wasn't sure at first, but it's like this 'ere: when they thought we was too bad they didn't trouble about us, but somebody must have been watching, and seen you beginning to pick a bit, and that's made them think that it's time to look after us, so they have planted a chap outside as a sentry.'

'How horrible!' whispered Archie.

'Well, it's bad, sir; but it's good too. He's got a big spear and one of them crooked daggers stuck in his rolled-up sarong; and them's just what I want.'

'Yes; but you can't get them, Pete.'

'I dunno so much about that, sir. If I get out I might be able to drop down upon him from the roof and help myself to his tools before he knew where he was.'

'What! murder the sentry?'

'Not me, sir. It's only war now. 'Sides, I won't hurt him if he will give in quietly. It strikes me that if I could manage to drop down upon him sudden he would be so scared that he would be ready to cut. But don't you bother about that, sir. You leave that to me. You have got nothing to do now but eat and drink and sleep till you are fit to take command.'

As the day wore on the heat of the place grew half-suffocating. They had both been too ill to notice this at first, but now it grew to be insufferable.

'I wonder how the sentry stands it,' thought the young private; and taking advantage of the Malay being very quiet—for not so much as a step had been heard for quite an hour—Peter made a sign to his companion not to take any notice, and then crossed to the other side of his prison, and after walking to and fro slowly and quietly a few times, he raised one foot to a bamboo cross-piece, sprang up, caught at a second bar, and held on just long enough to get one glance through the hole, before dropping lightly down again.

'Look at that, now,' he muttered, for he had had time to see that the sentry was squatting down upon his heels, his chin buried in his breast, and evidently fast asleep. 'What a chance if I was outside!' thought Peter; and he climbed quickly and silently up now to have a good look at their guard, just in time to see him start up erect and catch hold of the spear he had leaned against the tree that shaded him.

At the same moment Peter Pegg grasped the fact that the ·Malay had not been disturbed by *his* movements, for he was gazing right away down the forest path facing the big door.

'It must be somebody coming,' thought Peter. 'He sleeps like a weasel, with one eye open.'

He had proof the next minute that he was right. The steps became audible, and a couple more spear-armed men approached; there was a short whispered conversation, and one of them took the sentry's place.

'Changing guard,' muttered Peter. 'That's imitation of what they have seen us do. Wonder whether they are going to carry that on all night.'

In due time there was another visit from the party which had brought the fruit and water, the surly-looking leader having the door unbarred, to give a look round, and then, on their being satisfied that the prisoners had an ample supply of provisions, the door was closed again, to Peter Pegg's great relief, for he placed his lips close to Archie's ear and whispered:

'Oh, I have been squirming! I was afraid they would begin to hunt for the spear they left behind.'

'Spear left behind?' said Archie.

'Yes; didn't I tell you? They forgot one last night, and it's tucked in behind you, under the leaves.—Now then,' thought the lad, 'what's it going to be—sentry by day only, or one all night?'

The latter proved to be the case, for after the two prisoners had partaken of an evening meal— Archie making no opposition now—Peter Pegg peered out from time to time, to see that the sentry had drawn nearer to the door; and there he was, plain enough, till it grew too dark to distinguish anything a few yards away, when at last the silence became so profound that the lad began to hope that the watch was given up. He whispered his belief to his fellow-prisoner, and said that he was going to see whether it would be possible to creep out by way of the roof, when his hopes were dashed by a cough; but on peering out he could see nothing, and, full of disappointment, he walked slowly to where Archie lay, and whispered to him again.

'I can't see anything,' he said, 'but I have watched him so often that I could make it all out. He's been taking a bit of one of them betel-nuts out of a bag, and then taking a sirih-leaf from a sort of book, and laying it on his hand before he opened his little brass box full of that wet lime. Then he smeared some of the lime over the leaf, laid the bit of nut on it, rolled the leaf up into a quid, and tucked it in his cheek, just like a Jack-tar. Nasty brute! Making his teeth black and the corners of his mouth all red. 'Tain't as if it was a bit of decent 'bacco! Well, perhaps when he has had a good chew he will go to sleep.'

'It will be impossible for you to try to get out to-night, Pete.'

'Impossible, sir? I'll just show you! I'm not going to be kept shut up here like a tame hanimile in a cage, I can tell him.'

'But supposing you do try to break through the thatch, he is certain to hear you.'

'Suppose he does, sir! How will he know but what I'm one of them big monkeys as they send up trees to pick the cocoa-nuts, or one of the wild cat sort of things as the jungle's full of? You let me alone, sir. I mean to make a beginning. Sha'n't do much till you get stronger, sir. Then we shall get out together, and make straight for the camp.'

'But how about finding our way?'

'Well, sir, between ourselves, I have got two plans. One is, to get down to the river and find a boat. You see, once aboard that, all we have to do is to let it float down till we come to Campong Dang.'

'Yes; that sounds simple and easy. But you said that you had got two plans.'

'Yes, sir. That's the wet way; t'other's dry. You haven't seen because you have been too bad, but they keeps helephants here, and I know one of them.'

'You know one of them?'

'Yes, sir; he's been to see me twiced.'

'Are you dreaming, Pete?'

'Yes, sir—with my eyes open. I have thought it all out. I want to get him here some night, and then break a way out and get you on him—I knows how to ride like a mahout—and I'll make him take us to headquarters. What do you say to that?'

'Say to that, Pete!'

'Ah! don't you get talking like an unbelieving heathen, sir. You don't know what a lot of sense there is in one of these 'ere helephants. Once I get you on board—I don't suppose there would be a howdah, but you could hold on to his ropes—I've got a spear to guide him, though he wouldn't want no steering once I got him into one of those paths. They all lead to one or other of the campongs, and if we don't get into the right one at first we will try again.'

Archie sighed.

'Ah, you think I can't do it, sir; and you are low-sperrited because you ain't strong enough.'

'It all sounds so wild, Pete,' said Archie faintly.

'Course it do, sir. Helephants ain't horses.'

'Thank you,' said Archie, with a faint scintillation of his old ideas of fun.'

'They are wild beasts, and big uns, too, at that.'

'Yes, yes; but this all sounds nonsensical.'

'Course it do, sir. That's the best of it. You can't grarsp it because you have been lying there onsensible and don't know what's happened. I didn't believe it myself at first; but you remember about the review and the big Rajah's helephants?'

'Yes, of course.'

'Well, when I was off duty for a bit I goes and makes friends with one of the swell mahouts—him as drove the Rajah's own helephant. The mahout let me feed him, and the big beast was quite chummy with me—took me up in his trunk, and set me up astride on him.'

'Well, suppose he did,' said Archie peevishly; 'what's that got to do with our position here? Where is your chummy friend?'

'That's what I want to tell you, sir. He found me out here, and he comes and shoves his trunk through that hole as you can't see now because it's dark. "How are you, old man?" he says. "Who'd have thought of seeing you here? Tuck one or two of them bananas in the end of my trunk and see me eat them, and I will show you;" and I did. Then he says, "Give us a drink of water;" and so I did, and he played it into himself just as if he was a portable fire-engine. What do you think of that?'

'I think,' said Archie faintly, 'that if I was like I was in the old days, Peter, I'd punch your great, stupid head. What do you mean? Do you think I'm as weak as a child, and that you must try and please me by telling me all that flam?'

'Haw, haw!' laughed Peter Pegg softly. 'I knowed you'd say that. But it's all as true as true. I don't mean to say that he talked to me like that in plain English, but he chuntered and grunted and squealed, and ate nearly all the bananas and bread, and drank up the water before he went away, and come again for more.'

'Oh, I could believe that. But what makes you think it's the same elephant as the one you saw before?'

'Oh, I did doubt it at first, sir; but I am sure now.'

'Why?'

'Because of his size. He's the biggest one that came to the camp; and he knowed me again by the smell.'

'Bah! He smelt the fruit.'

'But the smell of the fruit wouldn't make him stroke me down all over and talk to me in his way. You wait a bit till he comes next time. He will soon show you how friendly he is to me. Why, it was only yesterday, I think—though the time goes so rum here, where one sleeps so much—he come to see me, and one of the Malay chaps as was taking him to the water tried to drive him away, and, my word, you should have seen him chivy the chap off and call him a hinterfering blackguard, in helephant! He's my friend, sure enough, sir; and it will take a bit of time to settle matters, but I think I can make him understand what he's got to do, and start off some night and carry us to Campong Dang.'

'Ah, if you only could, Pete!' said Archie faintly; 'but it all sounds to me like a dream, and '——

There was a deep breath, and silence.

'And what, sir? What were you going to say?—Why, I'm blessed if he ain't asleep!' muttered Peter. 'Well, so much the better. Now I'm going to see if I can't get out; and if that beggar hears me I must try and gammon him. Wonder whether I can come that *chicker, chicker, chick, chack, chack, chack,* like one of them big monkeys. I did manage to imitate it pretty fairly time back when I teased that one as Captain Down used to make a pet of. Well, why shouldn't I now ?'

CHAPTER XXII.

PETER PEGG SAYS 'YUSS.'

'YUSS,' said Peter Pegg, as he sat in the profound darkness, for it was some hours before the moon would rise, and he was solacing himself with a piece of the bread-crust, which was terribly dry and exceedingly hard—'yuss, this is precious nice tackle for a fellow's teeth. Wants nibbling like a rat. Yuss, what I have telled the young governor sounds 'most as easy as cutting butter, only not quite. I can get the helephant up to the door here, and I don't see much hardship in mounting him and riding off; only how am I to manage to get him here at the right time? Ah, well, I'm getting on. The governor's better, and I have got a spear, and, so to speak, I have got a helephant, and a fine one, too. So I am not going to give up because some of the job is hard. This 'ere bit of bread is as hard as wood, but I am getting through with it, and that's what I mean to do about our escape. Where you can't take a fair bite at anything, why, you must nibble; and I must go on nibbling now to find some way of getting out of this here ramshackle place. If I can just contrive a hole so that I can climb on the roof whenever I like, and be able to cover it up again so that these beauties don't know, I don't feel a bit doubtful of being able to slide down to the eaves, and then hold tight and get my toes in here and my toes in there, and climbing back'ard till one gets to the ground. As to getting back again—oh, any one could do that. He will do it as well as I can as soon as he is better. Now then, ready? Yuss. Then here's to begin.'

He rose softly, stepped quietly over the leaves, and deftly climbed up the door again, where he applied his eye to the ragged lookout.

'My, it is dark!' he said to himself. 'There must be a regular river fog floating over the place. I can't see a star.'

He stopped peering out and listening, but everything was so black that he could not even distinguish the tree opposite to him beneath which the sentry had taken his post.

'So still,' muttered the lad, 'that I don't believe he can be there. If he was, everything is so quiet that—— Whoo—hoop! What's that? Like somebody learning to play the key bugle without any wind. Here, I know: it's one of them long-legged, long-necked birds with a big beak, that stands a little way out in the river and picks up the frogs. Yes, that's it. Now it's all right, so here goes.'

He crossed to the other side of the building so as to be farthest from the tree where he had last seen the sentry, and, as quietly as he could, he began to climb the back wall of the great stable; and, as he had anticipated, this did not prove difficult, the crossbars and uprights, interlaced with cane and palm-strip, furnishing plenty of foot and hand hold, so that, without making much rustling, he drew himself up and up till his head came in contact with one of the sloping bamboo rafters, to which battens of the same cane were lashed with thin rotan ; and, as he expected, upon these battens lay a dense thatch of so-called attap——that is to say, large mats of palm-leaves were laid one over the other till a thick cover, which would throw off the most intense of the tropic rains, roofed the building in.

Standing with his toes well wedged into the side, the would-be fugitive raised one arm and began feeling about in the mats above him, and chuckled.

'Why, it's just nonsense,' he said. 'Talk about escaping. Why, one has got nothing to do but shove these up a little way and creep through. Then the attap will all fall back again, and no one will see as the place has been disturbed. Then there is the getting down again. Well, that's just as easy as it is to get up. Oh, don't I wish Mister Archie was all right ! These 'ere Malays must be fools to think of shutting up a couple of English young fellows in a place like this. Well, it's awful hot here. The mats are quite warm still with the sunshine. I will just let in some air.'

He began thrusting the attap thatch a little upward, and there was a loud scuffling and beating of wings.

'Birds,' he muttered ; 'and a good roost, too. Wonder what they are.'

Then there was a puff of cool, moist, night air seeming to be sucked into the building as he made an opening.

'Ah, that's just prime,' he sighed ; and he raised himself a little more, and then, as he thrust out one hand to get a fresh hold of the bamboo batten, he stopped short, silent and motionless, and with cold perspiration breaking out all over his face, for his hand had closed upon one of the battens, which felt cold and scaly; and but for the fact that his left arm was hooked over one of the sloping supports of the ridge-pole, he would have dropped heavily back on to the floor of the elephant-stable.

As it was, his legs felt as if they were hanging paralysed downward, and he was conscious of the fact that the batten that he had last grasped was slowly gliding through his right hand and getting thinner and thinner, till it passed rustling away right in amongst the palm-leaf thatching.

'Oh dear!' sighed Peter Pegg, 'could that have been fancy? It felt just like a big snake. Phew! How hot it is! And yet I feel quite cold. Is it fancy? I know snakes do climb trees, but what could a snake be doing up here in the thatch? Oh, murder! It's all right enough. I know! Didn't the Doctor tell Mister Archie that they crawled up the walls and had their regular runs so that they could catch the rats and birds?'

He made a movement, as he began to master the strange feeling of dread, to replace his feet in the rough trellis into which his toes had been thrust, and then woke to the fact that his legs were not swinging downwards, for the half-paralysing sensation had been caused by sheer dread.

'Think of that, now!' he said. 'I thought they would give way. Here, let's get down out of this. Shouldn't be at all surprised if there's snakes swarming all over the place. That one didn't bite me, did it? Don't know that I should mind a

honest bite, but some of these things are poison.
Here, I have had enough of this;' and he felt
about with a strange feeling of creepiness for the
batten that he had not touched.   This he grasped
shrinkingly.

'Oh, this ain't a snake,' he said.   'Bamboo; and
a thick un, too, for here's a knot.   Here, don't be
such a coward, Peter.   Go on, comrade.   That there
snake's gone, and it was more afraid of you than
you were of it.'

Gaining fresh courage, he had very little difficulty
in creeping out from beneath the great mat and
drawing himself upwards till he lay out in the
darkness upon the roof, panting heavily as he
breathed in the soft, cool, night air.

'Now, can I find this hole again?' he said to
himself.   'Oh yes, all right.   And what's this?'
For his hand encountered a good-sized stone secured
in its place by a thin rotan bound over it, and passed
through the thatch and under one of the battens.
'That's all right,' he said to himself, as he began
to crawl up the slope towards the ridge; and in
doing so he found that flat, rough, slaty pieces of
stone followed at intervals to weight the roof, and
formed supports for his feet, so that he was able
to creep with the greatest ease right up to the
ridge.

'Be quite jolly,' he said, 'if it wasn't for the
feeling that I may be crawling over millions of
snakes.   However, I am in for it now, and I must
chance'it.   Now about getting down.'

He lay upon the back slope of the building, resting with one arm over the ridge, listening intently,

knowing that he must be gazing in the direction of the sentry; but the silence was as intense as the darkness, and he still hesitated as to whether he should lower himself down again in the direction from which he had come.

Feeling, however, that if he descended from there it would be into the jungle, which he knew from experience was one tangled and matted mass, impervious to human beings, he decided to go on, and proceeding very cautiously, he began to lower himself down towards the eaves by the help of the many stones which offered support to hand or foot.

'Why, it's just like going downstairs,' thought the lad; and then, as if to prove it was not so easy, one of the stones, upon which he was bearing with his foot, slipped from its rotan tie and began to rustle loudly down before him.

Then there was a sharp hiss, which made the lad cling tightly and begin to feel a return of the paralysing shudder which had unnerved him a few minutes before. The hiss was repeated, and followed by a sound like a quick reiteration of the word *Yah;* and then Peter Pegg's heart began to palpitate heavily as he realised that it was a human utterance coming from the direction of the sentry's tree, and followed by a quick movement as of some one advancing towards the stable door.

'You brute! How you frightened me!' said the lad to himself, as, obeying his next impulse, he tore a stone that was held in its place by the thin cane, raised it above his head, and hurled it with all his might in the direction of the sentry.

'There's a fool!' he muttered to himself as he lay full length, listening to a gabbling, threatening utterance from below, which was slurred with hisses and dotted with angry ejaculations. 'He's a-swearing at me in his ugly lingo,' thought Peter. 'Can't see him, so he can't see me, and of course he can't tell who it is up here. Here, I know,' he continued, as there was a series of hisses such as would be uttered by one who was trying to drive some obnoxious creature away.

'Hississh!' cried the sentry again.

'Blest if he don't think I'm a big monkey up here,' thought Peter. 'Monkeys throw sticks and stones. What a lark! Wish Mister Archie was here with me. I'll let him have another;' and feeling for the next stone, he threw it from him sharply. 'Frighten the beggar away,' he muttered.

But it had the contrary effect of arousing a fresh burst of hisses, stamps, and subdued yells.

'Oh, get out with you, you idgit!' said the young private, in a whisper, to himself. 'Wish I could recollect how that big ape Captain Down used to keep chained up went on when he teased it. Chance it,' he muttered; and raising both hands to his mouth so as to speak between them, he sent forth his imitation of an angry monkey, spattering through the night air, his utterance being produced with wonderful rapidity:

Chick, chick, chick, chick, chick, chick, chuk, chick! *Chick, chuk, chack!*

Errrrrr! growled the Malay.

Chick, chack, chuk, chack, chick, chack, chuk, check, check, chuk! snarled the imitation monkey.

What evidently meant in the Malay tongue, 'Be off, you ugly beast!' came from below, followed by a pant as of somebody exerting himself; and simultaneously Peter Pegg felt a tug at one leg of his trousers, and a slight scratch which made him dart his left hand down and feel the bamboo staff of a spear which had passed right through his garment and had pinned his leg down to the thatch, in which the spear was deeply buried.

'You cowardly beast!' panted Peter softly. 'This is getting a fellow's monkey up in reality;' and without pausing to reflect upon what might be the consequences, he began to reach for and tear out every stone he could find, to hurl them with all his might in the direction from which the hissing and growling came.

The first must have gone pretty close to the angry sentry, the second startled him, and the third produced a yell as it struck him full in the back, for he had already begun his retreat; and after sending two or three more with all the vigour produced by anger, Peter Pegg lay back on the roof, listening to the distant pattering of feet, and laughing with suppressed mirth till the tears ran down his cheeks.

'Took me for one of them big monkeys,' he panted at last; and, in closer imitation than ever, he sent forth a final *Chick, check, ckuk, chick, chick, chack, chack, chack,* after his retreating enemy.

'Don't be a fool, comrade,' he said at last. 'He can't hear you. Poor old Job Tipsy! He always said me and the governor were just like a couple of schoolboys with our games and larks, and I suppose he was right. Poor old Bully Bounce! But I do wish he was here now to help us two out of this hole, and a dozen of our chaps at his back, for it's rather a different sort of game to what it used to be when we got found out. Here's poor Mister Archie lying down below badly hurt, and me stretched on the top of this attap roof, pinned out like a jolly old cock butterfly meant for a specimen. Think of it,' he muttered, as he sat up and began feeling down his leg. 'Shied a spear at me. It hurts, too. Good job it didn't hit me in the middle. It's a bit wet, but it can't be bad. Scratted a bit, and then it went through the leg of my trousers. Well, I call that a narrow escape.'

As he muttered to himself he began tugging at the spear-shaft, only about two feet of which stood out above the cloth; and from his cramped position the young private found that, tug as he would, the weapon was too deeply buried in the thick thatch for him to draw it out.

'Well, this 'ere's a nice game,' said the lad softly. 'Won't come out, won't you? All right! More ways of killing a cat than hanging it. Go in, then;' and reaching upward with both hands, he began to press upon the butt of the spear, and drove it a little farther in. 'If you can't pull a spear or a harrer out, the best thing to do is to shove it through. That's what I'm a-doing; only, as you may say, I'm walking off it.' As he spoke he raised his leg up, holding on to the attap roof the while, gave two or three sharp kicks, and threw his leg off the spear-shaft and let it fall free upon the slope, where he lay now upon his back shaking with laughter.

'Oh dear! Oh dear!' he said. 'What a game! Pinned down like a specimen! I can't stop it. Just like it's often been when we have been on the march, feeling half-starved and empty, and I have made the lads turn savage, and bang me on the back, and call me all the fools they could lay their tongues to, as they kept telling me to leave off, when I couldn't. Pinned down like a cockchafer! 'Tention! Oh, I say,' he gasped out excitedly, 'I never thought of that! Here was I wondering how I was to get hold of another spear, and it's come flying at me. Where are you?'

He felt about till his hand came in contact with about two feet of the haft standing out of the thatch, and he began tugging at it to draw it forth. 'Won't come, won't you? All right, then, go;' and catching hold of the bamboo staff with his left hand, he doubled his fist and turned his right into a mallet, thumping the butt, which readily yielded and went farther and farther through, till he struck the bamboo and mat together, when a final blow sent the weapon right through, and it was gone.

'My!' he muttered at last. 'Suppose Mister Archie was just underneath, listening! Not he, poor chap! He'll be fast asleep,' thought Peter. 'Well, there's no considering what I ought to do next. I have just got to get back and pick up that there spear. Mr Sentry will never think it's gone through, and if to-morrow he comes to look for it, he will think that there monkey has carried it away sticking in his back. Phew! My leg

smarts; and that ain't the worst of it. I have got
to get up to the ridge here, and down the other
side to where I crept out; and that's where there's
snakes.'

It took a little resolution when the lad had reached
the loose portion of the mat, and he hesitated and
kicked about a bit, to scare any enemy away, before
raising the mat, passing his legs through, and lowering himself partly down.

A few minutes later he was holding on with one
arm, having wedged his toes into the side of the
stable wall, while he carefully drew back the thatch
into its place.

Directly after, he stood listening amongst the
rustling palm-leaves, then crept to Archie's side, to
hear him breathing heavily, fast asleep; and then,
after refreshing himself with a draught of water, he
began to search for the fallen spear. This he passed
several times before he found it sticking upright
in the floor, gave it a hug of delight, and was
about to carry it to thrust it in beside its fellow,
when he paused.

'That means if they find one they will find t'other,'
he said to himself, 'so that won't do.'

This thought resulted in his finding another hiding-
place for his newly acquired treasure.

'We are getting on,' he said in a satisfied way—
'only got to smug a couple of krises, and there we
are. I say, my leg smarts, and I should like to
have a look at it; but I won't light a match, because
it would be risky in amongst these leaves—and I
ain't got one. Well, that will do for to-night, so
good-night. I am beginning to think I am tired.'

Before five minutes had elapsed Peter Pegg proved the truth of his assertion by the utterance of a very regular snore, which kept time with his breath till broad daylight, when he started up.

'*Réveillé*, comrade!' he cried aloud; and then, 'Blest if it ain't that helephant again!'

CHAPTER XXIII.

MORE ABOUT A FRIEND.

'ALL right, old man,' cried Peter Pegg, as he sprang up and crossed to the door, where his visitor was chuntering, as the lad called it, and making a succession of peculiar snorts as he waved his trunk up and down. 'What's the matter? Want some breakfast?' And after a moment's hesitation he stretched out his hand and began to stroke the great, prehensile organ that was now passed over his shoulders and down his sides. 'You won't hurt me, will you, old chap? That'll do. Steady, and I will get you some breakfast.'

The quiet, soothing tone of the lad's voice seemed to convey his meaning, for the elephant curved the end of his trunk right upwards and began to trumpet.

'Hear that, Mister Archie?' cried Peter, as he made for where the fruit-basket stood.

'Yes,' replied the subaltern, raising himself slowly and painfully. 'Is anything the matter?'

'No, sir; only my friend come to see us.'

'Your friend?' said Archie wonderingly.

'Yes, sir; the helephant. Can't you see him?

'No,' said Archie. 'Oh yes, I can see its trunk.

'That's right, sir; come for some breakfast;' and the young private strode back, breaking up the cake and placing a goodly piece within reach of the extended trunk, for it to be taken and disappear through

the opening, when the trunk quickly returned ready
for more.

The business was repeated again and again, and
the pieces of bread were followed by bananas and a
fair-sized vegetable which might have been either
pumpkin or melon.

The trunk curled round it directly, but this proved
too great in diameter to pass altogether through the
hole, dropping from the trunk and being dashed at
by its donor.

'Well caught!' cried Peter. 'You must wait a
minute, old chap,' he continued, pulling out his
knife, with which he divided the small pumpkin in
four, each portion being quietly taken and drawn
through, to disappear in the monster's cavernous
interior, to be followed by several more bananas,
Peter dealing out his gifts deliberately so as to make
more of what in its entirety was a mere snack for
the visitor.

'There,' he cried at last; 'that's all you'll get,
so you had better toddle.'

Hoomph! grunted the elephant.

'What do you mean by that?'

Phoonk! came in a hollow-sounding grunt.

'Oh, why didn't you speak plain? Want water,
do you? Can't spare any. My young governor
wants a good wash. Go on down to the river.
There's plenty there. Good old chap,' he continued,
softly stroking the trunk; and after a low, muttering
sound the elephant submitted to the caresses, and
then began to respond.

'Take care, Pete!' said Archie in a low whisper.

'All right, sir. He knows me.'

'But he may turn spiteful. A blow from an elephant's trunk would dash you across the place.'

'Oh, he isn't going to dash me—are you, old man?'

'Take care!' whispered Archie hoarsely, for the great serpentine trunk glided completely round Peter and drew him close up to the hole, raising him from the ground, so that he hung three or four feet above the dried leaves.

'Ah-h!' sighed Archie, with an ejaculation of relief, as the elephant lowered the lad again and withdrew his trunk through the hole, and the two young men heard the soft movements of his huge, yielding feet as he slowly shuffled off, making a deep, low, muttering sound.

'There, Mister Archie, what do you think of that?'

'Think!' said the lad excitedly. 'I was afraid the brute would crush you to death.'

'Not he, sir. Didn't you see what friends we were?'

'Oh yes; but they are dangerous friends.'

'He isn't going to be dangerous to us, sir. I am glad you woke up. I wanted you to see him; and now you know how easy it will be for us to escape. Once I get you on his back, he will take us to camp as easy as you please.'

'Yes, once we are on his back,' sighed Archie. 'But how's that to be managed?'

'Oh, you want your breakfast, sir. You've got the dismal empties bad. Now, what do you say—a cup of water and a bit of bread to soak in it, or shall I give you a wash first?'

The great serpentine trunk glided completely round Peter and drew him
close up to the hole.

'A wash! Oh Pete, if you could only bathe that place on my head first, I feel as if it would be so refreshing.'

'All right, sir. Plenty of water. That's why I wouldn't give any to the helephant. You've got a handkerchy, and I shall have to trouble you, for that there tie as well; that silky thing will do to bathe the place nicely, and the handkerchy to dry you with.——No, it won't. I never thought of that.'

'Oh yes, take them,' said Archie eagerly. 'The tie will soon dry again.'

'Yes, I know that, sir; but your puggaree would have been better, only you lost that along with your cap.'

'Never mind. Make haste; the place is so hot and stiff.'

'Yes, sir, I know; but the wash must come last.'

'Why?' cried Archie irritably.

'Because this 'ere ain't a bath-room, sir, and there ain't no washhand-stand. You see, I have only got that there big jar of water, and a cocoa-nut shell to drink out of. You must have breakfast first, and here goes.'

Archie remained silent while, taking the cup, the lad fetched the great jar, which was half-full of water.

'There you are, sir,' cried Peter, as he filled the cup. 'What do you say? Think you could sit up now, or shall I help you?'

In response, wincing a little from pain and feebleness, Archie sat up, took the cup, and drained it with thirsty haste.

'That's good,' cried Peter, taking and refilling it. 'It does me good to see you, sir. Oh, you are coming on fine. Slep' all night, didn't you?' he continued, as he steadied the cup.

'I suppose so, Pete,' said Archie, with a sigh. 'I don't remember anything.'

'That's a good sign, sir. Now then, have another, or will you try a little soaked bread first?'

'No,' said Archie decisively. 'You drink that.'

'No, no, sir; after you have done.'

''Tention! Drink first,' said Archie, speaking more firmly.

'Oh, if you give commands, sir,' said Peter, 'I must do it;' and he drained the little vessel, with almost as much avidity as his patient. 'Fine tap, ain't it, sir?' he continued, as he drew breath.

'Yes. Now give me another cup and a piece of bread, so that I can break it and soak it.'

'Hooray! You are getting hungry, sir;' and the lad broke off some of the bread from the big cake that was left, handed a piece to his subaltern, and watched him with intense satisfaction as with trembling fingers he held a wedge in the cup, keeping it there till it was thoroughly soaked.

'Now then, you do the same,' said Archie.

'Oh, I can wait, sir. I ain't in no hurry.'

'Obey your orders, sir,' cried Archie sternly.

'Right, sir,' was the prompt reply; and the private followed his officer's example, this being repeated in each case, with results doubly satisfactory to Peter Pegg. 'They make capital bread here, sir, don't they?' he said, smiling, as he partook heartily of his share of the food.

'Yes,' replied Archie quietly. 'I seem to be able to taste it better this morning.'

'That's good, sir. Ready for a piece more?'

'Yes; about half as much as you gave me.'

The repast went on till Archie refused another portion.

'Give me some more water. I think I can manage,' he said. 'Now,' he continued, after drinking, 'take as much water as you like.'

'Sure you won't have some more, sir?'

'Quite.'

''Cause there won't be another chance till the niggers come with the next lot.—Oh yes, I didn't think of that,' cried Peter; and after drinking a couple more cupfuls, he placed the brimmed shell upright in one corner of the stable, before proceeding carefully to bathe his companion's face and hands, and ended by applying a succession of drenched pads to the painful, stiffened wound.

'How does that feel, sir?' he asked after a time.

'Oh Pete, I can't tell you! It's something heavenly. Go on, please. The necktie keeps getting so hot. Ah yes, better and better,' he sighed. 'There, that'll do,' he said at last. 'You must be tired now.'

'Not me, sir,' replied the lad. 'It's easy enough. I could go on for a week—only I am glad you cried halt.'

'Yes; I thought you must be weary,' said Archie.

'No, sir, 'tain't that, I tell you. There!' and he withdrew the silk necktie, dripping, from the bottom of the jar. 'That's sucked up the very last drop, sir. Hold still, sir, and let me lay this just on the top, and as soon as you begins to feel it too warm I will take it away and hang it up to dry. I won't dab the place with the handkerchy, because it will feel cooler if you let it dry by itself.'

'Why, Pete, you are as good as a nurse.'

'Oh, I don't know, sir. Tidy, like—tidy. You see, I have had two goes over the chaps in horspittle, and one can't help picking up a bit.'

'No nurse could have done better,' said Archie in a tone full of relief.

'Well, sir, 'tain't much to talk about. You see, I ain't got no proper tackle—not so much as a sponge. Now, if Dr Morley was here he'd put on some lint and a bandage.'

'Yes, I suppose so. Is the wound very big?'

'Quite big enough, sir. Might be bigger. Worst of it is, it's so much bruisy-like. But you are getting better, sir, splendid.'

'Ah, and I have been so selfish, thinking only of myself. You must be longing for a wash, and there isn't a drop of water left.'

'Oh, I don't mind, sir. I shall crumble up some of them leaves and have a dry wipe, for I suppose my skin don't look very cheerful.'

Archie held up his hand.

'What's that, sir? Somebody coming?'

Archie bowed his head, and Peter Pegg went on tiptoe to his observatory, and drew himself up, holding back as much as possible, to see a Malay, whom he recognised as the previous night's sentry, standing back at some little distance, shading his eyes with his hands as he looked upward, and then changing his position time after time as he seemed to be sweeping the roof with his eyes, before hurrying away.

'Why, I'd 'most forgotten that,' said Peter to himself. 'He was looking up there to see if he could find where that there spear's sticking in the roof, and,' he added, with a chuckle, 'it ain't sticking there a bit. I suppose he's afraid of being hauled over the coals by his sergeant for losing his weapon. Sarve him right! The beast! Why, he might have sent it right through me.'

This thought seemed to suggest what he had gone through over-night, for after taking a final glance in the direction of the retiring sentry, he dropped softly down to where the broad patch of light lay upon the leaves, drew up the leg of his trouser, and examined an unpleasant-looking wound.

'Might have been worse,' he thought. 'Only wants leaving alone. Just a wash and a dab of old Jollop's sticking-plaister; and it won't get neither, for it will heal up by itself and be something to show,' he chuckled—'P. P.'s first wound in the Malay Expedition!'

Getting up actively enough, for he fancied he heard a sound, he climbed to the hole once more, and found he was right, for the Malay sentry was returning, shouldering a fresh spear.

'Now, where did he get that?' thought the lad. 'It's wonderful to me how quiet everything is here. There must be houses, or huts, or something, and a fairish lot of men; and, of course, there's helephant-sheds. Only where are they? Jungle, jungle, jungle, without so much as a squint of anything else. Wonder what Mister Archie thinks about it.'

The lad dropped down again, after noticing that the sentry was now leaning on his spear, scanning the roof once more; but as Peter stood listening and laughing to himself, he muttered:

'He must have thought it was a big monkey!' and he mentally pictured what had passed in the night, when a smart tap caught his ear which sounded as if the shaft of the spear had been brought down with a rap upon the ground. This was followed by a step or two.

'Coming here,' thought the lad, and he stepped quickly over the leaves, to throw himself down close to Archie as if he were asleep, but keeping one half-closed eye fully observant of all that passed.

The sunlight was streaming in through the sides of the building in several places, and the watcher was conscious of the movements of the man by his shadow crossing first one and then another of these openings, one of which he directly after darkened.

'Don't you stir, Mister Archie,' he whispered. 'Sentry's squinting through one of the holes.'

There was no reply, and Peter watched till the light struck in again through the darkened hole. This was followed by footsteps.

'You see him, didn't you, sir?' said Peter, turning in his fellow-prisoner's direction.—'Look at that, now! I was shamming sleep, but, my word! he's off again, sound as a church; and that means he's getting well. I feel better too after that bread and water. Now then, some of that fruit.'

He went gently to the basket, which held a still ample supply.

'Might have given old Two-tails some more,' he

muttered. 'This won't do. We shall eat some, but there will be a lot to spare, and if they come and find the basket like this they will grow stingy; and I can use any amount for our friend.'

Taking up the basket, he carried it to one corner, raised a few leaves, and placed part of the bananas in the clearing, before lightly covering them up, taking the basket back to Archie's side, and placing several of the yellow fruits close to his hand.

'I might go to sleep,' he thought, 'and they will be ready for him.'

Then settling himself down near the empty water-jar, which he carefully wiped out and turned upside-down to dry, he began to munch his own share of the fruit, making up his mind the while to think out thoroughly a good plan for their escape.

'One helephant,' he said softly, 'two spears, one officer, and one private who knows how to use the spears. Wanted: two krises and how to get away. Well, there's nothing like thinking, so here goes.'

CHAPTER XXIV.

'R-A-A-A-AH!'

THREE weeks had passed away. Morning had come at last, and Archie Maine was beginning to breathe more freely, after passing a very bad night. For, as if it had scented an easy prey close at hand, a deep-voiced tiger had startled him from his watch about an hour before midnight by a deep-toned roar which had made the young subaltern stand half-paralysed for a few minutes, feeling as he did that there was nothing but the partly woven, fence-like wall of the big stable between him and the most savage beast that ranges the Eastern jungles.

The lad was stout-hearted enough, but he could not help feeling that though the building was strong of its kind, it would prove but a frail defence against the mighty arms and tremendous claws of a furiously hungry tiger; and after the first shock he crept cautiously to the hiding-place of one of the spears and drew it out, to plant the butt against one retired foot and hold it with the keen blade about breast-high in the direction of the bamboo uprights and palm lath slats that were woven in and out in duplicate.

That deep-toned roar was followed by a silence that was awe-inspiring in its way, and as Archie listened it seemed to him that he could hear the snuffling breathing of the savage animal that must have scented him during its rounds.

That silence lasted about a quarter of an hour before it afforded some amount of encouragement to the listener. The loneliness was awful, for he was sure that he and his fellow-prisoner were correct in coming to the conclusion that very soon after sunset the sentry had crept silently away, this terrible roar suggesting itself as an explanation of the reason for the elephant-stable with its prisoners being left without a watcher during the night.

Several times over, since he had been sufficiently recovered to sit wakefully chatting with Peter Pegg as to the best way of making their escape, he had heard snarling cries, shrieks that were thrilling enough in themselves, and which the two lads had set down to be the utterances of some ape that had been scented out and pounced upon by one of the cat-like creatures during its nocturnal search for prey. They had heard too, and rightly judged what were the authors of, other night cries, some of which, coming from a large kind of stork or crane that lurked upon the banks of the neighbouring river, were horrible and weird in their intensity. But though the jungle was supposed to contain plenty of tigers, it was only once that the prisoners had heard what they knew for certain to be the huge cat's roar.

Archie felt that he would not have cared upon the present occasion if Peter Pegg had been by his side, and in imagination, as he stood with the lowered spear, he saw himself taking turns with the

young private in stabbing at the savage beast as
it was snarling, tearing, and trying to force its way
through the tangled side of the big stable. But to
do this alone, it seemed to him, would only result
in irritating the beast and make it more furious
at his efforts to drive the sharp blade into a vital
part.

'We might have settled it between us,' he thought;
and then, in the midst of the weird darkness, he
shivered, for a fresh horrible thought assailed him,
which made the palms of his hands grow damp and
the moisture gather upon his brow.

What did it mean—this savage monster making
its way close up to his prison that night of all those
that had passed? Could it be that it had tracked
stealthily, after the habit of its kind, and pounced
upon poor Peter Pegg, dragged him down, and
hidden his body somewhere in the dense thicket,
and now, guided by its keen scent, followed the
flair to where *he* stood with the cold perspiration
now beginning to trickle from his temples and the
sides of his face?

There was not another sound, and after a sturdy
battle with his feelings, Archie began to force himself into the belief that it was his weakness that
made him imagine that such a catastrophe had
occurred. But all thought of sleep had passed away
for that night. He felt it would be impossible, and
he stood with every sense strained, listening for
some movement; but it was quite an hour later,
and after he had begun to feel overcome by weariness
from standing so long in one position, that he took
a deep breath and began to walk lightly up and

down the building, fully expecting that the rustle of the palm-leaves would excite the tiger into some fresh demonstration of its proximity.

But the beast made no sign, and beginning to indulge in the hope that after its roar it had crept stealthily and silently away upon its cushioned, velvet paws, he made his way to the stone jar, felt for the cocoa-nut, took a draught, and began to think of what had passed during these many weary days and nights of his struggle back towards recovery.

There was not much to dwell upon, for it had been terribly monotonous, that time, and sadly punctuated with either mental or physical pain. The mental was all embraced in the one painful thought of Minnie Heath and what had been her fate; the physical was mingled with the pain caused during the healing up of the horrible contused wound above his temples; while when he had not been suffering from this he was burdened by a series of wearing headaches, which would wake him from a refreshing sleep somewhere about the middle of the night, and not die out again till just before it was light.

Then day after day there had been the trumpeting sounds of the elephants shuffling by the prison on their way to water, the regular visits of one of their number, Peter's friend, to thrust in his trunk for a fresh supply of bread and fruit.

The dwarfish little Malay whose task it seemed to be to drive the great beasts to their morning bath, from which they returned muddied and dripping, had twice over, to the recovering lad's knowledge, shouted at and tried to drive Peter's friend from the stable door, but on the second occasion he had been so nearly caught by the huge beast that he was satisfied to leave him to his own devices, and Rajah, as Peter had christened him, came and went as he pleased.

Then, after the heat of the day had passed, the head keeper, as Peter called him, came with his followers to bring a fresh supply of their monotonous food and water; and it was he who, at irregular times, would come to change the sentry, peering through one of the holes to make sure that his prisoners were safe, and then going away as silently as he had come.

All this was discussed, as Archie grew stronger, again and again by the two prisoners, and they came to the conclusion that they must be deeply buried in an out-of-the-way part of the jungle from which it would be impossible for them to escape, and that that was the reason for so little attention being paid to their security.

'That's it, Pete,' Archie had declared. 'They know we can't get away, or else there would be more regularity about our guard, and whoever is on sentry would not disappear as soon as it is dark.'

Peter's answer repeated itself with additional force on this particular night of Archie's watch, for the lad had said, 'They know 'tain't safe, sir. It's my belief that if the sentry kept guard there one night, he would never do it again.'

'Poor Peter!' thought Archie as, refreshed by his draught of water, he began slowly to pace the rustling floor again. 'In such a silent night as this,' he mused, 'one's thoughts ought to flow easily enough, and I was hopeful that when he came back I should have hit out some better plan for our escape; but ever since that horrible night all power of thinking seems to have gone. Sometimes I do get fancying that the power is coming back, but it is only for me to seem weaker again, and—— Oh, I wish I had not let him go! I am too cowardly now to be left alone, and '——

R-a-a-a-ah!

Archie started into his old position, for once more, apparently from close at hand, came the deep-toned, savage, snarling roar of some huge tiger that had approached the big stable without a sound, and in imagination Archie could see its fiery, glaring eyes distended with a gaze that seemed to pierce the woven wall, as, with the soft white fur of its under parts brushing the earth, it gathered itself up ready to dash like some living catapult clean through the frail partition to his very feet.

'To impale itself, if I am lucky,' thought Archie. And then the silence continued for what seemed to be an hour, before, in the hope that the monster had once more stolen away as silently as it had come, the young man once again ventured to recommence the duties of his lonely, rustling beat. And now again he was attacked by his former horrible dread. The imaginary picture was in all its force. Poor Peter must have been followed by the tiger and dragged down helplessly to a horrible death; and, yes—for it was all too clear—this was indeed the reason why they were not guarded at night.

There was the temptation for them, had they

known, to attempt to make what would seem to be an easy escape; but for what? One sudden blow from a tremendous paw—and death.

The thought was sufficient to prostrate a man in the full vigour of his health and strength, and hence it was more than enough to cause a weak lad, slowly recovering from the fever and suffering from the shock of concussion and wound, to lean heavily upon the staff of the spear he held and feel at times that he should sink down in a heavy swoon.

It was a terrible night—one which seemed as if it would never end; but he fought bravely on, proving in himself that hope springs eternal in the human breast, and driving back what he called to himself his coward thoughts, till at last, after twice more being startled by the coming of the tiger, he did sink down heavily amongst the rustling leaves, and buried his face in his hands, that had quitted their hold of the spear, to receive the quivering face that now lay motionless upon them.

But it was no new coming of the enemy that had banished sleep and set every nerve pulsating before it seemed to lie weak and slack. It was one strange, twanging cry that he recognised at once as the call of the argus pheasant, far away in the jungle, and it meant so much—the fading away of the black darkness, and the glowing golden red of the rising sun to tell him ere long that it was morning and that the disturber of his would-be restful watch must have slunk away; and Archie Maine crouched there with his face still buried in his hands, quite sensible, for his lips were quivering and his breath coming and going more strongly, and causing a slight rustling of the dry leaves beneath. And then there was a whisper of thankfulness, as the lad now slowly rose from his knees with a weary sigh.

CHAPTER XXV.

'LIKE AN OLD TOM-CAT.'

THERE was nothing but the suggestion of the faint light of dawn stealing through the Rajah's hole, as Peter called it; but Archie knew well enough the way to the cocoa-nut and the stone jar for a refreshing draught, after which he pulled himself together, and began to wonder at the different phases of the night.

'I don't think I should have been such a coward before that dreadful night,' he said to himself. 'What horrors one can imagine at a time like this!'

For there seemed to be a something in the coming of day that brought with it the flagging hope that had passed away, and minute by minute there was something to take his attention.

He felt that there was no occasion to carry the spear any more, and he crept to its hiding-place and thrust it in where it would be safe, before crossing to the door and making use of Peter's steps as he drew himself up to peer out and breathe in the cool, soft, refreshing air.

And now the varying notes of birds came more often—cries of stork and crane, the whistle of the smaller parrots, the harsh shrieks of those of larger growth; and then he seemed to hear nothing, for all his feelings were concentrated in thoughts of his fellow-prisoner, in repetitions of how they had canvassed one particular thing, how he had objected, and how Peter Pegg had fought for and won in his determination that he would creep out from the roof, lower himself down, and make an expedition that should put away doubts and prove to them what their position really was, how near they were to their guards, and where the stables of the several elephants that passed their prison lay.

'You see, Mister Archie, sir,' Peter had insisted, 'we must do something. You are getting well on your legs now, and if we don't make a heffort we may be kept here for months. You are my officer, and I take my orders from you, but I do beg and pray, sir, as you will let me have a try. I can get out easy enough, and I can get in again. An hour or two would do it.'

And Archie had at last given way, to find that the hour or two had not done it, for the night had passed; it would soon be broad day, with the elephants being driven to water and a sentry resuming his post; and a chill was beginning to paralyse him, while hope grew more and more dull for the searcher for the way to freedom.

There was a faint tint of red now right away over the top of the distant trees, and what seemed to be a mountain appeared above the jungle; but it brought no return of the hope. To Archie, as it grew redder and redder, it looked blood-like—a forecast, as it were, of the horror and despair that were soon to come upon him in the shape of a dreadful truth. For Peter had not come back; and even if he were to come now, it would only be to be seen and made a closer prisoner; the secret of his way out would be known, and they would be more carefully imprisoned. He must be seen now, for there was the distant trumpeting of the advancing elephants, and it was quite light enough for the sentry to make his way along the forest path to take his place beneath the tree, and perhaps come to peer in first to see if his prisoners were safe.

Archie thought that perhaps the elephants might come by first, and then contradicted himself as he felt convinced that it would be the sentry; and as he peered forth from the hole, with the cold chill of despair increasing, there, far down the path, came the squat figure, with the light playing upon the end of his spear.

'It's all over,' thought the prisoner; and then he almost fell from the hole, and turned to stare wildly up at the mats which sloped down to the eaves of the building, and saw a leg thrust through hastily, then another, and the next moment Peter Pegg's toes were kicking at the wall as he struggled, hanging by one hand, to rearrange the attap mat of the roof, and then, panting and breathless, he lowered himself down and dropped at Archie's feet.

'Oh, I say!' he groaned. 'That was close! Sentry's coming down the path.'

'Yes, I saw him. Did he see you?'

'No. I was creeping along like an old tom-cat to get round to the back, and, my word, ain't I scratched! Talk about thorns!'

'Oh Pete, how you frightened me!' said Archie faintly.

'Frightened you, sir? Well, didn't he frighten me?'

CHAPTER XXVI.

MUST CHANCE IT.

THE sound of a step outside made Peter Pegg throw himself quickly down in a pile of the crushed leaves, burying his face in his hands, while Archie began to walk slowly up and down, conscious the while, through the shutting out of the morning light, that their guard had come up to the side of their prison and looked in, before going back to the sheltering tree, where he squatted down, to watch carelessly the coming of the elephants, one of which made for the hole, and was in the act of thrusting its trunk through, when it was charged by its big companion, the Rajah, who uttered a fierce squeal and drove the intruder away, before inserting his own trunk as usual, making no scruple about taking his customary refreshment from Archie's hand, having during the past few days grown accustomed to the subaltern's presence, and ending by giving the lad a few of the friendly touches that he was in the habit of bestowing upon Peter Pegg.

As soon as the elephant had gone, and after giving a glance at their guard, Archie, who was burning to listen to what his fellow-prisoner had to say, lay down beside him, under the impression that weariness had kept him from rising to attend to the elephant's visit.

He found him so soundly asleep that he did not even respond to a sharp shake of the arm which Archie gave him on receiving no reply to his whispers; and then he had to contain himself till evening, when their usual visitors came; and it was not till long after, when they were once more alone, that the young private suddenly started up.

'Have I been asleep?' he said half-wonderingly.

'Asleep! Yes; and I want to know what you have found out.'

'Let's have a drink and something to eat first. I feel half-starved.'

'Yes, of course—of course. Go on.'

'Now,' said Peter, after a ravenous attack upon the bread and fruit. 'Oh, here, this is good! Only I think it's time we got some meat. I'd give anything for a bit of commissariat bacon. You want to hear what I did, sir. Well, it was next to nothing but crawl like a slug in and out amongst trees, scratting one's self with that long, twining, climbing palm, and not once daring to stand up and walk.'

'Well, but what did you find out?'

'Nothing at all, sir, except that there's a bit of a lodge here which seems as if it might belong to the Rajah, and be where he lived and slept.'

'And was he there?'

'Oh no, sir; there's nobody there, only about a dozen Malay chaps, besides them as come to see us; and then there's a very big helephant-shelter, like this, only quite new and good, at the end of that there left path; and right away beyond that, in a sort of clearing where the jungle has been cut down—if I didn't tell you before—there's some big trees and a sort of scaffold of bamboos that looks like a shelter such as any one would climb up to shoot tigers, and under it some bones, just as if a buffalo had been tied up for a bait.'

'Yes, I see,' said Archie.   'Well, go on.'

'What about?'

'About what you found next.'

'I didn't find nothing next, only paths—helephant-paths that go right away somewhere.'

'Yes.   Go on.'

'Well, I did go on as far as I dared, sir; but it was all dark, and I couldn't do anything so long as the Malay chaps were talking, and when they were quiet I was afraid to stir for fear of waking them up.'

'But didn't you find out where the paths led to?'

'No, sir.   I did try.'

'Well, but didn't you strike out into the jungle?'

Peter chuckled.

'Strike out, sir!   Why, you're shut in every-where, and it's like trying to break through a sort of natural cane basket.'

'Then you really have done nothing?'

'No, sir; only found that this seems to be the place in the forest where somebody comes to shoot tigers.   And talk about them chickens—that's why I did not go so far as I might.   Every now and then I could hear one of them calling to its mate; and the first time it scared me so that I swarmed up a tree into the shelter or scaffold sort of place, where you could sit down.'

'Well, what then?' said Archie impatiently.

'Well, sir, I sat down.'

'Naturally,' said Archie.

'And then, when I thought it safe, and I was going to climb down in the dark to have another look, *mi-a-o-u!* There was that there great pussy again—and he was a whopper!'

'But you couldn't see him?'

'No, sir; it was too dark. I knew he was a whopper, though, by the size of his squeak. But I am pretty sure that he could see me, for he seemed to come and sit upright in the middle of the clearing, and began to purr. Blessed if he didn't sound just like a threshing-machine out in the fields at home after harvest-time.'

Archie was silent for a few moments, and Peter Pegg went on quietly and thoughtfully:

'Yes, sir; it sounded just like that.'

'Then you stopped up in that shelter for long enough?'

'I just did, sir—for hours.'

'Did you go to sleep?'

'Did I go to sleep, sir? No! Never felt so full of wide-awake in my life. Why, if you had heard that there thing roar'——

'I did hear it roar,' said Archie quietly; 'and it kept me awake all night.'

'Hark at that now, sir,' said Peter. 'My word, Mister Archie, sir! wouldn't one of them be a fine thing to train young recruities with, and teach them how to keep awake on sentry?'

'But you said something to me, Peter, about having to make our escape by daylight. Why?'

'Why, sir? Because as soon as you try and

travel out in that there jungle, it's so dark that you can't tell which way to steer.'

'But we should have to trust to the elephant—if we could get him.'

'Oh, that wouldn't do, sir. We should have trouble enough with it all clear daylight. I've thought it all over till my head won't think, and it's all as clear as crystal. We must wait for morning, when the helephant comes for his titbits before one of these chaps mounts guard, and then slip out and chance it. I believe in chance, sir —chance and cheek. You can often do things by risking it when you makes all sorts of plans and fails.'

'Well, Peter,' said Archie wearily, 'I can propose nothing better.'

'I wish you could, sir.'

'So do I,' said Archie. 'Well, we must try; and if they catch us, why, they can but bring us back. I don't think they dare use their spears, for fear of what might follow when our people come to rescue us.'

'Oh, they won't dare to savage us, sir. I believe these are Rajah Suleiman's men, and he wants to keep friendly with the Major.'

'There I think you are wrong, Pete. If he wanted to keep friendly, he would not have set his men to attack our boat.'

'I don't know, sir,' said Peter solemnly, 'for there's a deal of cunning and dodgery amongst these krisy chaps, and you never knows what games they may be at; and as to waiting for our Br'ish Grenadiers to march up and find us, I'm thinking that we may wait till all's blue. My old woman used to say—my granny, you know, as brought me up—"Peter," she used to say, "I am going to give you a moral lesson, boy: don't you wait for people to help you, my lad; you help yourself."'

'That was very good advice, Pete,' said Archie, smiling, and uttering a deep yawn.

'Yes, sir; and that's what I used to do.'

'Help yourself?'

'I didn't mean that, sir. I used to hear it so often that I used to do as you did just now.'

'What do you mean?'

'Yawn at it, sir.'

'Oh!' said Archie. 'Well, but, Pete, that tiger you talked about kept me awake all night.'

'So he did me, sir.'

'Yes,' said Archie, laughing; 'but you've slept all day since.'

'Right, sir. That's one to you, Mister Archie. Well, sir, that's our game, just as I say. We'll lay up a good stock of rations—I mean save the fresh and keep on eating the stale, and be all ready for the right morning, and when it comes, nip outside, mount the helephant, and away we will go—I mean, that is, if you think that you can creep up same as I do, and lower yourself down from the roof.'

'I think I could now, Pete.'

The lad grunted.

'What do you mean by that?'

'It means I don't, sir. I know you'd *try*, but *try* ain't enough. You must *do*. Still, it don't mean that we are going to start to-morrow morning;

and a good job, too, because there's grub, and our sleep-chests is pretty well empty. We must both be as fit as fiddles, sir, and then we can play a tune that will make the niggers stare.'

'Yes,' said Archie, after lying in silence for a few minutes, with the darkness rapidly approaching. 'We will worry our brains no more. This plan is simple. We will be prepared, and then good luck go with us. We will make our start.'

'Bray-vo!' cried Peter. 'That's talking like our own old Mister Archie. I say, sir, you are picking up!'

'Am I, Pete?' said the lad sadly. 'Feel my arm.'

Pete ran his hand down his companion's limb from shoulder to wrist.

'Well, sir, that's all right.'

'All right! Why, I feel like a skeleton.'

'Well, but the bones is all right, sir. You went for ever so long without eating anything at all but water, and there ain't no chew in that; and when you did begin to peck, what's it been? Soaked bread, and 'nanas and pumpkins. You couldn't expect to get fat on them. Just wait till we get back to camp, and you are put on British beef and chicken, and them pheasants as you officers shoot. My,' said the lad, with a smack of his lips, 'couldn't I tackle one now—stuffed with bread-crumbs and roasted! I should be sorry for the poor dog as had to live on the bones. A bit of fish, too, fried, sir— even if it was only them ikon Sammy Langs. Here, stow it! I only wanted you not to fidget about being a bit fine. You get your pluck, Mister Archie;

and you are doing that fast. Never mind about the
fat and lean so long as you feel that you can hit
out with your fist or tackle a kris chap with one of
our spears. Doing a thing, sir, is saying you will
do it and then doing it in real earnest. I say, how
soon it has got dark! Now, what do you say to
a bit of supper, and then finishing up our sleep?'

'Agreed, Pete. But what about keeping watch
for the tiger if it comes?'

'Ah, I didn't think about that, sir; but we've
got to chance getting the elephant here and riding
away before the sentry comes.'

'Yes; we've settled that we must chance that.'

'Yes, sir; and we must chance the tiger if he
comes, which maybe he won't, for we haven't heard
much of them chaps before.'

CHAPTER XXVII

'DID you hear anything in the night, Pete?' said Archie the next morning.

'There he is, bless him!' whispered Peter, from where he was peering through the lookout-hole.

'What do you mean?'

'That Malay chap, sir—the big one with the squint. I should like to drop upon him and smug that kris of his. Just think of it! As soon as we made up our minds to toddle the first time we can get the helephant here before they mount sentry, here he comes, just as if orders had been given for that to be done regular.'

Peter dropped down from his lookout-hole, and began to pick out the worst of the fruit for the elephant when he came.

'Seems hard on a friend, Mister Archie, but I don't suppose the Rajah minds them being a bit over ripe.'

'Not he,' replied Archie; 'but I meant, did you hear anything in the night?'

'Oh, you mean the tiger, sir? Yes, I heerd him three or four times, but I was too comfortable to sit up and bother about him. Did you hear him?'

'I suppose I did, but it all seems as if it was part of a dream.'

'That's all right, then, sir. I say! Hear 'em?

Here's the helephants coming. You get up and look.'

Archie mounted to the hole, and saw, following steadily one after the other, four of the great beasts, with the little, squat driver seated on the neck of the last; and after they had passed, loafing carelessly along as if he were too important and disdained to be driven, came the Rajah, muttering as if to himself, and walking straight up to the big stable door before going on to take his bath.

Archie dropped down, after seeing that the sentry was quietly rolling up a fresh betel-quid, and Peter stood aside for his companion to take his place by the basket.

'Never mind me, sir. Let him stroke you over as much as he likes; and you mustn't mind if he smells you too much with the wet end of his trunk. I want you to be as good friends as me and him is.'

The result was that Archie fed the great beast, and was caressed, the sensation being upon the lad, as he listened to the flapping of the elephant's ears, that the beast's two little, pig-like eyes were piercing some crack in the door and watching him intently.

Then, as if quite satisfied with his share in the provender, which he must have taken as a dainty addition to the vast quantities of jungle grass and leafage which formed his real support, the elephant swung off, bowing his huge head and muttering softly, to overtake his companions, while Peter gave his officer a very knowing look.

'There, sif,' he said, 'that's just what we want, only no sentry. You will have to creep out with the prog and the spears, and the krises when they comes, which we shall have all ready, while I'm feeding him, and then go on yourself giving him some bread which we will save up for him. I shall join you, and tell him to kneel down; up we gets. You will crawl on and hold on by the ropes while I settle down with my legs under his ears. It will be just as easy as A, B, C.'

'*IF*,' said Archie, in capital letters.

But the days passed wearily on; provisions were stored up, and there had been no chance of securing a kris, let alone two, and Peter declared that it was all out of aggravation that some sentry or another always took up his daily task before the elephants came.

'They are making a regular custom of it, sir,' he said. 'Cuss them!'

'What's that, Pete?'

'I only said *custom*, sir. I warn't swearing. I won't say what I might have said if you hadn't been here.'

That very afternoon, as if fate had become weary of fighting against them, Peter, who had been watching the sentry's weapons with covetous eyes till it was beginning to grow dusk, suddenly uttered an ejaculation.

'What is it, Pete?'

'Look here, sir. Be smart, before it gets dark. I have been watching this 'ere chap for a hour. He has been nodding off to sleep all the time, and now he's off sound.'

'What of that?'

'Kris, sir,' said the lad; and crossing the floor of

Trapped. Q

the great building, he climbed cleverly up to the thatch and passed out, and Archie heard a faint rustling, and then sat listening in the dark till, after what seemed to be an impossibly short space of time, the rustling began again, and a few minutes afterwards Peter, panting heavily, dropped down on his knees by the subaltern's side.

'Well, was it still too light for you to venture ?' asked Archie.

'Poof !' ejaculated the lad. 'Ketch hold 'ere, sir ;' and he thrust the pistol-butt-like handle of a kris into his companion's hand. 'Sound as a top, sir. Ain't that prime ! Don't I wish he had had a mate, so that I could have got two !'

'But he will miss it as soon as he wakes,' exclaimed Archie.

'Not 'im, sir ; and if he does, he 'll think that one of his mates has been larking. Wait a bit, and I shall get another chance, for we ought to have two.'

But Fate was going to smile again, for the very next morning, in a wild state of excitement, the lad gripped his young officer's hand tightly between his own.

'No larks, sir,' he half-sobbed. 'Don't gammon me. If you don't feel strong enough, say so, and we 'll wait.'

'What do you mean ? What 's the matter ?' whispered back Archie.

'Look there, sir ! The helephants are coming, and there ain't no sentry.'

'Oh !' ejaculated Archie, wild now with excitement, 'I 'm strong enough for anything.'

'Then take it coolly, sir, just as if we weren't going to make a bolt. That chap must have been a bit sick last night, or been taking bhang or something, and he's overslept himself this morning. Now then! Spears—kris—victuals. Ready for action. Let's get part of the prog on to the thatch. You hand it up to me, and then mount yourself.— Oh dear, we sha'n't have half enough time!'

'But suppose the sentry comes?'

'Lie down on the thatch. You will be out of sight.'

The low muttering of the elephants was heard as Peter scrambled up to his hole in the roof. Archie handed up the spears, which the lad took, and used one to help him in drawing up the basket of provisions, leaving Archie to follow with a couple of cakes thrust into his breast; and by the time the young subaltern was climbing along the thatch preparatory to lowering himself down, five of the elephants had shuffled by, with the squat little driver mounted on the last, and disappeared round a curve of the narrow elephant-path.

As usual, their great fellow, Rajah, as Peter called him, was coming muttering up, apparently only seeing the ground just where he was about to plant his feet, so that he started and prepared to swerve as he suddenly caught sight of the private standing waiting for him, this being something entirely fresh.

But Peter did not lose his presence of mind; he called him by name and held out a piece of the cake, when the great animal uttered a loud grunt, stopped short, and extended his trunk, not to grasp the tempting offering, but to bring to bear his wonderful sense of smell before he was satisfied.

Then he passed his trunk over the lad's chest, muttering pleasantly the while, and taking the piece of cake, transferred it to his cavernous mouth.

'Now, Mister Archie, sir, bring what you can, and never mind the rest. We haven't a moment to spare. Come gently, whatever you do.'

Archie was slowly descending the slope of the great thatched roof, which seemed to be a perfectly easy task, but so novel to one who had not had Peter's experience that when he had nearly reached the eaves and was planting his feet carefully, in preparation for lowering himself down the eight or nine feet of perpendicular wall, whose trellis-work would afford him support, the tied-in piece of flat stone upon which he had planted his foot suddenly gave way, and slipped from the thin cane. A faint cry escaped from the young officer's lips as he grasped at the brittle attap mat, which gave way at once. He slipped over the ragged mat which formed the eaves, and the next moment, *crack, crack, crack*, he was hanging feet downwards, and then fell heavily in a cloud of dust bump upon the trampled earth, in company with a snake about six feet long, which began to glide rapidly away.

'You've done it, sir!' panted Peter; and then loudly, 'It's all right, old man,' he continued, as he held out the rest of the piece of cake. 'That's only his way of coming down. Whatcher frightened about? Oh, I see; it's that snake;' and catching up one of the spears which he had leaned up against the big door, he used it pitchfork fashion

to the writhing reptile, and sent it flying upward
on to the roof, for it to begin scuffling away amidst
the leafy thatch.

Phoonk! said the elephant; and he slowly turned
himself as if upon a pivot, and extended his trunk
to the coveted cake.

'Don't say you are hurt, sir!' whispered Peter.
'You can go on, can't you? Oh, do say you can!'

'Yes, yes,' panted Archie confusedly; 'I think I
am all right.'

'Then here goes for it, sir. I don't feel a bit
sure, but I am going to try as soon as I have fed
him a bit more. Don't you bother about the prog.
I am going to make him carry it as inside passengers.
It will please him, and if he will carry us we will
eat leaves or grass.—Come on, old man. Here you
are! Ripe 'nanas, and one of them pumpkin things.
What! rather have the pumpkin first?' he continued, as the great trunk curved slowly towards
the golden-hued, melon-like fruit. 'Can't swallow
that all at once, can you? And I don't want to
stop and cut it. What! you can? Oh, all right,
then. I forgot you'd got grinders as big as meat-
tins.—Good-bye, pumpkin.—Now, Mister Archie, I
am not sure, but I think I can say what the mahout
does when he wants him to kneel down. Then
don't you stop a moment, but climb up and get
hold of them ropes that he has got round him, pull
yourself up, and hold on. Ready?'

'Yes,' said Archie dreamily; but he was shaken
up and confused by his fall.

'Now, Rajah, kneel down!' cried Peter, in the
nearest approach he could recall to the Malay

mahout's command; and, to his great delight, the huge beast swayed from side to side and sank upon the earth, at the same time curving his trunk towards Peter as he raised his head.

'There you are,' cried Peter, as he passed a couple of the bananas he held ready, and the moment these had been grasped and the trunk lowered again, 'Now then, up with you!' cried the lad; and planting a foot upon one of the corrugations of the wrinkling trunk, Archie began to scramble up, passing over the animal's forehead, up between the extended ears and over the rugosities between head and neck.

He nearly slipped as he reached for one of the ropes that girdled the animal's loins, but recovered himself, and, to Peter's satisfaction, seated himself, holding on tightly by the howdah-stays.

'Here you are!' cried Peter again, and this time he handed a great lump of cake, which the elephant took contentedly.—'Now, Mister Archie, sir,' he cried, as he seized the two spears and handed them up, 'take hold; I'll carry one by-and-by.—Now, old chap,' he continued, 'it's my turn now. Up with you!' And once more his memory served him in giving some rendering of the mahout's command, for in his slow, lumbering fashion the monster began to sway.

'Hold tight, sir, whatever you do,' cried Peter.

'Yes. Are you going to walk?'

'Not me, sir; but I do wish that we hadn't got to leave that basket behind.'

By this time the towering beast was once more upon its feet, and Peter was puzzling his head for an order he had forgotten; but just as some misty notion of the Malay words was hovering in his brain the great trunk encircled his waist, he was lifted from the ground, and the next minute he was gliding safely into the mahout's place, his widely outstretched legs settling themselves behind the monster's ears.

'Now, Mister Archie, give us one of them spears. Got it! Now then—talk about a mahout!—*Geet! geet!* Netherway!' he cried, using the words familiar to him from the days when he used to watch the carters and their teams. 'What are you up to now?—Look at that, now, Mister Archie!' For, to the lad's great delight, the elephant had swung himself round a little, the effect being to Archie that of a heavily laden boat in a rough sea, and reaching out with his trunk towards the basket with the rest of the fruit, he had picked it up, and then began to march solemnly and sedately in the direction taken by the other elephants every morning since they had passed the great shed.

'Can you hold on, Mister Archie?' said Peter.

'Yes; pretty well. Are you all right?'

'Oh, I'm all right, sir; but 'ware trees as soon as we get into that path in front. Mind as the branches don't wipe you off.'

'I'll try.'

'I say, sir, don't the Rajah know how to take care of hisself!' cried Peter, carrying his spear diagonally, and looking as if he was prepared to use it if any one should present himself to stop their way. 'Now what do you think of our plan, sir?'

'Oh, it's splendid,' replied the young officer. 'But never mind me. Don't talk much, for I hurt my head a little when I fell.'

'Don't think about it, sir. It will soon pass off,' cried Peter without turning his head, and then muttering, 'Think of me talking to the poor fellow like that!—Now then, go ahead, Rajah! Best leg foremost, old man. Headquarters, please; and I hope you know the way, for I'm blest if I do. All I know is that I don't want to see that little chap again for him to go and fetch some of them guards.'

The elephant slowly shuffled along for the next ten minutes or so, before the first difficulty that presented itself to the amateur mahout appeared in front; for after they had pursued the regular elephant-path beyond the clearing for some little time, there in front was a dividing of the road, and upon reaching this the elephant stopped as if in doubt, and began slowly swinging his head, ending by planting the basket he carried upon the earth and helping himself to another of the coarse melons.

'Which way?' growled Peter, as he looked down each path in turn, the one being fairly trampled, but green with the shoots of the cane; the other showing the regular holes, and being wet and muddy in the extreme.

'All right,' thought the lad. 'That must be the way down to the river where t'others have gone for their bath. Right!' he cried, as the elephant raised the basket again and inclined his head slowly as if to follow the muddy path, from some distance down which came the grunting of the other elephants, when, in his excitement, Peter uttered a savage 'Yah-h!'

This did as well as the purest Malay order meaning to the left, for the elephant turned his head in the other direction at once, and then planting his great feet carefully in the fairly dry holes, he began to follow the greener path.

Squash—suck—squash—suck, on and on through the forest shades, and as the boughs of the jungle trees hung over here and there lower and lower in the great tunnel of greenery, so cramped in size that there seemed to be only just room for the elephant to pass along, Peter kept on looking back nervously, half-expecting to see his companion swept away from his precarious perch.

CHAPTER XXVIII.

PHOONK !

'I'M getting better fast, Pete,' cried Archie Maine, his voice sounding clearly above the *suck, suck* of the elephant's feet in the deep old tracks, and the *whish, whish* of the green cane-sprouts that shot out on either side from the wall of verdure.

'That's right, sir. You do comfort me. I've been thinking that it wasn't fair of me to be riding comfortable here while you've got nothing but a bit of rope to hold on by except your balance. But, I say, it ain't all best down here, for, my eye, ain't it 'ot !—quite steamy.'

'Yes; this tunnel is steamy and hot,' replied Archie.

'Oh, I don't mean the tunnel, sir. I mean Rajah's neck and these two great fly-flaps of his keeping all the wind out. I tried lifting up one of them, but I suppose it tiddled him—fancied he had got a big fly about him, I suppose. I say, Mister Archie, ain't it prime ! He don't seem to be going fast, but, my word, with these long legs of his how he does get over the ground ! But, I say, look ye here; wouldn't this be a jolly place if we was out for a holiday, instead of being like on furlough without leave ?'

'It's beautiful,' said Archie; for after they had travelled for some time in deep shadow, completely covered in, the jungle suddenly opened out, and their way was now between two perpendicular walls of dense green verdure. Just in front a couple of brilliantly green-and-gold, long-tailed paroquets suddenly flashed into sight as if about to alight, but, startled by the elephant, they flew off with sharp screams.

And now time after time large, wide-winged, diurnal moths and glistening butterflies flew up from where they had settled on the dew-drenched herbage and fluttered before them. Not far onward a flock of finches flew from the tops of the green banks, twittering loudly as they displayed the brilliance of the blue and yellow and green of their plumage and its varying shades. But this was only for a time. The jungle growth rose higher on either side till it shut out the sunshine, and once more the elephant-path wore the aspect of a deep, shadowy tunnel, while the air grew more moist and steamy, seeming stagnant to a degree.

'All right, sir ?' cried Peter, straining to look round.

'Yes, yes, Pete. My fall shook me a bit, and seemed to bring back the old aching in my head. But don't mind me. I feel quite happy now that we are getting farther and farther from our prison. We are free, and if I could only feel that we were going in the right direction I should not care.'

'Oh, don't care, sir ; don't care a bit. It 's chance it—chance it. Old Rajah 's taking us somewhere, and why shouldn't it be to headquarters ?'

'It 's not likely, Pete.'

'Very well, sir. Then I will have another go. What do you say to its being to the Rajah's palace ? I don't know where it is—only that it is somewhere in the jungle, not very far from the river. You've never been there, have you?'

'No, Pete, I haven't. But, as you say, it is not far from the river.'

'Well, sir, we can't be far from the river. It must be somewhere off to our right flank, and old Rajah here must know his way, or else he wouldn't be going so steadily on; and the beauty of these places is that when once you are on the right road you can't miss your way, because there ain't no turning.'

'But we passed one turning to the right.'

'Yes, sir. That's where the helephants went down to drink, and you see if we don't come to another farther on. But this is splendid travelling. How he does get over the ground! And if it warn't for the commissariat department one could go on day after day, just making a halt now and then for this chap to take in half a load of growing hay and suck in a tubful of water, and then go on again.'

'Hush! Don't talk so, Pete.'

'Why not, sir? I am doing it to keep up your sperrits.'

'But I want to listen.'

'Hear anything, sir?'

'I am not sure. But I keep expecting to hear some of the Malays in pursuit.'

'Not likely, sir. If they are they must be coming on one of the other helephants, and I don't believe any of them can walk as fast as this one does, so they are not likely to overtake us. We are safe enough so long as we can get old Rajah here to keep on. The only thing that fidgets me is the eating and drinking.'

'I should be glad to have some water,' said Archie, 'but I can wait till we come close to the river.'

'That's right, sir; but what about something to eat ? Old Rajah seems to have thought that all that was in the basket was meant for him, and he's tucked it inside and chucked the basket away. So don't be hungry, sir.'

'I have two of the cakes, Pete, inside my jacket.'

'What ! Oh, who's going to mind ? That's splendid noos, sir.—Go ahead, old chap. What are you flapping your ears about for ? Think you can hear water ?'

'There, Pete,' said Archie eagerly, 'I am nearly sure now I heard a faint cry far behind.'

'Oh, some bird, sir. Don't you get fancying that. We are miles and miles away from where we started, and as most likely we are pretty close to the river, it's one of those long-legged heron things, and if you hear anything else it's like enough to be one of them big frogs or toads. If it was to-night instead of being this afternoon, I should say it was one of the crocs. But I should know him pretty well by heart.'

The great elephant went patiently trudging on, mile after mile, with the heat so intense that Archie Maine had to fight hard to keep off a growing drowsiness, and he now welcomed the fact that the portion of the jungle through which they were being carried kept on sending down trailing strands of the rotan cane and other creepers which threatened to lasso him and drag him from his seat.

But no further cry or note of bird came to suggest danger from the rear, and as ⸢the drowsiness at length passed away, the question began to arise : what was to happen when darkness came on ?—for the afternoon was well spent.

It was after a long silence that Archie broached this question.

'What are we going to do when it's dark, sir ?' said Peter. 'Well, I've been a-thinking of that— not like you have.'

'How do you know what I've been thinking ?' asked Archie sharply.

'Well, I ain't sure, of course, sir, but I should think you are wondering what we should do if we come across a tiger. It strikes me that we needn't mind that—at least, not in front, for Mr Stripes wouldn't face these 'ere two great tusks. One of them would go through him like a shot. What I'm thinking of is the making of a halt, first clearing we come to. But if we do, who's going to tie up Rajah so that he sha'n't go back ? He might take it into his head to stop by the riverside for some water, but it strikes me, sir, that as soon as we got off he'd go back to the old stable to see if he couldn't find something to eat and drink.'

'Hush, Pete !' cried Archie excitedly.

'What for, sir ? Afraid he will understand what we are saying ?'

'Hush, I say !'

'All right, sir,' said Peter, speaking in a whisper. 'But he does keep cocking up his ears and listening.'

'Yes,' said Archie; 'I was in doubt before, but

I am sure now. It's some one keeps on hailing us from behind. Drive him on faster, for I am sure we are pursued.'

'What! make him gallop, sir? Why, it would chuck you off directly.'

'No; I think I could keep on. We must try and leave whoever it is behind. I couldn't bear for us to be taken again.'

'We ain't a-going to be, sir, so long as we have these 'ere toothpicks to fight with.'

'That's a last resource. Try to hurry the beast.'

'He won't hurry, sir. 'Tisn't as if I'd got one of them anchors, as they call them; and even if I had, poor old chap! I shouldn't have the heart to stick it into him as the mahouts do.'

'It wouldn't hurt him more than spurring does a horse, with such a thick skin.'

'But I ain't got one of them boat-hooky tools. Look here, sir; hand me that there kris. Ain't poisoned, is it?'

'The Doctor says they are not.'

'Let's have it, then, sir.—Why, what game do you call this?'

For at that moment, before any experiment could be tried with the goad, a faint, unmistakable hail was heard from far behind, running as it were along deep, verdant tunnels, and Rajah, after flapping his ears heavily, uttered a low, deep sigh, stopped short, and began to tear down green branches from overhead and convey them to his mouth.

'Oh, this won't do!' cried Peter angrily.—'Get on, sir—get on!'

The elephant uttered what sounded to be a sigh

and raised one huge leg as if about to step out, but only planted it down again in the same deep hole, went through the same evolution with another leg, subsided again, and went on crunching the abundant succulent herbage.

'It's no good, Pete,' said Archie bitterly. 'They are in full chase. The elephant recognises the cry, and you will never get him to stir.'

'An obstinate beggar!' grumbled Peter. 'Makes me feel as if I could stick that there spike right into him, though he is fanning my poor, hot legs with these flappers of his. Well, Mister Archie, I suppose it's no use to fight against him. He has got the pull of us, and there's only one thing for us to do now.'

'What's that, Pete?'

'Act like Bri'sh soldiers, sir,' said the lad through his set teeth. 'Hold the fort, and fight.'

At that moment the cry was more audible, and the elephant gave his ears a quicker flap and said, *Phoonk!*

CHAPTER XXIX.

PETER'S RAJAH.

'AIN'T it been a mistake, sir?' said Peter Pegg. 'We ought to have risked it both of us together, stirred him up with the spears or the point of that kris, and made him go on.'

'No mistake, Pete. He would have turned savage, and dragged you off as easily as he lifted you up, then knocked you down with his trunk and perhaps trampled you into the mud.'

'Perhaps you are right, sir; and it wouldn't have been very pleasant. But hark! There's a helephant coming, and you can hear the *suck, suck, suck* of his feet in the mud plainer and plainer. I wish whoever they are upon it would holloa again. I want to know how many that helephant's got on board.'

'I think only one,' said Archie.

'Oh, well, we are not going to give up to one, sir. I was afraid—I mean, 'spected—there'd be a howdah full, all with their spears and krises, and a mahout as well. Have you got any orders to give me, sir, about dismounting?'

'No; we must do the best we can from where we sit. What could we do if we got down into this narrow path full of mud-holes?'

'Nothing at all, sir,' replied Peter. 'I think just the same as you do. The helephant's getting very close now, so keep telling me what you see from up there, for I can see next to nothing where I'm sitting. Now, sir,' whispered the lad, 'can't you see him yet ?'

'No; the path bends round.'

'But you must see directly, sir.——Here, you keep quiet, Rajah, and leave them boughs alone.'

'I can see now, Pete,' said Archie eagerly. 'It's the smallest elephant, with a tiger pad on its back.'

'Yes, sir; but who's on it ?'

'Only one man—the mahout, in a turban.'

'Oh, him ! That little, squatty driver ! I can finish him off with one on the nose.'

'No; I think—yes, it is the mahout who rode into camp at the review.'

'What ! him, sir ? That's Rajah's own mahout —I mean, Rajah's his helephant. That's why he stopped. *Phee—ew !*' whistled the lad. 'Why, he's a friend of mine. I say, sir, we are not so bad off as I thought.'

'You've met him before, then, Pete ?'

'Course I did, sir—day of the sham fight. But I didn't know he was up yonder. He must have been there all the time, though he didn't show up. That little, squatty chap used to do all the work of taking the helephants to water, while he stopped back, too big to do any of that dirty work, and ready to ride when he was wanted.'

It seemed plain enough now that when the big elephant was missing, his mahout had come in search of the huge brute himself, and directly after the small elephant he was now riding bore him close up, butting its head against Rajah's hind-quarters and uttering a squealing, muttering sound, while, without turning his head, Rajah seemed to answer, and went on breaking off succulent boughs of leafage, to go on munching as if quite content.

But, heard directly above the gruntings and mutterings of the two elephants, the fierce-looking little mahout raised himself as high as he could in his seat and burst into a furious tirade in his own tongue, not a word of which could be grasped by his hearers, but its general tenor seemed to be a series of angry questions as to how dare these two English infidels take away his elephant, and bidding them get down directly.

'Can you understand all that, Mister Archie?' said Peter as the man paused to take breath.

'No,' was the reply. 'Can you?'

'No, sir; but it's all plain enough. Now, will you drop upon him?'

'I think you had better.'

'So do I,' said Peter, changing his position so that he could stand up on Rajah's neck, steadying himself by one of the pendent boughs, and resting the butt of one of the spears upon the animal's neck.

He had just finished this when the mahout, who had evidently prepared himself for his journey by donning his turban and his showy yellow baju and sarong, recommenced his torrent of abuse.

'Yah!' roared Peter as loudly as he could. 'Hold your row, you ugly, snub-nosed, thick-lipped, little cock-bantam of a man!'

The mahout stopped short and sat staring in wonder, with his mouth wide open and the corners

of his lips ruddy with the juice of the betel-nut
he had been chewing.

'How dah you?' roared Peter, in the loudest
and best imitation he could produce of the Major
in one of his angry fits. 'How dah you? I say.
How dah you? You flat-nosed little run-amucker!
Speak like that to a British officer!' And he
emphasised his last words by raising the spear and
bringing the butt down again heavily on Rajah's
neck, his energetic action making the great elephant
stir uneasily, so that the speaker was nearly dis-
lodged. 'Quiet, will you?' roared Peter, making
a fresh grab at the branch he held. 'Want to
have me overboard?'

The elephant grunted.

'Yah-h-h-h-h!' roared Peter, raising the spear
he held; and poising it after the fashion he had
learned from the Malays, he seemed about to hurl
it at the little mahout, whose head and shoulders
he could see plainly now just beyond Rajah's shabby
little tail. 'You dare to say another word, and I
will pin you where you sit, like the miserable little
beetle you are! Now then.——Here, steady, Rajah!
——Hold tight, Mister Archie! I am coming to you;
but just you make a show of that other spear.
You needn't get up, but make believe to be about
to chuck it at him if he isn't pretty careful.'

Archie held on more tightly to the rope girths
by which he had kept his position so long, while
Peter rather unsteadily joined him, bringing himself
so much nearer to the mahout that he could have
pretty well touched him had he extended his spear.

'I say, Mister Archie,' he said, 'if old Rajah takes

'You dare to say another word, and I will pin you where you sit, like
the miserable little beetle you are!'

PAGE 276.

it into his head to move on now, I shall pitch right on to old Chocolate there.—Yah-h!' he roared again.

The mahout, who had apparently begun to recover from his astonishment, had changed his ankus from one hand to the other, and was in the act of drawing his kris, when Peter yelled at him again and made so fierce a thrust with his spear that all the little fellow's pugnacity died out, or, as it were, passed away in a shriek of fear.

'Ah, that's better,' cried Peter. 'Now then, you have got to do what I tell you.'

The mahout's eyes rolled as he thrust back his kris into its sheath, the man's face turning from a rich, pale-brown hue to a dirty, pallid mud colour.

'Here, give us that kris, Mister Archie,' continued Peter in a blustering tone.

'You are not going to use it, Pete?' half-whispered the subaltern.

'You will see, sir,' cried the lad fiercely; and then he almost roared, 'He'd better not give me any of his nonsense!' And taking the kris in his hand, he held the blade threateningly towards the mahout and beckoned to him to come.

His gestures were so plain, and the manifestations with the little, wave-bladed dagger so easily comprehensible, that the poor, shivering, little wretch dragged himself out of his seat and knelt upon the head of the smaller elephant and bowed down with his hands extended as if asking for mercy.

'Ah, you know you deserve it!' roared Peter. 'Now then, give me that weapon—quick!'

The man raised his head a little and looked up at the lad, who was making a horrible grimace and rolling his eyes; and then seeming to fully grasp his meaning, he quickly drew kris and sheath from the folds of his sarong, and held them out to Peter, who snatched them away and handed them to Archie.

'Now then,' shouted Peter, 'don't you pretend you can't understand plain English, because if you do I'll'—— He raised the spear on high and made as if to deliver a thrust, with the effect that the mahout uttered a shriek of fear and banged his forehead heavily down between his hands. 'Now get up,' roared Peter; and the man raised his head and displayed a face and lips quivering with fear, shrinking sharply as the lad reached out and laid the blade of the spear upon the thinly covered shoulder. 'Now, you understand: if you try to play any games you will get this. D' ye 'ear?'

The poor fellow uttered a few words in his own tongue, and raised his hands together towards Peter as if begging for mercy.

What followed took some considerable time and proved a difficult task, for the mahout was almost beside himself with fear; but as soon as he grasped Peter's meaning he set to work excitedly, and with the cleverness born of experience he loosened the ropes of the tiger pad upon the lesser elephant, unlaced them, and with Peter's assistance dragged it on to the back of the larger beast, Archie having changed his place to Rajah's neck, where he sat facing the workers with a spear in each hand.

'Don't look so good-tempered, sir,' Peter stopped

for a few moments to say. 'Squeege your eyes
up, sir, and show your teeth, as if you meant to eat
the little beggar.'

'Oh, nonsense!' replied Archie. 'You have
regularly mastered him now. The poor little wretch
is half-dead with fright.'

'Yuss!' growled Peter, turning to give a savage
look at his panting little companion. 'He knows
what Great Britons are, sir; and it's lucky for him
he does.——Now then,' he roared, 'let's get this job
done.'

The mahout winced, and after a time the task
of securing the big, comfortable pad was finished,
and, in obedience to Peter, Archie took his seat upon
it, while the mahout made a gesture as if asking
whether he should go back now to his old seat on
the lesser elephant, which all the time was following
Rajah's example and making a hearty meal of the
succulent leaves.

'What does he mean by that, Mister Archie?'
whispered Peter. 'No, no, don't tell me! I see;'
and turning to the mahout, he roared out 'No!' and
pointed forward towards Rajah's neck. 'That's your
place,' he shouted; and the little fellow, grasping
Peter's meaning, crept past Archie and took his seat,
settling himself, with a sigh, with his legs beneath
the great beast's ears.

The big elephant, though apparently intent upon
demolishing as many leaves as he could contain,
proved himself to have been busy with his little,
pig-like eyes the while, for as the mahout took his
seat he began muttering and chuntering again, and
dropping a bunch of the green food, he turned up

his trunk and began to pass it over the body of his rider.

The look of fear had died out of the mahout's countenance as he turned his face to the two Englishmen, and he nodded and smiled rather pitifully, as he seemed to be feeling now that his life was going to be spared.

'All right!' shouted Peter; and the mahout winced again as he drew his ankus from where he had tucked it in the folds of his sarong, as if to signify that he was ready to perform any duties his masters wished.

'That's done it, Mister Archie,' said Peter. 'One can't understand everybody's lingo, but good, loud English goes a long way if you put plenty of powder behind it. You see now.—Forward!' roared Peter, and the mahout, who had been nervously watching his every movement, turned and spoke to Rajah, when the monster moved on at once into the deep, rich glow that was now penetrating the tunnel-like road, while the lesser elephant stayed for a few minutes to collect a good-sized bundle of twigs, and then moved after its fellow as contentedly as if everything were right.

'Then you are going to make him take us right back to camp, Pete?' said Archie.

'Yes, sir; that's the marching orders, if we can do it; but it won't be very long before it's dark.'

'Yes; it will soon be sundown. How long do you think the elephant will go on?'

'I d'know, sir. It's chance it—chance it, just as it's been ever since we started this morning. I say, though, this 'ere's more comfortable than riding barebacked, holding on to a rope, sir, eh?'

'Pete, my lad,' said Archie, with a sigh, 'it's wonderful! How did you manage it all?'

'Oh, sir,' said the lad modestly, 'it's only having a bit of a try. One never knows what one can do till you sets to work, and when you puts your back to it and goes in for chance it as well, it mostly turns out pretty tidy.'

'Yes, Pete; but what worries me now is what we are going to do when the elephant stops to rest or sleep.'

'Don't you worry your head about that, Mister Archie. I know you are weak and pulled down, but just you pay a bit more heed to what I say. It's what you ought to do now, and what we must do—chance it, sir, chance it, same as I'm doing about something else.'

'What else?' said Archie wearily, as he let his aching body sway with the movement of the great steed.

'About whether this is the right way or the wrong, sir. I don't know; you don't know. But perhaps old Rajah does, so what we have got to do, as I said before, is to keep our eyes on that little bantam of a Malay, and chance it, sir—chance it.'

CHAPTER XXX.

A JUNGLE NIGHT.

IT was just as the shades of night were coming on that the great elephant stepped out of the tunnel into comparative light. The wall of verdure opened out on either side, and a natural clearing lay before the travellers, while, still bearing what looked like the pale stain of sunshine, there flowing from right to left was the river.

There was a regular track marked out by the various animals that frequented it; and the mud-holes formed by the elephants grew deeper and more given to spurt out water as the great animals passed on till the edge of the river was reached, when they plunged in on to what now seemed to be firm, gravelly soil, with the clear stream pressing against their sides, till the smaller elephant was pretty well breast-deep.

Here Rajah stood, setting the example and drinking deeply, while those he bore began to suffer the pangs of Tantalus as they saw the clear stream gliding by.

'I can't stand this much longer, sir,' said Peter. 'Think there 's any crocs up here ?'

'It is impossible to say, Pete.'

'Yes, sir; but I am ready to risk it. But what I want to know first is : are we going back, or is this 'ere a sort of ford, and the path goes on the other side ?'

He had hardly spoken before Rajah uttered a
snort and went splashing on towards the opposite
shore, with the water growing shallower and shallower
till the two beasts were walking on firm, gravelly
ground, the water flying up at every step, and they
soon stood out on dry ground, with the dimly seen
track going on before them.

Here, at a word from the mahout, both animals
stopped short, and Rajah kneeled, when the mahout
descended nimbly and began trotting back to the
water's edge.

'Not going to cut and run, is he, sir?' began
Pete. 'No; it's all right. I can't quite see, but
ain't that a cocoa-nut he's stooping to dip?—Yes;
that's right. Good old chap! He's bringing us
a drink.'

This proved to be the case, and the little fellow
brought the refilled half-cocoa-nut-shell he had taken
from somewhere in his baju, and it was handed up
to the two lads four times, before the little fellow
went back to the river, filled it for himself, and
finally returned to his place and climbed up once
more.

Directly after, the elephant rose and continued
along the track to where, in the darkness, it was
evident the marshy land began, and beyond it seemed
the jungle once again.

Peter was ready enough to begin his favourite
advice soon after, and bid his companion chance
it, as on this side of the river the open land grew
more moist, and in the darkness the elephant's
huge feet sank in deeper and deeper, till at every
step they plunged in quite four feet, and it needed

a sturdy effort to withdraw them. Then all at once the Rajah uttered a grunt, half-turned as if to retrace his steps, and then stood fast, while his companion, making use of the prints he had left, half-turned likewise as if to meet him; and then both stood fast, pressing their heads together with a grunt.

'What does this mean?' said Archie with a look of wonder.

'I d' know, sir. Looks to me as if they are going to sleep.'

It was soon proved that the lad was right, for the animals, after uttering a low sigh or two, remained perfectly still, with the mahout dimly seen in his place and his head lowered down upon his chest.

'Well, sir,' said Pete, 'this is all plain enough, and it looks as if we may as well go to sleep too.'

'Sleep!' said Archie. 'With the risk of falling off this pad?'

'Oh, we sha'n't do that, sir. We must take it in turns.'

'Will they stand like this till morning? said Archie.

'Suppose so, sir. They can't fall over sideways, because their legs are stuck fast in these holes. Here, you have first go, sir, and I'll keep watch. Think this is a tigery sort of place?'

'They are fond of the river-side, Pete,' said Archie sadly; 'but I was thinking about crocodiles.'

'Haven't heard anything of them, sir; but, anyhow, we are safe up here, and we have got to chance it.'

'Oh,' exclaimed Archie impatiently, 'how sick I am of hearing you say that!'

'Yes, sir; you're a bit sleepy now. Just you slip one arm under this pad rope, and lie right over on your side, and you will go off. You may trust me, sir. I won't go to sleep.'

Utterly wearied out, the subaltern began to make some opposition, but he obeyed his companion's order, and five minutes after Nature had asserted herself and he was fast asleep.

How that night passed he could never afterwards recall, but he had some dreamy notion that he woke up and took Peter's duties of watchman, telling him to slip his arm under the pad rope and lie over upon his side so as to get his turn of rest. But it all proved to be imaginary, for the poor fellow, weak and still suffering from the effects of his wound, did not start up until the great elephant had begun to drag his legs out of the deep holes, when he trudged on towards where the track ran once more between two walls of densely matted palm growth; and he stared in wonder at his companion, hardly able to collect his thoughts so as to put the question that was troubling him and say:

'Have I been asleep all night, Pete?'

'Yes, sir; like a top. Feel better now?'

'No!' cried the lad passionately, for the confusion was passing off. 'I trusted you.'

'Yes, sir. All right. I have been listening to one of them great cats singing and purring right back on the other side of the river, and I never slept a wink.'

'Oh!' ejaculated Archie; but Peter chose to misunderstand him.

'Oh it is, sir,' he cried ecstatically. 'Take another look before we are shut in amongst the trees. It's lovely! It's the beautifullest morning I ever did see'.

CHAPTER XXXL

AN AWAKENING.

'YOU can't be sure, Pete. These elephant-paths through the jungle are all alike. There's the same half-dark, dense heat, the tangled walls on either side, the overhanging trees and loops of prickly rotan suspended overhead ready to catch you. How can you be sure that this is one that you have been along before?'

'I d'know, sir. What you say is very right, but I seem to feel that I've been along here before, and old Rajah must have been, or he wouldn't go swinging along as if he felt that he'd got nearly to the end of his journey. Shall I try and ask Mr Bantam there?'

'Oh no,' said Archie wearily. 'It's so hard trying to make him understand, and I always feel in doubt when you have tried.'

'Well, sir, we shall soon know whether it is, for I don't believe we are more than two or three miles from headquarters.'

'I'd give anything for you to be right, Pete, for I am nearly done up.'

'I know you are, sir, and I might say, so am I; for long enough it has seemed as if the hinge of my back was giving way, and when the helephant gives one of his worst rolls it just seems as if he'd jerk my head off. But cheer up, sir! I think it's all right, and we have done splendidly. We might have had to pull up and fight all the Malay chaps from up there by the Rajah's hunting-box. Of course we should have made a good stand of it, but how are you going to dodge spears in a narrow place like this? There, cheer up, sir! When you look happy over it I feel as if I am ready for anything; but when you go down in the dumps I haven't a bit of pluck left in me.'

'It will be dark soon, Pete. If we have to spend another night out in the jungle I must lie down under some tree.'

'Mustn't sir. Cold, rheumatiz', and fever. You will have to stick to your warm bed up here. But talk about a warm bed—you should have tried sitting like a mahout.'

'It will be dark in an hour, Pete,' said Archie, who seemed to pay no heed to his companion's brisk chatter.

'Not it, sir. Two hours—full, though I ain't got no watch. Not as that much matters. Old Tipsy has got a big, old silver one, but he says you never can depend upon it in this damp place. We have got plenty of time to get there yet, and see how old Rajah is swinging along! I am sure he knows his way.'

'Don't—don't—pray don't keep chattering so! It makes me feel worse than ever.'

'You think so, sir,' said Peter stubbornly, 'but it don't; it rouses you up, sir, even if it only makes you turn waxy and pitch into me.'

'Yes, yes, I know, Pete. It's because I'm so ill. It's like having a touch of fever again. Then you

must think what a beast and a brute I am to you—
a regular burden. I could feel it in my heart to
slip down under the first big tree and go to sleep,
even if I were not to wake again.'

'Hah!' said Pete dryly. 'That sounds bad, if it
was real, sir; but it's only what you fancy. How's
your head now?'

'That old pain seems back again worse than
ever.'

'Wish we'd stopped an hour ago when we crossed
back over the river again, and had 'nother good
drink. That must have been about one o'clock, I
should say. I don't know, though—I've about lost
count. Ain't it rum, sir, how rivers wind about,
and how the elephants' paths go straight across
them?'

Archie looked at him piteously; his eyes seemed
to say, 'Pray, pray don't keep talking!'

The look silenced his companion, and for half-an-
hour at least not a word was spoken.

Plosh, *plosh*, *suck*, *suck* of the elephants' feet
went on in the same monotonous way. A gleam of
sunshine now and then lightened the gloom of the
tunnel-like path, but besides the dreary sound the
silence was awful. By this time Archie seemed
to be quite exhausted, and as Pete passed an arm
round him and lowered him back on to the pad
before slipping a hand into his waistband to ensure
his not slipping off, the poor fellow's eyes were half-
closed, while those of his companion were fixed with
the lids wide apart, and with a fierce, staring look
gazed forward over the mahout's head in the wild
hope of seeing something that he could recognise,

something that would prove that they really were on the path that led to headquarters.

'I'm about beat out,' said poor Peter to himself. 'A chap wants to be made of iron to keep this up much longer, and I ain't iron, only flesh and blood and bones, and them not best quality—— upper crust. Oh! if I could only'——— He stopped short with his lips apart, face down, and one ear turned in the direction in which the mahout was staring.

'Oh!' he panted once again, 'is it, or am I getting 'lirious? Ah! there it goes again—or am I wrong? What's a bugle going for at this time in the afternoon? I'm a-dreaming of it. No, I ain't! Hooray!—Look up, Mister Archie, sir! It's all right. Cheer up, sir!'

'What! What! Who spoke?' said the exhausted lad, making an effort, catching at Peter, and dragging himself up and sitting clinging tightly to his companion's arm.

'Close in, sir. We shall be at the campong in five minutes, and in less than another on the parade-ground. Hooroar, sir! There's no place like home, even if it's out in a savage jungle.—Here, what are you panting at, sir, like that? Don't do it! You ain't been running.'

'You're saying this to keep me up, Peter.'

'I ain't, sir; I ain't. Look! Look! You can see for yourself now. There, them's the big trees where all the helephants sheltered at the review, and —brave old Rajah! He's making for it straight. There's a peep of the river too, and you can see the hut above the landing-place where I kept guard that night and listened to the crocs. Now then, what do you say to that? Am I right?'

Archie made no reply that was audible, but his lips parted as he muttered two words in fervent thanks; and the next minute Rajah had increased the rate at which he made his strides upon hard ground, and the open space before them was becoming dotted with moving men in their familiar white jackets, in consequence of an order that had been passed after a glass had been directed at the advancing elephant; while, as the great beast, as if quite accustomed to the place, strode in beneath the sheltering trees and stopped short, to stand with slowly swinging head on the very spot where Peter had first made his acquaintance, a burst of cheers rang out from officers and comrades, who came up at the double to welcome back those who had been given up for lost.

One of the first to reach the elephant's side was the Doctor.

'Archie, my lad!' he cried. 'Minnie! My poor girl! Speak, lad—speak!'

Archie's lips parted, and his old look of despair deepened as he tried to answer; but no word passed his parched lips, cracking now with fever and exhaustion. He only looked wildly in the Doctor's imploring eyes and shook his head.

The Doctor uttered a groan, and then, as the elephant knelt in response to the mahout's order, the Doctor's despair died away to make room for duty.

'Now, my lads,' he cried, 'half-a-dozen of you help them down and carry them carefully into

hospital.—Cheer up, boys! I'll soon put you right.
—Ah, Sir Charles! You here? I can't go.—Hold
up, man!—Go up to my place and speak to my wife.
But after this—be a man, sir!—there's hope for
us still.'

CHAPTER XXXII.

IN THE DOCTOR'S HANDS.

'LIE still. What have you got to fidget about? I have done all I can, and made a decent job of your head. It looks quite respectable now, after what I have done with the scissors. That hair ought to have been cut close off first thing, so as to afford a place for decent bandages, and I feel quite astounded to see how kindly Nature has treated you. It must have been an awful blow, my boy, and if you hadn't been of the stupid, thick-headed breed, you would have suffered from a comminuted fracture of the skull. Can't you lie still?'

'No, Doctor. I want to get up.'

'And make yourself worse?'

'No; but after what you have done, I feel so much better and more comfortable that I want to be up and doing.'

'Nonsense! You have been doing ten times too much, and I tell you seriously, sir, that another day or two of what you have gone through in making your escape, and you must have been dangerously ill with fever.'

'But I feel so much better, Doctor.'

'Of course you do. I was just able to catch you in the nick of time, and now I have done my part, and you must leave the rest to Nature.'

'But I want to go out with one of the detachments.'

'What for ? To break down directly, and interfere with the good four or half-a-dozen of the lads would be doing, from their time being taken up in carrying you on a bamboo litter ?'

'Oh Doctor, I shouldn't break down.'

'Oh, wouldn't you ? Nice piece of impudence ! Here am I, who have devoted half my life to the tinkering up of damaged soldiers, and know to a tittle how much a man can bear, all wrong, of course ! And you, a young jackanapes of a subaltern, a mere boy, tell me to my face that you know better than I do !'

'No, no, Doctor ; I beg your pardon !' said Archie. 'I don't mean that. It is only because I want to be out with the fellows, trying to run that brutal scoundrel down.'

'Yes, yes, my boy, I know. But wait. Everything possible is being done, and any hour the news may come in that my poor child has been found and some one has been shot down. Archie, my boy, nothing would afford me greater delight than to see that lurid-looking heathen brought in half-dead, and handed over to my tender mercies.'

Archie burst out into a mocking laugh.

'What do you mean by that, sir ?' said Dr Morley.

'I was thinking, Doctor, you would set to at once attending to his wounds, and making him well as soon as you possibly could.'

'What ! A treacherous, cunning savage ! I'd—— Well, I suppose you are right, boy. Habit's habit. But the British lawyers would tackle him afterwards, and he would get his deserts. They'd put a stop to him being Rajah of Dang any more. There, I 've no time to stop gossiping with you.'

'But when may I get up, Doctor? It seems so absurd for me to be lying here.'

'That's what you think. Well, there, I won't be hard on you. If you keep quiet now, and are as much better to-morrow as I found you to-day, and you will promise to be very careful, I 'll let you get up. Now I must go and see to that other ruffian.'

'Peter Pegg? But you are not keeping him in bed?'

'Oh no. He didn't get it so badly as you.'

'I say, Doctor, he 's been hospital orderly before: send him to attend on me.'

The Doctor frowned, and hesitated.

'Oh, very well. He might do that. He was as mad as you are two days ago, and wanted to go off with his company.'

'Send him in at once, Doctor.'

'For you two to talk too much? There, I 'll see.'

A couple of hours later Peter Pegg entered Archie's quarters, looking very hollow-cheeked and sallow, and displaying a head that had been operated upon by the regimental barber till there was nothing more left to cut off, and stood holding the door a little way open, and showing his teeth in a happy grin.

'Ah, Pete! I wanted you,' cried Archie.

'Did you, sir? Here I am, then. Doctor says I am to do anything you want, only you are not to talk.'

'All right, Pete. Then tell me, what's being done?'

'Three detachments is out, sir—one under Captain Down, one under Mr Durham, another under old Tipsy.'

'Yes? Go on.'

'They're a-scouring the country, sir; and I hope they'll make a clean job of it.'

'Yes, yes; but tell me everything.'

'Ain't much to tell, sir; only one party's gone up the river in Sir Charles's boat, and he's with them.'

'Yes?'

'And another party's gone down the river to search Mr Rajah Hamet's place.'

'But I heard that he came up here and brought in my boat, and spread the news of our being killed.'

'Yes, sir; and the Major, when we came back, said he'd been gammoning him, and that he must have been in the business.'

'No, no,' said Archie thoughtfully; 'I'm sure the Major's wrong. Well, go on. Which way has Captain Down gone?'

'He has gone along the road to the Rajah's palace, to take him prisoner and make him give an account of himself.'

'Right away in the jungle, along that elephant-track? They have taken tents, of course.'

'I d'know, sir; but they've took possession of Mr Suleiman's two helephants.'

'Ah, capital!' said Archie. 'This is fresh news.'

'Yes, sir; and I suppose Mr Suleiman will never get them again. They ought to be prize money.

We took them, sir. My word, I should just like to have the old Rajah!'

'Of course,' said Archie contemptuously. 'Nice thing for a private soldier! A white elephant, Pete.'

'Why, he's a blacky-gray un, sir. Wish I could be his mahout.'

'Stuff! Where's Mr Durham gone?'

'Don't know, sir. Private instructions. Through the jungle somewhere, I expect, so as to take Mr Suleiman in the rear. But I say, sir, you don't mean to be kept in horspittle, do you?'

'No, Pete; I'm to be up to-morrow.'

'Hooray, sir! I'm all right too—ready for anything. Try and put in a word for me.'

'Of course, Pete.'

'Thank you, sir. You and me has had so much to do with this business that they ought to let us go on in front over everything.'

'We can't help it, Pete. Soldiers must obey orders. Still, there's one thing: they can stick our bodies into hospital, but they can't stick our hearts. They go where we like. Now, is there anything more you can tell me about what's going on?'

'Can't recollect anything, sir. But I shall pick up everything I can; you may depend upon that. I suppose you know, sir, that the Major's chucking out the orders right and left, and it's all just as if we were surrounded by the enemy.'

'No, chuckle-head! How could I know all that? You mean, I suppose, that the garrison is in a regular state of siege?'

'Yes, sir, that's it; only I couldn't put it like that. Don't be waxy with a poor private as old Tipsy says is the most wooden-headed chap in the company.'

'Now go on telling me.'

'Sentries are doubled, sir, and the chaps says it's precious hard now we are so short of men.'

'Then they should draw in the lines,' said Archie eagerly.

'Yes, sir; that's what they have done.'

'Oh, of all the thick-headed—— Here, I won't get cross, Pete. But you do make me wild. Why didn't you tell me all this?'

'Too stupid, I suppose, sir. But don't give me up. I will try better next time. Want to ask me anything now, sir?''

'No. Be off.'

'You don't mean you are sacking me, do you, sir?' half whimpered Peter.

'No-o-o-o! Be off. Go amongst the men and pick up every bit of news you can, and don't shrink '——

'Not me, sir.'

'And what you can't get from the men, ask any officer you meet.'

'I say, Mister Archie, sir!'

'Say you are asking it for me.'

'That's better, sir. Then I'm off.'

It was quite dark when Peter entered the room again, hurried to Archie's bedside, and then stopped short.

'Fast asleep,' he said to himself. 'Ought I to wake him? Oughtn't I to wake him? Chance it. —Mister Archie, sir! Asleep, sir?'

'What? Yes—no! Oh, it's you, Pete!'

'Jump up, sir. You won't hurt,' said the lad breathlessly. 'It's a beautiful, hot night. I've picked something up, and I've run up to tell you. Come to the window, sir, and look out.'

Archie sprang out and followed Peter to the open window, from which they had a full view of the landing-place, where lights were moving and their bearers could be seen hurrying to and fro.

'What boat's that?'

'Resident's, sir. I have come up to tell you.'

'Yes—be smart! Tell me what?'

'Sir Charles and his party have come back, sir.'

'From the up-river expedition?'

'Yes, sir. I got hold of one of the chaps who went with him.'

'Well, go on; I'm burning to hear. What have they found out?'

'He says, sir, that the Major did not want Sir Charles to go, and they had words together. He heard Sir Charles say the attack was made on the boat up the river, as well you and me know, sir.'

'Yes, Pete,' said Archie, who was listening and watching the movements of the boat at the same time.

'And that he felt sure Miss Heath must have been carried right up-stream, and that they should find her in one of the campongs, or kept shut up in some place belonging to the Rajah.'

'Well, go on.'

'And then the Major said, sir, to Sir Charles that they weren't quite sure that the Rajah had done this, and that he should be obliged if Sir Charles would

stay, and let one of the officers go instead. Then
Sir Charles says that he's morally sure that it was
the Rajah's doing, and that he feels he must go.
And then they went, and they've been right up the
river as far as they could get the big boat; and they
landed over and over again and searched the campongs and examined the people, who all said they
did not know anything about it, and looked stupid,
as these Malay chaps can look when they don't want
to tell tales; and at last Sir Charles had to give
up, after he had been down with something like
sunstroke.'

'Yes—go on quickly,' said Archie.

'And he went onsensible like, and there was
nothing else they could do but bring him back.'

'And they brought him back ill?'

'Yes, sir; and those chaps you can see there with
the lanterns are coming back from carrying him up
to the Residency.'

'Poor chap! Poor fellow!' said Archie. 'Well,
go on.'

'That's all, sir. Don't you see they're tying
the boat up for the night? I thought you would
be satisfied if I picked up something.'

'Too much this time, Pete,' said Archie sadly.

'Too much, sir?'

'Yes. It's all bad.'

'But you said I was to bring everything, sir.'

'Yes, yes; that's quite right. But it is so dis-
heartening. They must have taken her up somewhere; for aught we know, poor girl! she may be
a prisoner somewhere in one of the places near that
elephant-shed.'

'Near what elephant-shed, sir?' said Peter rather vacantly.

'Why, where we were prisoners.'

'Oh no, sir. Didn't I get out that night and go and look everywhere?'

'No. There might have been scores of other buildings up there. You couldn't have seen much.'

'No, sir, I didn't. It was so dark, and there was that tiger.'

'Here, I've got leave to be up to-morrow, and I must see what I can do.'

'Don't think you could have done any more than I did, sir, that night.'

'I know that, Pete; but I want to be trying now all the same. Here, I know; I'll get the Major's permission to go up and join Sergeant Ripsy and make a better search up there.'

'Spite of the tigers, sir?'

'In spite of ten tigers, Pete, for I shall have men with me, and rifles.'

'Think old Tipsy will like it, sir?'

'I think Sergeant Ripsy is a stern old British soldier who would do his duty, Pete.'

'Well, yes, sir. He's a hard nut, but he's all that you say. I'd rather be under anybody else, but you talk about ten tigers: I'd go under ten Sergeant Tipsys if it was to bring Miss Minnie back.'

'I know you would, Pete. And poor Sir Charles was knocked over by the fever?'

'Sunstroke, sir.'

'Well, sunstroke. He's *hors de combat*, and we want to take his place.'

The next day Archie signalised his permission to be about by asking for an interview with his commanding officer, who congratulated him warmly, and then replied to his request with an imperative:

'No! Quite out of the question, sir. I have weakened my force too much as it is, and I cannot spare another man.'

'Horribly disappointing,' said Archie to himself as he came away—'but he did call me *man!*'

CHAPTER XXXIII.

A DESPATCH.

ARCHIE MAINE had been round visiting posts
in the faint hope of picking up some fresh
news from the men, after the hurried mess
dinner, glad to get out into the comparatively cool,
soft night air; for the Major had sat in his place,
hardly speaking a word to any one present, and
for the most part with lowered brows, deep in
thought.

The night was as beautiful as ever; the brilliant
stars that spangled the sky looked twice as large
as those at home, and the reflections, blurred by
the motion of the river, seemed larger still. The
fire-flies sparkled in every bush, and the distant
cries of the jungle floated softly on the night air.
But everything seemed to bring up thoughts of
trouble and misfortune. The native messengers
sent in from the search-parties brought no good
tidings, and to the lad, still suffering to some extent from his injury, everything seemed to suggest
despair.

'I can't help it,' he said to himself. 'I'm sure
I'm strong enough. I'll go round by the Doctor's
and beg and pray him to tell the Major that I might
very well go to the front, if it's only to join old
Ripsy. I might be of some help to him. Yes, Pete
ought to go with me. We know more about the
part there by the elephant-stables, and with him

and his men we could follow up some of the paths where poor Pete dared not go.'

On the impulse of the moment he turned back and made for the mess-room, to try there first, though half in doubt as to whether he might find that his chief had gone back to his own quarters, where he was now prone to shut himself in.

The lad had been sauntering very slowly and doubtfully before. Now he quickened his pace as he thought over his adventures when a prisoner in the elephant-stable; and as he recalled watching the going to and fro of the elephants, he felt more than ever that he ought to be there helping the surly old Sergeant.

'Not gone,' he said, as he came into sight of the open window of the mess-room, where the shaded lamp was casting down its light upon the stern-looking, gray head of the old officer, who had a paper lying before him, which he was scanning, while just at the other side of the table the lad could see the swarthy countenance of a native, whom he recognised at once as one of the followers of the regiment.

Archie's heart began to beat fast, for he grasped the fact at once. This was evidently the bearer of a despatch from one of the detachments, for a private was standing in the shade resting his piece on the floor, after bringing in the man handed over to him by a sentry.

As Archie passed into the veranda the Major heard his step and looked up.

'Who's that?' he said.

'Maine, sir.'

'Oh, just right. Come here. You may as well know. This is a rough scribble from Sergeant Ripsy.'

'Good news, sir?' burst out Archie sharply.

'Not likely, my lad—no. He writes of his safe arrival at what he calls the elephant-pens, and as a matter of course too late. The place is quite deserted —not a man there—and the elephants have all been driven off. But he adds that he is following up the trail as well as he can, and that it is very hard to trace, because the great animals always step into the old tracks, and you can't tell which are the new; but that he means to follow them until he comes up to where they have been driven. There, I have no more to say.'

Archie, seeing that his presence was not needed, stepped out into the darkness again, walking some minutes without any definite aim, till, finding himself near the Doctor's bungalow, he thought he would call in there and give him the news, such as it was.

But as he neared the gateway and saw through one of the open windows a bent figure just shown up by the lighted lamp, his heart failed him, for thoughts full of memories of the past came to him with a rush; and he stepped on, when, just as he was at the end of the creeper-burdened bamboo fence, a gruff voice exclaimed:

'Who's that? You, Maine?'

'Yes, sir.'

'What is it? Want me?'

'No, sir. I was only just going by.'

'Humph! That's a sign you're better. Why didn't you call in?'

'I hadn't the heart, sir. I could see Mrs Morley sitting there with her head resting in her hand, and it set me thinking, sir.'

'Good lad! Yes, of course. But she'd have taken it kindly, my lad, if you had dropped in to see her now that she is in such trouble.'

'But I was afraid she would think I had brought some news, sir, and then she would have been disappointed.'

'No, boy. She and I are both getting hardened to trouble now. We have pretty well given up hoping for anything good. There, come in, my lad.'

He laid his hand on Archie's shoulder, and they walked into the house together, Mrs Morley startling the visitor as he noted how thin and old-looking she had grown.

'Ah, Archie,' she said, as he saw by the lamp that the tears had started into her eyes, 'I am so glad to see you—so much better, too. But '———— She turned quickly away, tearing her handkerchief from her pocket, and the next minute she would have thrown herself sobbing in a chair but for the entrance of one of the native maids, who in her broken English announced that there were two people wanting to see the Doctor.

'Not the proper time for them to come,' said that gentleman. 'Who are they? People who have been here before?'

'Yes, sahib,' said the girl. 'It is Dula, with her husband.'

'Child bad again!' muttered the Doctor. 'Where are they? In my room?'

'Yes, sahib.'

There was only a little lamp, . . . but it threw up the figure of a slight,
graceful-looking native woman and a tall, fierce Malay.

T.   PAGE 307.

'Don't go away, Archie. Stop and talk to the wife till I come back.'

The Doctor passed out of the room, and Mrs Morley turned to Archie, to say imploringly:

'Have you brought any news?'

He shook his head.

'Nothing—nothing?' she cried, in a tone of voice which made the lad feel almost ready to reproach himself for being alive and well when his companion whom he had taken light-hearted and merry from that very room, so short a time before, was—where?

'Here, Maria—Archie!' came in a sharp tone of voice which made them both start. 'Here—quick!'

There was only a little lamp, which gave forth a faint light, upon the table of the Doctor's surgery and consulting-room, but it threw up the figure of a slight, graceful-looking native woman and a tall, fierce Malay; and, jumping at conclusions, Archie judged by the man's bandaged head that he had been wounded, and that his companion had brought him to the Doctor for help.

The Doctor sprang from his seat as his wife entered, drew his chair on one side, and thrust her in.

'Now, be calm, my dear. Be a woman! You know these people?'

'Yes, yes!' exclaimed Mrs Morley in agitated tones, as the woman stepped forward, to go down on one knee and kiss her hand, while the man muttered something and then drew himself up rigidly.

'And you think we can trust—depend upon what they say?' continued the Doctor, with his voice quivering.

'Yes. Speak! Tell me, what is it?' cried Mrs Morley excitedly.

'Well, be calm, then. Be quite calm and firm, as I am. Minnie is alive and safe.'

'Ah!' ejaculated Mrs Morley, as she sank back and buried her face in her hands; while the woman now fell upon her knees, catching up Mrs Morley's dress and holding it to her lips as if to choke back her sobs.

'And I told you to be firm,' said the Doctor pettishly. 'This man has escaped from up-country somewhere—I don't know the confounded place's name. He was overtaken and wounded by some of Rajah Suleiman's people, so that he shouldn't tell tales, I suppose. But he says he can show us where the young English lady has been kept a prisoner, and that she is quite safe.—Isn't that so?' he added, turning to the man.

The Malay stared, muttered something, and then turned to look appealingly at his wife.

'Oh, of course! You didn't tell me; it was she. Let's see. You are the man that came to me months ago for '—— The Doctor finished in pantomime by making believe to take hold of his own jaw, apply a key, and wrench out a tooth.

The man smiled and nodded, and the Doctor added a few words in the Malay tongue; while the woman now sprang up and began to talk volubly in her own language, uttering short, sharp sentences, which the Doctor punctuated with nods and:

'Yes—yes—I see—I see—exactly. But, hang it all, my good woman!' he exclaimed in English, 'don't talk so fast. I only know a smattering of

your tongue.—She puzzles me, my dear. It's all
tongue.—Who the British Dickens wants to know
that your little one is quite well again and strong,
at a time like this ?'

He spoke again in Malay, and the woman nodded
and began to gesticulate again, in company with a
fresh flow of words.

'Yes, yes, yes,' said the Doctor; 'I am very glad,
of course.—Now, my dear, this is not like you,' he
continued. 'Remember you are a doctor's wife.—
Did you ever see such a woman, Archie ?'

'Never, Doctor,' replied the lad, coming forward
out of the darkness to take Mrs Morley's hand and
kiss it.

'There, I am quite firm now, Henry,' said Mrs
Morley; and drawing the native woman towards
her, she kissed Dula on both cheeks.

'Now let's have a few quiet words together,' said
the Doctor.—'No, no, Archie; what are you going
to do ?'

'I thought I ought to go and tell the Major, sir,
at once.'

'Not yet. Wait a bit, my lad. We must have
a consultation here. I feel as you do, my dear
boy; I want to rush back with these people at once.
But this is a ticklish affair, and we must do nothing
rashly. You see, we have learned this. It's been
a bad case, and we must run no risks. We have
learned this—for certain now. It was Suleiman's
men who carried Minnie off and nearly killed you,
and, with all the native cunning, he sent his people
here to fetch me to doctor him for his so-called tiger
scratch. By Abernethy ! if I'd known, I'd have

poisoned it so that it wouldn't have got well for a year.—No, I wouldn't,' he grunted. 'I am getting a tongue as bad as that woman's. But steady, steady! We know for certain that he carried her off; and this man, being a fisherman, has been living at a spot up the river where our poor darling has been taken and kept hidden. And just think of it, Archie: how clever a blackguard needs to be when he's going to do anything wrong! Talk about Fate! See how busy the old girl has been here! The blackguard, with all his crafty cunning, hides her somewhere close to the place where two of my best patients live, and they have had an eye upon her ever since, and just when we were in our most despairing time come and tell us of her fate.'

'Yes, sir; and now'——

'Stop a minute, my boy. I just wanted to say to you, I am ready to draw the teeth of all the Malays in the district without fee, and I am prepared to say that some of them are as grateful as we can be ourselves.'

'Yes,' cried Archie; 'but business is business.'

'Thank you, boy; thank you for pulling me up. I can't help it just now. Poor Minnie is to me just as dear as if she were my own child, and I am quite overturned—hysterical as a woman, more shame for me! Here, it was only the other day you came whining to me about being all wrong because you are such a boy. You said you thought you were not as you should be—that you wanted to be a man. Didn't I tell you, sir, to wait—that all you wanted was a little real trouble, and that it

would come fast enough and make a man of you?
Well, do you feel like a man now?'

'No, sir, not quite; but I feel man enough to
start to-night as one of a strong party to go and
rescue Minnie Heath, even if we die in doing the
good work.'

'Well said, my lad; and I'll go with you, and
you sha'n't die, any of you, if I know anything of
wounds. There, I'm pulled up now, and ready for
anything.—Maria, my dear, see to these people—
rest and refreshment, anything they want—while
I'm gone; and you can set the girl to work talking
to this Dula here. Make her your interpreter.—As
for you—here, I know what you'll like.'

The Doctor took a cigar-box from the shelf,
snatched out three or four, pressed them into the
fisherman's hand, and then almost dragged him out
into the veranda, where he thrust him into a cane
chair and gave him a light. 'One moment, Archie;'
and he spoke to the man, who was smiling up at
him. 'That's right, Archie; they came in a boat.
Come along up to the Residency.—No; I'll go there.
You run on to the Major and ask for orders. He'll
find us a little detachment to take with us in the
Resident's boat. This means good business, my
lad, for we have found out the real seat of the
disease.'

CHAPTER XXXIV.

THE MAGAZINE.

'YOU don't say so, my lad! A Malay and his wife who have been patients of the Doctor bringing in such news as that! Why, it's grand! Poor, dear girl! Tut, tut, tut, tut, tut, tut, what she must have suffered! Well, Mr Rajah Suleiman will have to pay for it. Morley says he believes in these people. Not some trap, is it?'

'He feels sure not, sir. The people are grateful to him for all he has done for them. Oh, I am certain it is genuine, sir.'

'Don't be too sure, my lad. These people can't help looking upon us as their enemies, and they are as treacherous as they are high. Look at this Suleiman. I have been trusting him. I looked upon him as a sensual brute, but it was so much to his advantage to be friendly. The fool! He's given his country away. He will be either shot or made prisoner, and then another Rajah who is friendly to us will reign in his stead.'

'Rajah Hamet, sir?'

'No,' said the Major shortly. 'And look here, young fellow, don't you mention him to me again. He's your friend, and you have a strong bias towards him.'

'I can't help believing in him, sir.'

'Then you must, sir, as a British officer, working for your country's good. I presume you don't know that I have it on trustworthy authority that Rajah Hamet has been for some little time past strengthening his position and gathering his men, like the savage he is, to go out on the war-path? And all the time he has been educated in England! A young fool! Well, this news is splendid, but it comes at a horrible time. Here is Suleiman hanging about, dodging our men; Hamet in all probability waiting for us to be in a dilemma, and then he will come down; and my little force here depleted till we are as weak as weak. I ought to say I can't spare a man. I feel it's my duty to refuse to send an expedition to save that poor girl. It means sending up a couple of boats with not less than twenty men, for Suleiman is sure to have a certain number of the brutes in charge of the place. But of course it must be done, and they must start at once. Where's the Doctor?'

'Gone on to the Residency, sir.'

'Yes. And I want Sir Charles. Send a man to ask him to step here.—No; go yourself—save time.'

Archie was making for the door, when steps and voices were heard, and the Resident hurried in, closely followed by Dr Morley.

'You have heard this news, Knowle?'

'Yes; everything.'

'And you will send a party of men at once?' said the Resident in a half-suffocated voice.

'Directly we can man the boats.'

'Ah!' exclaimed the Resident, sinking into a chair, with his hand to his breast.

'But you are not fit to go with them.'

The Resident smiled faintly and made a gesticulation.

'It's no use to waste words, Knowle,' said the Doctor. 'I know better than you what he can stand, and I have told him it is madness to think of it.'

'Yes; and I am going to be mad,' said the Resident bitterly. 'If you have not given your instructions already, sir, pray do so at once. At all costs I must go.'

The Major shrugged his shoulders.

'I want two boats,' he said. 'I am going to take yours, of course. But one of my difficulties is, who is to take charge of the expedition?'

Archie started, and his lips parted to speak.

'I shall take charge of it,' said the Resident.

'Very well.—You are not fit to go, Maine?' said the Major.

'Oh yes, sir,' cried Archie eagerly.

'No, sir,' cried the Major; and the subaltern's brow puckered up in his disappointment. 'And I can't spare you,' continued the Major. 'But under the circumstances I must, for I can spare no one else. Of course there will be a sergeant and a corporal —and a nice state we shall be left in here!—You, Dallas, take my advice. If you really mean to go, leave all the preparations to the Doctor. But really I think you had better let him go in your place.'

'Yes,' said the Doctor; 'and it is my duty to my child.'

Sir Charles made an angry movement, and the Major was about to issue his orders, when he sprang from his seat, for a rifle-shot rang out on the still night.

'What does that mean?' exclaimed Sir Charles.

There was another shot, followed by another and another.

'Attack, and in force,' cried the Major, crossing to the side of the room, to catch up hurriedly his sword and belt; and he was busy buckling the latter as the bugle rang out the assembly.

By the time he was out in the front the sentries were being driven in, and announced that the Malays were advancing in force; and almost immediately two of the men hurried out of the darkness supporting one of their comrades, who was bleeding profusely from a spear-wound, the weapon thrown by one of the attacking Malays being carried by a fellow-soldier.

The men turned out without the slightest confusion, and fell into their places under the direction of the officers remaining for the defence of the cantonments, and so well had the arrangements been previously planned out that the rush of the advancing enemy from three sides of the cantonments was temporarily checked by the steady fire of the defenders; but not before two more of the sentries had been carried into the mess-room, where the Major, hurrying in to see what was being done, found the Doctor in his shirt-sleeves busily attending to the men's wounds.

'Oh, there you are, Major!' he said, speaking with a strip of bandage in his mouth. 'This looks like my taking command of the expedition, doesn't it?'

'Yes. Impossible,' said the Major. 'The brutes are coming on in numbers, and much as I regret what you must feel, I am only too thankful that your party has not started. But there, you see I can do nothing until we have driven these scoundrels back, and then——we shall see.'

'Yes, I know,' grumbled the Doctor.—'You can take hold of one end of that bandage yourself, my lad. That's right. Nasty cut; but you are not going to lose the number of your mess this time.'

'Oh no, sir!' said the wounded man excitedly. 'Tight as you can, please, sir. I think I can go back to the firing-line, and——ah!'

'I don't,' said the Doctor grimly. 'Poor lad— talk about British pluck!'

'Not a bad wound, is it?'

'Quite bad enough,' said the Doctor. 'An inch lower, sir'——

'Yes, I know,' said the Major, as the firing increased. 'Why, they've got muskets! There, Doctor, I felt that I must speak to you, and I am afraid you are going to have your hands pretty full.'

'But you should keep your men more under cover, sir,' said the Doctor pettishly. 'Look! They are bringing in two more.'

'Under cover!' said the Major angrily. 'Every fence, wall, and breastwork is occupied, and the men are holding the Residency according to orders. These poor fellows were speared at their posts.'

The Major hurried out, to busy himself with seeing that the various occupants of the place were provided with shelter in the officers' quarters and the other buildings of the cantonments, the upper windows of which were occupied by the little force, with instructions to retire to the Residency, which was so situated that it would lend itself well to being treated as a sort of citadel in case they should prove to be hard pressed.

Fortunately for the defenders, as the night advanced the smoke from the firing hung low, prevented as it was from rising by a gathering river mist; and as not a light was shown in either of the buildings, the firing of the Malays from the sheltering trees and cultivated gardens of the station had little effect, while of the many spears that were thrown after the first attack was made, hardly one found a victim.

The men, in obedience to orders, were now firing only from time to time at the sheltering Malays, who kept on creeping up to hurl a spear in at a dimly seen open window, more than one not being sharp enough in jumping back, for his activity was checked by a bullet which sent him tottering for a few yards before falling heavily with a groan.

This had the effect of bringing the flash and heavy, dull report of the old, cast-off military muskets which the Malays were using; and as these weapons flashed, the defenders of the various buildings seized the opportunity to return the fire, guessing at the enemy's position by the light.

Just about this time, when a loud yelling from the direction of the river suggested that a fresh party of the enemy were landing from boats, a dimly seen officer hurried through the darkness to one of the upper rooms.

'Who's in here?' he cried angrily.

'Me, sir—Smithers, sir.'

'You are wasting your cartridges.'

'Am I, sir ?'

'Yes. Wait till we get some daylight, unless you can make sure of your man.'

'All right, Mr Maine, sir. It is you, isn't it ? I was getting a bit excited-like. One moment, sir : have you seen my missus ?'

'Your wife ? No. Why ?'

'She told me she was coming up to help the Doctor.'

'Oh, nonsense ! She ought to be with the women. I will tell her if I see her.—There, look,' whispered Archie—'to your left ! There are half-a-dozen fellows at least creeping through that patch of fog.'

'They look big uns, too, sir,' whispered the man excitedly, as the indistinct figures were magnified by the mist. 'Would it be waste of cartridges, sir, to get two in a line and let go ?'

'No. Fire !'

Crack went the rifle, and the figures that had loomed up seemed to melt away. But as soon as the rifle had flashed there was the *pad, pad, pad* of hurried steps, something whizzed in at the window, and with a dull thud a spear stuck in the floor of the room.

Crack, crack came from Archie's revolver as he fired it twice in the direction of the spear-thrower, an answering yell suggesting that one of the shots had had effect.

'There, keep a sharp lookout, and only fire when you are sure,' said Archie as he made for the door, striking against the bamboo shaft of the spear. 'This didn't graze you, did it, Smithers?'

'No, sir. I was afraid you had got a touch by your whipping out your pistol so quickly. But please, sir, don't tell my missus to go into shelter. She likes a job like this, and she's very useful with a basin and sponge.'

'All right; all right,' replied Archie; and hurrying away, he took the mess-room on his way to the post he was about to visit, and stepped to where a faint light rose from behind a Japanese screen which shut off one corner of the big room.

There he came upon the Doctor busy over one poor wounded fellow whose head was resting upon the arm of a kneeling woman, who held a sponge in the hand at liberty, while a great brass lotah of water was at her side.

'Very useful with basin and sponge,' said Archie to himself, as he smiled grimly.—'Can I do anything for you, Doctor?' he said.

'Not unless you have come to help, my lad.'

'No, sir; I can't do that.'

'Well, you can stop some of these scoundrels throwing these abominable spears.'

'Not till daylight, I'm afraid, sir; and I fear that this light will be seen outside.'

'Can't help it,' said the Doctor. 'I can't play Blind-Man's Buff and stitch up wounds without a lamp. I want more help.'

'Shall I ask Mrs Morley to come, sir?'

'My wife? No. She is busy with the women and children, and running off now and then to give the poor fellows a drink of water. Here, I

know : set some one to find that ragamuffin Pegg.
He'd be worth anything to me now, for he's handy
over this sort of thing.'

'Yes, Doctor; but he's one of our best shots with
a rifle, and the Captain has posted him where he
covers the river path.'

'Oh, well, then, you can't spare him, of course.
But look here, Archie; the wounded are being brought
in too fast. Tell the Major that I say that he must
blaze away a little to hold the enemy back.'

'Do you want him to cut me down, sir? He's
in a furious temper.'

'Enough to make him. So am I. I nearly
stuck a lancet into Sir Charles Dallas a few minutes
ago for coming and worrying me about the possibility of a party of men stealing off to one of the
boats with him. The madman! All men are mad
when they're in love. Never you catch that
complaint.'

'No, sir,' said Archie.

'Well, I'm keeping you, my lad; but I'm glad
of a minute's cessation from this work. There!
I think he will do now, duchess.—What do you
say?'

'Poor fellow! You have done it all beautiful,
sir,' said Mrs Smithers, smiling, as she passed a cool,
wet sponge across the wounded man's brows.

'There, off with you, Archie, my lad. Keep out
of danger.'

'Of course, sir,' was the reply.

'I mean it, for you have had more than your
share of my attention lately. But I say, my lad;
feel very boyish now?'

'If you tease me again about that, Doctor,' said Archie, 'I'll never consult you again.'

'Till next time,' said the Doctor, with a chuckle. —'Great heavens! what's that?'

That was a tremendous puff of wind that knocked the Japanese screen over against the wall, and sent Archie staggering so that he nearly fell over one of the wounded men. Then almost instantaneously came a terrific roar as if a sudden burst of a tropical storm had followed the flash of light which blazed through the lightly built place, the walls of which had rocked, and seemed to be tottering to their fall.

'Anybody hurt?' panted the Doctor, his first thought being that he must render aid.

'I—I don't know, sir,' stammered Archie.

'Glad of it,' said the Doctor. 'The worst storm I ever saw.'

'Storm, sir?' said Archie. 'It's the magazine gone!'

CHAPTER XXXV.

THE FLIGHT OF A LIMBING.

IT was no rash assertion. The small erection that it had been the Major's pride to erect by means of the men a short distance back and just inside the jungle, and to which he had brought to bear all the ingenuity he possessed, so as to ensure safety—sinking it deep in the earth, protecting it by a *chevaux de frise*, and then thickly planting the outside with a dense belt of the closest and most rapid-growing of the jungle shrubs —had been levelled with the earth, and its framework was now blazing furiously.

The first few moments after the explosion, it had seemed to the besieged that defence now would be madness, and that nothing was left for them but to throw themselves on the mercy of the Malays. But that natural desire of the Briton to make the best of things exemplified in the Latin proverb *Nil desperandum* soon began to assert itself. A sergeant suddenly shouted, 'Look out there, my lads! Want to see the place burnt down?' And first one and then another made a rush towards the different buildings to pick or knock off fragments of burning wood and bright embers, cast by the tremendous force and scattered by the powder, that were beginning to threaten destruction on the roofs where they had fallen.

The example set was quite sufficient for the rapid stamping out of the fires.

Meanwhile the remains of the magazine were burning furiously, and though the river was so near, it was no time for any attempt at checking the fire's progress.

'Let it go, my lads,' the Major had said, 'and be ready to take cover again, for we shall have the enemy back directly.'

For, instead of taking advantage of the explosion and the temporary bewilderment that had been caused to the besieged by the shock, the Malays, utterly demoralised by the terrific roar, had to a man made for the shelter of the jungle.

The silence that had succeeded the roar was intense. Where, firing their clumsy old muskets and increasing the noise by their savage yells of defiance all round the cantonments, the Malays had been tearing about and rushing from tree to tree, peace now reigned, while the snapping and crackling of the burning wood, the deep-toned, half-whispered orders of the officers, and the talking of the men seemed to sound unnaturally loud.

In a short time now all risk of further spreading of the fire was at an end, and the question arose, to be discussed by officers and non-coms, as to whether, as the Malays seemed to have retreated, something should not be done in the way of extinguishing the flames by bringing entrenching tools to bear and smothering them out with earth.

'No,' said the Major; 'it will be useless toil. Let it burn out.'

'But the fire's getting brighter, sir,' protested Archie.

'Well, sir,' said the Major peevishly, 'that's plain enough; you needn't tell us that.   What then?'

'We shall be having the enemy back directly, sir, and all of us standing out against the light as a mark for their spears.'

'Tut, tut!' exclaimed the Major.   'How absurd! I had not thought of that.   But, all the same, the explosion seems to have completely scared them away, for I don't hear a sound.   Do any of you?'

There was no reply.

'Yes,' continued the Major sharply.—'Here, Sergeant; half-a-dozen men, and spades.   Do the best you can to smother the flames.—The rest take cover, for this can't last.   We shall have the enemy back directly.'

The Major's *directly* did not prove to be correct, and while a careful watch was kept on the surrounding jungle and the little patches of fire that were flickering here and there amongst the trees, where goodly pieces of the woodwork had been cast by the explosion, a little meeting was held to discuss their position and the consequences of the catastrophe.

'You had all your ammunition stored there, had you not?' said the Doctor.

'All but what was in the men's pouches,' replied the Major.

'Then what do you mean to do?'

'Fix bayonets,' said the Major quietly.

'And not surrender?' said the Resident.

'Not while we have any fight left in us, Sir

Charles. We have our women to protect; and besides, there are the three detachments out in the jungle. I begin to think that this explosion will prove to be a blessing in disguise, and act as a rallying-call to bring the men back and take the enemy, if they come on again, in the rear.'

'Yes, to be sure,' said the Resident, who stood half turned from his companions in distress, and was gazing hard in the direction of the river.

'Well, Sir Charles, I presume you agree with me that we must stand to our guns—or, I should say, hold to our bayonets—till the very last? Help may come at any hour now.'

'Yes, certainly, sir,' replied the Resident; 'but I am afraid'——

'I wouldn't say so, sir,' said the Major, with a bitter laugh.

'You know what I mean,' said Sir Charles sternly. 'I fully expect that we shall have another body of Malays, to join in the attack, from down the river—I mean, the Rajah Hamet's men.'

'Well,' said the Major, 'our little citadel will hold us all, and when the last cartridges are fired we can make such a breast-work of bayonets as I don't think, in spite of their spears, these Malay scoundrels will pass.'

'We shall do our best, I am sure,' said the Resident quietly. 'But what do you make of this explosion?'

'Ruin,' said the Major bitterly.

'No, no; I mean, what could have caused it? You have all your rules—no fire is ever allowed to approach.'

'Ah yes, to be sure,' said the Major sharply, 'what could have caused it?' and he looked round from one to the other. 'I have been so wrapped up in the consequences that it has never occurred to me to think of the cause. We could have no enemy within the camp.'

'Look here,' said Archie to the Doctor; 'one of these fellows is coming to say that the more they throw on earth the more the wood blazes up.—What is it?' he continued, to the shovel-bearing private, who now joined them, his streaming and blackened face showing plainly in the bright light.

'We've just come upon a wounded man, sir.'

'Why didn't you bring him in?' said Archie sharply.

'I don't mean only wounded, sir. He's all black and burnt. Seems as if the blow-up had sent him ever so far away, and he's lying yonder amongst the stripped trees.'

'Eh? What's that?' said the Major excitedly. 'Not one of my lads?'

'No, sir. As far as I can make out by what's left of his clothes, he's one of the enemy.'

'One of the enemy!' cried the Major. 'Why, we are coming to the truth, then. No one of the enemy could have been there—unless'——

'Look here,' said the Doctor in his busy way, 'you said wounded man, my lad?'

'Yes, sir; he's alive, for he moved when we touched him, and groaned. But he's got it badly.'

'Well,' said the Doctor sharply, 'a wounded man, whether he's one of ourselves or an enemy, is all one to me;' and he walked with the rest, after a glance or two in the direction of the silent forest, from which the attack had come, towards the still blazing fire, where a little group of the spade party was standing round a dark object lying at some distance on the other side of the ruins of the magazine.

The party drew back a little to make way for their officers, and Archie shuddered as he caught sight of the horribly blackened object before them.

'A litter here,' said the Doctor shortly. 'I will have him up into hospital, but I'm afraid it's a hopeless case.'

As the Doctor rose from one knee, something bright caught Archie's eye and somehow brought to mind the gold bracelet he had seen the French Count wear. Then thought after thought flashed through his mind, as he heard a deep, muttering groan, and the man who had brought the tidings whispered to his young officer:

'That's the same as he did before, sir—just cried "Lo-lo-lo!" or something like that.'

'Why, Doctor,' said Archie excitedly, 'did you hear the rest—"*De l'eau*"? He was asking for water.'

'Yes—for the love of Heaven! what does this mean? He can't be a Malay.'

'No,' said Archie excitedly. 'It's impossible to recognise him for certain now, but I feel sure it's the Rajah's French friend.'

'What!' said the Major excitedly. 'What could he have been doing here?'

'What could he have been doing here, sir, that night when Captain Down and I were startled by hearing some one outside the veranda—some one who must have been listening to you and Sir Charles when you were talking together?'

'Here, I don't understand,' said the Major petulantly. 'What could the Rajah's friend have been doing here listening to our talk?'

'Playing the spy, sir, in his master's interest.'

'Pooh!' said the Major angrily. 'This is no French friend of the Rajah's. He's a Malay. That's a piece of a silk sarong clinging to his waist, with a kris stuck in it.'

'Yes, sir,' said Archie; 'but those are European trousers he's wearing underneath, and—yes!' cried the lad, as he bent nearer and shrinkingly touched the blackened wrist, just as a fresh flight of flame rose from the ruined magazine—'I am certain that's the gold bracelet the Rajah's friend used to wear. It's got a French motto on it, which you could see if you took it to the light. But I know it by the shape, and I thought that it was a silly bit of effeminate foppishness on the part of a man.'

'Yes,' said Sir Charles; 'I remember thinking so too. Why, the scoundrel must have been in the pay of the Rajah, and played the spy here to pretty good purpose. I don't think you need search for the cause of the magazine being exploded.'

Further conversation was ended by the report of a musket, which served as the signal for several more, all fired from beyond the parade-ground, and doing no harm, though the *whiz* and *phit* of the bullets passed close by, and could be heard striking against the nearest buildings.

'Cover,' said the Major sharply. 'Never mind

the fire now. It will do them as much harm as it does us, for we shall be able to see its glint reflected in their eyes at the edge of the jungle. Quick, every one—cover!'

'Wait a minute, four of you,' said the Doctor. 'I want my patient carried in.'

'Your what!' said the Major fiercely. 'The renegade who has dealt us this cowardly blow?'

'I never ask questions about a man's character,' said the Doctor gruffly. 'If he wants a surgeon's help, that's character enough for me. If I save his life, and you like to prove all this is true, and court-martial him and shoot him afterwards, as a spy, that's not my business, and I shall not interfere.— But look sharp, my lads. These big musket-balls are coming unpleasantly near, and they make very bad wounds. I can't afford to get one in me, for I am afraid you will want your surgeon for some time to come.'

It was a horrible task, but the four men who raised the injured man to bear him in could not forbear a chuckle at the Doctor's remark.

But the order to take cover was none too soon, for the musket-bullets were flying faster, fortunately without aim; and as shelter was reached it became evident that the scare caused by the explosion had died out, for by the light of the burning ruins the flash of a spear-head could be seen every now and then at the jungle-edge, and as the enemy once more gathered as if for a rush, their threatening yells grew plain.

'Well, young Maine,' said the Major slowly, as he passed his hand over his grizzled moustache just as

Archie was going round from post to post, 'this seems rather hard for you.'

'For me, sir?' said the lad, gazing at his commanding officer wonderingly.

'Yes, because you are such a young fellow. There, go on. Don't let the men waste a cartridge, for they must be made to last until one or the other of our detachments comes in—I hope well supplied, for if they've been using what they have, they will be in just as bad state as we are.'

'Oh, they'll be coming in soon, sir,' said Archie cheerily.

'I don't know. I hope so, my lad, for everybody's sake; but it's tough work getting through the jungle—and there, look at that! These fellows have plenty of pluck, or they wouldn't expose themselves as they do. I expect to find that we have very little more ball-cartridge. Well, it will be bayonet against spear, and if it were only equal sides I should back our lads. As it is, Maine, we must hope, and pray for our lads to come in with a run. Have you any idea what time it is, my lad?'

'No, sir. But it can't be near morning yet.'

'I suppose not. There, let's go and see how the Doctor's getting on with his new patient. You are right, my lad; I am sure now. You young fellows jump at a thing directly. We old fellows want a good deal of thought over anything before we will accept it as a fact.'

'Are you looking for anything, sir?' asked Archie, as the Major walked close to the window and stood looking out.

'Yes, my lad; I was looking for morning, and I

can't see it yet.——Why, what'—— The Major went heavily against the side of the window, as a result of a violent thrust from Archie, who swung out his sword and struck up the shaft of a spear with one cut, sending the spear to stick into the upper framework of the window, his next stroke being delivered with the pommel of his sword crash into the temple of a Malay who had crept up in the darkness and made two thrusts at the gallant old soldier, who said dryly, as one of his men made a thrust with his bayonet and rendered the treacherous enemy *hors de combat*:

'That was very soldierly and smart, Maine. They're as treacherous as the great striped cats of their jungle. Well, I suppose I ought to thank you for saving my life, but we soldiers don't talk about this sort of thing.'

CHAPTER XXXVL

A STRANGE CONFESSION.

THE Doctor was busy with his patients in the heat of the day, loosening one poor fellow's bandage, and tightening another that an irritable sufferer had worked loose; while Mrs Smithers was thoroughly proving her ability at using basin and sponge over the brows of some poor, fevered fellow whose pillowless head rolled· slowly from side to side. Archie was taking the mess-room on his way to visit the chamber where Peter Pegg was stationed, and from whose window an occasional shot rang out from time to time, with the result of the gaudily robed Malay in a smart, cavalry-like cap, who had drawn the shot, being seen no more.

'How am I, Mister Archie, sir? Oh, it's rather hot here, sir,' said Mrs Smithers; and then, in response to a second: 'Yes, old lady, or, I should say, Madame la Duchesse'—'Now, please, sir, don't you get calling me names too. I don't mind from the Doctor, but it teases when it comes from a young gent like you. No, sir, I ain't cross, only a bit worried by the flies. They are terrible, and it's all due to its being so hot.'

'Yes, Mrs Smithers,' said Archie meaningly. 'It is hot, and no mistake. But how beautiful and tidy you have got everything!'

'Well, it is a bit better, sir. I have been collecting all the mats I could find for the poor boys. Do you hear any news, sir, of reinforcements coming up?'

'Not yet, old lady.'

'I do wish they'd come, sir; and oh, Mr Archie, can't I do anything for you?'

'Me? No! I am not wounded.'

'No, sir; but, oh dear, what a state you are in! Some clean things would be a blessing to you.'

'Oh, wait a bit. One's got something else to think about now. Where's the Doctor?'

'He was here just this minute, sir; and he's sure not to be long, for I never see such a man for watching everybody who's in hospital. There, I thought so! Here he is, with the mess water-can and a clean glass. He might have asked me to fetch some water if he wanted it. But he always will interfere with what's in my department.'

'Hullo, Maine, my lad, you here! You are just in time. I've been fetching a can of this clear, sparkling water for my poor fellows. Look sharp, for I can see several eyes looking at it hungrily—I mean thirstily,' he added quickly.

He filled the glass after the fashion of Dickens's butler, trying to froth it up with a heading of sparkling beads.

'May I drink this, Doctor?' said Archie.

'Drink it? Of course! You are one of my patients still.'

'Thanks. But ladies first.—Here, Mrs Smithers; you look tired and hot. I will have the next glass.'

'No, sir, please,' said the woman firmly. 'You want it worse than I do.'

'Don't waste time,' said the Doctor sternly. 'Drink the water, my lad.'

The deliciously cool draught trickled down Archie's throat till the bottom of the glass became top.

'*De*-licious,' he said.

The Doctor took the glass, filled it, emptied it, smacked his lips, and then refilled and handed it to Mrs Smithers.

'Your turn, nurse,' he said. 'Then take the can and go all round, and finish off by taking a glass up to the Frenchman.'

'Ah, I was looking round, sir, for him,' said Archie.

'Yes, I am getting too full here, my lad. I have had him carried up to that room where Pegg's on duty.'

'Oh, I'm going there, sir, and I shall see him.'

'One moment, Duchess; half a glass, please. I feel like a volcanic cinder.—As you say, my lad— de-licious,' he continued, as he handed back the glass. 'I am proud of that water, and so you ought to be.'

'I am, Doctor.'

'That's all due to me, sir. When we first came —you know the Major's way—"Nonsense," he said. "There will be three hundred idle men here with nothing to do, and they can fetch as much water as we want for the day's supply from the river." And I said, "No. In a hot country like this I want my men to have good, pure, sparkling well water, and not to be forced to drink croc and campong drainage soup. I want a thoroughly good well dug by an engineering company." I got it, too, just when he was red-hot over his idea for a magazine. And now, sir, there's my well, always full of that delicious spring water that will do the men more good than any medicine I can exhibit; and where's his magazine? You tell me that.'

'If he were here, Doctor, he'd tell you that he'd rather have the magazine intact than the well.'

'Never mind. I've got the water.'

'Yes, Doctor. But how's Mrs Morley?'

'Ah, poor dear soul!' replied the Doctor, and his eyes looked moist. 'Worked to death, thank goodness!'

'Thank goodness?' said Archie wonderingly.

'Yes, my lad. It keeps her from thinking and fretting about Minnie. I'll tell her you asked after her, my boy. It will please her, for she doesn't know what a reckless young scamp you are, and she always talks of you as if you were her own boy. Going?'

'Yes, Doctor.'

'All right and square, my boy? No shot or spear holes in you?'

'No, sir; I'm as sound as sound.'

'That's right. If you do get into any trouble, you know where I am; and though I don't want you, you will be welcome to our mess—and a nice mess we are in, eh, Archie?—Come, look sharp, you British soldiers, and clear away all this scum.'

'Only too glad, sir,' said Archie, and he hurried away to have a few words with the sentry who commanded the landing-place, and who was so intent at the window, watching the edge of the jungle, that he did not hear his visitor till he spoke.

'Got company, Mister Archie, sir? Yes; that

French chap. Doctor said if he was not brought up here where he'd be quiet he would go off sudden like.   Not very cheerful company, for he's awful bad, and when he does talk it's all in his *parly-voo*, *kesky say*, *pally wag bang* lingo that don't mean nothing as I can make out.'

'Ah, poor fellow!   I suppose he's very bad.'

'Oh, that's right, sir!   Poor fellow, and we are all very sorry for him and much obliged because he was kind enough to come and blow all our cartridges to Jericho, or elsewhere, as they say on the soldiers' letters.   You stop here a little while, sir, and you will hear him begin to jabber.   Talk about that mahout's *pa-ta-ta-ma-ta-ja-ja-ja*—this chap goes twice as fast.'

'Well, Pete, I can't stop talking to you.   I only wanted to take you in my round.   Are you all right?'

'Right as a trivet, sir; only I am getting awful short of ammunition.   I don't want to keep on potting these 'ere fellows, but somehow I took to rifle-shooting.   There's some fun in hitting a mark at a distance, and that's the only thing I ever got a kind word for from old Tipsy.   He said I could shoot.'

'Yes, you are a very good marksman, Pete; and that's why you are stationed here.'

'Yes, I suppose so, sir.   But 'tain't my fault that I'm a good marksman, as you call it.   It come quite easy like.   I suppose it's good for us, but it's very bad for these 'ere Malay chaps, and it does make me feel a bit squirmy when one of them gives me a chance, and then it's *crack, phit,* and down he goes, and me loading again. I don't want to shoot them. But then if I don't keep on knocking them over they 'll knock us over, and I 've got such a kind of liking for P. P. that I 'd sooner shoot one of them than that they should shoot me. Still, there is something a bit queer about it.'

'You are doing your duty, Pete, fighting for your country.'

'I say, sir, that ain't quite right, is it ? Seems to me that I 'm fighting for these 'ere people's country.'

'We needn't go into that, Pete. You are doing your duty—fighting for your comrades in defence of this station and the women and children.'

'There he goes again, sir. Just you listen. It makes me wish I could understand what he 's saying.'

Archie turned sharply, for from the part of the room where the Frenchman was lying upon one of the mats Mrs Smithers had placed for him, with another rolled up to form his pillow, came the quick, excited utterance of the terribly injured man.

He was delirious, and evidently in his wanderings was going over something that had impressed him strongly, and almost at his first utterances in his own tongue he attracted the subaltern to his side.

Archie was no good French scholar, but that tongue had formed part of his studies at a public school, and he had been somewhat of a favourite with the French master, who had encouraged his pupils in acquiring French conversation by making them his companions in his country walks.

The sufferer's first utterance was an expression of anger at somebody whom he was addressing, calling him an *imbécile*; and then Archie pretty clearly gathered his meaning. He was telling the man to be careful, and to give him something so that he could do it himself.

'No,' he said, 'you don't understand. I wish I could tell you in your own tongue. There, your hands are trembling; you are afraid. You hate these people, but not with the great hate I feel towards them, who am their natural enemy. There, give me the two bags. Yes, it is bad powder; not such as, if I had known, I might have brought from my own country. What is it? You hear some one coming? Lie down. No one can see us here, shut in behind these trees. You are afraid they will shoot? Bah! Let them! They could not aim at us in this darkness. Be brave, as I am. Recollect what I told you before we started to creep here: if we fire, it will destroy all their ammunition. They will be defenceless, and it will be easy for your prince to slay and capture all these wretched British usurpers of your prince's country. And I shall be the Rajah's great friend and counsellor, and make him great, so that he will become a glorious prince and reign over a happy, contented people. There, you are not afraid now. Your hand trembles, though. Well, help me to pour out what is in this bag in a heap over that pile of boxes. Do not tremble so. Nothing can hurt us now. That is good. Now stand there, behind those bushes, and tell me if you hear any of the enemy coming. That is good, and there is the good work done. Quick! Now the other bag. My faith, how you tremble! Now my hand—hold it tight and lead me through

the darkness back to the way we came—in silence,
so that the enemy shall not hear. No, no—too fast!
Do you not understand? You must lead me so that
I can pour the powder from the bag as I walk backwards and lay the train.'

The Frenchman ceased his utterance, and though
Archie missed some of his words, the scene that
must have taken place in the darkness of the jungle
surrounding the magazine seemed to start out vividly
and picture itself before the listener's eyes. Then
the sufferer began to speak again, in a low, quick,
excited way.

'Ah! Idiot! Clumsy! I could have done better
without you. Do you not understand? You have
trampled over the careful train I have laid, and I
must scatter more, or the plan will fail. Stay here
till I come back to you.—Curses! He has gone.
What matter? I can finish now. That is well.
There is plenty, and it cannot fail. Now the matches.
—Stop. Is the way clear? I shall have time—
and—yes, I can find my way as I did before. I
was mad to bring that shivering idiot. He has been
in my way all through. But no; he did carry the
bag, and the task that brings ruin and destruction
upon these English is nearly done. Now—the
matches. Ah! Confusion! The box must have
been wet. Now another; then quick! The moment
the fire begins to run. Confusion! Is it that the
matches are wet? No. I am all in water, and the
touch from my fingers prevents the match from
striking. Now—ah, that is better. But hark!
Could the sentry have seen that? No. I am
trembling like that coward Malay. Courage, my

friend. It is such a little thing to do. But I must
hasten, before the powder spoils upon the damp
ground, where everything drips with the heavy dew.
Courage, my friend—courage! It is such a little
thing, and for the glory of my beautiful France, and
for my great revenge against these English and their
officers, while my prince will rule in peace, and—
yes, my faith! I shall rule him now. Crack!
That match burns, and—*hiss*—the train begins to
run, and so must I. Ah! My faith! I am going
wrong. These trees catch my feet with their fright-
ful tangle, and the light dazzles my eyes. My faith!
My faith! I am lost!'

So vivid seemed the picture that the listener's
brow grew moist, and he turned shuddering away,
to see that Peter was watching him curiously ; and
both lads started now as a wild cry of horror and
despair arose from the rough pallet on which the
sufferer lay struggling feebly.

'I'd say as you would, Mister Archie, sir : "Poor
beggar!" for he must be feeling very bad with his
burns ; but he don't deserve it. It was his own
doing. Could you make out what he was talking
about ?'

'A great deal of it, Pete.'

'What was he saying of, sir ?'

'Poor wretch! He's quite off his head. He
seemed to be talking about how he tried to blow up
the magazine.'

'Said he was sorry for it, perhaps, sir ?'

'No, Pete ; I didn't catch that.'

'Ah, well, he would be, sir, because he didn't
get away fast enough. A chap who would do a

thing like that wouldn't feel sorry for it if he hadn't got caught.—I say, *pst!* Look here, Mister Archie.'

'What is it?'

'I was only just in time to catch sight of them. Think of it! I only turned my head to talk to you, but two of them took advantage and crept right close up behind that bush. Can you see 'em?'

'No.'

'Well, I can, sir, or think I can, because I saw them for a moment as they dashed in. You stand back from the window, sir. There's only shelter for one, and that's me.'

'Are you going to fire?'

'Don't quite know, sir. Depends on them. They must have seen you when you stood looking out before that Frenchman began to talk. I could send a shot right through the bush, and it might hit one of them; but then it mightn't, and I should have wasted a cartridge. I think I'll wait till they come out to shoot or chuck a spear, and then I can be sure. What do you say?'

'That will be quite right, Pete; and I will go on now. Why, Joe Smithers ought to be able to spot any one hiding behind that bush. I'll go round by where he's posted and see.'

'Ought to be able to see for hisself,' grumbled Peter; and as Archie turned to reach the door, unaware of the fact that he was exposing himself a little, Peter raised his rifle to his shoulder and fired a snap shot, just as simultaneously Archie started at the brushing by his cheek of a spear which came through the window with a low trajectory and stuck with a soft *thud* into something at the far end of the room.

'Missed him!' said Peter in an angry, impatient way. 'No, I ain't. It was only chance it, though. Ah! Would you?' For another spear flashed through the window, making one of the young men duck down, while the other started aside.

Then their eyes met in a curious look of horror, and for a few minutes neither spoke.

'Think of that, now, Mister Archie!' said Peter, as his trembling fingers were playing about the breech of his rifle.

'Horrible!' said Archie, as he recalled the confession to which he had listened.

'Yes, sir; 'orrid, ain't it? And that was a chance shot, too, though he meant it for you. I say, sir, he won't blow up no more magazines;' and Peter made a great smudge across his moist forehead with his powder-blackened hand. For the second spear had found its billet in the chest of the Frenchman, whose sufferings were at an end.

CHAPTER XXXVII.

THE DOCTOR'S CARTRIDGES.

THE position of the beleaguered occupants of the Residency grew worse and worse. There had been three different brief despatches from the detachments, but the information conveyed was very small. In each case the commander announced that he was in full pursuit of the Rajah, who had thrown off the mask and taken to the jungle; and after reading the despatches over to the Resident the Major had uttered a grunt and said:

'One would think there were three Rajahs instead of one.'

He had sent replies by native runners, urging upon his subordinates the necessity for an immediate return, so as to strengthen the position of the Residency, and stating that, from news that had come in, it was evident that Rajah Hamet had also thrown off the mask and was waiting, undoubtedly to make an attack in conjunction with Rajah Suleiman.

'We shall be hard pressed,' he said emphatically, 'and I must call upon you to rally at once. Sir Charles is sending a despatch to Singapore, telling of the uneasy state of the native princes, and the sore straits in which we find ourselves; but it will be some time before a messenger can reach the Governor, and Suleiman's men are pressing me hard.

As you well know, it must be many days before a gunboat can reach us here.'

No reply reached headquarters, for, however wanting in generalship Suleiman might have been, he took care that no messengers should pass his people in either direction, and, in fact, the Major's appeal to his officers never reached their hands, and the cunning Malays kept up the appearance of being in full retreat, leading the detachments farther and farther into the intricate mazes of the jungle.

Meanwhile it was not only the ammunition that was running out but the provisions. But there was an ample supply in the various stores of the settlement, and these under ordinary circumstances would have been largely supplemented at the little market held by the people of the neighbouring campongs. But after the attack by Suleiman's men not a single native made his appearance, and, as was afterwards proved, no Malay, save at the risk of losing his life, dared to approach the military quarters.

'It seems so hard,' said the Resident, 'that after Dr Morley and I had gone over the matter as we did respecting provisioning the place, we should not have made other arrangements for warehousing our permanent supplies. I felt that, with a strong military force for the protection of the storehouses, nothing more could be done.'

'No; nobody blames you, Sir Charles, for no foresight could have seen that the place would be denuded of troops, and that the enemy would close us in so completely that no man could approach a ware or store house without risking having a spear in his back.'

'Ah,' said the Doctor, 'it's lucky for us all that I beat you, Major, and got my well dug.'

'Yes, Morley,' said the Major sharply; 'and no one's more glad than I am. But you needn't tell us all about it quite so often.'

The Doctor chuckled, for in spite of the terrible demands that were made upon him he was generally in pretty good spirits.

'Well, I won't say any more about it, but you military men, who get all the honour and glory, might let your poor doctor have a little bit of praise.'

'Well, what's to be done? We must have a couple or more sacks of that Indian meal from the store to-day. We cannot sit here and starve. And at the same time more of the necessaries of life, or what we have in time come to consider necessaries, must be obtained for the women and children.'

'Yes,' said the Doctor. 'My hands are full with dealing with the wounded. I can't have the poor, starving women coming into hospital to be treated for exhaustion, and the children upon my hands dying like flies.'

'No,' said the Major; 'we must call for volunteers, Sir Charles, to cut our way through the enemy to the store.'

'No, no,' said the Doctor; 'I forbid that.'

'Why?' said the Major angrily.

'Because it means half-a-dozen or a dozen more wounded men to crowd my hospital.'

'Hah!' ejaculated the Major. 'And I can't spare one.'

'Then look here,' said the Doctor; 'call for your volunteers—or for one volunteer at a time. You see, with their cunning and subtlety they know beforehand that we must be ready to do anything to get at the stores, and consequently they keep the strictest watch, with spearmen ready to let fly at any poor wretch who approaches either of the buildings.'

'Yes, yes, we know that, Doctor,' said the Resident peevishly.

'Then why don't you meet cunning with cunning?' replied the Doctor. 'Surely the Major can pick up some clever, sharp fellow who will crawl in the darkness past the enemy's pickets and bring back something, if it's only one sack of meal.'

'That would be better than nothing, Doctor. —We'll try; eh, Major?'

'Of course; of course.'

The little council of war was being held in the hottest part of the day, when the attacking enemy seemed to have drawn off for a while amongst the trees, and most of the beleaguered were grouped around in the shadow of veranda and tree to listen to the discussion.

'Well,' said the Resident, 'I can't ask either of my native servants who have been true to us to risk his life for us. We should never see them again, for the enemy would be sure to make an extra effort to spear them.'

'Quite out of the question, Sir Charles,' said the Doctor.—'Now, Major, we must look to you again. —What's that, Mrs Smithers?'

'I was only going to say, sir, that my Joe is a big, strong fellow, and he'll volunteer to try and get a sack of flour to-night.'

'Eh? What's that?' cried the private.

'You heard what was said, Joe. What do you mean by shaking your head like that?'

'Oh, I'm not the right man,' he said. 'I can carry my rifle, but I'm an out-and-out bad one at carrying sacks.'

'Nonsense, Joe,' said his wife. 'You can do anything that a British soldier can.'

'Nay, missus,' said Smithers; ''tain't in my way at all. If it was my officers wanted a stone jar of rack or a dozen of bottled ale, I might manage 'em, but I'm nowhere with sacks.'

'Never mind, then,' said Mrs Smithers tartly; 'I'll go myself.'

'Nay, you won't,' said Joe, shaking his head more hard than ever.—'I'll go, gen'lemen. She wants to be a widow, but I look to you, Doctor, not to let her be if I come to quarters with a sack of meal pinned on to my back with a spear.'

That night Joe Smithers managed to crawl right round the outskirts of the settlement, got into the store from the other side, and returned by the same circuitous way with a sack of meal and such instructions to his messmates that two more men started at once and foraged with a like success. But that was only a temporary alleviation of the troubles of the beleaguered, and twice over, when off duty, Archie summoned Peter to accompany him to the lower part of the river, where they succeeded, at great risk, in wading off to a boat, fishing for three parts of the night, and returning after very fair success.

Then came a day when the enemy had been more energetic than ever, and three more of the Major's little force were carried into hospital suffering badly from spear-wounds, and this just at a time when, in a whisper, the announcement had gone round that there were very few cartridges left.

The Doctor had just finished tending his men with the help of Mrs Morley, for Joe Smithers's wife had broken down from being brought face to face with her well-scolded husband, who was carried in by two comrades and laid at her feet.

'Oh Joe,' she cried, 'how could you?'

'I didn't, missus. It was one of them ugly, flat-nosed chaps, who managed to put a spear into me; but I give him the bayonet in return. But ain't you going to tie me up?'

'Oh, yes, yes, Joe dear!' she cried, hurrying to fetch her lotah and sponge; while the Doctor came up from the other side, frowning severely, and then making a dash to catch the unhappy woman and save her from falling, for poor Mrs Smithers, the strong and never-tiring, had fainted dead away for the first time in her life. The consequence was that the Doctor's wife stood by his side till the last dressing had been applied, and then sat in the veranda to discuss with him a glass of his favourite water and talk in a whisper about the perils of their position.

'Yes,' said the Doctor; 'it's a very bad lookout, my dear. I have seen some bad times, but this is the worst of all, and you have no business here.'

'Why not, dear?' she said softly.

'Because our poor fellows are doing the best they can to protect us, but at any moment one of these savage beasts might make a dash and send his limbing flying and hit you.'

'Isn't it just as risky for you, dear?' said Mrs Morley quietly.

'Oh, but I am a doctor, and doctors don't count.'

'Nor doctors' wives,' said Mrs Morley quietly. 'I shall stay. Now, tell me, isn't it very strange that neither of the detachments have made their way back?'

'No, my dear. They are right out in the jungle, and that explains everything. Perhaps they are being lured farther and farther on by the Rajah; or perhaps,' he added to himself, 'the poor fellows have been surrounded and speared.—Oh,' he added aloud, 'we may hear a bugle at any moment, and see the lads come in with a dash. Don't you bother your head about military matters, but help me to bring the wounded round.'

'I will, dear,' said the poor woman quietly; 'but tell me this'——

'Is it military?' said the Doctor.

'No, no, no, no. I was only going to say, have any of the men seen anything of that big fellow, Dula's husband?'

'No,' said the Doctor. 'He and his wife disappeared during the attack, didn't they?'

'Yes,' said Mrs Morley. 'I'm afraid they lost their lives.'

'Humph! Maybe,' said the Doctor. 'It is quite enough for them to be seen here with us to bring upon them the enemy's spears. But don't, please, my dear—don't! I 've never said a word, but you know that I have felt it as cruelly as you, and I would have done anything to have gone up the river with those two people to try to bring back our poor child.'

'Yes, yes, I know; and I have tried, dear, to keep my sorrow to myself.—Hush, hush! Here 's Archie Maine. Not a word before him.'

Mrs Morley held out her hand to the young man as he came up, and the Doctor nodded shortly as he saw the lad's contracted, anxious face.

'Anything fresh, boy?' said the Doctor.

'No; only the old bad news: we are coming down to the last cartridge for the rifles, and we officers have only too few for our revolvers.'

'Well,' said the Doctor, 'you know what the Major said. There are the bayonets.'

'Last cartridges,' said Mrs Morley thoughtfully.

'Yes, my dear. It 's no use to hide anything from you. The poor fellows' pouches are pretty well empty.'

'Oh, by the way,' said Archie quickly, 'those three poor fellows who were just brought in—what about their pouches?'

'Oh, the bearers pretty well fought for them,' said the Doctor bitterly, 'and divided the spoil. Two men got one apiece, the other a couple.'

'But, Henry dear,' said the Doctor's wife, laying her hand upon his arm, 'what about your double rifle at home?'

'Double gun, my dear, and one barrel rifled. I haven't done much sporting with that lately. I was to have a tiger-shoot. But what do you mean? Do you want me to begin potting at the enemy?'

'No, dear; I was thinking about the cartridges.'

'Yes, Doctor,' cried Archie excitedly. 'You must have a lot of cartridges.'

'I had four boxes, my lad—two of shot, large and small, and two of ball cartridges for the tigers. But I haven't the least idea where they are.'

'But I know, dear—on the store-room floor. I put them there to be dry.'

'Good girl! But they're no use for our men's rifles.'

'The powder would be, Doctor,' said Archie; 'and you might let us have the rifle for one of the men.'

'Yes, of course,' said the Doctor bitterly. 'But how are you going to get them here?'

'Yes,' said Archie thoughtfully; 'how are we going to get them here?'

'Why, my lad,' said the Doctor, 'to reach the bungalow you would have to go through a little forest of spears, and if our lads managed to cut you out it would be only another patient for me to heal —if I could,' he added softly—'and the one we could least spare.'

'Poor boy!' said Mrs Morley as Archie went slowly away. 'I wish I hadn't mentioned the cartridges. Surely he won't dream of trying to get them?'

'Oh no; it's an impossibility. He would never be so mad.'

'I don't know,' said Mrs Morley. 'After what

has been done by the men in volunteering to fetch in food, he will be offering to make some such dreadful venture.'

'Then he sha'n't,' said the Doctor fiercely, 'for I will make it my duty to put the Major on his guard.'

CHAPTER XXXVIII.

AFTER LAST POST.

MEANWHILE Archie, faint with heat and weariness, had made his way slowly to Peter, who was at his old post, doing double and quadruple duty as the sentry who commanded the approach to the landing-place; and as Archie entered the room he looked up eagerly.

'I was thinking about you, Mister Archie, sir.'

'And I was thinking about you, Pete.'

'Thank you, sir. Have a drink, sir,' he continued eagerly, pointing to a brass lotah and a cocoa-nut shell. 'It's nice and fresh, sir. Mother Smithers only brought it up about two hours ago, because she said this was the hottest place in the station; and it's splendid stuff, sir. It's kept me awake many's the time, when I've felt as I must snooze.'

Archie took the cup mechanically, filled it, and handed it to his man.

'After you, sir, please.'

Archie raised the cup and drank.

'Don't it put you in mind, sir, of the stone jar and the helephant-shed ?'

'Yes, Pete. Ah, it's rather warm, but very refreshing;' and he refilled the cup and held it to the man.

'No news, I suppose, sir ?'

'Yes, Pete. More bad, of course; three more men down.'

'Three, sir! Well, I suppose we have all got to get a taste of them spears, just have our dose, and—good luck to him!—the Doctor will set us up again.'

Archie was silent for a few moments.

'One of the men is poor Joe Smithers,' he said at last.

'Joe Smithers!' cried Peter, letting his rifle fall into the hollow of his arm. 'Joe Smithers!'

'I didn't know you cared for him so much, Pete,' said Archie, as he saw the big tears gathering in the lad's eyes.

'Oh, I liked him as a comrade, sir. He's a good chap, and fought as well as the best of them. But it makes me feel ready to snivel, sir, about old Mother Clean-shirts. Why, it will about break her heart. Why, she was here a couple of hours ago to bring me that drinking-water, and looked as chirpy as ever.—Poor old girl!' continued Peter, as Archie told him what had passed. 'It's a bad, bad job, sir; but we soldiers has to chance it, for where there's a lot of bad there's always a lot of good. And look at that now! Who's Joe Smithers as he should have such a stroke of luck and have a nurse like that?'

There was silence for a few minutes, and the two lads sat gazing out of the window.

'Extra quiet this afternoon, ain't they, sir?' said Peter. 'Think it means that they are making up some fresh dodge to wake us up?'

'I don't know, Pete,' said Archie sadly. 'You

ought to be able to bring that fellow down,' he added, pointing.

'Yes, I could cripple him, easy, sir, though it is rather a long shot.'

'Then why don't you fire?'

'Only got two cartridges left, sir,' replied the lad, looking at the speaker wistfully.

'Cartridges!' said Archie, starting. 'That's what I came to talk to you about.'

'Go it, then, sir, please, for there's nothing I should like better to hear.—Hooray!' ejaculated Peter softly, as Archie related what had occurred. 'Talk about corn in Egypt, sir! Well, we must have them.'

'The Major won't let us go, Pete.'

'No, sir, I suppose not. Says it's too risky.'

The lad was silent for a few minutes, and then went on:

'Yes, 'tis a bit risky, sir, for the niggers are as thick as thieves all down that way; but you and me always did like a lark with a bit of spice in it— when we was boys; and that ain't much more than a month or two ago, sir. I should just like to get them cartridges; shouldn't you?'

'Yes, Pete, dearly; and it might be the saving of a good many lives.'

'To be sure it would, sir.'

'But it would be like acting in defiance of orders if we were to attempt such a thing.'

'Well, if you look at it like that, sir, I suppose it would. And the Major would never forgive us— if we didn't get them.'

'No,' said Archie.

'But if we *did*.'

'Yes, Pete, if we did he'd shut his eyes to our breach of orders.'

'Well, sir, we always did like a bit of spice, as I said just now—just a bit of risk over a lark; and this is only like a serious lark to do a lot of good as well as giving us a bit of fun. I'm game, sir, if you are.'

Archie was silent for a few moments, and then he said slowly:

'It's for the benefit of all, Pete. With a couple of hundred cartridges, even if half of them are small shot'——

'We could kick up such a row, sir, as would make the niggers think we had no end of supplies. Let's get them, sir.'

'How, Pete?'

'Oh, that means you are on, sir. How? Well, that wants a considering-cap and a little bit of thinkum-thinkum. How? Don't quite see it yet, sir; but if you sets your mind on a thing, and comes to me—it always did end in our seeing how to do it, and that's how it's going to be now.' Peter began to whistle softly and then sing in a whisper about—

> 'Some talks of Alex-ander,
> And some of Hercules,
> Of Hector and Lysander,
> And such brave chaps as these.

—Here, I have got it, sir.'

'Yes—how?' cried Archie.

'A boat, sir.'

'Bother! I have been thinking of boats and

sampans and nagas and gunboats, and all the rest
of them. How are we to do it with a boat?'

'Don't be waxy with me, Mister Archie, sir. You
are in such a hurry with a chap. I said boat.'

'I know you did,' said Archie gruffly.

'And then you chopped me off short, sir, when
I was going to say—and chance it.'

'That's what you are always saying.'

'That's true, sir; but you can't say but what it
sometimes turns up trumps.'

'Well, go on. What boat?'

'Any boat, sir. Anybody's boat. Why not
smuggle the one we had when we went fishing?'

'We can't do that again. There's a fresh rumour
that Rajah Hamet is bringing his men up there;
and we may have an attack from the lower river
at any time.'

'Oh, that settles it, then,' said Peter. 'We must
have them cartridges before those fresh reinforcements come. All right, then, sir. We must creep
round right away outside the camp, and get to
the water-side half a mile beyond the spot where I
was on duty and hailed you that night. There's
sure to be boats up there.'

'Very likely. What then? But if there are
they will be anchored right out in the river. How
are we to get one?'

'Swim,' said Peter laconically.

'And the crocs?'

'Chance it,' said Peter.

'Ugh!' ejaculated Archie.

''Tain't tempting, sir, but I'm game. Look here,
Mister Archie,' continued the lad; 'they say British

soldiers are odd fish——and so they are——but bad as we want cartridges, ain't four hundred of them, all new, and waiting to be used, at a time when every lad's pouch is empty, a big enough bait to make any British soldier bite ?   Come on, sir ; chance it !'

'I will, Pete ; and if one of those hideous reptiles takes me down——well, I shall have died for my country.'

'I won't, sir,' said Peter fiercely, 'but I'll die for him.   I mean, I will disagree with him this 'ere way.   Of course I should leave my rifle at home, but I should go that journey with a naked bayonet in my belt, and it will go rather hard before he settles me if I don't find time to put it into his fatigue-jacket here and there.'

'Yes, Pete ; and, as you say, we will chance it. But when we have got the boat, what then ?'

'Lie quietly in the bottom, sir, and let it float down till we are off the foot of the Doctor's garden, and then one of us will hold it ready and drop down the anchor-stone or the grapnel, and there we are.'

'But suppose some of the Malays are already in the house.'

'No, we won't, sir.   We are not going to suppose anything of the kind.   We are going to chance it, sir.'

'That's right, Pete.   When shall we start ?'

'What do you say, sir ?'

'I say to-night, directly after Last Post.'

'Last Post it is, sir.'

Peter had not lost the memory of differences of position, but he was thinking of two men binding themselves upon a perilous compact that might mean death to both, as he slowly stole forward a very dirty hand.

The young officer to whom it was extended on his part did not see in his companion a private, but the brave, tried comrade, as he caught Peter's powder-grimed hand in a warm grasp.

And Archie's hand was just as grubby.

CHAPTER XXXIX.

A DARK EXPLOIT.

'IT seems so stupid, Pete, going all this way round in the black darkness to get at the bungalow, when ten minutes at the outside would have taken us there.'

'That's right, Mister Archie. What was it—five hundred yards?'

'Somewhere about; but if we had tried to walk there, how far should we have got before we had spears through us?'

'About five-and-twenty, sir, or thirty; and then we shouldn't have got the cartridges. But, I say, this is about the darkest dark night I ever remember. Glad I ain't on sentry-go. Can you make out where we are?'

'Yes. Can't you?'

'No, sir; we come such a long way round. But as far as I can make out, we are somewhere at the back of them big trees where they fed the helephants on Sham-Fight Day.'

'Yes, I think that's right,' whispered Archie, as they knelt together whispering. 'But let's get on; we must hit the river somewhere.'

'Hope so, sir. It will be softer than hitting your head against trees. I did get a poke just now when I went down, and it has made my nose bleed wonderful.'

'How tiresome! Let's get to the river, and the cold water will soon stop it.'

'All right, sir.'

They had been creeping along for the most part on all fours for the past hour since starting, so as to avoid friends and enemies, for they had been expecting at any moment to hear a challenge from one of their own outposts or receive a thrust from a Malay spear. But so far success had attended them, and Peter had just caught hold of his officer's arm to whisper that he could smell the river, but he said instead:

''Ware hawk, Mister Archie!'

And the next moment there was a rush of feet, a rough-and-tumble scuffle, the sound of blows, and Archie was down on his knees, panting and trying hard to get his breath silently so that he should not be heard.

'It's all over,' he thought, 'unless I can do it myself. Poor old Pete! I wonder where he is.'

He crouched a little lower as he heard the rustling of bushes a short distance away, and he did not stir till the sounds died out, when, guessing more than knowing where the river was, he made a slight movement, and felt himself seized by the throat.

'You stir, and '——

'That you, Pete?'

'Mister Archie! My! You have done me good! Let's lie down, put our heads together, and whisper. There were three of them, I think, and one may have stopped back.'

'It was our fellows, wasn't it?'

'Yes, sir; and I know who one of them was. Didn't you get a crack on the back?'

'Yes. Drove me forward on my face. I think it was done with a rifle-butt.'

'That was it, sir. You know who it was— Scotch Mac. He always says "Hech" when he hits out.'

'Yes, of course.'

'Well, wait a bit, sir. Some day I'll pay him back. I'll make him say "Hech" out louder. Hurt you much, sir?'

'Only made my arm feel a bit numb. Stop a minute and listen. What's that?'

'A splash!'

'Some one rowing?'

'Croc, perhaps, sir, with his tail.'

'Then we are close to the river.'

'Splendid, Mister Archie! Then it's going to be easy, after all.'

At the end of a few cautiously taken paces the two lads found their progress arrested by bushes, and they stopped short, trying hard to pierce the gloom; but it seemed darker than ever.

'Can you tell where we are, Pete?' whispered Archie, with his lips close to his companion's ear.

'No, sir; but take care, or we shall step right off the bank into the water somewhere. Think I might strike a match, sir, and chuck it before us?'

'No. If you do we shall be having a spear this time instead of a rifle-butt.'

'Right, sir; but I don't see how we are going to find a boat unless we wade in and chance it.'

'Let's get on, and creep through the bushes.

It may seem a little lighter close to the water's edge.'

Hand-in-hand they pressed on, the bushes brushing their faces but yielding easily for a few minutes, and then, as if moved by one impulse, they checked an ejaculation and stood staring straight before them, for all at once a bush they had reached sent forth a little scintillation of light, and as Peter struck out with one hand, he started a fresh sparkle of tiny little lights, as a flight of fire-flies flashed out for a moment, and left the surroundings blacker than ever.

'That's done it, sir,' whispered Peter. 'I saw two quite plain.'

'I saw quite fifty, Pete,' whispered back Archie.

'Boats, sir! Stuff—fire-flies!'

'Do you mean to say that you saw boats?'

'That's right, sir. Just a glimpse—tied up, not half-a-dozen yards out in the river. Come on, sir; I'll lead; only keep hold of hands and be ready to step down into the water. These bushes hang quite over, you know how. Ready, sir?'

'Yes.'

'Then come on.'

Two or three cautious steps were taken, which disturbed the occupants of one of the clumps of low growth, which sparkled vividly as the nocturnal insects were disturbed, and then the two adventurers were standing breathing hard, hip-deep in the cool water which was flowing by them.

'Hear anything, Pete?'

'Only the ripple-pipple of the water, sir. You see the boats this time?'

'Yes, for a moment, quite plainly, away to your left.'

'We can reach them easy, sir; but it will get deeper. You must be ready to swim. Say the word, sir, and I will lead.'

'No, no; I'll go first.'

'That's wasting time, sir.'

'Right.   Go on.'

The words had hardly passed the subaltern's lips when he felt a sudden snatch and a wallow in the water as if Peter had stepped out of his depth; but the lad recovered himself directly and stood firm, panting.

'All right, sir,' he whispered.   'Bay'nets!'

In his excitement Archie had forgotten the crocodiles, and he now tore the sharp, triangular blade from his belt, his imagination turning the ripple and plap of water against the nearest boat into the movement of an advancing reptile.

But all the time, short as it was, Peter, with extended arm, was moving sideways in the direction where the boats had been seen, with the bayonet-holding hand stretched out in the direction of his goal, the other clutching Archie's left with a force that seemed crushing to the owner's fingers.

Step after step was taken sideways, with the water each minute growing deeper, and as they passed quite clear of the bushes they had left, the water pressed more and more strongly against their breasts, so that they could hardly keep their feet; while as the darkness above the flowing stream seemed to be growing more transparent, Archie turned his head to gaze back in the direction of the overhanging bushes, in the full expectation of feeling a thrust from a spear, when he felt another sudden snatch and tightened his grasp of his comrade's hand, for Peter had reached deeper water and was borne off his feet, dragging Archie sideways.

Then there came a sharp sound as of metal against wood, a splashing or wallowing that suggested the rush of one of the loathsome reptiles, and Peter gasped out in a gurgling way, as if he had been under water:

'All right, sir. I've got hold. Let yourself float down, and make a snatch at the side.'

How it was done Peter did not know, and did not want to. It was enough for him in the darkness that he could feel that his companion had hold of the side of the boat, which had careened over so that the surface of the rippling river was within a few inches of the edge; and there they clung, listening with straining ears, trying to make out whether they had been heard.

'It's all right, sir,' said Peter softly, as they now rested with their arms over touching the bottom of the boat.

'I don't know,' said Archie. 'I think the stern's covered in. Is anybody on board?'

'Like enough, sir; but chance it;' and raising himself with a sudden movement which made a loud wallowing and sent a shudder of horror through his companion, Peter drew himself over the rough gunwale, rolled into the bottom of the boat, in company with a gush of water, and then, bayonet in hand, crept over the thwarts and under the attap-covered stern.

'All right, sir,' whispered the lad; and he crept to the far side of the boat, trimming it so that it made Archie's task of joining him easier to achieve. 'Ready, sir?'

'Yes. What about the moorings?'

'I was going to cut the rope, sir,' whispered Peter, 'but I won't. Perhaps it's a grapnel, and we shall want it again.'

Creeping right to the bows, he began to haul on a roughly made fibre line, which came in readily as the water rippled more loudly against the stem, and the line became more and more perpendicular, till something struck against the frail woodwork of the bows, and, panting with his exertion, Peter drew a little, clumsily made anchor into the big sampan.

'That's done it,' he whispered. 'Hear anything, sir?'

'No; but we are floating down.'

'Lovely, sir. Now then, we shall have to look out, for we mustn't pass the Doctor's garden.'

Crack—creak—scrape!

The two lads dropped at full length into the water that was washing about the bottom of the boat, and lay motionless till they had scraped past a boat that seemed similar to the one they had boarded. But it was evidently unoccupied, and they raised themselves up into a sitting position again, and strained their eyes to gaze in the direction of the shore they had left, where all was perfectly still. Then Archie felt his companion's hand touch his arm. .

'Talk about a lark, Mister Archie!' whispered Peter.

' A lark ? '

' Yes, sir. I forgot all about the crocs. They must have been asleep.'

Plash—wallow! came from just ahead, as there was a slight jar as if something had been encountered, and a tiny shower of water flew over them.

' Doesn't seem like it, Pete,' said Archie softly.

' No, sir ; and the brute needn't have done that. I was quite wet enough before. I suppose you are a bit damp ? '

' Don't, Pete—don't ! ' whispered Archie. ' This is no time for trying to be funny.'

' All right, sir. I thought it was, for I 'm in precious low spirits. Think we can manage to stop opposite the Doctor's garden ? '

' We must, Pete ; but I can make out nothing. I suppose we are a long way above the landing-place.'

' Oh yes, sir ; and perhaps it 's all for the best as we can't see, for if we could, whoever 's ashore would see us ; and that would mean spears, for none of our chaps would be about here.'

' Look here, Pete, we must both watch ; but you get right in the bows with the grapnel in your hand, ready to drop it over silently when I say *Now !* '

' Right, sir ; but we must have ever so far to go yet, eh ? '

' I am not sure, Pete.'

' No, sir ; but you will have to chance it.'

Archie uttered an angry ejaculation, and then clutched sharply at the side of the boat, which shivered from end to end and nearly capsized as it glided up the slanting rope of a larger vessel with which it had come violently in contact. But it righted itself quickly, and scraped along the side, with the lads crouching lower as they listened to the angry, muttering of voices and the scuffling of people moving. But the next minute the river had borne them clear, and the muttering died away.

'That must have been a naga, Pete, from the size of it, and having men on board.'

'Suppose so, sir. I thought it meant a swim for us. But, I say, it must have spoilt somebody's beauty snooze. But look there, sir! That must mean gardens.'

'What, Pete?'

'Can't you see them glow-worm things sparkling?'

'Yes.'

'Well, sir, ain't you going to say *Now?*'

'No, Pete. We cannot have passed the big landing-place yet. If we have, only just. Yes, that must be it, and this must be the spot. Oh! if we could only see a spark of light from the Residency we should know where we are.'

'Yes, sir; but it's no use to look out for lights. Still, we must be getting somewhere near, sir, and I'm ready when you are. I must leave it to you, for you know more about boating on the river than I do. It only seems to me that it can't be long before we shall be opposite the Doctor's beautiful garden and the little steps at the bottom, where you used to land.'

'Yes, Pete, I must guess, for I can see nothing.'

'Nor me neither, sir; but don't be huffy because I say what I am going to say.'

'No.   Speak out.'

'Then just wait, sir, till you think we are as near as we shall get, and then chance it.'

Archie made no reply as he reached over the side, and, unconscious of the fact that the stream had turned the boat completely round so that she was dropping down now bow foremost instead of stern, he suddenly uttered the word 'Now!' and his command was followed by a faint splash and the rattle of the rope passing over the bows, till there was a check, and then they were conscious that the sampan was swinging round again, and Archie uttered a low, groan-like sigh.

'What's the matter, sir?   Didn't I do it right?'

'Right, my lad?   Yes, you were right enough, but I was all wrong.   The boat has been gliding along stem first, and I have been confused and looking at the farther shore, seeing nothing but the faint twinkle of the fire-flies.'

'Yes, sir; that's right enough.'

'No, no; it's wrong enough, my lad.   I'm quite lost.   I don't know where we are.   You will have to haul up the grapnel again.'

'But what for, sir?   She's swung round now right enough, head to stream—and look—look!' he whispered.   'I can see trees quite plain.   We must be close inshore.'

'Close inshore, Pete!'

'Yes, sir.   Can't that be the Doctor's garden?'

'Hist!' whispered Archie; and there was a sound as if his companion had given his mouth a pat, for

Trapped.   X

from pretty close at hand there was the low babble of voices.

'Hear that, sir?' whispered Peter again. 'Our chaps?'

'No—Malaya.'

CHAPTER XL

'WHAT ABOUT VICTUALS?'

FOR a few minutes it seemed as if the success that had attended them was to be completely dashed, though it had become evident that, by a wonderful stroke of good fortune, they had dropped the grapnel of the boat so that they were swinging nearly opposite to the part of the river-bank which had been their goal. For then Fate, which had been filling their breasts with hope, seemed to have withdrawn from them behind a darker cloud than ever.

The voices were so near that they dared not whisper or stir, only wait in the full expectation of being seen and welcomed with a shower of spears; but by degrees the talking ceased, and the silence was so profound that it became evident that the enemy, whatever had been their object in coming there, had silently crept away.

'Do you really think they have gone, sir?' whispered Peter.

'I feel sure of it,' was the reply.

'Then don't you think we could get out the poles and work the boat closer in?'

'I'm afraid to try, Pete. The stream seems running so strong that we might be swept away.'

'Oh, I don't know, sir, close inshore like this. I think we might manage it. Hadn't we better try?'

'Well, yes,' replied Archie, after a little hesitation.

'We must use the poles when we go away, unless we try going down-stream.'

'Oh, that wouldn't do, sir. It would be running right into Rajah Hamet's nest, even if we didn't meet Suleiman's men; and if we didn't do neither we should have to carry the boxes through them who are surrounding the Residency.'

'We must get them somehow,' cried Archie impatiently.

'Yes, sir. But we ain't getting them like this.'

For answer Archie seized one of the poles that lay along under the thwarts of the sampan, passed it over the side, and, to his great delight, found that close in to the bank the eddy was so strong that there would be no difficulty in working against the current. This discovery made, the grapnel was pulled up and the sampan thrust in close under the bank at the bottom of the Doctor's garden.

'Nothing like trying, sir,' said Peter; and landing, he carried the grapnel in to the full extent of the rope and pressed its flukes down into the earth.

This was not done without noise, and the two lads stood listening for a few minutes before proceeding farther. Once satisfied that there were no fresh occupants in the bungalow, Archie led the way in, and the rest of their task proved delightfully easy.

He knew enough of the interior of the Doctor's home to make for the store-room at once. Everything was open, just as it had been left in haste, and in spite of the darkness they easily found the little, square boxes of cartridges lying exactly as Mrs Morley had described; and each securing two, they were about to hurry down to the boat, when Archie remembered the gun, which, he knew, was hanging over a cabinet in the Doctor's study.

Placing his two boxes on the floor, he made for the Doctor's room, took the gun from the hooks where it hung, and hurrying back to the room where he had left the boxes, he found himself alone, for Peter had hastened off with his portion of the load.

There was nothing for it but to wait; but at last his ears were gladdened by the sound of his companion's hurried footsteps, and together the remainder of the objects of their search were borne down to the boat, which was cast loose, the poles were seized, and they began to stem the current.

The work proved easier than they had anticipated so long as they kept close inshore; but this, they felt, was incurring the greatest peril, for an occasional voice warned them of the presence of enemies close at hand; and after one narrow escape, consequent upon their being hailed by some one in the Malay tongue, they pushed off in despair, to make for the farther bank of the river.

This portion of their journey was not achieved without losing ground, for out beyond the middle there were times when, in spite of the length of the long bamboo poles, they could not touch bottom. But once more close inshore, they began to make better progress, and as they paused for a few minutes' rest in the thick darkness in a place closely overhung by trees, the question arose as to how long it would be before daybreak, for both felt that the night must be pretty well spent.

'What do you say, Pete?' said Archie.

'Don't want to say nothing, sir,' was the reply.

'Why?'

'Don't want to put you out of heart.'

Archie was silent for a few moments.

'You mean that it must be nearly morning now. Speak out.'

'Something of the kind, sir; and I was thinking that it seems too bad to have to make a mess of it at the end.'

'Ah! You think that though we may get across and land with our load on our side of the river, we should have daylight upon us before we could get anything like back to the Residency?'

'Wish I was as clever as you are, Mister Archie,' said Peter in a low, grumbling tone, as he thrust with all his might at the end of his pole.

'What do you mean?'

'You saying just exactly what I was thinking about, sir. How you come to see it all I don't know.'

'Oh, never mind that, Pete. It's very horrible, and when we are missing in the morning there will be no end of an upset, and they will think that we have deserted.'

'Haw, haw!' grunted Peter, with another thrust of his pole which hindered the straight course of the sampan. 'Them thinking you had deserted, sir? Likely! You ain't me.'

'Well, Pete, let's get as high as we can past the place where we got the boat, and then the moment we think that daylight's coming let's get across, tie the boat up somewhere under the trees, and lie in hiding till night.'

'Won't do,' said Peter shortly. 'Boat belongs to somebody as ain't our friends, and when they find it gone they will come hunting along the water-side till they find it, and like as not tell the enemy where we are.'

'You are right, Pete. Then we will find a snug place, and lie in waiting till it's dark again; and we shall know by then pretty well where we are, and take our measures for a fresh start.'

'That's right, sir. Glad I was able to do some good—and, I say, it's getting close to morning.'

'How do you know?'

'By them things as we have heard howling out in the jungle over and over again.'

'I've heard nothing,' said Archie.

'I have, sir; and they're getting quiet now. I heard a tiger once, and crocs over and over again, but I wouldn't say anything.'

'I had too much else to think of, Pete,' said Archie, as he toiled hard at his pole, causing an eddy more than once, as if some river-dweller had been disturbed.

It was not long after when the notes of the birds began to proclaim the coming day, and the surroundings began to appear so plainly that at the first favourable opportunity the boat was run in beneath the shelter of the overhanging trees and made fast; while, as the day broadened and they peered out across the river, Archie found they were so high up that no object on the farther bank was familiar; and he said so.

'Well, sir, I must leave that to you,' said Peter. 'I ain't done much boating, and have never been so

high as this before. Well, from what you say, I
suppose we shall be safe till night, and then we are
going to get across and land them cartridges somehow or another where they are wanted. We've got
a lot of hours to wait, though, first.'

'Yes,' said Archie, with a weary sigh.

'Well, then, sir, what about victuals?'

CHAPTER XLI.

'IF THE POWDER AIN'T DAMP.'

MORNING came with a rush, the rays of the sun seeming to do battle with the mist that floated over the surface of the river. The golden arrows of light cut and broke up the one dense, gray, heavy cloud into portions which floated slowly along, separating more and more, the dull gray growing rapidly silvery, then golden, and the gold becoming suffused with soft light. So beautiful was the scene that, while Archie gazed thoughtfully at its beauty, even commonplace, powder-besmirched Peter sat with his lips apart, staring hard, and then, forgetting himself and their risky position, with its need for concealment, he clapped his hands softly.

'Just look at it, Mister Archie!' he said. 'Blest if the place don't look just like the inside of one of them big hyster-shells that they get the pearls out of!'

'Hush!' said Archie softly.

'Mum!' said Peter. 'I forgot; but don't it look as if the river was boiling hot and the steam rising, and the fire that hots it was shining up through the cloud? I say, nobody could hear me say that,' he whispered.

'I hope not; but for aught we know boats may be floating down, hidden by that mist.'

'Mist—of course, sir! But it do look like steam, and it makes me think of rations and hot coffee. I say, if one feels like this just at daybreak, how's it going to be by night? Here goes to tighten my belt.'

Peter suited the action to his words, and moved the tongue of his buckle up two holes.

After this the lad sat peering through a dense, green curtain of the beautiful tropic leafage, till by degrees all the mist had floated away with the stream, leaving the water glittering and sparkling in the bright sunshine, and giving the watchers a clear view of the flowing river and the jungle that bowed its pendent branches so that they kissed the water, while farther on tall, rigid palms shot up and displayed their feathery tufts of great leaves, to sway gently in the hot sunshine.

'Let's see, Mister Archie; don't seem to be many paths where helephants and things come down to drink. I don't believe if we were landed there we could get through those woods. I wonder what makes them call them jungles. I suppose it means because the trees are all junged up together so that you can't get through. If they called it tangle there'd be some sense in it. But that ain't the worst.'

'What is, then, Pete?' replied Archie, speaking so that his companion in misfortune should not think him surly and distant.

'Why, we have got to carry them four little chesties and the gun right through it in the dark. Well, we've got 'em, sir, and that's what we come for.'

'Yes, Pete; and it will be a relief to get them to the Residency.'

'Yes, sir; and we have got to do it; and that means we shall, somehow.'

The lad ceased speaking, and bent down to shift the four square, solid-looking boxes a little, and as he did so he uttered a low grunt.

'I say, sir, it's been so dark that we couldn't tell what we were doing, but lookye here. These 'ere two bottom ones are standing right in the water. It's to be hoped they are tin-lined, or else what about the cartridges? What do you say to laying them two bamboo poles right across the boat for the day, and standing the boxes on them?'

'Good idea, Pete!' And the two lads busied themselves in placing the boxes so that the moisture would drip away, with the possibility of their getting dry in the sunshine, which was already beginning to fill their shelter with semi-horizontal rays.

'Here, I say, sir, if we had known what a ramshackle old wreck this 'ere sampan is we should have stepped along pretty gingerly while we were poling—at least I should, for it looks to me as if you could shove your foot through anywhere. Look at the sides! Why, they are half-rotten!'

'Yes, Pete; it's a wonder that the boat did not go to pieces when we ran up against that other one in the night.'

'That it is, sir. Why, if I'd known I believe I should have liked to travel outside, hanging on, with my legs in the water.'

'As a bait to tempt crocodiles, Pete?'

'Oh, I say, don't, sir! You give one the shivers.'

As the lad spoke he peered over the side of the boat and half drew his bayonet from his belt.

'Might be one of those beauties under the bottom now, sir,' he said half-apologetically. 'Nice morning, though, ain't it? Talking about hanging one's legs over the side, we might lay them up a bit to dry;' and he set the example of stretching his own out on the seat-like thwart, and sitting silently for a while gazing through one of the openings across the river.

Then, as if being silent wearied him, his tongue began to go again.

'Suppose you can't make out exactly where we are, sir, can you?'

'No, Pete; the river winds about so.'

'Of course, sir. Well, no wonder—it ain't got anything else to do. Got your watch, sir?'

'Yes;' and Archie drew it out from his pocket.

'What time is it, sir?'

'One,' said Archie dryly.

'Can't be, sir. Why, that means afternoon, and the sun's only just up.'

'It means that it was one o'clock when we waded into the river, and the water got in, Pete.'

'Stopped! I'm blest! If you had thought of it, sir, you'd better have left it at home. "Home, home, sweet home!"' hummed the lad. 'But this ain't home, and I'm precious hungry; but I'd a deal rather be here, after all, than in the old whitewashed barracks where we were stationed last, with nothing but drill, drill, drill, till one felt as if they had drilled a hole right through you. Feel anything of your head now, sir?'

'Yes, Pete; but not much.'

'That's the same with my hurt, sir; but one can't expect what we got to get well directly. Wish we'd got something to do, if it was only to clean one's buckles and lay on a bit of pipeclay. Is my face dirty, sir?'

'Horribly, Pete. Is mine?'

Pete showed his teeth in a broad grin.

'Well, it would be all the better for a wash, sir, before you went in to mess. We might have a bit of a sluice. But I suppose it would be risky to try and get closer in to the bank?'

'You couldn't, Pete. It would be impossible to force the sampan through this tangle. Why do you want to move? We are in a capital place.'

'I was thinking of getting some soft mud out of the bank to use instead of soap. It's wonderful cleansing, sir. I know what I should like to do.'

'Not talk, Pete, for you are doing that now?'

'Yes, sir, I know,' said the poor fellow sadly. 'I feel as though if I didn't go on saying things and thinking of doing something, I should go half-dotty.'

'Nonsense, Pete! See how beautiful it is all round.'

'Yes, sir, lovely! But who's going to enjoy it when your inside keeps on saying, "Soup and 'tater—soup and 'tater—soup and 'tater," and there ain't none? Plenty of croc soup, of course. But, I say, Mister Archie, sir, think it would be safe to bathe?'

'No; but I think you must be half-*dotty*, as you call it, to propose such a thing.'

'Right, sir. Of course! It does look very pretty about here, but one can't help feeling that one of them pretty, smiling creatures may be lying in there, just where the leaves touch the -water, and watching us all the time. Here, I should like to murder some of them. What do you say to fixing bayonets on the end of them bamboo poles, and then pitching leaves or bits of dead wood into the water as a bait for them reptiles, and having a bit of sport to pass away the time?'

'I don't feel much disposed for sport, Pete.'

'Course you don't, sir; but, you see, we've got hours and hours to sit here till it's dark. One feels as if one must do something. Here, I know! Capital! I've got no tackle but green leaves. I'll clean that gun.'

'No cleaning-rod, Pete.'

'Must be, sir.'

'Of course; but it will be hanging up somewhere in the Doctor's bungalow.'

'Might cut a young, thin bamboo, sir,' said Pete, looking sharply round, and feeling in his pocket for his knife.

'I can see no bamboos,' said Archie—'nothing but crooked boughs.'

'Well, anyhow, sir, we might rub the specks of rust off with leaves. Would you like to have first turn?'

'No, Pete. I feel as if I could do nothing but sit still and rest and think.'

'What about, sir?'

'What they are saying about us at the Residency. I suppose they will give us the credit of not deserting.'

'Course they will, sir. They will be saying that we are lying speared somewhere not far from head-quarters. My word, sir, won't Mrs Morley take on about losing you, sir! And, oh dear! nobody won't miss me—except old Tipsy. Haw, haw, haw! He'd like to have me to bullyrag when he gets back to headquarters again.'

'Will nobody else miss you, Pete?'

'No, sir—I d' know, though. Yes—old Mother Smithers, next time she has a chance to have a turn at the wash-tub. It will be, "Now, Pete, fresh water, please." Wish she'd got some of what's in this precious boat! Talk about a leaky sieve! Why, it's coming in everywhere. We shall, have to begin baling soon, Mister Archie. To be sure; that will be next job after I've rubbed up the gun, and—— This 'ere ain't a fruit-tree, is it, sir?'

'Absurd!'

'Suppose it is, sir. I was thinking of cocoa-nuts and getting one down to bale with. I shall have to use my cap. It's wonderful how it's stuck on. I ketched it slipping off twice, though, when we were creeping through the wood.'

Peter reached for the gun, and began to rub the barrels with such leaves as he could pick; but after trying to polish for some time, he shook his head in despair.

'Only making it worse, sir.—I say, Mister Archie, you are not going to sleep, are you?'

Archie, who was resting one hand on the side of the boat and bending down sideways, rose quickly.

'Hist!' he whispered. 'Listen.'

Peter sat motionless for some little time, and then, looking full in his companion's eyes, shook his head slowly. Then a look of intelligence came into his face, and he nodded two or three times quickly, leaned forward, and placing his lips close to his companion's ear, he whispered:

'Poles! Boat coming up-stream.'

The two lads sat thinking of their own slow advance as they had punted upwards in the darkness, and fully understood the effort that was being made to force the advancing boat against the running water.

Then the same thought must have animated both, for after peering through the leaves by which they were surrounded, each lay back upon the thwart he occupied and cautiously began drawing one of the thick boughs that touched the water closer in so as to increase the shelter; but no sooner had Archie begun to disturb the water at the side of the boat than there was a violent disturbance, and something dashed out into the open river.

'Croc,' whispered Peter, 'or some large fish. Wish I had him on my bayonet, sir. I could eat him raw.'

'Hist!' whispered Archie, for the sound of splashing poles was giving place to the regular beat of oars; and crouching low, wondering whether their shelter would be pierced by the keen eyes of the enemy, they lay waiting, listening to the steady plash and the muttering of voices, which grew louder, and, looking bright in painted gold, with the rowers' silken bajus gleaming gold and yellow in the sunshine, a large dragon-boat glided by, so close to the lads' hiding-place that the rowers' blades on their side nearly swept against the leaves, and they could see the gleam of the eyes and glint of spears, for the boat was crowded with armed men, and beneath the palm shelter in the stern they could note the gaily plaided silken sarongs of the principal leaders of the party of Malays.

Feeling that they must be seen, the lads hardly dared to breathe till the gilded stern of the naga had passed; and even then it seemed as if the steersman was looking back straight through the hanging leaves so that he must detect the boat.

At last both were breathing freely, for the plash of oars was growing more distant, and Peter, who had found it horribly painful to remain silent so long, hazarded a few words.

'Felt as if my heart was in my mouth, sir. But do you know what I was thinking all the time?'

'That they must see us, Pete?'

'Of course, sir; but something else.'

'Speak lower, man!'

'All right, sir; they can't hear. But can't you guess?'

Archie shook his head.

'Well, I'll tell you, sir. Here's a double gun; there's four boxes of cartridges. Why haven't you got it loaded and ready to blow a couple of the enemy overboard, and then *click*, *click*, shove in two more cartridges, as I should hand to you, ready for two more shots? That would be enough to send them to the right-about, for they wouldn't know

Trapped.   Y

but what there might be half a company of us
hiding here.'

'How are we to get at the cartridges, Pete?' said
Archie, brightening up, for his companion's words
sent a thrill of hope through his breast, and their
position seemed not half so defenceless as before.

'I've got my knife, sir.'

'What! to cut through the lid?'

'No, sir. It's screwed down. I think I could
turn the screws with the big blade.'

Taking one of the boxes on his knee, he brought
the blade to bear, but dared not put forth all his
force, and for some time he could not get even one
of the fastenings to move, for the water had made
the wood swell.

'It's no use, Pete.'

'Oh, ain't it, sir? They are in precious tight,
but we have got lots of time; and look—the top
of this box is steaming, and it's drying fast. I
shall do it if I don't break my knife.'

Click!

'There, now, if half-an-inch of the blade ain't
gone! And I thought it was a bit of the best stuff
in our company. Well, there's a bit left to work
with, and I must try and cut through.'

'No, no!' cried Archie eagerly. 'Try if the
broken blade will not go into the ends of the
screws.'

'What! and use it as a screw-driver, sir?' cried
Peter joyously. 'Why, it will be quite easy now.
Call mine a head! Why, it's as thick as a bowl.
Here, take it coolly, sir! Here's one coming out as
easy as easy.—There's one! Don't shout "Hooray!"

sir, for sound runs along over the water like a skate on ice. Why, my knife is like a real tool. Couldn't have broke off better, sir, and in half-an-hour we shall be all right if '——

'If what, Pete ?'

'The powder ain't damp.'

CHAPTER XLII.

'DON'T YOU KNOW ME?'

TO the great satisfaction of both, the upper layers of the cartridges proved to be quite dry, and, at Peter's suggestion, they made sure of having a couple of dozen handy by bestowing them in various pockets.

'All right for present use, sir,' said Peter; and placing in a few leaves to refill the box, he lightly screwed down the lid again.

'It's a pity to do that,' said Archie.

'Think so, sir? We have got to get those boxes down to the Residency, and it might happen that we should be obliged to hide them somewhere. Anyhow, what we've got out will be handy. Now then, I want it to get dark. What do you say to one of us taking an hour's snooze?'

'By all means, Pete. It will help us to get through the long watching before night. There, I could not sleep now. You lie down while I keep watch.'

'Oh no, sir; you first.'

'Don't argue, Pete. I say, lie down,' said Archie sternly.

'Right, sir. But you will play fair? Rouse me up in an hour, and let me relieve guard.'

'I will, Pete. We both want rest, and we shall do our work the better afterwards.'

Peter promptly prepared the only dry place he

could find, which was in the stern of the boat, by dragging down a portion of the bamboo and palm-leaf awning and laying the pieces across so as to form a little platform, where he stretched himself out, and before a minute had elapsed he was breathing so heavily that his companion began to peer up and down the river and think of the possibility of the sleeper being heard. But nothing was in sight downward, and he now found that by changing the position of the boat a little he could command a long reach upward—quite a mile.

The guessed-at hour grew into what must have been two, and amidst the annoyance of flies, and troubled by the intense heat, Archie sat watching and thinking, and wondering whether it would be possible as soon as it was dark to thread their way among the bushes of the opposite shore and carry their burden to the help of their friends.

'It's all what Pete calls chancing it,' he said to himself; 'but we may succeed—and we will.'

At last, just as he was thinking that it might be wise to awaken Pete for an exchange of places, he suddenly caught sight of a large boat in the extreme distance, gliding round a slight curve, and after watching it increase in size as it came rapidly down, he laid a hand on Peter's arm, and the lad started up, fully awake.

'Relieve guard, sir? Right! Give us the gun,' said the lad quietly; and then, following Archie's pointing finger, he realised the new peril, and withdrawing his hand, he drew out his bayonet and replaced it ready for instant use.

A glance showed the pair that they could do

nothing more to add to their concealment, and with the boat rapidly nearing, they sat and watched, Archie with the cocked piece lying across his knees ready for their defence in case of need.

During the first part of the time their impression had been that it was the dragon-boat they had seen going up, but as it drew nearer they made out that it was manned by Malays, evidently of the poorer classes, but well armed and in all probability followers of some minor chief.

To the lads' great satisfaction, it seemed that they were hugging the farther shore, and they passed by travelling slowly, without even looking in their direction, and glided out of sight.

'Lucky for some of them, Mister Archie,' said Peter, as he stretched out his hand for the gun and crept forward. 'There you are, sir. I feel like a new man. Have a good sleep, sir. It helps the time along beautifully. How did you guess an hour, sir?'

'Never mind about the time, Pete. You guess another as nearly as you can; but wake me, of course, if there is any danger.'

'You trust me, sir,' was the reply; and Archie lay down, feeling that the position would be restful, but certain that he should not be able to sleep.

Five minutes had not elapsed, however, before he was sleeping heavily, but ready to awaken at a touch and sit up, to stare about him wildly.

'Why, Pete,' he said angrily, 'I have had more than an hour.'

'Well, just a little, sir. Feel all the better for it, don't you?'

'Why, you scoundrel,' cried Archie as he reached for the gun, 'it's close upon evening—close upon night! How dare you disobey my orders? Why didn't you wake me up?'

'Hadn't the heart, sir,' said the lad quietly.

'But I said '——

'Yes, I know you did; and I was going to wake you up half-a-dozen times, but I knowed how weak you were, and that you would want every bit of strength for what we have got to do to-night; and I didn't want you to break down.'

'Am I your officer, sir, or am I not?' said Archie fiercely.

'Yes, sir, of course; and I know I ought to obey the word of command. But you don't want me to do impossibilities, now, do you, sir?'

'What do you mean?'

'Why, sir, you don't want me to carry you and the cartridge-boxes too?'

'No; I should carry my share, of course.'

'Yes, sir; but I should be having Paddy's load. You would be carrying the boxes, but I should be carrying you and the boxes too.'

'Pete'—— began Archie fiercely; but he was checked by the lad's action, for with one hand he pointed up the long reach, and with the other he placed the gun across the subaltern's knees.

'A boat!' said Archie.

'Two on 'em, sir;' and they sat gazing up through the gathering gloom of their shelter at what the last faint rays of the setting sun showed to be a large sampan coming down the river, urged by a couple of Malays who were steadily using their poles, while some distance behind a boat about double the size was following them, propelled by oars.

'It will be all right, sir,' said Peter. 'By the time they come by here it will be getting dark. Look at that farther one. The attaps looked red just now, but they are turning brown already.'

'Yes; and look there. Why, Pete—am I right? It seemed as if one of the Malays in the front of the far boat stood up and threw a spear.'

'Right you are, sir, and no mistake. There goes another. Can you see how many there are in the first boat?'

'Three, I think; and one's a woman.'

'I thought two of them,' said Peter; 'and there's eight or ten or a dozen in the other. Well, sir, the far-off one must be enemies, and the little boat must be friends. I know which side we ought to take, and we can now.'

'What do you mean? Fire?'

'That's right, sir.'

'But we shall show where we are.'

'Of course; but we can't help that, sir,' cried Peter excitedly. 'Here they come. They'll over-take the little un directly. You've got bullet cartridges, sir, for I tried one. But I don't know whether this double gun will carry so far; so you had better wait.'

'One barrel's rifled, Pete, and it will,' said Archie, drawing himself into a kneeling position and resting the barrels upon a horizontal bough.

'Look sharp, sir! Oh, murder—there goes another spear! I couldn't hardly see, but it must have gone close to that woman who is handling the bamboo. Oh, do fire, sir!'

There was the sharp report of one barrel, and then, as the smoke rose, Archie fired again, and opened the breech and rapidly inserted the cartridges that Peter handed to him; while, as if startled by the reports, the rowers in the far boat laid on their oars, and those astern started up, and the lads could dimly see their spears bristling in the gathering gloom.

'Give them another, sir—only one—and reload. You missed first time. You must bring down a couple now.'

Archie fired again, and this time one of the Malays seemed to spring out of the boat and drift behind.

'That's good, sir. Here's your cartridge. Now then! Give them two now. They are coming straight for us where the smoke shows. Quick, sir!'

Bang, bang went the double gun, the reports almost simultaneous, for in his excitement Archie had no thought of reserving one shot; and as he hastily reloaded he could see in the rapidly dimming light that the rowers were changing the course of their naga, as if to get out of the line of fire, and were beginning to make for the opposite shore; while the big Malay in the small sampan had ceased his efforts to pole his boat more swiftly along, and was using the bamboo to steer the little vessel, which, gathering force from the man's efforts combined with the swift stream, plunged right in through the hanging boughs behind which the two lads crouched. There was a heavy crash, mingled with the breaking of twigs, and the two lads were driven headlong into the bottom of their boat.

Archie struggled up at once, holding his double gun on high to keep it out of the water, with which he was drenched; and the first thing he could make out through the wide opening torn in their shelter was the naga and its occupants gliding rapidly by, the rowers pulling as if for dear life, and the spearmen crouching down in the bottom, half-hidden by the awning. Then they were gone.

Meanwhile Peter was struggling to free himself from the encumbrance of the big Malay, who had been shot from his own vessel right upon him; and the next thing that met Archie's eyes, as he gazed through the crushed-down leafage driven before the lesser boat, was Peter's bayonet-armed hand with the weapon raised daggerwise, and beyond the Malay, who was holding out his hands, the native boat with the Malay woman, pole in hand, panting hard as if from exertion. Then his eye caught the figure of the other woman, kneeling in the stern.

'Pete, look out! Quick! We must climb into this boat. She's cut us down. Quick—before it's too dark to see!'

'Here, I don't understand, sir. This fellow knocked me down, and'——

'Understand! Can't you see we are sinking? It's deep water here.'

Before he could finish he dimly made out that the big Malay had struggled clear and seemed to be much higher as he dragged at Peter, hoisted him right up, and jerked him behind; while at the same time the panting woman was holding out the pole she used, at which Archie grasped, just in time, as he felt the water was gradually bearing him away.

The next minute he was being dragged over the side of the sampan by the two Malays, and as they lowered him so that he lay upon his back, Peter's head suddenly appeared between the two strangers, with the eager question:

'Have you stuck to your gun, sir?'

'Yes; all right, Pete. What a horrible accident! Where's our boat?'

'Rotten old cocoa-nut shell,' cried Peter savagely. 'There's the last on her just going down;' and he pointed to a spot a few yards away, where, dividing the pendent branches of their shelter, was the attap roof of their sampan. 'And do you know what that means, sir?'

'Utter wreck, Pete,' said Archie, breathing hard from excitement.

'Yes, sir; and my four boxes of cartridges with all them blue pills gone to the bottom to feed the crocs.'

'But what about the other boat?'

'Why, we are in it, sir. Can't you see?' said Peter sourly.

'No, no—I mean the enemy's.'

'Oh! Out of sight, sir. Gone down the river just as if you were peppering them still.'

'Eh? What?' cried Archie, as he became aware of the fact that some one else had spoken, and that a bough of one of the trees that overshadowed them was being pressed aside; and, half-stunned in his astonishment, the young officer grasped the words that seemed to be coming in the confusion of some strange dream:

'Archie! Don't you know me? I'm Minnie Heath.'

CHAPTER XLIII.

THE ENEMY'S WORK.

ARCHIE MAINE and Minnie Heath sat in the
darkness, hand clasped in hand, the poor
girl sobbing bitterly, nearly overcome with
emotion, after, in a low, excited voice, asking questions about her aunt and uncle and Sir Charles.
After learning that all were alive and safe, she burst
out in so wildly hysterical a fit that there was a low,
deep growl from the darkness at the far end of the
boat.

'Silence, Pete!' whispered Archie sternly.

''Twarn't me, sir. It's this 'ere Malay chap. I
think he means that you oughtn't to make so much
noise at that end. I wanted to say something of
the kind, but I didn't want to be rude to the young
lady.'

Minnie was silent directly; and close to the spot
where Peter had been speaking a curious rustling
noise arose, which Archie could not understand, till
almost at once the edge of the moon appeared above
the night mist and lit up the interior of the shelter,
and then it was plain that the big Malay fisherman
was busy at work cutting down branches and laying
them across the boat, in which a pile of leafage was
beginning to appear.

'What does he mean by this?' whispered Archie.
'I suppose he means the branches to disguise the
boat.'

'I don't know,' said Minnie. 'I suppose so. I don't think we need ask. He and Dula have saved me, and have been most kind.'

'But can you talk now?'

'Yes, yes; I will not break down again if I can help it.'

'I'll wait,' said Archie.

'No, no; go on talking, pray,' half-sobbed the girl. 'It keeps me from thinking. What were you going to say?'

'I was going to ask you how you knew that we were in hiding here.'

'Knew! Oh no! It was like this. Dula and Pahan were bringing me down in their boat, believing that they could reach the bungalow in the darkness and hide me there. Of course you did not see in the dusk that I am wearing Dula's baju and sarong.'

'No; it was all too dark and confused. But I did think you were a native woman.'

'That is good,' said Minnie. 'Dula brought me down to the creek where the boat was lying, and Pahan meant to pretend after dark, if we met any of the Malays, that he was taking in fruit for the Rajah's men. But we were seen too soon. One of the Rajah's boats came in sight, and the chief with it called to us to stop. Then Dula said I must lie under the attap mats, as they were going to pretend that they did not hear the call. They began poling the boat along as hard as ever they could, hoping, as the stream was with us, that we could escape; but '—— The poor girl broke down with a sob.

'Don't talk about it, Minnie—dear sister,' said

Archie quickly. 'Sit quiet and try to believe that you are safe. Pete and I will die sooner than harm shall befall you now.'

'Yes, yes, I know,' said the poor girl, stifling her rising sobs; 'but I must talk. Don't stop me. It helps me to grow calm again after the horrible excitement of that race for life. Oh,' she shuddered, 'it was terrible! For they kept gaining upon us, till they got near enough to begin throwing spears, two of which passed through the attaps; and I crouched down, praying that the darkness that was so near would come down and hide me so that Pahan could run the boat in somewhere amongst the bushes. At last, when it seemed all over, and I was feeling that I must bid good-bye to life and jump into the river before I saw these dear people speared to death, my poor heart gave one great throb in answer to the sound of your rifle, while Dula uttered a cry of joy, knowing the shots at the Malays could only come from friends, and helped her husband to force the sampan right in amongst the trees where we saw the smoke rising; and then—— Oh Archie! oh Archie!' She broke down, and as she clung to her old companion, the lad made what sounded like a dreary attempt at a mocking laugh, as he exclaimed:

'Upon my word, Minnie, it was too bad! Here were we trying to save you, and you dashed in, sank our boat, sent all my cartridges to the bottom, and nearly drowned us into the bargain.'

'Don't—don't try to make a laughing matter of it, Archie! I can't bear it now.'

'Of course you can't. Forgive me for being such

a fool. I say, your what's his name—Pahan—he's getting quite a stack of green stuff aboard, and——Hang it all! Look at the moon!'

'Yes; I am looking,' sighed Minnie. 'I've watched it many a time since I have been in hiding, and I never thought to look upon it peacefully again. Oh Archie! go on talking to me. Tell me more about Sir Charles, and what you have all been going through at the station.'

'Can't. It would take a month.'

'Oh! do tell me something.'

'Breaking our hearts about you, then—everybody in the place. Even poor old Mother Smithers sat down and cried like a child; didn't she, Pete?'

'Gugg!' said the lad, out of the darkness. 'Can you get at your knife, Mr Archie? Mine's turned into a screw-driver, and I want to help this nig—Malay gentleman to cut sticks.'

'Here you are, Pete,' said Archie, after a hard struggle to get his hand into the pocket of his overall, and a harder struggle still to get it back with the knife.

'Thankye—gugg—sir! Blest if I don't believe I'm going to have a cold!' And the cutting and rustling of thick, leafy branches went on.

'Now, Minnie, tell me, what do they mean to do?'

'Yes,' said the girl quickly. 'Dula told me—she can say a few words in English, and I know a few Malay sentences as well, so that we managed to understand one another—she said her husband thought he could get the boat down to the foot of our garden in the darkness, and then we could all carry baskets of fruit, and so pass through the Malays to a spot where we could make a dash for the Residency, where we should be safe, if some of the soldiers didn't shoot us down.'

'Ah,' said Archie slowly, 'you needn't be afraid of that, Minnie.'

'What's the matter?' cried the girl sharply.

'Oh, nothing. I am only very wet.'

'You are trying to hide something, Archie,' said Minnie earnestly. 'You called me sister a few minutes ago.'

'Well,' he said sharply, 'that's what you are to me.'

'Then is it brotherly to keep something back?'

'Oh, all right, then,' said the lad. 'It was only because I didn't want to give you more troubles to think about.'

'What is it, then? I know: Sir Charles is wounded, or perhaps'——

'No, no. He's been knocked about, like the rest of us. I was keeping it back that our men haven t got a cartridge among them left to fire. Pegg and I were at the bungalow last night to smuggle out your uncle's double gun and the cartridges, and we had got in here to wait till night came again before we landed and tried to make our way back to the Residency.'

'Say, Mister Archie, sir,' grumbled Peter, as Minnie sat pressing her old companion's hand in token of her gratitude for what he had said.

'What is it, Pete?'

'I can't understand what this chap says, but he made me shut up your knife, and has put away his own, so I think he means we have got as much green stuff as we can carry.'

'Yes, that's it, Pete.   Well, what?'

'Only this, sir.   You see the moon there?'

'Of course I do.'

'Well, is it a heclipse or an echo, or anything of that kind, over yonder?'

'Where?   What do you mean?'

'This 'ere way, sir.   You are looking t'other.'

'Nonsense!'

'You are looking the wrong way, sir.   Hold them branches back.   Yes; it's getting wuss, sir.   Blest if they ain't burning the Residency down!'

CHAPTER XLIV.

THE FISHERMAN'S PLAN.

PETER'S conclusion was only a guess, but it soon became evident that a fire was raging somewhere in the direction of the station. But this did not seem to trouble the two Malays, who shifted the position of the boat by pushing it clear of the trees, to one of which they secured the sampan so that it swung in the stream, while they rearranged the greenery that had been collected, and worked hard in the bright moonlight so as to give it some semblance of a market-boat carrying down supplies from higher up the river.

This done to the satisfaction of the owner, whom Peter had been working hard to help, the lad uttered an apologetic cough.

'Look here, Pete,' said Archie impatiently; 'if you are going to say that we had better remain in hiding on account of the moonlight and the glare of that fire, you had better be silent, for we must trust to these people to do what they think best.'

'I warn't a-going to say nothing of the sort, Mister Archie, sir,' protested the lad.

'Then what were you going to say? I know that that cough or grunt of yours means that you are going to object to something.'

'No, sir; it's not a object to anything unless you say I can't have it. I was only going to ask if

Miss Minnie didn't say something about having fruit aboard this 'ere craft.'

'Yes, yes!' cried Minnie excitedly.

'Well, miss,' said Peter, with a sigh of relief, 'if you won't think it rude of me, I should just like to say that Mister Archie here ain't had a mossel of nothing to eat since the day before yesterday, and P. P. ain't much better.'

'Oh Dula!' exclaimed Minnie; and she uttered a few words in the Malay tongue that sent the woman rustling past the cut boughs beneath the attap awning, to return directly and gladden the eyes of Peter with a basket containing a heap of bananas and a couple of native-made cakes.

'Ah!' sighed Peter. 'Don't they look lovely in the moonlight! Tlat!' he added, with a hearty smack of his lips.—'No, thank you, sir. No water, please,' he continued, after a busy interval. 'I never feel sure what you might be swallowing when you have a dip out of the river. It's all very well when the sun shines hot, but when it's the moon it don't make you thirsty—least it don't me.'

It must have been a couple of hours later, during which the occupants of the boat had been watching the rising and falling of the fire as they swung slowly to and fro at the end of the rope, when Minnie, who had been speaking in a whisper to the boatman and his wife, turned to her companions and said:

'Pahan thinks that we may risk floating down the river now. The excitement of the fire will be pretty well over when we get abreast of the bungalow, and we have a long journey yet; and then if he

makes the boat fast, as he says he can, at the foot
of the garden, he thinks no one will notice it. But
we shall have to lie hidden, and, if necessary,
covered up with the boughs.'

The covering over with boughs fell to the share
of the two lads, the shelter of the attap mats and
her Malay dress seeming likely to be sufficient for
Minnie's protection if they neared any Malay boat,
that most dreaded being the naga whose occupants
had been put to flight—though even if that were
encountered, the sampan was now so transformed
that it was not likely to be recognised; and once
more the little party were in motion, floating down
towards the station, the Malay poling the boat and
keeping as near as possible to the farther shore.

CHAPTER XLV.

'CLOSE UP!'

'DON'T you think we might make a bigger peep-hole, Mister Archie?' whispered Peter.

'No,' was the abrupt reply.

'All right, sir; you know best; only it is precious smothery. I'm as hot as hot.'

'Can't help it, Pete. We must bear it, and above all now that we are getting so near.'

'Yes, we are near; aren't we, sir?'

'Very near, Pete.'

'Can you make out anything more about what is burning?'

'Yes—the Residency.'

'That's bad, sir. Thought we was to retreat to there when things got too hot at the orspittle.'

Archie had been raising the boughs that concealed them as they drew nearer the upper landing-place, dropping very slowly along, their progress being checked by the manipulation of the boat's grapnel under Pahan's clever management, for he controlled the rate at which they were carried downward on the swift stream by using the rough little anchor as a drag.

As far as could be made out in the moonlight, the river was quite clear of boats, and, to their surprise, they glided on into utter silence, while not a moving figure could be made out.

Archie had, in a whisper, given such information

to his companion as he could, and attributing the position to their still being at a considerable distance from the scene of the conflict, he had crushed down in his own breast the feeling of dread that the worst had occurred. He had just come to this conclusion when Peter made a horrible suggestion.

'Mister Archie,' he whispered, 'ain't it all very quiet?'

'Yes. Perhaps the enemy is waiting for broad daylight, to make another attack.'

'More fools they, sir, when they might catch our poor chaps quite done up in the darkness and without a shot to fire. But you don't think, sir, as we are too late, and the niggers have made a rush, carried all before them, and ended up by finishing our lads off?'

'No, I don't,' said Archie shortly; 'and now don't talk. What's the use of making the worst of things?'

'Quite right, sir. There, I've done; but I'd give anything to get to work again. Just tell me this, sir: how much farther have we got to go?'

'A very little way,' whispered Archie, as he raised his head a little and peered through the boughs, to see that the fire was burning low and that they were now gliding into comparative darkness, evidently caused by the river mist keeping down the smoke, which hung low and partially obscured the light of the moon.

And now the big Malay was evidently busily using his pole, and thrusting hard to force the boat into the position he had marked. Then, as far as the listeners could make out, he had hauled up the little grapnel so that it hung over the side, worked hurriedly with his pole again, and then laid it leaning against a pile of boughs so that the two lads could hear the water dripping where they lay.

Then the grapnel was lowered again, and the boat swung round; and as Archie raised his head once more, it was to find that they were close up to their old position whence they had made their successful capture of the cartridges. And now it seemed as if they had suddenly glided from silence into the noise and turmoil of the fight, for from the shore came the shouts and yells of the Malays, who were evidently engaged in a savage attack upon the defenders of some portion of the station, and Archie, in his excitement, uttered a low:

'Thank Heaven!'

'What did you say that for, sir?' whispered Peter excitedly.

'That horrible silence, Pete, made me afraid that you were right.'

'Ah, yes, sir; and that all our poor lads were wiped out. It's all right, sir, only that we ain't got no cartridges. But what are you going to do, sir? We can't go on lying here.'

'No, Pete, of course not,' whispered Archie, though there was no need, for the noise and tumult would have drowned his words even had they been spoken aloud.

He raised the boughs, but nothing was to be seen, for the bungalow was hidden by the smoke and mist now being borne by the faint breeze of the coming daylight in their direction. But he could make out enough to determine that an attack must have just commenced upon the mess-room and its surroundings, while, in spite of the stillness in that direction, the lad could gather that the defenders must be still holding their own.

A sudden sharp rustling and movement of the boat made Archie turn sharply.

'Don't say nothing, sir,' panted his companion, whose voice sounded as if he had been running hard. 'I couldn't bear it no longer, sir. I was being smothered. Can't you hear, sir? They ain't cheering, but our chaps is at work with the bay'net.'

'Yes, yes, I hear,' said Archie hoarsely.

'Well, sir, we are close inshore, and with a sharp run we could get in and help.'

'But it would be madness, Pete, to try and land with Miss Minnie now.'

'Who wants to land with Miss Minnie, sir?' cried the lad fiercely. 'She's safe here. You tell her to lie low, and say that what's his name is to pull up his anchor and run her a bit lower down, or across the river out of danger till all's safe again.'

'Impossible, Pete. We are almost unarmed, and it would be like forsaking the poor girl at a time like this.'

'What you talking about, sir? Here's two of us, and there's our poor chaps dropping before these niggers' spears. Come on, sir! I must speak, for I feel it's our duty to be there.'

'Yes, Pete,' replied the subaltern in a voice that he hardly knew as his own; and rising clear of the bushes, he made his way to where he could dimly make out the figure of Minnie kneeling beneath the attap roof.

'Minnie,' he whispered, 'our men are fighting to defend the station, and our place is there. Tell the Malay to get the boat across to a spot where you will be safe. Don't ask me to stay. I can't.' Turning from the girl as she made a snatch at his hand, 'Now, Pete,' he said, and grasping the gun, he sprang over the side into the shallow water, and then, as he dragged himself out by the help of the nearest bush, a quick panting from the gloom around told him that Peter was by his side. Then old discipline asserted itself. 'Forward! Double!' he cried; and falling into step, the two lads ran almost blindly in the direction of the shouting and yells, which acted as their guides to the quarter where the conflict was going on.

Those next minutes were to the lads like a brief period of blind confusion, and at one time they were hurrying between trees where the smoke was thickest, rising from places where firing was going on and the mist hung low but seemed to be lightened here and there by the flickering of fire, whose pungent odour of burning wood assailed their nostrils. Then Archie was conscious of finding himself rushing through a crowd, at whom he struck right and left with the barrels of his gun, and of hearing a piercing yell somewhere to his right, followed by a grim, stern voice growling:

'You've got it, then!'

And at last, with a bound, the two lads stumbled, nearly fell, and then leaped together over a rough breastwork, and fell heavily amongst the dimly seen defenders who were left.

'Friends — friends!' yelled Peter, and then, 'Mister Archie, sir, where are you? Ah! That's done it!' For no reply came in answer from his panting companion, who was being partly held up by one of those whom he had joined, and who gasped out a cheer.

'That's right! Hooray it is!' cried Peter. 'Here, give us a rifle. I've got a bayonet.' And Archie heard the *click, click* of the keen weapon being fixed.

This brought back his failing powers, and the next minute, finding himself in the little line of defenders who were dimly seen in the smoke that was floating from the levelled Residency, he raised the gun he still clung to, fired twice into the bearers of so many bristling spears, and began to load again, asking himself the question, 'Are the cartridges wet?'

The little, hurriedly thrust-in rolls answered for themselves with two more sharp reports, and these four shots resulted in checking the enemy's advance and in raising a wildly exultant, though feeble, cheer from the defenders along the little line; for, trifling as was the addition to the failing force, the shots seemed to give as much encouragement to the enfeebled men as dismay to their enemy.

'Fire, sir—fire, Mister Archie! Don't stop to aim, sir!' panted Peter. 'I've got a lot more ready. Fire till the barrels are too hot to hold!' And, trembling with excitement the while, Archie fired as fast as he could drag the cartridges from the pockets where they lay.

And as he fired again and again the Malay attacking party hung back, dropped a little more to the rear, and began turning their spears into missiles, which began to whistle past the defenders, who were finding their voices more and more, and cheered hoarsely.

'Here y'are, sir! Old England for ever!' cried Peter. 'I've got about a couple of dozen handy. Ketch hold.'

'Who's that firing?' came in a familiar voice from Archie's right. 'You, Maine! Great heavens! I thought—— Here, distribute some of your cartridges to the men.'

'No use, sir. This is a shot-gun,' panted Archie hoarsely; and he fired again twice, snatched at a fresh supply from Peter, and was in the act of closing the breech again, when the Major exclaimed:

'Stand fast, my lads! It has given you a rest. Bayonets!'

There was another cheer at this, and the men stood fast as ever—a dwindling party, hard beset, of the defenders of the mess-room veranda, their breastwork for the most part consisting of the bodies of the slain.

'Steady, my lads! Close up!' cried the Major. —'That you, Sir Charles? Good! I didn't know you could use a bayonet like that.'

There was a tremendous yell from the front now, and it became plain that the enemy had recovered from the check given by the recrudescence of the long-stopped firing, little though it was, and were now coming forward in greater force.

'Close up, my lads!' he said again. 'God save the Queen!'

The cheer that burst forth was only faint, but it was true as the British steel with which the men stood ready to deliver their final thrusts.

'The last two, Mister Archie!' panted Peter in a low tone. 'Let 'em have 'em, sir, and then be ready. I've got another rifle and bay'net. Fire, and chuck the Doctor's gun at them and hooroar! We will die game!'

'Close up!' roared the Major desperately, as he stood sword in hand, ready to give point. 'Stand fast, and let the black-hearted cowards spit themselves upon your bayonets. — What's that?' he cried.

'A fresh body of 'em, sir, coming round to right and left.'

'That you with your bad news, Sergeant?' cried the Major half-laughingly. 'Good-bye, my lad! Good man! Brave soldier! But we've done our best, and they'll say it was bravely done at home.— Form square! Rally!' he roared, as he now raised his sword on high.—'Well done, subaltern—and you too, boy,' he added, as right and left, with lowered rifles, Archie and Peter helped to close him in.

Yell, yell, yell, came in a savage roar, as, like a dark wave flashed with scarlet and amber yellow, two lines of spear-armed Malays in admirable military order charged round the two angles of the mess-room right and left; and as the tiny square stood firm, it was to see the new-comers dash wildly past and tear away right before them in a fierce charge upon the advancing enemy, whose attack that had meant the extinction of the brave defenders was now turned into a repetition of the sham fight's rout, as they scattered in wild retreat across the parade-ground and made for the jungle.

The defenders stood, with presented blood-stained bayonets, in bewildered silence for a time, and too much astounded to cheer as they watched the smart, bright military charge of the new enemy, for it seemed impossible to believe that these were others than a fresh party who were making some terrible mistake.

They watched then as the fresh, bright line with glittering spears tore on, driving the enemy before them, till the latter began to plunge in amongst the jungle trees, or made for one or other of the paths, when all at once a wild, shrill cry rang out, and, as if by magic, the new, well-drilled force stopped short as though in obedience to the loud, familiar sound of a British bugle. This was answered by two more, one from the path nearest to the river, the other away from the direction of the village campong; and in response to these three calls came as many crashing volleys, while as the smoke arose it was to display a motley crowd of the enemy returning in wild excitement, driven back by the check, to be met in their retreat by the spears of their new foes.

What followed was a short and desperate encounter, in which the retiring foe turned wildly again to reach the shelter of the jungle, but only to meet the quick, scattering fire of the advancing detachments, which, as if from some carefully planned manœuvre, but which Peter called chance, were now advancing in the nick of time.

The fight was over, for, hemmed in now, Rajah Suleiman's despairing force threw down their arms in appeal for mercy, crushed, beaten, half-destroyed.

The commanding officers of the three detachments were in turn grasping
the hand of the quiet-looking young leader of the
well-drilled Malays.

T.

CHAPTER XLVI.

'HOO-RAY!'

IN the midst of the wild bursts of cheering given
out again and again by the rescued men, wounded
(who were many) and sound (who were very
few), to those who had succoured them in their
direful time of need—shouts that were echoed and
re-echoed by the wearied and weather-worn comrades
warmly shaking hands and almost ready to embrace
old friends—there were other meetings and heart-
stirring incidents. Not the least interesting was
that in which the commanding officers of the three
detachments were in turn grasping the hand of the
quiet-looking young leader of the well-drilled Malays
who had come up from the rear and literally flung
back Rajah Suleiman's savage warriors on to the
bayonets of the returning force.

'I don't know how to thank you enough, sir,'
said Captain Down.

'Nor I, sir,' said Lieutenant Durham.

'You, Ripsy,' cried Captain Down again—'you
understand these things better than we do. Did
you ever witness a better advance and charge? You
saw it, didn't you?'

'Yes, sir,' said the old Sergeant, 'just as we were
all out of breath and were struggling out of the
jungle path.'

'Well, say something to the Prince, man.'

'No speaker, sir,' said the Sergeant-Major gruffly;

'but I should have been a proud man if I had had the drilling of such a body of men.'

'Oh, gentlemen, gentlemen,' said the young chief, 'it is all imitation, and the teaching of an old non-com. whom I have had with me ever since I came back from England. Only too glad to have come in time. But I should like to say a few words to Major Knowle and Sir Charles Dallas before we retire to my boats.'

'Oh, we will talk about that by-and-by,' cried Captain Down. 'I see they have been playing havoc here while we have been tricked and deluded into following no end of false and lying guides who professed to lead us to the place where Suleiman and his men were retiring before us. Come along. Good heavens! I had no idea that the Major had been pressed like this. The Residency gone, too! And look, Durham—it was time we came!'

The officers and the young Rajah quickened their steps across the parade-ground, dotted now with fallen Malays, wounded and dead in the final *mêlée;* and Captain Down uttered a groan as he ran to grasp the hand of his chief, who took a step or two forward by the help of his blunted and rusted sword, while the relics of the defenders stood round, cheering hoarsely and feebly, and trying to cheer again, but breaking down in the effort and lapsing into silence, each man craning forward eagerly to listen to what was said.

'We had no messages, sir, from headquarters, or we should have been back long before. All we could gather was that the Rajah was fleeing before us; and Durham was told the same. Here—the

Sergeant too. He was led on and on by people who showed him the tracks of Suleiman's elephants, and'——

'No more—no more,' said the Major hoarsely. 'I knew you'd have come, and that there must be some good reason. I thank Heaven that it was no worse, for in my despair I was ready to agree with my true comrade here, Sir Charles Dallas, that each detachment had been led into some trap, and my brave lads slaughtered to a man. As you see, we have had pretty well to fight to the death, and I'm too weak and ready for the Doctor's hands to grasp everything. I want to know, though,' he added feebly, 'how it is that this brave little native force came to us at the last pinch and turned our defeat into a victory.'

'What! don't you know, sir?' cried Captain Down excitedly.—'Here, Rajah Hamet, speak for yourself.'

'Rajah Hamet!' cried the Major and Sir Charles in a breath; and the young man took a step forward as the group of officers drew back to give him place.

'Oh, don't say anything, Major,' said the young man, smiling. 'I have always been your friend, but, somehow, your caution and the malignant lies and jealousy of an old enemy made you distrust me. But there, I remember a Latin saying at my English school. It was, to speak no evil of the dead.'

'The dead!' said Sir Charles, who looked startled.

'Yes, sir, of the dead—the man who plotted to rob me of my country, and make you believe in him and mistrust me.'

Trapped. 2 A

'But you said dead,' cried Sir Charles, who spoke with difficulty, as he supported a wounded arm with a bleeding and roughly bandaged hand.

'Yes, sir. Rajah Suleiman died bravely in his final charge.'

'Are you sure of that?' said Sir Charles excitedly.

'Yes, sir; I saw him fall. But one word, Sir Charles: I should like to hear from your own lips that you believe in me now.'

'Believe in you, Prince! You have proved that my suspicions have all been wrong. I ask your forgiveness, sir; and let me be the first to hail you as the new Rajah of Suleiman's dominions, combined with your own.'

'You mean this, Sir Charles?' cried the young man, who for the moment lost his calm, Eastern composure.

'Mean it, sir? I repeat it in the name of Her Majesty the Queen, whose representative I am. —Yes, what is it, Major?—Quick, some one—the Doctor! He is fainting.'

'No, no,' said the Major feebly; 'only a little overcome. Water, from the Doctor's well. Don't fetch him. He has too many brave fellows to attend to yonder. Ah! thanks, Rajah. You carry a water-bottle, then, as we do.'

'I was never more glad to follow a good old English custom than now.'

'Ah!' cried the Major, after a hearty draught. 'That's like new life. I had half-forgotten. Everything's been swimming round me. Now tell me, some one—you, Sergeant—did not Mr Maine come suddenly upon us, as if from the dead, to help us at the last?'

'Yes, sir; and young Pegg as well,' said the wounded Sergeant, saluting, as he supported himself upon the rifle and broken bayonet he held. 'But'——

'Ah!' cried the Major excitedly. 'Don't say that'——

'No, sir, I hope it's not that,' said the Sergeant huskily; 'but they were both amongst the missing as I tried to call the roll.'

'Wrong, Sergeant!' cried a husky voice, and all turned and saw a grim-looking private sitting with his bandaged head resting upon one hand.

'What do you know, then, Joe Smithers?'

'Only here they come,' growled the poor fellow, as he flung up his disengaged hand and cried, 'Hoo'——

He meant to say 'Hooray,' but his feeble voice was drowned in a fresh burst of cheers, as from the direction of the Doctor's bungalow Minnie Heath appeared, nominally led by Archie and Peter Pegg, but partly supporting them as they tottered on either side.

At that moment a wild cry of joy rang out, and Joe Smithers's wife, who had dropped a great brass lotah of clear, cold water which she had been to fetch from the Doctor's well, hurried in to announce that the commanding officer was down, and had brought the Doctor with his wife to attend to their brave old friend.

Poor Archie and Peter had to snatch at the nearest hands, as, with a cry of joy, Minnie sprang to her aunt; while, after an interval devoted to embrace and welcome, the Doctor turned to Archie and began to examine his hurts.

'Quiet, sir!' he cried, as he passed a hand hastily across his screwed-up eyes. 'I've no time for all this nonsense with all these wounded on my hands. I've kissed her, boy, and said I was glad; and her aunt and Sir Charles here will do all the rest. Now, Archie, my lad, no nonsense; lean on me. Do you think I've been wounded too? I haven't a scratch. I say you shall have first turn, and—I say, wasn't I right when I prescribed that day? Do you feel anything like a boy now?'

'Oh, I say, Doctor, don't!'

'What!' cried the Doctor, purposely misunderstanding him. 'What! going to play the woman? Bah! I'm going to hurt you far more than that.'

THE END

Edinburgh:
Printed by W. & R. Chambers, Limited.

CPSIA information can be obtained at www.ICGtesting.com
Printed in the USA
LVOW091007010912

296976LV00005B/143/P

9 781142 069247